M000199504

APOCALYPSE IDAHO

Dear Future me,

This is the first one ever published.

Love,
    Rich Lundeen

Apocalypse Idaho

Rich Lundeen

ISBN: 978-0-9861113-0-3
eBook ISBN: 978-0-9861113-1-0

"It's better than a couple books I've read so far." -my wife

PROLOGUE

The human sprints through the forest with the coordination and agility of a billion years of evolution. Despite the dark and uneven Idaho National Wilderness terrain, he is at top velocity. Stumbling through blackness, his feet always manage to find basically correct footing. Instinct helps him run as fast as he is possibly able. When he ricochets off a large tree in his path he dives behind it for cover.

Everything is black. He hears himself breathing anaerobically and attempts to force himself quiet, but every decibel is amplified in silence and he can't help but make sputtering noises. He tries to will himself to stop making sound, but every leaf crunch is like someone trying to open a bag of Cheetos in a movie theater. Every time he stops breathing, it only comes back louder when he has to inevitably gasp in more oxygen. Despite his noisy human body, he manages to hear the stream in the distance. "That's the distance to safety," his spinal cord brain tells him, "the stream".

The big problem I have with the modern horror flick is always the characters. They run upstairs instead of outside. They fumble car keys. They have a last night on earth make-out session. It's unrealistic. These characters make bad decisions when it matters. And sure, there might be some of that, but I bet more people than you'd think would do well in that type of situation.

The big man in the forest is not overly fat or tall or lean. He's a large square, and if there's fat on him it's a layer over solid muscle. In his mid-40s, he's leather tough from a lifetime of outdoors. He has a permanently sunburnt face with deep lines where it's hard for anyone to imagine him smiling. He knows the woods like few people do. Even compared to others in Idaho where outdoor recreation is common, he knows this place better. He's spent a full lifetime in the dirt. It's laughable now that tonight he had been outside for fun. Weekend warrior recreation.

He remembers how large the forest is, a million acres of cold nature. For all the distorted minutes he's been running, is it possible he could be alone?

The fact is that people have evolved this ability to do incredibly well under pressure. The hunters who tripped when a saber tooth tiger was chasing them were eaten. Our ancestors were not these people. Our ancestors are the ones who never tripped – not when it mattered. Evolution: It's all about the fight or flight.

Night is unnaturally dark, as if it isn't only the absence of light but a black coating over the world. There's a substance to it, like if he moved his hand quickly he'd feel an oily texture. No stars are visible, no clouds, and no way at all to distinguish shapes or objects using sight. There is

2

darkness in the darkness.

In this time of danger, the large man doesn't think about his family, or what he has to live for, or God. His thoughts are reptile thoughts. He thinks about what *it* is, and more importantly, *where* it is. His brain works efficiently and uses heuristics. It attempts to maximize the probability of survival. With higher thought shut down, the mass of jumbled neurons has considered climbing trees, toyed with the idea of hiding, weighed the advantages of running, and braced itself for fighting. This number crunching has led to a single conclusion. If he can get to the truck parked by the stream, he will be safe.

His truck is where he keeps his gun.

The sound of the stream is the natural sound a stream always makes, and it seems out of place for some reason, coming from exactly where it's supposed to be. A spark of hope ignites and is almost tangible. If the world weren't coated in this oppressive blackness, the spark might even be visible.

As a species, we do not drop our car keys. Not when it matters.

The man's muscles pump acid as he sprints. His energy is so focused on the vehicle he stops breathing. His brain sends the electric commands through his nerves to his fingertips, letting every piece of him know the danger he is in. Even his lungs are flexed. His toes detect the rocky ground with relative precision, and he glances off debris and trees and sage brush with quietness. In the darkness he stumbles, but he trusts his feet to recover and they always do. Before he is able to form the thought his keys are already in hand. By the time he reaches the car they are perfectly positioned to unlock the door.

The sky is dark, but in the openness where the truck is parked he can see some of the colorless world, everything changing from black to gray. Running into truck steel, he moves his hand along the cool body until he finds the keyhole, and when he does the key slides smoothly into the passenger lock. The two hundred and sixty pound man throws himself into the truck head first, rotating to his back as he slides in. He grabs the loaded revolver hidden behind the seat like it's the Second Amendment.

The car door sensor is sticky, and it can take up to two seconds for the dome light to turn on after the door opens. By the time there is light, the man is already positioned with his back braced against the locked driver-side door facing the creek. With hands steady as rock he points the loaded revolver at the opening toward nothingness.

He is unable to see into the darkness outside. Where the light from the truck should be piercing the darkness, it seems to be doing the opposite. The darkness pulses like it has energy, as if it's penetrating the light rather than the other way around. If anything, the light is making it more difficult to see because it's keeping his eyes from adjusting. Blinding him, almost.

The man makes a move to close the open door. He moves with quiet deliberation, struggling to hear any noise. He never lowers his gun.

Yes, but it's been a long time since people have had to run for their lives. Maybe we've had enough time to breed in some fumbling-of-keys under pressure.

His breathing is conscious, but he is unable to make it

slow. His hands begin to tremble, surely due to his tired shoulders. His eyes scan the darkness until they're unable to focus. The shaky gun never lowers.

It is only in the relative safety of the truck that the thought enters his head. *What if this is in my mind?* This *being in his head* seems logical in nearly every way.

But there had been those eyes. Those animal eyes, reflecting an eerie yellow, not unlike some giant African predator. Eyes adapted to see in the darkness. But rather than cat-like, there was something alien about the eyes. A self-aware kind of intelligence. A demonic hatred.

Every instinct in his body had told him to run, and he is the kind of person who has always trusted his instincts.

All through his long sprint to the truck the hateful eyes had quietly followed him, reflecting unseen light. Surrounding him. They had been at his side and in front of him, appearing for barely a moment, causing him to change direction and then doubt if he had ever seen them at all. Even now, those hateful eyes are in his mind. In the darkness he had lost all sense of north. How much time had he spent running? And even with his Lewis and Clark sense of direction, how is it that he eventually managed to find his truck running blindly through the forest?

The word *herded* comes to mind.

Was the supernatural part his imagination? It had to be.

All he had sensed was a strong wrongness. The eyes could have been any number of things.

His finger never leaves the trigger.

Spending his life in the woods he has seen real predators, but never something like this. As the minutes pass he thinks about all the things it could have been. A cougar. A bear. His imagination. *What else could it be?*

He lowers the heavy gun. Breathes out. Seated in the truck cab, he awkwardly wiggles his hand into his jean pocket, but the keys aren't there. His heart sinks as he remembers that in his hurry to open the door and defend against the forest he had left the keys dangling in the passenger door keyhole. *Shit.* For some reason the inside of the truck feels safe in comparison.

"There is no rational reason to be afraid," he says out loud and tries to swallow as he peaks his head outside.

Darkness fills the surrounding air and he immediately forgets all the reasons he shouldn't be afraid. The grayness has once again turned to black. Hairs stand up on his body and his hand clenches the revolver white-knuckle tight.

There's movement. Although it is slight he does not hesitate to aim and fire a single silence shattering bullet. There is no perceivable change in the situation except the high pitched tinnitus already ringing in his ears.

He yanks the keys out of the door and scrambles back into the truck, pulling the door shut behind him. *Start*, he thinks as he turns the key and pumps the gas pedal three times. Chemical electricity from the battery churns the heavy engine. The truck roars loudly to life as the fan belt squeals.

Something is wrong, but the old vehicle shifts reliably into drive and bounces into motion without a problem. As soon as the truck is moving he exhales slowly, but it takes almost a minute before he starts to loosen his grip on the steering wheel. It's something about being inside the metal armor of a moving vehicle maybe. Accelerating down the road seems almost anti-climactic. In a good way. Driving away in the truck was the goal, so mission accomplished.

The road is bouncy and narrow, the kind of road where you have to Indian-leg-wrestle over who has to back up when someone is driving the opposite direction. It's difficult to see the way ahead, even with headlights. The air seems covered with a dark fog, similar to a winter ice cloud, except it reflects black rather than white or gray. He turns on his useless windshield wipers, which don't help with visibility but they do make a distracting noise. When he turns on his brights it only makes things darker.

He drives as fast as he dares, but the speedometer rarely rises over 30 mph. He tries not to think too much about the possibility of something chasing him. He tries not to. He turns on the radio. The reception isn't perfect. *Sweet home Alabama* is playing, and he turns it up to compensate for the ringing in his ears and the white static. He likes the sound of the music and can put up with the white noise for now.

Relax, he thinks. He forces himself to focus on the dirt moguls in the road. He tries to think about his family. *Don't think about those inhuman alien eyes.* His wife would be out with her friends right now, eating and drinking and smiling. She's changed a lot since they were married over twenty years ago, but those orthodontically straight teeth still sparkle white. He thinks about that, her smile.

But his grip on the steering wheel is still too tight. His neck

7

is still flexed.

Although the thing jumps into the bed of the pickup with ninja silence, the driver notices movement in the rearview mirror and reacts instantly. He slams on the brakes with the complete force of thick quadriceps. The biomass slides forward and there is the sound of absorbed impact against the back of the cab. It is not the tangible deadweight thud he had been hoping for.

The man pushes the accelerator pedal to the metal in an attempt to buck whatever it is out of the pickup bed. The jolting of uneven terrain jars him sharply forward and backward while all his senses focus on the sliding scrambling sound of the unanchored mass behind him. In the sudden acceleration up the dirt road he is close to losing control. He switches from accelerator to decelerator. By the time the truck stops, one wheel is spinning uselessly in the air above ground. The truck would be capable of freeing itself from this situation, given time, which of course is something he is short on.

He looks behind him and sees nothing.

A sharp tap on the dashboard and he spins his head around. As soon as his vision is forward there is another sharp tap behind him.

The man's eyes are wild, darting from object to object at full alert speed. There isn't enough room in the truck cab to point a handgun properly, so he awkwardly holds it close to his body, pointing it in whatever general direction he hears noise. He is focusing his eyes into the darkness.

Nothing.

The windshield wipers are still on, going back and forth at rhythmic speeds. Rubber spreading dirt and the bodies of dead insects. But something else...

The sound of friction between fingernails and car steel and windshield glass. The sound happens in places he can't quite see: *tap tap tap, claw, scratch, tap*. He turns his head in every direction looking for the source, and although he catches movement in the periphery, very little is clearly visible.

The passenger door was left unlocked from when he climbed in, so he moves to lock it. As he reaches for the lock he sees a hand. Although it is weird in a way he can't place, it is distinctly human. The man pushes the lock down, but the foreign hand does not retreat from vision. It presses against the glass with a palm, probing the smooth surface. It taps on the glass, scratches the glass, tests the glass. The owner is underneath the window, just out of view.

His breath catches mid exhale. *A person?* His instinct had not prepared him for this. A monster, maybe, but a person? *Gun or run?*

The hand takes its time as it makes its way down and out of view, evidently finding the handle and pushing the release button as if to test the locked door.

Gun.

The man aims the loaded revolver and waits. When the human hand reappears flat against the glass it has an arm attached, and attached to that arm must be a torso. Everyone has a heart. He squints to shield his eyes from broken glass and pulls the trigger four times.

9

His ears were ringing before, but he is legally deaf now with sounds completely muffled. But he is confident in his aim, at least two bullets to the heart, and he has shot enough guns to be confident of where a corpse will be.

He slides over to confirm the kill, but before he can open the passenger door the pale white hand bursts through the splintered glass, grabbing him by the head like a cartoonish player palming a basketball. The man is pulled through the window head first.

His neck does not break.

The man fights with all his life force. He kicks at the thing until it breaks his legs. He attempts gauging out its eyes, until he realizes it has broken some piece of him responsible for moving his arms. In his last moments he tries biting until his brain becomes unable to connect the signals for even that simple task. He stops feeling pain and everything goes cold. He stops breathing. *Finally,* he thinks, remembering a few moments before when he was trying so hard to be quiet and stop breathing. It is a joke only he would ever get.

When no part of him is alive but his brain, he thinks about love and regret. But it is hard to think clearly while dying. He tries to hold on to a picture of his wife's smile as darkness takes even that.

Yep. That's exactly what this world needs. More survival of the fittest.

CHAPTER 1

It hurts a lot.

Johnny Sparks sits across the room from this woman, his wife. She is still his wife. Cigarette smoke hangs between them in the air and she sits, secret and deadly with her long legs crossed. Perfect pale legs. Her full lips wrap around the cigarette and she inhales as if she's been doing this her entire life. Johnny has never seen her smoke a cigarette before. He used to think she didn't wear skirts because she was slightly self-conscious about her legs. That reasoning seems ridiculous now.

Her left hand is cut. It's cleanly wrapped in sticky white gauze, but blood is seeping through the edges and it won't stop bleeding. It's oddly un-messy for the size of the wound, as if her blood is too thin for her skin. Johnny keeps waiting for her to look away so he can steal a closer look, but she never breaks eye contact.

Instead of asking about her injured hand, he says, "Can

you please at least let me take a pair of keys?"

Compared to his unusually large size she's a fragile little thing, like how Uma Thurman in *Kill Bill* is a fragile little thing. She looks breakable like a shard of broken glass looks breakable.

When she doesn't answer he keeps talking to fill the gaping silence. "So this guy. Do you love him?"

She blows a perfect smoke ring that looks like it took a lot of practice, and she lets it hang in the air before answering. "I don't know. I suppose not." She looks relaxed except for her eyes. Her pale blue eyes are sharp. Focused. "I definitely like him enough though. Obviously."

The cigarette has no filter, she rolled it herself. She took out a precise-looking amount of tobacco and spread it evenly. Her yellow hair spilled over her face as she rolled the paper carefully and licked one side like a sunset Mexican cowboy. She's smoking like she's been to prison or something.

Not knowing what to do with his hands, Johnny sticks them in his pockets to nervously jingle keys that are no longer there. "Why are you being like this? Did I... do something?" He doesn't want to hear more, but like anyone who's been wounded by infidelity, he keeps asking questions anyway. "I need to know what I did. What I could have fixed."

"Did you do something that made me have sex with this specific person? No Johnny. You didn't. I didn't mean to hurt you so can we drop this?"

Even clean shaven and well groomed, Johnny Sparks comes on as a great grizzly bear. Thick and hardy. Even sitting, he towers over Autumn. His clothes were clean in the morning, but they're already greasy from a day of manual labor and hard work. He's had to buy every shirt he owns at special stores for giants, and even these stores never carry Johnny's size in stock. He has to special order everything.

His voice is soft, but it booms deeply, "Who is he? You owe me that much, to at least tell me who he is." The furniture reverberates with his voice.

She meets his stare with caffeine eyes. "I really don't want to be having this conversation."

"After four sentences? Normal people tend to have a conversation about this sort of thing."

"Since when do you think of us as *normal people*?"

She's right of course. Thinking of Autumn as a normal girl is not a mistake he should make. Her frightening intelligence and cold beauty are anything but normal. She was always sharp, yes, but never like this. And he loved that. He loved her.

And now he's losing her.

She says, "It's time for you to leave."

Something hot rises in his throat. Why should it be him who must leave? After all, he is the one who built this house with his own hands. He is not the one who is sleeping with other people.

He swallows, and is left with only a sense of awkwardness. Embarrassment almost. He feels like an intruding stranger in his own house. But no, it was never his house. It was always hers. There was never any question about that.

"No, no, no, no," he says out loud. He had a plan. He had her. What is his life now? What is his life without her?

"You're entire body language says no, but your double negatives say yes. Let me get the door."

She doesn't move toward the door or anywhere else. It's Johnny who can't stop moving. He stands up and paces the length of the room. His room. His house. Her house. There are skeletons hidden here. He sits down. He stands up. He sits down.

The blood on her bandage bunches together, slowly forming a crimson droplet that snakes past her white knuckles. Johnny imagines a deep and thin slice. He forces himself to not look at the blood. She smokes with her right uninjured hand.

Johnny wants the key to the house, wants it more than he has ever wanted anything. If he can get the keys from her, that means he's still welcome in her house. He would still respect her privacy, and always knock, and never ask about her hand unless she brings it up first. But if he has the house keys, it means this is only temporary, her hand is fine, and maybe one day he can come back. "Can I please have the keys?"

"It's better for us if I keep both sets."

His airless chest collapses on itself. "Tell me his name," he says, and for the first time a hint of darkness touches his voice. "You owe me that much."

She does, and adds, "Not that it matters. You don't even know him."

In slow motion, a blood drop falls from her fingertips onto the hard linoleum floor. It splatters across the ground so hard it's audible. Autumn never acknowledges it.

"I should go," Johnny says, doing what she's been asking him to do this whole time. Leave. On his way out he can't help but say, "You can be a horrible person."

He walks outside with a hole in his left pocket where the house key should be. He doesn't throw anything or slam the door or hit her with the back of his hand. He imagines she almost says wait, but she doesn't.

CHAPTER 2

Apocalypse Wednesdays.

To Johnny Sparks, Autumn Sparks says, "There is no way at all I would attempt to rescue you in this type of situation."

The zombie faces are gruesome makeup. Autumn and Johnny watch as rotten wooden teeth tear through people flesh like undercooked rotisserie chicken. There are hundreds of them, an undead horde the size of a high school prom gone horribly awry. Every zombie is unnaturally fast and sped up in time. No arms, no legs, no problem. The American humans are helpless against them.

"Who says I'd need rescuing?" he says.

"You'd better not need it, because if you do, and if you happen to need it, that's one thing you're not going to get. Not from me."

She is sitting next to her husband while he is still her

husband. Autumn and Johnny Sparks two weeks ago are happy. Comparatively happy anyway, compared to today.

In the zombie world of science fiction tomorrow, there are only three remaining survivors from the original ten. Everyone is doomed. For the moment, the zombies seem distracted eating recently dead man meat, but the horde is large, and a zombie stomach is never satisfied. The remaining three humans are out of bullets and they are trying to barricade themselves into some place that doesn't look like it's built to withstand zombies throwing their own corpses against it. There are glass windows, unreinforced drywall, etc.

"In fact," she continues, "there are very few scenarios where I would save you."

"Is that right?"

"Not if I had to risk myself. Sorry Charlie."

As Johnny and Autumn watch the zombies eat human guts, the intestines look exaggerated but real. Everything is black and white.

They say this type of gore is something you can adapt to if you see it enough. If that's true, then Johnny hasn't seen it yet. Regardless, he enjoys his time here with Autumn. It's a blood spattered car wreck that's disgusting but he can't pull his eyes away.

Two week ago Autumn and Johnny hold hands and stare unblinking at the massacre. The normal sized seat is far too small for Johnny's square body. His muscles are hard from a tough life, not a gym. He likes the feeling of Autumn's slender fingers inside his massive ox hand.

Now is the climax. The horde looks unstoppable, but although the remaining three survivors have made a lot of mistakes, they've also proven themselves to be extremely lucky. Everything has led up to what happens next. But Johnny already knows. There are no happy endings in apocalypse stories.

"What's the long term plan here? What do they plan on doing about those little things like food?"

Apocalypse Wednesdays. That's what they call it at the Rockwell Valley Cinema. They have a poster and everything. Johnny glances around and wonders how long they'll keep calling it that, as empty as it is. Every Wednesday the cinema will show exclusive flicks about the end of the world. It's after Cry Baby Tuesdays where you can bring your screaming kid, but before Mystery Science Theater 3000 Thursdays, where audience members are encouraged to shout out jokes.

This Apocalypse Wednesday there's no one else in the theater watching the old zombie move besides Autumn and Johnny.

She says, "My biggest fear in any apocalyptic flesh-eating zombie type scenario is not people going extinct. I mean, if you look at a monster that fast or that big, the thing is a Ferrari. These gas guzzlers take a lot of energy. The whole monster thing just isn't self-sustainable. When food runs low, the monsters start to die. Maybe the less fast type zombie will survive and evolve to live on less human and more tomato. What I'm trying to say is I'm pretty sure that some guy and his family shelled up in a North Dakota bomb shelter will probably survive to repopulate planet earth."

"That's what your biggest fear isn't."

"My biggest fear is that the monsters will wipe us back to the stone age. The most important thing after your own skin is to save the information. I would be high tailing it to Google. Or Wikipedia. To save the information."

"Google?"

"Or Wikipedia."

She's repeating herself all over again. They've had this conversation nine hundred times before and Johnny doesn't care. This is the point in the dialog where thought experiments follow. They discuss advantages and disadvantages with respect to buildings to barricade themselves inside. What food supplies might be available, what's escape route C, do they have enough bullets, etc.

"Of course, Autumn, it depends on the type of monster. If the outbreak stems from a pig virus like in this particular movie, you might have a point. But if we're actually talking about the 'undead' here, you can throw physics out the window right there."

"I don't even know how to respond to that."

Johnny likes zombies and he loves Autumn, but the truth is he could like almost anything. If Autumn wanted to go to Mystery Science 3000 Thursdays instead, Johnny would be up for that too.

In some ways she saved his life. But he's having a hard time figuring out what to do with it now that it's saved.

Not being passionate about anything is everything Johnny Sparks hates about himself right now. Not to be confused with passion, which is a characteristic Johnny does have. He never wants to be one of those people who when they talk about their dreams they're only ever talking about the dream they had last night (and the dream usually doesn't even involve naked). Johnny wants to dream big. He just hasn't found something worth dreaming big about yet, other than Autumn.

"So I still can't believe you would leave me. I'm pretty sure you'd want me around to help start repopulating the planet." He says this with the careful confidence he's trying to project to a girl he sees growing distant.

"I'm sorry. Humanity needs my brain."

The analog projector clicks above, filling the room with mechanical sounds and flickering light above the actor's screams and all the things left unsaid. Johnny talks to his wife with a nervous and mathematical first-date charm where the words are calculated and punctuated with too many smiles. "Well," he says, "I would come back for you."

"Even after knowing that I'm not coming for you?"

"I would find you or die trying. Even then I'll probably be the walking undead, so I'll probably continue to hunt after you. Undead or not, you couldn't keep me away if you tried."

He moves his mouth in an upward shape, but the smile never reaches his eyes. His face is full of foreshadowing. He says this sort of thing a lot. Variations of the same theme. New jokes on the same observation that Autumn won't come for him, but he'll come for Autumn. Even if he's the undead.

The people on screen are celebrating their temporary reprieve. There's a guy and a girl who have chemistry, and it's pretty obvious they're about to pull a *last night on earth*. Little do they know, the third member of the group is using his long sleeve shirt to cover a suspicious looking wound on his forearm.

"When you look at this zombie survival party," he points at the screen, "or any zombie survival party really, there's rarely any logic. I understand people aren't rational creatures, but when it's getting obvious that there's an undead epidemic that spreads by biting, and when you have a big infected bite on your forearm, why are you trying to hide it? Except for the rare occasion where you're a main protagonist or love interest, you're completely hosed. If you have a zombie bite, instead of killing all your friends wouldn't you rather... like... go out fighting zombies like the Alamo?"

Autumn shrugs. "The point is that everyone is their own main protagonist or love interest."

"Wouldn't the survival instinct kick in for the rest of the gang? If I were in the middle of a zombie survival party and somebody new showed up, the first thing I'd do is make them get naked so I could look for bites."

"Johnny, if you ever find yourself in the situation where you're at a zombie survival party and when someone shows up on your doorstep the first thing you do is force them to get naked so you can look for bite marks, congratulations – you are probably part of some very crazy cult."

She kisses him with passion and smiles broadly. He pulls his head backward slightly, and Autumn has to pull herself all the way up to his height. He doesn't close his eyes for the kiss. He glances at the door, and then up at the opening where the person running the projector could potentially be looking in. His eyes cover every fire opening that a zombie might enter from. With her lips pressing against him in the dark movie theater, he doesn't press back. His feet are stuck to the movie theater floor, and he can't help blushing.

It's not that he doesn't love her.

Johnny likes Apocalypse Wednesdays because the cinema is always empty. He usually doesn't like going out to movies at all because as tall as he is he's always hated blocking other people's view. When somebody bumps into him in the aisles, he's always the first one to mumble, "Excuse me" or "Pardon me". On the drive to the theater he almost never passes anybody unless he has to. He drives defensively and has really good car insurance rates.

If a movie patron were to drunkenly punch him in the face for being tall, Johnny would say, "Excuse me."

That's why he doesn't kiss Autumn back, and she knows it.

CHAPTER 3

At first it's hard. He loves her and that hasn't changed and might not ever change.

She's *having sex with someone else*. That's how she said it. Not that she's been *sleeping with someone else* or *cheating*. "Well, I'm not having sex with someone else right this moment," she had clarified, "what I mean is I've *BEEN* having sex with someone else on a regular basis for some time now."

Johnny uses a thready rag to wipe sweat from his forehead, and folds it automatically, placing it in the same drawer where sandpaper is sorted from rough to roughest. The metal dust of the machine shop feels comfortable. Engine heat and the smell of oil is rubbed into everything here, including Johnny. He likes the cool concrete and safety goggles required. This is a place with the certainty of a job as secure as tenure. The cords are orange and the lights florescent. Every sledge hammer, screwdriver, and Stanley socket wrench has outlines traced with permanent marker for exactly where they belong. These are where the tools should be returned to, and this is also exactly where each tool can be found again. There is a process for lost tools. If something is lost for more than a day, Johnny will send out a departmental email asking about it. If it's lost for more than a week he'll put in a requisition for a replacement tool, but this doesn't happen often. This is Johnny's shop, and in here he makes the rules.

Moving metal around, his wedding ring is constantly in the way. It's gold but looks brass with age. He struggles to twist it off, muddy oil under his short nails, but his huge ring finger is swollen underneath and the ring won't budge. His hands look older than he remembers. The skin is cracked and rough. He would forget that he's not young anymore, except for his hands.

The things Autumn said to him hurt a lot, and she said a lot of things. She's decided she doesn't believe in marriage anymore. There are the tax advantages, sure, but she's decided to make a lot of money, and no offense but she doesn't want the kind of liability from anyone, and she doesn't get why Johnny is so upset about this. It's about how she feels and it has nothing to do with him. She says Johnny has stagnated. She says that maybe she wouldn't mind having sex with him in the future if he can get over some of his uncompromising nature. She says he has potential but not enough passion. Her words were poisonous.

The giant is working on a ski boat tower for one of the professors at the university. The professor has two teenage boys, and in the summer the family is on the water nearly every day. Soon the tower will be bolted onto the sides of the professor's twenty-one foot boat where it can be used for extra storage and for towing wake boarders at a more vertical angle. Buying from a store, a decent boat tower is several thousand dollars. Good stainless steel, on the other hand, is significantly less expensive. Johnny volunteered to build the tower in exchange for material cost. The professor didn't want to put Johnny out but Johnny insisted. The professor wanted to pay Johnny for the work but it would be against university policy to use state-owned workshop equipment for a profit, and Johnny doesn't need the money anyway.

The exact phrasing Autumn used would sound trivial to an eavesdropper, but the precise words and the carefully constructed sentence structures were the things that cut deepest. Hours later, he's still running the meaningless-sounding words through his brain. She knows him the way only a wife can. She was the only person on earth who knew exactly what would hurt him most and she said some of these things. It's a cut nobody can possibly give except the people you love who really know you.

He knows her too though, like only a husband can. It kind of makes things worse. *She cuts deep because she thinks she's helping me.*

A past conversation from a third or fourth or fifth date flashes back:

"Why would anyone want to do something like that?" He can't even remember what they were talking about. Skydiving maybe.

Autumn had shrugged, "Why not?"

"Ok… but why?"

Autumn had looked at Johnny with axiomatic clarity. "That's the difference between you and me. You live your life for why. I live mine for why not."

Almost complete, Johnny is welding the final joint. This tower will be stronger and lighter than one the professor could have bought from a store. A tower from a store is generic. One size fits all. But Johnny was able to build this tower as an exact fit for the professor's fifteen year old boat. Johnny turns off the welder and the flame consumes the last bit of fuel instantly. Stepping back, the tower looks good. He double checks the details. Stainless steel shouldn't rust, but in a few days he will still apply a clear coat for extra protection. Water is a pretty tough environment for mechanical parts.

"It's him or me," he had said to Autumn.

"Him," she said without any sort of hesitation, not even the pretend kind.

"You… aren't even going to think about it?"

"I'll always love you, but I'm never going to choose someone who makes me choose."

For all the grief, when he looks back at how he treated her, he was the best husband he could ever be. He was always kind to her. He laughed with her and never took her for granted. He was never rich, but he had provided. They never went hungry, and they had been financially stable enough to buy the fancy brand of cup o' noodles. For their short time together, he was a good husband. It's time to move on, so he puts her out of his mind. Johnny Sparks is nothing if not pragmatic.

Looking at the boat tower, even in his darkest hours, Johnny is able to create something that makes the world a little better. This is not a trait that Autumn mentioned when she told him to leave.

Logistically, there are a few things. He wants the divorce taken care of quickly, which should be simple enough. Autumn has always been independent and wanted everything separate. They have separate checking accounts and they both do their own laundry.

Johnny never leaves his tools out of place. He returns the welder to where it's supposed to be. He moves the tower into the area of the workshop he's designated for unfinished projects, and grabs a broom to sweep up.

His metal mechanical watch ticks to 2 in the morning. He's usually at work by 6:30, but in a university environment the schedule is pretty flexible. Usually, he'd just come in late tomorrow. Usually, he'd pick up the phone and leave a voice mail for the college receptionist upstairs. He would say tomorrow he'll be in after lunch. Nobody would care. Everybody likes Johnny, and he's responsible and hard-working. He's not some kid who punches in a time card.

"Shoot," he nearly cusses, because of all the days he could get some sleep, he can't be late tomorrow. Tomorrow's the big day.

Next thing, he needs a place to rest, and even though the practicalities of not being able to go home are harder than ever, the hole in his pocket where his keys should be no longer feels so empty.

He grabs the jacket and hat he brought with him. He puts on the gloves he leaves in the shop for when it gets cold and he doesn't bring gloves. When he opens the garage door to step outside, the cold air stings the way it can after a hot summer.

The small extension campus in Rockwell has three buildings. As an offshoot to the bigger campus thirty miles away, this campus caters to undergraduates who are interested in college but have a hard time making the windy drive to Inkdon every day. This is the beating heart of the tiny city, if there is such a thing.

They call the open area between buildings *the quad*, even though it's not rectangular and doesn't even really have four sides. The clean cut grass still has green parts, but it looks crisp with cold. With a few more days at this temperature, almost all vegetation will turn completely brown. Neat cement paths connect the building, and crisscrossing between them is the dead grass and dirt where students and faculty actually walk. The campus has a feel like the mascot should be an Aggie, and there's a certain vibe that screams, *we lack accreditation*.

There is a motel named *University Inn* across the street from the extension campus. Johnny has never stayed there, but he doesn't exactly have many options.

He walks through the quad on the dead grass. The cold hurts his ears.

Lights are always on throughout campus. Bulbs sit on top of poles with big red buttons. The lights look like they might be sirens. Painted on the side in hospital red is the word EMERGENCY. These are rape lights, designed for students to push when they're getting raped, or ideally before they're raped. The blue light shines brightly, and makes it impossible for Johnny's eyes to adjust to the darkness.

The university extension at Rockwell is the exact opposite of a party school. People come here to learn and save money by living with their parents. The campus empties completely at night, which is when the wildlife invades. The word *wildlife* is not slang for fraternities or some other college thing. Wildlife is literal - night is when raccoons and deer move in. Johnny regularly sees deer. *A pack of deer? A herd? A gosling of deer?*

There are no deer tonight.

About twice a year the campus police issue a cougar email alert that circulates to students, faculty, and staff in the Rockwell area. The campus police are two curmudgeonly ninety year olds who watch over the dangerous Rockwell campus extension district. Although most of their job consists of issuing parking violations and looking angry, they also occasionally respond to the cougar emergency. "It's okay everyone," the emails read, "The campus police are scouring campus with night vision goggles in search of the cougars. We won't rest until we've found them."

It's funny in a way that makes you laugh when you're sitting back at your office, but makes everything terrifying by yourself at night when nothing is visible.

A dark civil war cannon rests on a pedestal at the center of the quad, covered in shadow. Old and brassy, it looms heavily over the cement walkway. During the day it's easy to forget it's an ancient instrument of death. But now... this late at night...

It hits him that he's afraid.

Something isn't right. Every outline looks like the shadow of some terrible thing. It feels like a spider creeping on his neck. He traces shadows in the darkness, and with every step the dark outlines seem to stalk along.

Johnny Sparks walks on the dead grass, watching out for a cougar. Or a gosling of cougars, even.

Is someone there? It sounds like footsteps are walking behind him. Barely an echo. When he stops the footsteps stop too. When he takes three quick steps it takes three quick steps, or maybe only two steps, and maybe they're a fraction of a second off. He looks around but only sees shadow.

Even this late, it seems like at least a few stragglers should be wandering home. *Where is everyone?* His only companions are the crepuscular trees, bare of leaves now, stretching out with clawed hands that grasp with lazy malice in the breeze. Head on a swivel, he looks for anybody who might be using the university labs to finish a late report on a Tuesday. There's nobody.

Did I miss the cougar alert?

His stomach is so tight he could take the sucker punch that killed Houdini. He can feel the quiet and he's walking on the fronts of his feet. University Inn isn't far and he's not being reasonable. Television is misleading. In real life a cougar is only around the size of a dog. TV or not, dogs are usually less scary than cougars.

He walks outwardly casual to convince himself there's nothing to worry about. He tries to hum a song, but it comes out tuneless and he stops immediately. He moves his head from side to side at the beat of an absent rhythm.

There is no noise at all other than the sounds of his casual steps and his shotgun heart rate. *And those other footsteps that are just a millisecond too slow.*

In radar detection mode, his eyes dart from object to object, looking for anything that might be alive. *Trash can. Stupid little sculpture thing. Shrubbery.* He wants to sprint, but he has never in his existence had to run for his life. His brain associates fight or flight with amusement parks and zombie movies. Fear is an emotion set aside for apocalypse Wednesdays.

So he walks casually, identifying objects.

Another shrubbery. A big landscape rock. A stump.

The boulders have black slits for eyes that are following him. The trees have twisted mouths set forever in their screams. Everything looks like some hideous demon from hell. Or a cougar.

The rape lights on campus are evenly spaced like a residential neighborhood, but they don't seem to produce enough light. Johnny's shadow stretches out a long way in front of him eventually fading into nothing at a rate that's a calculus story problem waiting to happen.

Sinister Tree. Evil Shadow. Horrific Rock. Possessed Tree.

Everything visible has a long moving shadow. Johnny can't see more than a few feet in front of him and with every step he has the feeling that something is silently waiting to jump out. He has the feeling he's being hunted.

Lamp post that looks like a person. Shadow that looks like a person. Human Being that looks like a person.

Wait.

Even squinting, the human shape doesn't turn into a shadow or a lamp post or a garbage can. There is an evanescent, almost ghostly quality as it stands, perfectly dark and still in the space between rape lights. For some inexplicable reason, this person standing there seems impossible. Not necessarily against the rules of physics, but against some convention or natural law, like overhearing a Mexican speaking Mandarin. Johnny can make out a head, two arms, two legs...

There is something sinister.

"Hello?" Johnny blows out his cheeks at his own words and shakes his head. The volume feels wrong – he's almost yelling but trying to talk in a normal tone. The human shape must be 150 yards away and his voice sounds too loud in the quiet campus. "Hello?" Johnny's stranger voice cracks, and it sounds like he's hearing it through a recording.

The shape doesn't respond or move. The smell of dirt rises to his nostrils, mud even, although there is no water.

Somehow Johnny knows this shape is looking at him, and pumping through his cold blood he feels a horror he has never felt before.

Forgetting to feel foolish, Johnny runs toward University Inn and away from the human shape.

He reaches the sidewalk, huge boots pounding against concrete. University Inn is on the other side of the empty street. Instinctively, Johnny turns toward the direction of the human shape to see if anything is following him.

There's nothing there.

He double checks his reference points. Yes, the garbage can next to it is where it should be. Yes, he is looking in the right place. But where the human shadow was is now empty space.

Johnny puts his head down and sprints across the street to University Inn. His strong legs pump acid against the pavement and his broad arms pump like truck pistons. He goes straight for the double wide lobby door.

He pulls hard, but the lobby door doesn't open. It's locked.

CHAPTER 4

Derek Darius drinks his coffee black.

Ashley the Barista has the shift from three in the afternoon to closing, which here at the College Market House of Coffee usually means three to seven. Except now it's past one o' clock in the morning and here she is.

She takes extra care making this single cup of coffee. She tries the Kona beans this time, and she uses the French press ritualistically. Never grounds, not for him. With how particular Derek Darius can be, he never tells her what she's doing wrong. She wants so badly for him to be happy with his coffee, or at least not get angry.

He's been angry before.

Ashley has never had a problem getting tips. Her dark hair is shoulder length and streaked with blue. She has a hundred different hats, and ten different fake lip rings. She often wears a scarf to go with her boots. Tonight she's waiting on only one person, Derek Darius.

He's been here for hours.

Derek Darius types quickly on his ten thousand dollar laptop. Hunched over his computer he looks lost in thought, glaring at the monitor. She has made a few attempts to look at his screen, but it's gibberish to her. It looks like math and science and alien.

He's wearing a black leather duster in the 72 degree climate controlled environment. He's wearing red-rimmed sunglasses indoors, at night.

Clack clack clack, Derek Darius clacks his keyboard, *clack clack CLACK CLACK CLACK CLACK.* Keys are melting.

He takes a moment to sip his coffee slowly.

Then he's typing again in a fury. Every finger hits a key so hard it sounds like an IBM model M from the eighties. Even with modern rubber to ergonomically soften the risk of carpal tunnel, the click clacking is spring loaded and mechanical. Ashley turned off the music long ago, right after she turned all the chairs upside down on the tables. Every key pressed is an explosion in the closed room.

Sometimes he laughs out of nowhere. This is not a polite first-date chuckle, but rather he'll throw his head back with hearty laughter. Sometimes he smiles at the screen, as if in a conversation.

He only needs a coffee refill about once an hour, giving Ashley plenty of time to work on important things like counting toothpicks and staring at walls. She looks for shapes in the texture, and she always seems to make human faces. Two dark blotches are the eyes, and the mouths are twisted and gaping.

Everything about the billionaire is sharp. His perfect jawline is angular, and his black hair jets into needle points. It's difficult to place an age for Derek Darius. His face is full of youth, with light lips and a slanted nose untouched by age. But the appearance of youth never reaches his eyes. His eyes could be a thousand years old.

Whenever Derek Darius comes into the coffee shop, people are terrified of him for all the wrong reasons.

As he clacks at his laptop with sharp fingers, those ancient eyes have all the intensity of an obscure Olympic sprinter who has one last chance to set a world record. It may not be a coincidence that he always wears sunglasses. Derek Darius's eyes have that Olympic kind of intensity all the time.

The city sign to Rockwell says, "Welcome to Rockwell. Population 13,700. Home to Derek Darius."

To the audience, Derek Darius always wins the race. He's already world famous. He's already powerful. But his unblinking eyes never change to those of a champion. They're always old underdog eyes. Maybe in his own mind he's never won.

When people first see Derek Darius, they think of money and television. "Did you know he can memorize a page in the phone book in five minutes," people say. "You can ask him three days later what the phone number is for Elizabeth Beck or anyone else and he'll just know."

They ask if they can have his autograph, if they can gather the courage.

"Did you know when he was six he could divide any two numbers in his head faster than someone could type them into a calculator?"

"I heard he got his first PhD when he was sixteen."

There are around seven stages of running into Derek Darius. Every time Ashley the barista sees him she's scared at first. Fear is stage one. She knows every line of his angular Time Magazine face. Even this time of night his white skin looks like it was just airbrushed.

She never knows where to look. He's someone she obviously recognizes, but despite his perfect memory and all the times he's come to College Market House of Coffee, she doesn't know if he recognizes her. She suspects he chooses not to. She always ends up looking at the ceiling or a wall. He can remember Elizabeth Beck, a random name from a New Jersey phone book, but he hasn't bothered to remember her name.

"He's only a man," people say who have never met anyone famous and powerful and consistently ranked in Cosmopolitan's fifty sexiest whatevers.

The next stage of Derek Darius is anger.

He takes a break from clacking at the keyboard to light a cigarette.

"You can't smoke in here," she says reflexively. The words bite off, feeling as fake as her lip ring. She moves her tongue around the back of her teeth looking for absent chewing gum. She always has gum, but not now. She had swallowed it when Derek Darius walked in the shop.

He glances her way and a humorless laugh blurts out. It's

a sound more irritated than malicious. He keeps smoking.

"Seriously, you can't smoke here. I could lose my job if my manager smells smoke."

She used to describe herself as confident.

"Oh Christ, you're actually serious." He rolls his head from shoulder to shoulder. Inhaling again, deeply, he blows a perfect smoke ring. He inhales one more time and slowly exhales in her direction. He puts out the cigarette on the wooden table next to him, and leaves the cigarette butt there half burning.

She bites at her fake lip ring so hard it pierces her skin. Folding her arms across her chest, she waits until he looks back at his laptop before she starts shaking her head. Her mouth tastes bloody. She swallows. If not for him, tonight would have been amazing. Seven hours ago her plans were as complex as watching Gilmore Girls, but now she builds them up in her mind. She would have invited friends over maybe. Gone out to dance. Eaten something. Right now she's starving. Her shrunken stomach has turned in on itself.

The only food handy is coffee shop chocolate. She takes a bite and hates Derek Darius. Ashley is not remotely fat, but it takes a lot of work for her to stay skinny. This sort of hate is the next stage of running into Derek Darius. According to her bathroom scale, she's gained two pounds over the past two weeks, plus or minus two pounds. While Derek Darius's attention is elsewhere, she's glaring at the side of his face. Even then she has a hard time looking directly at him. She takes another bite of chocolate. *You're the person making me fat.*

The celebrity stops typing, grabs the coffee mug, and holds it out like a sultan of Abu Dhabi. This is his way of saying he wants another cup. He glances at her like she's some kind of subspecies, his eyebrows raised with expectance. *Servant! More Coffee!* But as soon as he sees her standing there with arms folded into an annoyed posture... it's a god noticing a mortal. Behind his red rimmed sunglasses his eyes narrow in annoyance as he peers into her soul.

She pales, but not in time to hide the scowl she was wearing a second ago. Derek Darius knows what she was thinking, and she knows he knows. The celebrity can always read people's thoughts. He sees through their faces.

"Well, look at you, barista, you certainly look intimidating. No one would fuck with you. Or French kiss. Or probably cuddle."

She opens her mouth but no words come out. Her long-sleeved shirt has holes cut out for thumbs. Eyes wide, she's grasping the shirt holes as if for support.

"Get me another cup of coffee."

Like a beaten dog, she gets him another cup. She walks with slumped shoulders and looks at her feet. Feeling contrite is the next stage of running into Derek Darius.

It's two thirty in the morning and Derek Darius says again, "More coffee."

"Sir." She doesn't know how to address him. "We close at seven." *Should I have called him Derek. Or maybe Derek Darius?* On television they always call him Derek Darius

39

and never just Derek.

His cup is held out, waiting for his goddamn coffee.

All the things she's thought about saying to Derek Darius in her head disappear. She sputters, "You're the only one here. I didn't know you'd be here this long and… I… didn't bring a book. I don't have anything to do." The words come out whiney, like a baby. She stares at the floor where she was counting tiles. There are thirty six of them, she knows by heart she's counted so many times. She stares at the wall where she was looking for faces. She looks at everything but Derek Darius.

He stares at her cold and sharp.

The small amount of dark brown liquid in his mug is hardly coffee anymore. It's cool with bits of used grinds. Slowly and deliberately, he stretches out his hand and dumps the quarter cup of brown liquid onto the carpeted floor away from his feet.

Ashley's heart stops beating and her mouth hangs open in the surprised gape of one of the wall faces.

Dumping the coffee is not in anger. It is calculated and precise and cruel. But even calculated it's an action that hints at strong passions barely hidden below a logical surface. The coffee dump is a rattlesnake's rattle. Maybe next he will burn the College Market House of Coffee to the ground.

Not many people risk making Derek Darius angry.

With his polished black shoes, he grinds the coffee into the carpet. He smiles with his mouth. "Now you have something to do. But do it after you get me a cup of coffee."

She pulls out the French press and decides she'll go with the full-bodied Columbian beans this time. She grinds eight scoops worth of beans, because he might like the coffee darker. Her movements are practiced and professional, leagues above coffee hobbyists. Fresh brown liquid bubbles up as she pours it halfway into the press. This time, she will try using the heavier mug because it might bring out the flavor better. As she pours, her nose fills with the aroma of a really good cup of coffee. She almost smiles, if only for a second.

But when she turns around the College Market House of Coffee is empty. Derek Darius is gone.

Money is a funny thing. The celebrity's wealth is public record, and Ashley has calculated that while he was typing away at his computer his carefully aggressive investments have made him more money than the gross domestic product of most countries - there's always a market open somewhere in the world. Ashley makes four dollars and fifty cents per hour plus tips.

Derek Darius did not leave a tip.

I don't care. At least he's gone and I can go home.

She's still holding the heavy coffee mug as she walks to the glass entrance. Outside it's dark like how only the late fall can be. Darker than that, even. She's clutching the coffee mug too tight. Her old 1988 Ford Mustang LX is parked across the street in the university parking lot - a ten minute walk from the College Market House of Coffee. She never would have parked so far away if she would've known how late she would be here, or how menacing the

41

night would look outside. There aren't many street lights on that walk.

She hesitates to open the door for some reason, but decides it's only her imagination. On the door, there's an old yellow bell that lets the employees know when a customer has entered or exited the College Market House of Coffee. When she opens the door, there's the familiar ring, but something's wrong.

When Derek Darius left, the bell on the door never made a sound.

CHAPTER 5

Johnny Sparks bangs against the University Inn lobby doors. "Open the door! OPEN THE DOOR!"

His moose sized heart is pounding at ten thousand beats per second with all the ferocity and desperation of somebody with a horde of zombies at his back.

"For the love of God somebody please let me in!"

An intercom is to the right side of the double doors. There's no voice, but for half a second there's static, the sound after somebody says "over" on a walkie talkie.

"Let me in!" Johnny doesn't need to look behind him to know there's something right there, almost breathing on the back of his neck. He doesn't need to look to know there's not much time.

A tired and confused voice squeaks out of the intercom, "Uh. Are... you here for a room?" Crackle. Over.

Johnny is pounding the industrial glass with insane jerky movements usually reserved for straitjackets and hobos, "LET! ME! IN!"

The automatic lock clacks open and Johnny shoves the door open, lunges inside, and shoves the door back shut again. Even with all his big weight behind it, hydraulics or something makes the door compress shut at a leisurely pace.

He glances around the cheap lobby. Five steps away is a fireplace and next to it there's a fireplace poker. Johnny is there in one step. He grabs two of the heavy iron sticks and pushes one through the locked double door handles. He keeps the heavy sharp one for himself.

Standing with the sharp fire poker positioned like a hitter waiting for the pitch, he tries to look through the semi-clear door, but all is black outside. The glass that should be transparent is a reflective one-way mirror where he can't see a thing except himself staring back with crazy-person eyes. No way is that lobby door strong enough to keep out... whatever it is. His muscles are flexed with the long fire poker. There are windows as well as the main entrance. The giant tries to position himself so that all the entrances are visible.

The sleep faced college student working the late shift, the concierge or whatever, he walks up to the doors and presses his face against the glass. No hesitation. He puts his hands up to shield his eyes from the interior light, standing motionless for a few seconds, looking outside. Johnny Sparks stands with his neck muscles flexed, expecting something to burst through the plastic glass and eat the concierge.

"Uh," the red headed kid turns around. "So... do you want a room or not?" He talks with a voice cracked as puberty.

…

Obviously, Johnny Sparks can't sleep.

The motel room is dastardly, and it's displayed like a horror movie set. The yellow incandescent light bulb flickers as it does a terrible job of lighting up the room. Before doing anything else, Johnny had checked all the cobweb corners, and looked under the dusty bed and behind the rusty shower curtain. His biggest complaint is that the room has a small defenseless window. The concierge/college student said that having a window couldn't be helped, but what he could do is get him a room on the top floor of the three story building, which he guesses might be hard for a mysterious monster type thing to get at. And to answer Johnny's question, yes, although the janitor's closets technically do have heavy doors and no windows, it's against hotel policy to rent them out. Insurance reasons.

It's almost three o' clock in the morning.

Johnny Sparks drags furniture across the room, positioning it snugly against the front door, which is the most solid door out of the "hotel's" three vacant rooms. All the doors used to be the same, but the concierge assured him, this door was just replaced after the old door was kicked in as part of a police raid. He doesn't remember what type of wood it's made out of. Something old, he said. Like oak.

The furniture does not drag quietly. *I hope there's not anyone in either of the rooms next to me*, he keeps thinking, *or in the room below me, or in two rooms below me.* With the world famous Derek Darius talking at the

45

university extension tomorrow, occupants are packed into the building.

Initially, Johnny had wanted to raise the alarm, to go from shabby motel room to shabby motel room, warning the people sleeping inside. But warn them against what? The concierge had treated him like a crazy person, and maybe that wasn't far off. What's more likely? That there's a creature of the night outside, some supernatural demon? Or there is only a man, sleepless, kicked out of his own house and ravaged by lovelessness, who maybe heard a raccoon and overreacted.

Yet Johnny just keeps dragging heavy objects from A to B. Whenever he makes an especially loud noise he drags more slowly, which without fail just makes the loud sounds worse. Cardboard wood against stained carpet and plastic linoleum, no matter what he does there are high pitched screeches or wooden crackling. He continues to move the furniture around anyway.

He looks out the window every few ticks. Everything is so dark he can't even see the ground below. All the windows in all the rooms were like this, black like there's black construction paper plastered against them. They look like they should be washed off, but scrubbing them doesn't seem to help. Physics has gone crazy. He has gone crazy. Something. The darkness is unnaturally penetrating the light.

A leaking full sized fridge, a detachable stove, two stained queen size mattresses with wooden frames, a toilet cover, a five hundred pound CRT Television, a recliner, a wooden chair, a table, a folding chair, an ironing board; these are some of the things barricading Johnny inside his room.

Most of them are pressed against the front door.

The door does feel solid. Johnny wants to disassemble the wooden bed frame and nail the boards into the door and over the window. He still has the sharp fire poker, and he could use that as a hammer. Nailing is something hard to do quietly so he decides against it.

He looks at his watch. 3:01 in the morning.

His veins are gorged with blood and adrenaline. Time is passing at a strange marijuana velocity. Everything is too loud and too clear and too slow.

He looks at his watch. 3:00 in the morning. *Wait, what?*

With furniture piled in front of the door, Johnny wipes his hands on his jeans and takes a step back to examine the defensive situation. Hundreds of zombie movies have made him something of an expert. The walls feel thick like they're made out of solid World War II cement. The material is all asbestos and steel and lead paint, which is good. The whole building has a solid dilapidated late 1940s early 1950s cold war feel, like it should be able to withstand an atomic bomb.

The three story window is the weak spot. *What if something is able to climb or jump really high?* The stuff in front of the door that's intended to stop a super monster thing is starting to look more and more like junk blocking his only escape route. *How do I know there isn't a fire escape or an easy way for it to climb up to the window? I tried to check, but I can't see anything outside...*

Johnny walks to the window and presses his forehead against the dark reflective glass.

Outside looks strange because he can sort of see, but he can't see well. His wild brown eyes, usually so sharp at night, are unable to focus. Everything looks grainy like he's looking at the world from a video cassette tape playing on an old black and white television. There's a useless street light less than a block away that doesn't seem to be doing anything but retreat.

Reflective light from the room is blocking the view, so he runs to the other side of the room to flip off the light switch, dodging some of the fortified clutter. It doesn't help.

Three stories below, light from the street lamp is scattering into a thousand separate pixels at three hundred million meters per second. The air is confusing static.

He glances at his watch. 3:01.

What's that?

Somewhere in the randomness are distinct patterns of movement. It's fast. He blinks, and then it's gone. A photo of bigfoot caught in the corner of your eye that you know is fake. A memory that's already fading. Except his body remembers. The hair on his arms is standing up again.

Johnny can't explain away this feeling. Whatever the concierge's reaction, in his arteries he knows he's seen something sinister. It's a feeling in the pit of his stomach like the opposite of how he knows God exists.

Fear overruling his dutiful sense of politeness yet again, Johnny begins the process of dragging most the furniture back across the room to barricade the window. He starts with the ironing board which covers the window nicely. He begins the process of disassembling the wooden bedframe so he can use it to nail the window shut.

The whole time he's dragging furniture and nailing things into the wall he thinks about his motel neighbors unfortunate enough to get a room adjacent to the lunatic. "I am so sorry everybody."

The joke is on Johnny, because there's not another soul at University Inn he might wake up, no matter how loudly he pounds the bed frame screws into the wall.

CHAPTER 6

"Are you there 8 a.m.? It's me, Nathan Montgomery."

According to *National Lampoon* and verified over and over by *American Pie* three through eighteen, college should have bi-weekly toga nights, beer in red plastic cups, and topless girls gone wild hot tubbing. Also, there should be whipped cream involved somehow. And scuba gear? Specifics are vague.

For years, Nathan Montgomery fell for this sort of college fantasy.

The only way he was even able to make it through high school, which was terrible, was by thinking that college would be this completely different and better world. Whenever his mind would drift, it would drift to thoughts like how in college girls would like smart guys and not just idiot football player assholes. The fact that with college things haven't changed much is evidence that the rest of his life might be like this. Terrible. Filled with loneliness and genuinely mean and nasty people.

"Don't worry about being lonely," Nathan tells himself, "The trick is to just to keep being myself, but with money."

In his closet-sized dorm room, he can hear his neighbors having sex or something, bouncing against the institutionally cold and bleached concrete walls and screaming. Things are tipping over and banging. They've been at it all night. It's like he's been locked in an insane asylum.

At first he puts the pillow over his face, trying either to kill himself by smothering or maybe at least block out noise. As a noise blocker the pillow is useless, and he can still breathe so he wonders if it's even really possible to kill yourself by pillow smothering or if it's one of those things you need another person for. *Do you need to be old to die like that? I only ever hear about grandmas being pillow smothered.* He's trying to will himself to sleep but he's stuck thinking about tomorrow's 8 a.m. Derek Darius lecture. This is not something he wants to be tired for. *There's a reason I went to bed at ten o' clock.*

When he first laid down he was too excited to sleep. Now it's so noisy he's skeptical anyone could sleep.

With every crash outside, he clenches his slightly crooked teeth a little tighter. He tries to go to his happy place of how things will get better in the future, maybe after college, but he's fairly certain he doesn't believe that anymore. By now his teeth are clenched with the force of a crocodile.

I need to make an investment in ear plugs and sleeping pills. He's thought this a hundred times before but can never remember to actually do it when he's not trying to sleep.

He wishes he could move back to his room in his parents' house, which is a bicycle ride away. Unfortunately, Mom and Dad think Nathan living on his own will help him grow into a responsible adult like they are, apparently. They have already converted his bedroom into a "craft room", making it "impossible" for him to move back. As far as Nathan is concerned, moving home is more of a money thing. It's what a lot of the other kids going to school at the University Extension are doing. At the rate he's going, by the time he finishes graduate school he'll be a billion dollars in debt and make a scientist salary. His parents don't help him with school, but they make enough money that he's ineligible for most scholarships and government aid. Either that or he sucks at getting scholarships and government aid, who knows.

"I worked my way through school," his dad who grew up in a different economy likes to say, "and so can you." Like withholding a payment to a starving boy in Africa to teach the child an important life lesson.

At least here in the good old dormitory I have my own room where I can sleep, he thinks bitterly as the walls pound and pound. Nathan isn't sure what "craft room" means, a place to put together scrapbooks maybe.

An irregular knocking comes from the door, as if someone is either trying to talk to him or might have just accidentally run into it as part of some massive hot tub toga party orgy he's not a part of.

Nathan stops breathing. *I'm not home whoever you are.* His door has no peep hole so he can't see outside unless he opens the door. He thinks about the underwear he's wearing. Old whitey tighties with the elastic stretched out and broken. There are several holes, and without elastic, the underwear can barely stay up against his bony hips. *There's no way I'm answering that door.*

Nathan went to a party once. His friend who was also a nerd talked him into going. A lot of people were there and it reminded him of being a sardine. That was the first time Nathan had ever tried beer and it tasted awful, but he sipped it deliberately. He didn't know anybody and his friend disappeared somewhere. Lots of people were dancing, so Nathan bobbed his head with what he hoped passed for rhythm. For a long hour Nathan went to the corner and sipped on the awful beer like he was enjoying it, enjoying himself, enjoying the music, etc. He smiled and gave several thumbs ups to people passing by. Eventually he left by himself. He didn't drive so he walked home. He would later wonder if people ever gave thumbs up to each other.

Nathan's face is as skinny as the rest of him. If his nose is too long, well, at least it's straight. If his side-parted blonde hair makes him look like Rick Moranis, well, at least he has hair. That night when he was walking home from the party, he had hoped every car that drove by would be the girl of his dreams, or at least a girl looking to have sex with a nice, decent looking guy. He might not be a great looking guy, but at least like a five. Maybe a four.

Most rooms in the Rockwell dormitory are shared, two people to a cell. In most rooms there is a sink and a mirror and a window and an old single pipe steam radiator used for heat. There are usually posters and textbooks and computers that fill these rooms. Beds are moved about in pretty much every configuration imaginable, sometimes residents even manage an impromptu bunk bed with cinderblocks. There is always a flag, the most common from China and Texas. The Rockwell dormitory inmates are jailed by nature as much as anything.

The dormitory is the tallest building in Rockwell. There is also a twin women's dormitory that's four stories, but slightly shorter. Nathan's room is a closet with a bed. He is on the top floor, the fourth floor, but the room looks like it belongs in a basement. There are no windows here, and no artwork hangs from these bare walls. He has his empty room to himself. At the beginning of the semester, he went out of his way to ask campus officials if any dormitory rooms were available that were not shared. Without extra cost there isn't in general, but with enough repeated phone calls and annoying enough people, Nathan managed to get himself his very own closet at half the price of a regular shared dorm room. It doesn't have real heat and is less than half the space of double occupancy rooms, but since it's located in the middle and there are no windows, it keeps the climate at a generally habitable temperature. There is enough room for a bed as wide as his shoulders and a cramped desk for his computer. What more does he need?

The fourth floor is full of Chinese exchange students. It's not racist, it's just quieter. Usually quieter. Nathan has an Idaho flag he ordered on the Internet hanging on his wall. It's the only Idaho flag in the dormitory.

Something knocks against Nathan's door. He thinks it's a knock. It's difficult to distinguish since the whole floor seems to be full of shouting and Mandarin and running into things. No doubt there are drugs involved. There's no way he's going to be able to sleep through this. The noise is getting louder. The shouting, more hysterical.

Starcraft II it is.

He gets out of bed in his underwear, logs in, noise cancelling headphones on, and he's ready for time to speed up. Nathan wants the hours before Derek Darius's talk to pass instantly. Whenever he plays Starcraft II his mind always goes into a sort of hypnosis like a long Interstate drive in the dark. As he moves his cursor over his zerglings, the noise outside fades into the background. His brain empties itself of the world, going to thoughts of defensive strategies, offensive strategies, and Korea. *Freaking Koreans. I play this game enough hours to make it a full time occupation and you still beat me. Get a life!*

His screen goes black.

Power outage. He removes his headphones.

Inches away from the other side of his dormitory door, there's a scream that would make a wine glass shatter. It's so full of gut-wrenching terror that it's more animal than Chinese. The shrieking lasts longer than it should. When the sound dies down it's replaced not with silence, but with a terrible gurgling sound, and also the sound that fingernails make when they dig deep into white coated concrete walls.

Nathan kicks the side of his desk and says fuck. Some party prankster downstairs must have flipped the breakers and cut all electricity to the dorm. Nathan just doesn't know how to handle these crazies on the fourth floor. *Why the heck are they screaming right outside my door?* He was just about to try his new swarming rush strategy, and it's not as if Starcraft II is a game where you can just save.

55

CHAPTER 7

Ashley the barista searches every corner for Derek Darius, rich fuck head. There isn't anywhere to hide in the College Market House of Coffee, so searching doesn't take long. He must have left, but there's this sliver in her mind she can't get rid of. The bell on the door always rings whenever it opens. That bell never rang. She's sure of it. Pretty sure. Like ninety percent sure.

Well, he isn't here now.

The thought of running into Derek Darius outside makes her skin crawl. She waits until she's sure he's gone. After that, she waits a few more seconds. She counts to sixty. *How long does it take someone to walk out of sight?* Derek Darius is one person she absolutely does not want to run into on her way out. She counts to sixty again and again. After each number she says "Mississippi".

Perhaps the celebrity opened the door slowly. That's surely one way to keep the bell from ringing. She approaches the door herself, looking at it skeptically. She grabs the door handle carefully, giving her best effort to keep silent. Yet still, as she pulls the door deliberately open, the bell rings. The quiet air outside is crisp dry ice. Water in her lungs crystalizes and freezes solid. The days are getting shorter and the nights longer. Autumn air has killed the garden tomato plants and now it's after humans, making them catch colds and whatnot. Flu season.

She's thinking she should start wearing her winter coat and other thoughts that don't much matter. What she's not thinking about is something waiting quietly in the shadows. No one thinks about things lurking in the shadows in Rockwell. She never in her life goes to survival mode, no matter how many cougar alerts there may be. The last time somebody died here it was from slipping on the ice and it was two years ago and that old lady was ninety three. People go into town to die in hospitals. Death is not a regular visitor here.

At the College Market House of Coffee the most popular drink is called la mode Americana. It's a comfortable six dollar cup of American coffee that sounds kind of Italian. People pay for it because it tastes better and comes with free wi-fi.

All it takes is three steps outside the shop.

One. Two. Three.

She's hit with the force of a diving ninja football linebacker.

Whatever tackles her opens what looks like a human mouth but it just keeps opening well past where a human jaw should stop, unhinged unnaturally wide. The motion is fluid with no joint detachment. The row of teeth fits nicely over her throat. It squeezes shut with the power of a crocodile, ripping through arteries and tissue and muscle and wind pipe. There's so much blood it could be a scene from an eighties action movie, *Robocop* vs. *Rambo III*. When the powerful jaws pull back there's a mess of body mass and spinal cord where a slender girl's smooth throat should be.

This happens before she can react in any conscious way, like scream, although she does manage to make a sort of groaning sound. Before she can even think, *oh my God it's coming right for me,* everything is already black.

If she had the capability of thinking anything anymore, Ashley the bloody barista would probably be blaming Derek Darius for this. After all, he is the reason she was working late in the first place. First it was making her miss *Gilmore Girls* and then it was yelling at her and now this. If she could've gotten to her car, it probably wouldn't start either, and that would be Derek Darius's fault too. It's one of those nights.

Statistically though, she might be comforted to know that the reason she's dead has nothing to do with the fact she worked late. By now pretty much everyone she knows is already dead too.

CHAPTER 8

The screaming outside stopped eventually. That's when the deafening silence started. For hours, there haven't been sounds of people waking up or snoring. No neighborly students getting up to take a leak. Even whirling appliances and clicking furnaces have been absent. *Deathly silent.*

Now that it is morning, Nathan wants to be the one screaming so he can give these fourth floor motherfuckers a taste of what it's like to try and sleep through a loud flat mate.

The cell phone screen is the only source of light in the windowless and electricityless dorm room. The room layout is still new enough to Nathan that he can't remember where the light switch is. He gropes at the walls feeling for it, and when he does find it, he flips it uselessly. Yep, no electricity alright.

Some towns have rodeos and others fireworks. Rockwell

has the annual Derek Darius technology talk. Nathan needs to leave soon. Every twenty three seconds, he presses the button on his phone so he can see the time. In his mind he's already set the exact minute he should start getting ready. He needs to be at the talk at least 2.5 hours early, well before the crowds from Inkdon start lining up. This event is a big deal, and the place is going to be a madhouse.

Nathan struggles in the dark to find basketball shorts and a t-shirt, something to wear on the way to the community restroom and shower. Yet another one of the fantastic amenities of living in the dorms is that the home bathroom is also a public bathroom. They should use that as an advertising slogan.

Looking for the door handle, he runs into the computer desk. His room is so small that the door, which opens inward, bumps into the bed. He has to open it part way and squeeze past the desk chair to get outside. The mis-weighted door automatically swings shut behind him.

When he turns to look at the common area his face is slack. His expression never changes as he tries to comprehend what he is seeing. The only thing that moves is his eyes.

Floor four of the university dormitory looks like a crime scene. Light and air are pouring in from a shattered window. The rubber-duck yellow Naugahyde chairs are tipped over and shredded, like something with claws dug into the fabric. The metal trash can is knocked over and there is garbage scattered across the carpet. Wind from outside is blowing some crumpled paper around like tumbleweeds, which it can do now because there is no window to stop it.

"What is wrong with these people? They don't have any respect for where they're living at all."

Despite his bone skinny frame, Nathan is wearing a sky blue extra-extra-large t-shirt. On the front it says, "GNU's not Unix". Even his pale face is frail, with smooth skin stretched over breakable cheek bones. Next to the trash can there's a mass of something red and squishy that looks like undigested food. With myopic clarity, he tries not to look directly at it as he makes his way to the common area restroom.

At the best of times, this bathroom reeks of an underpowered fan and students who can't aim. After a night like last night, Nathan isn't sure what kind of horrors to expect. He breathes deeply and holds his breath like it will be his last as he pushes open the door.

If anything, the bathroom is worse than he expected. He tries not to identify the biological objects growing inside. Something furry that looks like a scalp is wadded up next to a sink, and the grout between the tiles is teaming with some unspeakable ecosystem. Something like vomit and blood is smeared all over the wall. Maybe it is vomit and blood.

Disgusting.

With no windows, the institutional bathroom is dark. The thought of getting clean here is laughable. He showers out of habit. He has to search the darkness to find the valve, and when he turns it on, the water still works. At least it isn't freezing. When he steps inside the stall, through his sandals he feels some gunk with about the consistency of dog shit. The humid air in the stall smells like old refrigerated pork. Context matters. This naked smell in the shower is so much more horrible than the exact same smell would be while cleaning with latex gloves and a gas mask.

The shower is quick, and the whole time he tries not to touch anything.

…

Outside, the sun is coming up and glaring into his eyes. The morning is crisp and freezing and dry. He can see his breath crystalize in the cold air. He hides his hands in the sleeves of a heavy winter coat that is several sizes too big.

The cafeteria is in a small building located between the girls' and boys' dormitories. It opens at five, usually. There's someone who sits at the front of the building to scan his student ID and stamp his hand, usually.

He looks at his phone. 5:17.

What surprises Nathan is not that the glass windows to the cafeteria look closed and dark. It is that even with the closed dark windows the door is unlocked, and Nathan is eerily by himself. There isn't anyone eating an early breakfast, like there usually is. There isn't anyone to scan his student ID, like there usually is. He searches for a sign hanging up that might offer some sort of explanation, and hopefully directions on where to get breakfast.

He re-checks his phone.

What kind of a party was that last night? Was I the only person not invited?

He walks into the cafeteria with crooked glasses and an open mouth, looking like some sort of nerd *Far Side* character. The cafeteria is always crowded. Most mornings he has to fight for a seat, and with Derek Darius talking in just a few hours it should be bustling. Being here by himself, it feels like being thrown into the middle of Disneyland with no power and no people, sneaking through the *Indiana Jones* ride while some hapless security guard is working to find him out. There is an overwhelming sense that there should be people around.

"Hello? Is anyone here?"

Food is important for Nathan. He eats it almost every day. Despite a diet consisting mostly of Doritos and Cherry Vanilla Dr. Pepper, he looks almost anorexicly skinny and needs a lot of calories to keep even the weight he has. He would have a nice body if he were a female model. Unfortunately for Nathan, the lesbian population percentage in Rockwell, at least ones who have come out of the closet, is zero. Besides, the whole him having a penis thing might put them off.

In the cafeteria there should be cereal and oatmeal and someone making omelets. There should be someone making smoothies. He walks behind the stainless steel counters where people usually serve him food, hoping to find something. He's not allowed back here, but Nathan is a rule breaker. Some people just wreck themselves before they can check themselves.

Nathan has been described by his mom as an "absent minded professor", and he's the first to admit he is not the most observant person. But there's a cloud of wrongness descending, and even the oblivious Nathan is working hard to put pieces together in a morning where everything seems wrong.

He glances at his phone clock again, and his gut sinks. *What if everyone went directly from the party to the Derek Darius talk?* He needs to leave, and he doesn't have time to keep searching for someone to tell him what is going on. If he leaves now he'll arrive at the talk earlier than he had planned, but waiting around for almost three hours is no problem. Not with a Pac Man phone app for that. Also, Angry Birds is for wussies.

His stomach growls at the thought of not eating until lunch.

On his way out he opens several closets until he finds what he is looking for. There is a mountain of non-perishable food items. He has never stolen anything in his life, but tuition is too high and his coats have deep pockets. This stuff is waiting to be taken. He thinks about his great grandma, who lived through the depression. She was quite a lady. Every time she went out to eat with the family she would stuff her purse with free sugar packets and ketchup.

CHAPTER 9

His hair is wild.

He's tried to comb through it, but the plastic hotel comb was no match at all. His flannel shirt is tucked tightly into jeans as if to compensate. Even one day without proper care and the hair on his head starts to curl crazily. His stubbly beard is already thick and black.

Johnny Sparks stands at the University Inn checkout counter, looking like a hulking maniac. There is a bell to get somebody's attention. He rings it again.

He stretches his back, stiff from sleeping on the seventies shag carpet. *God, I wonder how much University Inn is going to bill the credit card they have on file for disassembling their bed and nailing it to the window.*

Despite doing his best to tidy up, the room upstairs is in as much of a mess as his hair. Stuff still piled high, there are traceable gashes that start in the linoleum floored kitchen

65

and continue all the way to the topsy turvy refrigerator braced against the window. He silently rehearses his *no really, the bed was completely torn apart when I got here* speech.

Johnny's mind is reset back to zero. The monsters of last night are far away and irrational. The memories of her are closer than ever, and it's hard to believe that she left only yesterday.

I need to call her.

He tried to call her from his room, first thing, but he can never figure out hotel phones. He had pressed nine. He had pressed zero. No matter what he did, there was no dial tone.

When he pictures Autumn, all he can see is her sliced-open hand, dripping blood.

Time to pull myself out of the I've-just-woken-up-in-a-strange-motel-room-where-I've-barricaded-myself-inside-for-protection-against-imaginary-vampire-monster-right-after-the-woman-I'm-still-in-love-with-left-me-and-also-I'm-questioning-my-sanity Tuesday blahs.

He shakes his head hard enough to dislodge these lower order thoughts from his brain. *I can always call her later.*

He needs to get to work.

His job is a government university job. Unless it's a fiscal recession year and you're caught looking at pornography it's a very difficult job to lose. But this morning is the *Derek Darius* talk. The whole reason Rockwell campus exists is because Derek Darius lives here. He is one of the most powerful people in the world. Think lines of black

66

limousines and dark Chevy Suburban decoys and motorcycle escorts with bulletproof glass, and it's not like that, but only because Derek Darius doesn't want it like that. He is the motorcade without the motor.

This talk is the type of thing people have been working on for months so that everything goes without a hitch. It will be broadcast and recorded and put on the Internet and have a sound bite on the front page of international newspapers. Johnny is the go-to guy. He is the one who mounted the projector and fixed the broken chairs and built tubing to keep Ethernet cables tidy. If something goes wrong and Johnny isn't there, he'll be blamed even if it is unrelated to anything he's done; a situation where not even his boss or his boss's boss or the governor of Idaho himself could save his job. There's this stress and pressure for what essentially amounts to a one hour talk.

No matter how many times he rings the service desk bell, nobody responds.

After glancing at his digital wristwatch, he decides he'll go to work and come back to the University Inn later. He doesn't like leaving the loose end of a destroyed room upstairs, but keeping his job is more important. Even more important is calling Autumn. On the other side of the counter is a phone that is not a confusing hotel telephone. He'll just call her, hear her voice, and then he can leave. He has to suck his stomach in to squeeze through the half door leading behind the counter.

When he picks up the phone, there is no dial tone.

His stomach drops, and the room suddenly feels uncomfortably cold. Has the temperature dropped? The dusty chandelier hanging in the lobby isn't giving off any light. He hasn't seen anyone since morning. If the University Inn had so few vacancies last night, shouldn't there be people?

Johnny desperately wants something in his hand – a weapon. He remembers the fireplace in the lobby from last night. The fire poker would be a decent weapon. Solid. Close. A fire poker is about the right weight for swinging hard. It should be just behind him and to his left.

When he turns, the poker is laying almost right where he left it. There is one difference however. The hard iron has been bent into a deformed pretzel.

CHAPTER 10

Nathan has no signal on his cellular telephone.

This isn't the type of thing that's usually a problem. It's not like he uses his phone a lot. He did call a girl that one time, but he eventually hung up when she said, "For the last time creep, who is this? I can hear you breathing! That's it, I'm calling the police." To be fair, that was taken completely out of context. And also, he knows for a fact his phone was on mute and it would have been impossible for her to hear him breathing.

There's nobody here at the engineering building.

Nathan is wondering as hard as he can if he is in the wrong place altogether, but there's no way to check without his phone. *Could they have changed locations due to the power outage? Where would they send an alert like that to? The cougar alert email alias?*

No carrier signal is mostly just how things operate here.

Rockwell is a canyon community and building a cell tower here would not be cost effective to telecommunication companies. Usually Nathan could check these sorts of details on his cell phone through the wireless access points, which are plentiful. A very, very fat Internet pipe runs into Rockwell. With a small population of only around 14,000, the cost effectiveness argument could also be applied to fat pipe bandwidth, but there is an invisible gorilla hand in the room. The largest tubes in the civilized world run into Rockwell, a place with no good cellphone tower, because Derek Darius wants a fast Internet connection. The billionaire doesn't carry a cellphone. He thinks they're a rip off.

Usually access point only Internet is fine. Usually it's more than fine. But with no power, there is no way for Nathan to determine whether or not he is waiting around by himself in the dark at six forty-five in the morning at the wrong place.

He says out loud to his phone, "You hunk of junk, the only thing you're good for is telling time." Pause, as if listening. "No phone, how could I play *Pac-Man* at a time like this!?"

The engineering building should be packed by now. There should be a long line of dedicated Derek Darius fans who camped out overnight. Dozens of people wearing "Derek Darius for President" t-shirts should be elbowing each other and having arguments about saving spots and cutting.

Instead of this, in walk Julie Black and Tim Scott, the second and third people to arrive.

Nathan smiles awkwardly at the newcomers. Maybe he is in the right place after all. The relief doesn't last long. Julie and Tim are looking around like they don't know where they're going. Worse, it seems as if they've stumbled in together. Like they're a couple or something.

Julie is wearing a black t-shirt with a logo nobody has ever heard of. Maybe a band or possibly a bicycle brand. Her skin is covered with tattoos, both arms snaked with tribal design sleeves of black and red and green. Nathan wants to look at these in more detail, but instead is swallowed by the green depth of her round eyes. She opens her mouth to speak.

Instead, it's Tim who speaks. In an accent from North Virginia he says, "Is this Derek Darius?" According to Nathan Montgomery, he knows everything he needs to know about Tim. Tim has a confederate flag in his dorm room. On his face is thick stubble in the beginnings of a sandy blonde beard, and when he's older he'll have a full beard for sure. He's the kind of person who drinks Budweiser and talks about the hotness of girls and argues about which brand of pickup truck is best. He is a first year computer science student who before that was a liberal arts major and before that he was something else. Both he and Nathan usually sit at the back of the same classes.

Peering into the dark engineering building that looks like it is closed, Julie Black's eyes dart around the empty room. "Are we in the right place?"

Nathan has noticed that she always smiles genuinely when she talks, even when she's asking a question or has nothing to smile about. With skin as smooth as a paperback book, she barely wears any makeup. Her brown hair is cut so short it doesn't even reach her ears, and she seems to do something different with it every day of the week. According to Nathan Montgomery, he knows

71

everything he needs to know about Julie Black. She's cute and she's a girl going into computer science.

"This is where it was scheduled yesterday. Maybe they cancelled or moved it because of the power outage."

Julie and Tim nod, but Nathan has already pulled his phone out so he has something else to look at. It isn't long before they're mumbling to each other incoherently while they flirt. Nathan didn't even realize they knew each other. He had always thought of Julie Black as single. His imaginary version of Julie Black likes writing poetry and developing advanced science in her spare time. She does not flirt with southern rednecks. Back in the real world, these two love birds would probably be happy if the Derek Darius talk were cancelled. They'd probably spend the time French kissing or something.

There's a useless electronic card system and most of the doors are locked, so the gang is restricted to the hallway with no chairs. Tim takes off his army-green-looking jacket and sits Indian-style on the linoleum. He's the type of guy who wears t-shirts all year round. He's tan in that healthy Southern California kind of way, not in that Kentucky Fried Chicken kind of way. He has teenage boy forearms with long brown arm hair and roping arteries. His neck muscles give the impression that he's spent a lot of time throwing bales of hay. He rolls his head and neck bones crack.

Nathan hates him.

He thinks of how his own shirts all button up at the front, and how his own arms are white and bony. His own arm hair is so thin and blonde it's invisible to the naked eye.

In most computer science classes, Julie sits in the front

row. Nathan knows the back of her head well. She answers a lot of questions the professors ask. He can imagine the sound of her voice even when she's not around. It's a beautiful voice, rich and seductive. The long computer science words most people only ever read, she enunciates like she's had practice saying them out loud. Smiling, Tim touches her leg while they talk. She doesn't move his hand away.

Ugh.

Tim says to Julie, "I need a neck massage, and I'm willing to trade for it. Whatever you want, return massage, lap seat, sexual favors. Seriously, I'll trade whatever." He speaks twangingly.

"Maybe you should try and trade someone money for a neck massage. People do that sort of thing for a real job and everything."

From the far corner of their conversation Nathan says to Tim, "I can give you a neck massage." Nathan says it seriously and nobody knows him well enough to get the joke. Nobody laughs and the words come off creepy.

There's no doubt about it, the morning has been a strange one.

On his short walk to school there's an old single-lot house situated by itself in the middle of the campus. Old people live there. It has a white picket fence to keep the college kids with their longboards and roller skates and fireworks off the lawn. They have this annoying giant poodle dog that must live in the yard, because every time Nathan walks by, it charges at the fence and yaps something high pitched and menacing. When he walks by at three in the morning, it barks. When he walks by at three in the afternoon, it barks. Christmas. Martin Luther King Jr. Day. Whatever. The fence is waist high and the dog looks like it could jump over and go for Nathan's throat if it wanted. The poodle is always there to charge at Nathan.

Except for this morning. This morning, the dog was not there.

Nathan interrupts the flirting couple mid-sentence. "Did either of you notice any dogs or cats on your way here this morning?"

"Nope. No dogs or cats noticed," says Tim.

"I think something's wrong." The way Nathan stares at the ground it looks like he's talking to himself. Pieces are falling into place. There are a hundred things that are standing out. The broken windows and the powerless cafeteria and the dormitory garbage and the missing poodle. He blurts out, "I think everyone's gone."

With her smile fading, Julie asks, "What do you mean you think everyone is gone?"

"I don't know... Out of town, like for an emergency or something. Or maybe they're dead. Maybe they went white water rafting, who knows."

I shouldn't have used the word dead.

"Where did you come up with that idea?"

"My brain. It's the same place I usually come up with all my ideas."

Tim and Julie don't revert to flirt talking. Julie's eyebrows are crinkled in thought, and Tim is leaned far enough forward that his sandy blonde hair tumbles over his face. *They feel it too, the wrongness.* The room is melancholy and hypnotic - standing quietly around a camp fire and staring into orange flames. Dodging smoke.

Tim finally nods. "That *would* explain a lot."

"You're both making patterns from nothing." Julie shakes her head viciously. "This is the same line of thinking makes moon craters into the man in the moon."

"Then why is it that you came over to my house this morning?"

"This is the line of thinking that makes water vapor clouds into penises," Julie continues. "Some clouds might look like penises. It doesn't make them into actual penises."

She's right. When you take all this noisy input from the world and try to make a pattern, it can so often be wrong. But there's a reason people evolved to do this type of thinking anyway. If, hypothetically, there were an undead creature on earth silently destroying the world, the human mind would be pretty well adapted to notice and extract this sort of pattern from the mess of information, just like a penis shape from a cloud. To back up his point that it's better to be on the safe side even if something is completely stupid, Nathan says, "Nobody has ever died for thinking Dan Brown books were realistic."

Julie and Tim both say, "What?"

"Like… the Knights Templar…"

The conversation is cut short as someone bursts through the Engineering building door.

The shop manager's presence is massive. He is an ox of a man. Old scars line his face, one prominent above his upper lip, one below his eye. There is a wild look to his movements, and whenever he takes a step his hundred metallic keys jingle. Nathan has never seen someone as big as the shop manager, or a face as granite. He looks like a dad from an older, tougher generation. His asymmetrical caveman eyebrows are ugly, and his flat nose makes him look dangerous. Even when the giant was a teenager, Nathan bets that he looked like a dad.

The giant's eyes sweep the room. Johnny Sparks asks, "Where is everyone?"

CHAPTER 11

The room is dark. The room is light.

At the front of the class, Johnny Sparks can't seem to stop moving. He paces one way, looks at his watch. Paces the other way, looks at his watch. The room is quiet, so the walls echo every time his oversized feet thump against the institutional linoleum.

In the back row, Julie twirls the plastic blind stick with her fingers seductively, opening and closing the room's access to sunlight outside. Next to her is a single window in the otherwise windowless computer lab, and also two Computer Science boys ogling her out of the corners of their eyes. She looks like someone who knows she's pretty; even when not smiling she seems to be barely suppressing a secret smile. There are fifty nine empty ergonomic office chairs complete with metal rests. Each station is equipped with a nice computer with powerless dual monitors and useless optical laser mice. But sitting in the back of the class, she has the stage. In that way, she reminds him of Autumn.

Seven forty-five in the morning. The Derek Darius talk is supposed to start in fifteen minutes. Johnny Sparks isn't concerned about the human-shaped monster he thought he saw last night, but he is worried about how he didn't check his email and wasn't available on his home telephone since yesterday morning. He's listening to his other survival instinct, the one he uses to make money and hold a steady job. He's thinking thoughts like *What if there was an emergency and they were trying to get hold of me* and *how could I be so stupid* and *I did this to myself.*

The blinds open and shut between Julie's forefinger and thumb. Clockwise to counterclockwise, she rolls her fingers in perfect rhythm. Since the single window is the powerless room's only access to light, the finger movement is turning the entire room from darkness to light and back again. The Computer Science boys are glancing at her sideways. Their mouths hang open.

"Can you stop? Please? Thank you." Johnny says to her. She stops twirling the blind stick and she renders the room completely black as the blinds happen to land in a darkness phase. "Actually, just one more time?" She opens and shuts them so the room stays dark. "No." but he trails off and with heavy feet walks to the back of the room to open the blinds himself.

The computer lab is what people call this room, as in *let's meet in the computer lab to do homework* or *Johnny Sparks is going to be fired in the computer lab.* The giant has poured sweat into making this place the way it is. When he first came here it had been full of old professor boxes. He built the stage, upgraded the wiring. Old

78

buildings like this have character. There are no hovering floors to snake copper through. He had to make the room adapt.

He stomps back and forth while the three Computer Science students watch in captive silence. If her twirling the blinds is something to look at, Johnny is something to not look at. He walks past the podium computer, the white boards, the recording equipment, and then back again and then again. The stubborn whiteboards have been wiped clean with professional elbow grease. There's an expensive backup microphone packed with rechargeable batteries so the famous words can be recorded even without power. Check one. Check two. Everything is prepped and ready for the Derek Darius talk.

Johnny Sparks looks as if he's trying to do long division in his head. He keeps pulling out his secondhand flip phone to check for a nonexistent signal. There are fifteen minutes until the talk is supposed to start and the audience so far consists of three people, all of them quietly trying to not watch Johnny stomp around. Johnny is pretty sure that every single one not watching him is autistic. Especially that kid with the glasses. Nathan.

What computer scientist isn't a little autistic?

He stops pacing and faces the room. "What's going on? I won't be angry, I just want to know what's happening. Why isn't anyone here except you three?"

The small audience sits there, looking everywhere but in Johnny's eye. The computer lab is full of nervous energy.

"You. What's your name?"

"Julie Black," the words escape her mouth too cheerfully. She says them through fake smiling teeth like she wasn't ready to talk, but the words came out automatically.

"Okay, Miss Black, what's going on?"

"Is this not where the Derek Darius talk is?"

"It is indeed, Miss Black. So where is everyone?"

"Isn't that something we should be asking you? Aren't you supposed to work here?"

She's right. Johnny Sparks isn't much older than these people, but he is the one who works here, not them. He should be the one with the answers, and he doesn't take that responsibility lightly. All of his thoughts are adrenaline thoughts, much too loud for this classroom silence. He stomps out of the computer lab without a word. In the administration offices across the hall, he starts making a lot of loud crashing noises.

…

Nathan is in love. What is it with girls and sticks that's so attractive? It doesn't even look like a penis, and even if it did he isn't sure he'd like the twisting anyway… On the other hand, he doesn't see why he wouldn't like it.

The CS students can hear Johnny Sparks across the hall jingling keys. He's opening and shutting doors too loudly. Stomping.

Tim asks everybody, but mostly directs the question at Nathan, "What's this talk supposed to be about anyway?" Somehow, Tim has made it into the talk that will likely have over fifty million YouTube views and he doesn't know what he showed up for.

Nathan cracks his knuckles. Actually, only three of them can crack. He isn't sure why. It might be genetic. "It's one of the Tuesday Tech series they have every month. They have a brochure they hand out that's a standard template. It has fields like speaker, bio, and description. Under Derek Darius's talk it just had TODO written."

"How many people usually show up?"

"Like a gazillion."

Julie Black starts twirling the blind stick again rhythmically. There's a cheap wooden necklace she's wearing that's beautiful on her, resting over her green collarbone tattoos. The room goes light to dark.

In the other room it sounds like Johnny just knocked over something heavy, like a file cabinet.

White to Black.

"So Nathan," she stops his heart by saying his name. "Everyone is gone huh? Or dead."

"Yes, but it isn't all bad. The test on Friday will probably be cancelled."

"The test?"

"In computer architecture."

She doesn't register any sort of understanding, and she stares at him blankly.

"The class we're in together?" He tries to clarify. "You sit in front of me?"

"Oh… right."

Tim taps his chewed fingernails against the wooden desk like a miniature baseball stadium wave. His pinky starts the tap, which ends with his trigger finger. He shakes his surfer hair out of his eyes. "Well, that's awkward."

Nobody laughs or smiles. Stating that the conversation is awkward somehow fails to make the conversation un-awkward. Nathan opens his mouth once and then shuts it again. He starts having eighties style flashbacks to the three times he's bunglingly tried to ask girls out.

"But seriously," Julie eventually gets out, "do you really think people are gone?"

"Or dead?"

Julie stops breathing when Nathan says the word dead.

"You know, yeah. I do."

Light and dark, the quiet this time is contemplative and a little scared. There is no finger tapping and the blind stick comes to a stop – it stops on dark. It always seems to stop on dark. Nathan wonders whether it's a coincidence or if they're being drawn to it. Her eyes are glued to Nathan and so are Tim's.

The silence is broken by a non-visible Johnny Sparks across the hall. It sounds like he hit his head and he's angrily muttering unintelligible words. Julie starts to twist the blind stick again. Open. Shut.

Hypnotic.

Slouching in his chair with his legs against the wall, Tim is the only person watching the blinds. It seems to be out of thin air when he gets up from his chair and says, "Whoa whoa whoa whoa whoa."

Everyone freezes. Nathan has no idea what Tim is talking about. Julie has one round eyebrow raised.

"Who's that black person? I don't mean black like Julie." Julie's last name is Black. "Or the skin color."

The single window in the near-windowless computer lab points at the quad. The grass is white with frost and there are wisps of mist slowly evaporating.

Nathan crowds at the window. Looking outside at the center of the quad, he can hardly see anything. Despite the complex glass structure of his bifocals, his eighteen year old eyes are useless. He squints like the only person not able to see the 3-d boat in a magic eye autostereogram. He crosses his eyes and focuses. *Relax, you can only see the picture pop out if you relax.* He opens his relaxed eyes.

"There it is."

"Yeah, we all saw him like five minutes ago."

It is a black silhouette against shadows. Bent at the waist with sharp predatory hands, it stands in a posture of restrained animal aggression. It is hidden in plain sight with shadows pooling around it. Although the sun is out, the light never seems to reach this creature. Strong and mechanically still. It's hard to see clearly, but its claw fists look clenched. It's impossible to tell for sure, but the shadow face looks inhumanly malevolent. Like it's staring at them staring at it with pure hatred.

The creature is black like evil. It is not black like Julie. It is not black like the skin color.

"Hi," Nathan whispers and waves.

Some people like to personify Death. They sometimes call it a reaper. Terrifying. Unrelenting. Inevitable. This thing looks like that.

"A vampire," Julie says, and the word doesn't seem funny or strange when talking about this thing standing outside.

"He wasn't there a second ago." Tim talks with wide gestures and expressive arms. His disproportionately big hands and big feet now look more gawky than strong. "Julie twisted the blinds open while I was looking right at the window. Julie closed the blinds, and when she opened them again BAM, that dude was standing there like a flexing statue."

"Are you sure?" Nathan says skeptically, "That's like two hundred yards of grass. With most supernatural beings it would take at least two blind flips for them to get all the way over to the middle. Unless it's like a... magician."

"Dude, what the hell are you talking about?"

"Magicians can disappear... and appear."

"Open blind closed blind open blind. That's how long it took for him get there."

"So if Julie flips them again does he go away?"

...

Walking into the room, Johnny Sparks starts to interrupt but stops short. He was going to tell everyone how the phones aren't working, and how there doesn't seem to be power on the rest of campus either. Instead, his eyes slide to the window and lock onto the dark creature that is still standing motionless outside. It appears to be glaring into the window, and into Johnny. The feelings of yesterday night are suddenly back. The thing stalking him. The alien wrongness. Johnny's huge hand clenches and his sandpaper face hardens.

The ox man moves at surprising speeds. With reaction times rivaling Nathan's South Korean Starcraft competitors, Jonathan Sparks is outside the computer lab before anyone else can stand. Durable rubber boots against classroom linoleum, his steps thunder down the hallway. Going down the stairs he takes them five at a time. A detour: he opens his unlocked workshop, passes some tools, a drill, a saw, a screwdriver. He grabs the seldom used but occasionally essential sledgehammer. Johnny doesn't know what to expect, but the core part of his brain is telling him it is evil enough for the sledgehammer.

What he is not doing is second guessing himself. He is not going outside to see what the dark creature is because he knows enough of the answer already. The only question he has now is how resilient the thing is to sledgehammer forehead bashing. Most things, even unfathomably evil things, have the common weakness of not functioning well without a head.

The inside of the exterior doors have no knobs, they push open. Tim, Nathan, and Julie make it down the stairs just as Johnny kicks the door open while holding the humongous sledgehammer over his head with both hands.

Something is in the path of the opening door, but it moves out of the way at an unnatural speed. The skin on the door-evader's face is white as frost. Where his eyes should be there are red reflective sunglasses. He's wearing a dark Keanu Reeves trench coat and is surrounded by cigarette smoke.

Derek Darius?

Johnny pushes past the celebrity standing there. He scans the quad for the shadow creature that was there a moment before, but the quad is now empty. There's nobody there but Derek Darius.

CHAPTER 12

She laughs to try and hide her sadness.

"The fact that only three of us showed up to your talk isn't the only thing that made me think that something was… off. There are a hundred nasty little things I know will sound unimportant and small when I say them out loud, but there's a reason that I believed Nathan when he said people in town might be dead. It's not the kind of story I would believe every day. I'm not that gullible. I'm not like… from Texas or anything."

Julie Black has deep circles under her eyes. Below a mid-thigh skirt she's wearing pantyhose, black and ripped at the top. She keeps reaching down to pick at the tears. Her triangle jaw almost turns into a smile as she says Texas. She says it like she's trying to relieve tension. It doesn't work.

"Every morning, without exception, my mom wakes me up. This has been happening since I was a kid. When I say without exception, what I mean is if I have plans to get up at 4:00 in the morning to go skiing at Pebble Creek, she wakes up at 3:45, puts on her robe, and turns on my light. Every morning. Every single time. If I don't wake up right away she whispers my name until I say something or open my eyes. She's an atomic alarm clock, my mom. She's never been late or forgot, not once. So this morning when I woke up and my light was off..."

She swallows sad sounds in her throat. There are restrained tears reflecting the cool sunlight, and she's barely holding them back. She's gripping and releasing her hands in the air.

"My bedroom is below ground and the basement window is tiny, but it was letting in enough light for me to know right away that it was already morning. I laid there for two seconds until I remembered the Derek Darius talk and the fact I was supposed to be awake. Maybe my mom forgot – there's a first time for everything. I tried to ninja jump out of bed by arching my back and jumping to my feet. I fell backward off my bed, which hurt. When I managed to flip the light switch, nothing happened. There was no power."

Her brassy nose ring twitches as she sniffs, nearly breaking into a sob. She breathes deeply before continuing. One deep breath turns into five distinct stuttering breaths.

"I was running behind schedule and I was pretty angry at Mom – I thought she had forgotten to get up. I went to my parents' room and opened their bedroom door, knocking first but opening the door at the same time. Nobody was in the room and the bed wasn't made. Nobody was in the kitchen, either, or the living room. I checked both bathrooms four times. My dad, he leaves the house early but at five in the morning, he should have been home and reading the newspaper. My brother is unemployed and living at home so he should have been sleeping but his room was empty too.

"Tim, he lives next door. It was early, but the phones weren't working and I didn't know what else to do... thanks for walking me to school Tim."

She never cries. In Tim's direction she smiles a sad smile that disappears almost instantly. Her eyes are wet, but not a single teardrop zigzags its way down her vulnerable face.

"My mom, she always makes her bed. She didn't this morning."

On-the-lookout Johnny Sparks has moved the group against one of the engineering building's concrete wall for safety, and is holding the sledgehammer protectively. He sees Nathan and Tim gazing at Julie with expressions full of empathy. Johnny reaches out to put a hand on her shoulder, but then pulls it back.

Derek Darius is standing hands on his hips, bobbing his head like his time is being wasted. "So you're telling me that a total of only three people showed up for my talk?"

Johnny towers over the celebrity. "This is no joke. Our lives could be in danger. I saw something similar last night."

At well over seven feet tall, Johnny is almost a foot taller than Derek Darius. But Derek Darius looks down at the giant. He looks at Johnny and Johnny looks away. "Do I not look serious? Let me assure you, I am as serious as testicular cancer."

Nathan Montgomery says, "That... actually kind of sounded like another joke."

The way Derek Darius said it, it actually did not sound anything like a joke.

Johnny Sparks is a person who looks people in the eye and has a firm handshake. But the celebrity's sunglasses are reflecting the world around him in a perverse way, and there's something about them where Johnny can't look him in the face.

The evil effect is just starting to hit Johnny. Up until now it had been a series of alternating adrenaline and self-doubt. Now, all of a sudden, he simultaneously isn't in immediate danger and also doesn't think he's crazy. His brain focuses on one thing. Autumn. His wife.

"My stupid dog was yapping like crazy early this morning. I wonder if that has anything to do with anything," Tim says.

Is she alive? Is she safe?

Derek Darius looks ready to leave. He is not wearing a watch, but he looks like a person who is continuously looking at his watch.

I would find you or die trying. Johnny had told her this a thousand times, always with a smile on Apocalypse Wednesdays. *Even with zombies I'll probably be the walking undead, so I'll probably to hunt after you. Undead or not, you couldn't keep me away if you tried.*

Nathan blurts out, "This is probably a good time to mention my Grandpa." He has a slumped over posture when he stands, and the slumping is more severe when he speaks.

"Did he also not make his bed? I am on the edge of my seat with anticipation," Derek Darius glares into his nonexistent watch. Look at the time. You aren't important.

"I don't know if he made his bed or not. I think he probably did."

Nathan tries to explain his grandpa used to be a metallurgist in the sixties and design the hull for space shuttles to compete with communists. Apparently, now he has too much time in his retirement. These days, the pigeon chested boy explained, Grandpa is always doing one Make Magazine project after another. One of his projects is apocalyptic ham radio. Nathan appears to have an undiagnosed speech impediment of some sort.

"My Grandpa taught this ham radio class. He put up flyers and stuff and ran it for free. Only two or three people came to the class and out of those I think only one actually got their ham radio license. He has emergency drills all over Rockwell. He has this safety patrol group, where they all wear orange vests with reflectors, and everyone takes a section of neighborhood to patrol. That means they go and knock on people's doors and stuff. Make sure they're alive."

"Your grandpa runs that? They knock on my door almost every month, on Saturday mornings," Johnny says.

"You should put up a ten thousand volt electric fence," Derek Darius says. "That will stop most solicitors. For me, it's worked quite well, other than the Mormon Missionary Incident of 2013." Sometimes, this type of thing is thinly veiled, as in *a thinly veiled insult*. With Derek Darius, there is no veil at all. "On the other hand, even with the Mormon Missionary Incident, I suppose the fence *did* technically succeed at keeping the missionaries away…"

"My Grandpa lives close to here," Nathan points south. "Also, he likes guns. And he has a bomb shelter."

Autumn or not, it's an obvious next step. I can get these kids safe and then find her. "Unless anyone has a better idea, we should go to Nathan's grandpa's house. There's also the parking lot that way, so we might be able to see if there's a car at the same time. That is, if Derek is done making zingers about testicular cancer?"

Derek Darius turns to Johnny with a face that looks like he's been sucking on a peppermint.

Johnny looks at his distorted reflection in Derek Darius's sunglasses and says, "I think we can all agree that this is serious. We should *all* should be taking it seriously."

Derek Darius takes off his sunglasses and his icy eyes, almost black, pierce into Johnny Sparks. Ancient eyes, it's as if thousands of souls were sacrificed to give them their depth. They burn into Johnny, and make the huge man feel small. He can't help but break eye contact again. Even looking at the ground he can sense the eyes looking through him, and piercing into his soul.

"So what are you supposed to be anyway, the janitor?"

"I'm the Engineering Shop Technician."

"So this random Black girl* has an anecdotal experience this morning where her mom apparently didn't make the bed. Yes, I understand this is all very sad to you for some reason. However, despite your feelings, a much better data point is how many people showed up to my talk, three in this case. There were over 2,000 in-person attendees last year and a similar number the year before. Even *if* the power outage is unrelated, a good estimate is at least half the attendees would still show up. I could go into more detail about how I came up with that number, but honestly, I don't even know why I bothered explaining this much to you."

He turns south, toward Nathan Montgomery's grandpa and the ham radio tower and guns and the bomb shelter. He starts walking without waiting for people to follow.

"Don't ever call me Derek," he says to the people behind him. They don't have much of a choice but to follow, so they are following. He knows they will. It's the obvious next step. "My name is Derek Darius."

*Black like her name Julie Black, not like the skin color

CHAPTER 13

They strut with their chests puffed out as if they had volunteered for some nationalistic war against evil. With the hospital red white and blue rape lights painting the way, they swagger upright and loud on their heels, each lugging tools for weapons and together looking like the world's shittiest boy band. They're stuck in this apocalyptic place where something is terribly wrong, like kids stuck in a candy store. Somehow it seems like there should be AC/DC playing in the background, and all their steps should be in slow motion. Except for Johnny Sparks in front and Derek Darius in the lead, everyone strolls.

But it isn't as if they aren't afraid.

The quad grass is cement hard and gray with cold. With each step is a crunching sound that's like snow except sharper. They should be starting to think how ridiculous it might look when the rest of the town sees them walking along with various wrenches and things. There should be safety in numbers, like how some things are scary by yourself but not so bad in a group. The foggy sunlight should be beaming down courage. It isn't. Instead, there is a sense of inevitability and a feeling of defending your home against the Communists/Terrorists/Fascists/*ists. The fear is turning into hopelessness already, and nothing has even happened yet.

The sky is crystalized white, but it is not cloudy.

Tim carries a non-adjustable wrench the size of a forearm. Julie has a hollow steel pipe, and Nathan has this ridiculous looking contraption he put together using a skill saw and some sort of robotic axel. Johnny still has his sledgehammer.

Derek Darius is holding a revolver in his right hand. Johnny wants to ask where he got it, and why he has it. The celebrity's fingers are tense - not a first dance nervousness tense, but rather like a trained athlete. The carbon steel gun looks natural somehow, an extension of his arm. If it were anybody else, Johnny would have asked about the gun by now.

Nobody speaks. Under their feet, the cement grass crunches. Under the empty sky, they walk alone.

Instead of asking Derek Darius for a gun, Johnny tells himself that if Derek did have an extra gun and if he wanted someone to have it, he would have said something by now. Why wouldn't he?

Derek Darius stops. He takes off his sunglasses and squints with his eyes, glaring into something that looks like nothing. A step behind, everybody else stops too. With his left hand, Derek Darius tosses his sunglasses aside and takes out a cigarette. He lights a strip club match. With the cigarette between his lips he lowers his head to the flame, and his intense black eyes never leave the spot.

Derek Darius's revolver has a hammer and a firing pin. Nobody sees anything move but there's an adrenaline tenseness seeping through the air that everybody understands. It's a stampede of energy that could bypass language and traverse species. The billionaire cocks the gun hammer with his thumb. Mechanical clicking echoes through the quiet nervousness much louder than it should, so much so that the world vibrates at the sound. Steadily, he raises his gun arm, pointing in the direction he's glaring at.

He exhales cigarette smoke.

Bullets explode from the barrel of the gun. In the same instant, a dark creature materializes silently from shadows a hundred meters away in a place it should not have been able to hide. It almost *was* the shadow. Most people picture materializing as a slow process, like fog to sunlight. This creature does not materialize slowly. It explodes into existence, like someone jumping out of a happy birthday surprise cake gone terribly awry.

Surprise! Happy birthday! Bang! Bang! Bang!

Nobody is more surprised at the sudden gunshots than Johnny, except for maybe the vampire taking three bullets in the face. Derek Darius would later say he fired slightly before the creature jumped out. He would say that that he anticipated it, by a millisecond, and that was why everyone heard the gunshot first. Johnny has a hard time accepting this. He is usually the first person to see anything.

The hollow point bullets are meant for killing people, and

every shot is a kill shot. The bullets should be expanding as they enter the skull, mushrooming out and ricocheting inside the brain cavity. Instead, every bullet passes through the creature's head like how it would pass through a carved pumpkin. The exit wounds that shouldn't exist ooze a black sticky tar.

Most everything about the creature looks human. It has an unremarkable human size and an unremarkable human shape. Its eyes are dark reptile eyes. Its skin, thin and white. One difference is the way it moves, which doesn't seem human or even cat-like as much as it looks like a Japanese computer generated ninja film. Another difference is that most people, when shot in the face multiple times, will at the very least slow down.

Armed with only his large wrench, Tim charges head on. Stupid college kid. Johnny lumbers after him, cursing for him to fall back.

Derek Darius is holding the gun with both hands in a professional gun range stance. The shots are a fluid dance with the recoiling and the aiming and the finger trigger twitching in constant harmonic motion. The creature is approaching in evasive rabbit zigzags, but every bullet is precise. With time slowed down, the bullets strike the chest, the stomach, the knee, the eye. In some places the bullets penetrate inside, and other places they uselessly ricochet off. Derek Darius is probing for weaknesses like he's fighting a video game ultimate bad guy. Every shot lands exactly where he wants it to land, but none of the bullets seem to matter much.

This doesn't stop Derek Darius from firing anyway. He shoots it in its obsidian eye, which seems like it should have worked. It was worth a shot. *Maybe both eyes?*

Tim is close to the line of fire, and Johnny Sparks a step behind. The rapid bullets appear to be annoying the creature because it's ignoring the front runners and traveling in a jig jag path aimed at Derek Darius.

Tim's face is an actor's snarl. His hair, windblown. When he is almost at the creature, his wrench is wielded back like a baseball bat. He swings with his hips and not his shoulders. He keeps his eye on the vampire head and he follows through.

The creature dodges strike one as an afterthought while trying to simultaneously dodge bullets. It seems trivial for it to reach out with claws and latch onto Tim's soft abdomen below the swinging wrench. The creature swings with its hips and not its shoulders. It follows through.

Tim's body hurls through space with dead limbs falling with the physics of gravity and air resistance. He's either unconscious or dead. He does not flail.

Johnny doesn't waste any time exploiting the creature, which is distracted with dodging bullets and throwing Tim. To a normal person the sledgehammer would be a lot bigger and slower than Tim's wrench, but Johnny is a lot bigger than Tim. The giant's hands are calloused and cracked in the cold northern desert air. His fingernails are dirty because they're always dirty. He's worked with heavy tools a lot. To Johnny's huge arms, the sledgehammer is light.

He swings the weapon as hard as he can.

The connection is solid.

There's no arguing with momentum in a car crash. Johnny Sparks easily towers over this vampire, and when the sledgehammer hits, the trajectory of the vampire is instantly reversed.

Johnny has no idea what this creature is, but it seems to have the wind knocked out of it. If it even breathes air. If this were *Street Fighter II* it would have stars circling its evil head.

And Derek Darius never stops firing. He seems to have an unlimited supply of ammo, grabbing fresh handguns in his trench coat. When one runs out, rather than reloading he tosses it aside and pulls out the next one. Right now he has two guns, one in each hand. Every bullet is fired with deadly precision.

Armed with their tools from the tool shop, Julie Black and Nathan Montgomery aren't far behind Johnny. Nathan's skillsaw blade spins on the end of the axel. Julie holds her steel pipe in front of her like a Roman spear. They work their way to the flank with their weapons in front of them like shields. Both are tentative. Taking the powerful creature head-on would be suicide, but not any more so than if the group fails. They look like they're trying to help but neither is entirely sure exactly how.

It takes a fraction of a second for the vampire to recover enough to snatch the skill blade end of Nathan's makeshift weapon and swing the handle around past Julie Black's metal pipe defenses, making her hit herself in her own face. It hits hard and she drops hard. A petite nerdy girl being punched in the face by Mike Tyson.

There is nothing but ten feet between skinny Nathan Montgomery and the vampire. He is weaponless now as it turns to face him. As it moves in for the kill its mouth opens to reveal sharply curved razor teeth. Its face is almost human. Its remaining obsidian eye stares with an intensity nearly matching Derek Darius. With monster teeth spread wide, it looks like it might be smiling.

Nathan's bladder releases. He takes a step back and puts his hands up to cover his face as if it will do any good.

Johnny rams forward to shove his hammer into the belly of the beast, shoving it back and away from Nathan. Johnny is in the direct line of Derek Darius fire now. Bullets sound close as they buzz by, with Doppler Effect high-pitch sounds turning to a lower pitch when they impact the creature in front of him. He doesn't want to think about how close these deadly projectiles are to hitting his back. Johnny isn't going to let the computer science kids get hurt if he can help it. The bullets fly through the gaps below his armpits and around his ears and in between his legs. Derek Darius doesn't waste a single bullet. Every shot is a hit.

Johnny shoves the comparatively small vampire thing around at the tip of the sledgehammer. He is utilizing the good-offense-is-the-best-defense cattle prod strategy. The vampire jumps around with an unnaturally quick and agile blur, and it doesn't take long for it to adapt. Through the bullets blazing, cattle prodding, it spins around the sledgehammer and toward Johnny. With the vampire climbing up the side of his sledgehammer, Johnny throws them both away.

The vampire lands gracefully on its feet. The hammer falls uselessly to the mushy frost grass with a thud. The Derek Darius bullets have stopped. Everyone is weaponless.

When the vampire springs at Johnny Sparks, Johnny leaps back with a protective sideways kick that fails to protect. The collision forces the big man's knees to buckle and he stumbles onto his back. The creature is on him in a millisecond, even before he hits the ground. The vampire turns its frown upside down, revealing terrible teeth. Johnny's tree trunk arms strain to keep any sort of distance between himself and the snapping mouth ready to kill.

As strong as his muscles are, they aren't anywhere near strong enough to keep this creature away. If Johnny is an ancient and immense redwood tree, then the vampire is spinning industrial steel.

Why are there no more gunshots? Is he finally out of bullets?

Johnny's arms tremble under the wriggling weight trying to eat him. The only thing keeping him alive is pure fear. He's the adrenaline woman lifting a Volkswagen to save her baby. His arms bend anyway. He doesn't have strength.

I'm sorry, Autumn...

With nothing but urinated pants and a visage of determination, Nathan Montgomery sprints toward the vampire. It isn't until after the first step that his expression fades to confusion, like he has no idea what he's going to do when he gets there. But resolution takes over as he seems to come to some conclusion within his head. He yells, "Mortal Combat!" with all the confidence of youth in his voice. He's yelling like his attack will pummel the vampire off of Johnny and into the ground.

It might be that he decided his strategy too late, or maybe he underestimated the difficulty of a drop kick, but the attack ends up as something between a terrible dance move and an off-handed punch. Nathan falls short and clumsily stumbles into the side of the vampire. His arms are flapping in a sad attempt at nerd balance just to stay upright.

The attack has the effectiveness of a two-year-old-toddler punch, but it does cause a diversion.

On his back below the vampire, Johnny sees Derek Darius walking toward him with a gun in each hand. He's walking purposefully, but not in a hurry. Derek Darius shoves his right hand gun below and up into a clavicle-like notch that's located about six inches above what might be a naval. In a human, the sternum and ribs protect some of the most important organs and innards like the heart. Derek Darius angles the left hand gun at a calculated angle to the first, pointing the bullet trajectory at the same spot. Quick, but not hurried. Not even the vampire has time to move.

The celebrity pulls the triggers. Point blank.

Johnny feels the compact strength of the vampire go flak and he throws the suddenly limp ragdoll off of him. The creature lands on its feet, barely. The way it lands is almost humanly awkward.

Julie Black has gotten dizzily back up in time to swing her pipe into the vampire's head, so she does. She swings so hard that if you took a picture it could have its own baseball card marketed to feminist softball leagues with the subtitle: *swing like a girl.*

Knocked over, the vampire scrambles backward to get out of range or maybe to regroup and re-attack. Derek Darius has reloaded bullets now and he's firing again, drilling the creature. The shots all land within a twenty-five cent grouping of the gaping point blank clavicle shot.

The vampire looks back, snarling and vile. Its insides seem to be full of gray goop.

Obviously hurt from the clavicle shots, it must see Johnny Sparks, the mountain, standing back up. It must see the unrelenting bullets from Derek Darius's gun. It must see too much for it to handle right now.

Johnny Sparks is shouting a primal battle cry. His screams are unintelligible animal sounds.

He realizes he has been screaming the whole time.

The creature turns and runs. At first on two legs and then on four. It runs with a limp.

Derek Darius is out of bullets with his right handgun. He throws it at the fleeing vampire. The gun spins wildly in the air, but somehow manages to bounce off the back of the vampire's leg.

"Well," Derek Darius says, "I didn't expect this to happen when I woke up this morning."

...

The time distorted battle took only thirty-six bullets worth of time, and that doesn't even account for the fact that some bullets were fired simultaneously with a gun in each hand.

Johnny Sparks is not a smiler, but his smile takes up his entire wide face now. He's alive and he thought for sure he would die. To the intensely melancholy Derek Darius, he exclaims things like "I don't know where you learned to shoot like that!" and "I almost felt the bullets when they whizzed by! I think I did feel the air!"

"I tried to drop kick a vampire," Nathan Montgomery says.

Everything about Johnny is big. His smile is giant with relief. "You just carry those guns around, like all the time?"

Without hesitation, Derek Darius spins the hammer cocked gun like a gunslinger to aim at Johnny's eyeball. "Yep, I carry them all the time." He lets the fear sink in for the necessary fraction of a second, and then he pulls the trigger.

Instead of a gunshot, there's the hammer click of an empty gun.

The retro-terrified Johnny Sparks is still wearing a vanishing smile. These things take time to register, the fact that someone put a gun to your head and pulled the trigger. You think you're dead and then you're alive and then you think you're dead and then you're alive.

For the first time since the skirmish, Derek Darius smiles. He even laughs. When nobody joins him he says, "Come on, big guy. That expression on your face... even the anti-gun people would be okay with what I did!"

Johnny's mouth is gaping open and he can't even respond.

"Hey Johnny, you want to hear another joke? Your attempt at trying to fight." He lets loose a second loud laugh directly into Johnny's face. Johnny can feel the celebrity's clean-smelling breath.

A joke. Ba-dum-ching.

"Stop joking around for one minute." Julie Black is looking around the empty quad with rabbit alertness, spinning in circles with energy. Her left eye is already swelling, and she shows no interest in Derek Darius's shenanigans. "What happened to Tim?"

CHAPTER 14

"I love science fiction. When I was a kid I liked reading everything, but when I started reading science fiction, I could never go back to other genres. I love the unexpected. When I'd try to read an otherwise decent book by like John Grisham or something, I'd turn every page secretly hoping aliens or dragons would happen."

Nathan's socks are mismatched, one is striped and one used to be white. He sits Indian-style on hard outside pavement, hunched over his knobby knees. Johnny is the only one within earshot. Nathan's eyes are blank and unseeing, and when he speaks, it's as if he is talking to himself or to a therapist.

"I've always been an outsider, which is probably another reason I like science fiction so much. These characters on these other planets have always understood me. They're funny and we share all these impossibly important experiences that really matter. I've always wanted to be part of that world… and now that it's happening… all I am is a redshirt."

The empathy in Johnny is an overwhelming lump in his throat. Despite having the lung capacity of an oil barrel, he almost can't breathe. He doesn't understand all the details of what being a redshirt entails, but it doesn't matter. He understands what it means to be an outsider. He absently runs a giant finger over the scar on his forehead, and then rests a palm reassuringly on Nathan. Johnny's meaty hand swallows the bony shoulder, and Nathan leans into it a little for support.

"Nathan, everything is going to be okay," Johnny says.

"All signs point to redshirt." Water glimmers across Nathan's eyeballs. "I have no strong connections, no love interest. At BEST I'm some sort of poorly conceived Jar-Jar comic relief!" Nathan's thin face is half retreated into his baggy coat for turtle-like protection. "I'm so depressed that these aren't the slow kind of zombies. Why can't these be the slow kind of zombies!?"

Johnny repeats, "We're all going to be ok."

There is an innocent sort of hope in Nathan's voice when he says, "We are?"

"Nathan, just because we were attacked by something doesn't mean we're part of a science fiction story. We're a group of Idahoans. You're with real people who care about each other. Yes, we've been through something none of us understand, but we won, and we're still alive. It's over. And even if it's not, even if there are more of those things out there, we can get through this together. If we're strong and we stick together, we can all make it out of this alive."

107

Nathan's eyes are intent. He's pretty much speechless.

"Johnny, are you fucking retarded? "

CHAPTER 15

The car window smashes into a thousand jagged pieces while Derek Darius sings songs written by *The Cure*. His face and hands are colorless. It's not so much that he has a pale complexion as his skin is in ageless mint-condition shrink wrap. It might not be new skin anymore, but it's been stored away and never taken out of the package. For the most part, nobody notices his too white skin unless they are racist or he's wearing the dark sunglasses. For some reason, without the red rimmed sunglasses there for contrast, the white skin just seems natural.

He sings, "Sometimes I dream where all the other people dance. Sometimes I dream Charlotte sometimes."

He wears these sunglasses a lot.

Tim can still walk and he says he's fine. He looks like the definition of shell-shocked in a very real way. The scruff on his face is messed up and homeless. His chin-length hair is damp, and has gone from Southern California surfer to

Seattle punk rock. The seeping cut in his armpit is the length of a hand, an angry slice that's a mat of sticky blood where there should be skin and hair. Perhaps more concerning is the two inch hole over his kidney, a gaping wound that's dripping ominously yellow blood. Whenever Tim moves his arm it makes a noise like sweaty skin peeling off a leather couch.

Johnny Sparks had cleaned the wound and he had applied pressure, using some of the layered clothes off his back. Both cuts are tied off with the blue bandages darkening red as blood seeps through. There is a first aid kit in his shop two hundred meters away, placed behind the hard hats in the supply closet, next to the electrical tape. It would take two seconds. The kit has the equipment to clean the wound properly, but Derek Darius won't go.

"You go right on ahead," the celebrity had said. Not a single hair is out of place. Thick black almost Japanese hair, it points out into movie star spikes. He's ready to walk the red carpet.

There is a strange sense of leadership the celebrity has gained through focused indifference. His active way of not caring about these people seems to have made him more dynamic in everyone's eyes except Johnny's. Derek Darius's confidence makes it look like he's the only person who knows what's happening. The innuendo is that if they go to get first aid, they won't be coming back alive. At best, they might come back as the undead or something.

"I'm fine," Tim says like a cowboy whenever people ask him if it hurts.

Julie Black has asked more than once.

"So you ended up being sliced open badly while the rest of us managed to fight off the vampire without serious injury. But don't beat yourself up, Barry Bonds. You still swung that baseball bat like a champ." Nathan seems to be enjoying survival. His posture is slightly less horrible and his movements are less jerky. He doesn't look embarrassed about the clearly visible urine stain on his pant leg below his large coat. He appears to have forgotten all about it.

Derek Darius swings the sledgehammer again, smashing the silence along with a green smug Prius's rear window. He pokes his head inside with a self-satisfied smile.

The hammer weapon has a precious bond with Johnny now. It's the first weapon he's ever used offensively to save human life, including his own life. It's something he would love to sleep with under his pillow, if only he could figure out the logistics. He never wants to let go of the sledgehammer again, it in one giant hand and Autumn in the other.

Except now Derek Darius has it and he's using it to smash windows.

"On that bleak track, see the sun is gone again, the tears were pouring down her face, she was crying and crying for a girl, who died so many years before," Derek Darius sings. The sound of shattering glass explodes like a Fourth of July firework finale.

"Give me the sledgehammer," Derek Darius had said with no explanation when they first reached the parking lot.

King Arthur had Excalibur and Rambo had that Soviet rocket launcher he found in *First Blood Part 2*. Johnny

Sparks had his sledgehammer.

"Come on big guy, you can trust me. No, really… You can… Nah, I'm just kidding." Derek Darius talks with his sunglasses on. Seared in Johnny's mind is a picture of the celebrity's eyes behind those glasses. Fire hot. Almost black. Johnny Sparks hopes the celebrity never takes those blood red glasses off again. "Seriously though. Give me the fucking sledgehammer."

He would rather hit Derek Darius with the sledgehammer than give it to him. There's something Johnny hates about the Rockwell billionaire beyond the persistent superiority complex and the complete lack of empathy. He is dangerous somehow.

Before giving Derek Darius his precious sledgehammer, Johnny Sparks thought about how fast a celebrity bullet could bring down a man of Johnny's size. He thought about how much damage the sledgehammer could cause with one swing. Vampires aren't the only reason he wants a weapon in his hand.

"Here, hold my gun." He had handed Johnny a gun, took the sledgehammer, handed him another gun, took the gun back, took the other gun back with a Bugs Bunny kind of trickery. All the weapons were now with Derek Darius.

Johnny's face was the very definition of concern. "Why do you want the sledgehammer?"

Apparently eccentrically smashing windows and singing: This is why Derek Darius took the sledgehammer and also why they couldn't go for a first aid kit to properly tend to Tim's bloody armpit and the gaping hole in his middle.

"Sometimes I dream. The sounds all stay the same."
Smash!

Johnny's dark curly hair is getting wilder. Thicker. The stubble on his face rises high on his cheeks, almost to eye sockets. If he were to look in a mirror, he would notice for the first time that some of the stubble is gray.

"Charlotte sometimes dreams a wall around herself. But it's always been love. So much love it looks like everything else." A blue minivan window shatters into sand with the force of the sledgehammer swing.

The celebrity's voice is annoyingly pitch perfect, and his swings of the heavy hammer are effortless.

The parking lot is close to the battle they had a moment ago with a vampire. There's a University building in the way, and around the corner are the faded yellow lines and cracked asphalt. This is parking for the university early birds and the handicapped. Every single tire on every single car is slashed. It was like that when they got here.

Not only in this parking lot either. There are cars visible in the street, where most people park when the parking lot is full. Their tires are flat too.

"How far does it spread?" Julie Black asks, "Is every tire in the whole city flat? Did the vampire get into garages and slash tires there too?"

"You said *vampire* not *vampires*," Nathan Montgomery replied. "What on earth makes you think there's only one?"

Johnny tries to remember what the vampire looked like, but the picture in his mind is generic and faceless, all sharp angles with no specifics. The bloodbath seems like a

113

dream to him now. Distant and fake. A movie colored by hand with Technicolor where every pixel is one of only two hundred and fifty-six distinct values. The realest remnants are Tim's bloody armpit and the flat tires. Already the only person who can remember the details perfectly is Derek Darius, whose memory is photographic. Even if he tried, Derek Darius couldn't forget.

Some of Tim's deep tan has drained away now, like his body can't supply enough oxygen to his skin. He says, "It's been half an hour and nobody has even asked, what was that thing?"

"That's because nobody knows, nitwit," Nathan replies.

"It's a good question Tim, but let's get everyone safe first," Johnny Sparks says, "Getting everyone safe should be priority zero." What Johnny does not understand is why singing and smashing windows is part of priority zero.

"Do you really think there's more than one of those things?"

"I'm just saying," Nathan says, "What if we used up all our best weapons and ammo to go beat the boss at the end of the game, but then it turns out it was just the mini boss at the end of the level?"

Every tire is flat, including the flat bicycle tires locked to the handrails with combination locks. It's too bad because Inkdon is only twenty five miles away and it's mostly downhill. Bicycles may have been a good option.

"This flat tire situation reinforces our earlier plan of going to Nathan's Grandpa's house," Johnny says with more confidence and authority than he actually feels. "If he has a generator and a ham radio we can call out for help."

Another window smashes and Derek Darius steps backward to examine his work. With a nod of a job well done, he tosses the sledgehammer aside like a used New York cigarette butt. The weighted hammer spins topsy turvy before settling on the parking lot pavement.

Nathan has shrunken into his coat. His hands are engulfed by the sleeves. His head is half hidden by the hood. "In this soft world where almost fifty percent of the population is fat, is it strange to anyone else that given this situation, we're paired up with an action hero gunslinger?"

"With any lottery," Julie shrugs, "somebody has to win."

Johnny has lost hope that the window smashing will produce anything useful. This is no time for group think. His thoughts automatically go to her. *Where would she go?*

From the depths of the car trunk Derek Darius produces a spare tire that's miraculously full of compressed air. He drops it to the ground with a spinning rubber thud. "And for my next trick, an iron wrench."

It doesn't take long before there's a drivable automobile, complete with four ragtag spare tires full of air. The car is an Eighties Ford Mustang LX. The LX means it has the same engine as the Ford Taurus, four cylinders of raw lawnmower-grade horsepower. The faded baby boy blue paint is peeling rust, and a Flying Spaghetti Monster Jesus-fish is stuck to the back.

"I'm surprised you didn't pick something flashier," Johnny Sparks says while he loosens a lug nut.

The Mustang LX's driver side door wasn't locked. The LX's

driver side door *doesn't* lock. The plastic handle is broken, and it needs to be pushed up and pulled down for the door to catch the lever that releases the hinge.

"What? Flashier than this costume jewelry?"

Johnny looks at the car critically. It has a lightweight frame and should be able to handle the small spare tires better in a pinch. The mechanics are simple, so maybe the starter is easier to hot wire than one of the newer cars. There would be negatives. The car's age. It's capacity. Johnny wonders what pros and cons went through Derek Darius's mind. The celebrity has a reason behind every decision he makes, and this group of survivors is not a committee.

"So I'm obviously the MacGyver of the group," Derek Darius says after it takes him less than thirty seconds to hotwire the car. "Really, is there anything I can't do? Why, I must be some kind of god."

They throw an additional spare tire into the back of the started car, along with the jack and Tim's weapon wrench. According to the gauge, which might be broken, the gas tank is two-thirds empty or possibly one-third full, depending on your level of optimism.

"I'm driving to Inkdon," Derek Darius says as he hops into the driver's side seat, "and realistically, this car can only hold four people."

"I thought we were going to Nathan's Grandparents'," Julie says.

"*You* are welcome to visit whatever retirement community you see fit. I, however, am driving my newly acquired Mustang out of town. I'd like to leave him." The celebrity points his requisite cigarette at Johnny. "The janitor."

"He's the engineering shop technician," Julie Black shoots back with angry eyebrows. "Why should we leave *him*? Why not... like... draw lots?"

It's quiet for a moment while Derek Darius appears to be thinking. He rests his chin in hand. "I have a nearly photographic memory and I can honestly say I don't know what a *lot* is."

Julie squints one side of her face. "They use it in soccer sometimes if there's a tie."

"So your question is, *why not do some soccer tie breaking thing to determine who dies.* First, we're in goddamn America and we don't draw lots in America. Second, if for some stupid reason we did draw lots then there's a twenty percent chance I'd be the one staying behind and I don't like those odds. Third, if you haven't noticed, Jolly Green Giant over there has to weigh over three hundred and fifty pounds. These old rubber spare tires are rated for a maximum speed of forty miles per hour. Going down the canyon pass I don't trust them to do much better than that under a normal load of four regular sized people."

"Can we not drive cautiously?"

"Little girl," Derek Darius says down to her, "The creature we were just fighting, do you not remember how fast it was?"

"After you shot it, it didn't look like it was in a position to be chasing us."

"I completely agree. I suspect that particular creature won't be chasing anything ever again."

117

Julie looks at Johnny with her huge round eyes, her face the definition of concern. "It doesn't seem fair to leave him behind."

"Do you know how many bullets I have left?"

"No, but…"

"I happen to know exactly how many bullets I have, but I understand your point. Wait… what was your point?" Derek Darius silences her with a hand gesture when she starts to talk. "Let's just assume I have infinite bullets. What happens if three creatures attack us next time instead of one?"

"Again, what makes you think there are more of them?"

"What makes you think there aren't?"

"That's circular reasoning…"

"This is not a debate." The Rockwell celebrity's expression clearly says indulging her questions up until now was a kindness that's being spit back in his face. He hisses, "If there weren't any vampires left, it wouldn't make any difference who we left behind."

Johnny Sparks has been thinking throughout this not-a-debate conversation and even before. There's a seed of thought in his head that's been growing since Derek Darius pulled out the first spare tire. Really, the thought has been growing since late last night when he was barricading himself inside University Inn.

"Julie, it's okay," Johnny says. "I'm not going. Derek Darius is right."

She does a double take.

"We might all be able to cram into the tiny car, but I weigh as much as the three of you combined. Those tires aren't meant for a car chase down a windy canyon with my kind of weight sitting in the front seat. Everyone is more likely to survive if I don't go. Including me."

Johnny isn't sure he believes the words coming out of his mouth. They're basically true, but it's not why he's staying. "Besides, there are other cars and more spare tires I can find. We'll meet up in Inkdon."

"Well, I don't want to go, either," Tim says.

"You need antibiotics."

"My grandpa's house is only two blocks that way." Nathan waves his hand vaguely to the west. "He has antibiotics. He probably has a better pharmacy in his kitchen than Inkdon Hospital."

Derek Darius hops into the driver's seat and looks at Nathan and Julie. "So. We don't need a speech every time one of you makes a decision. Kids, are you coming?"

Nathan climbs into shotgun without a word, head down. Julie looks at Johnny and Tim and back to Johnny. She seems to see through him, sees what he's really up to. She looks unsure as she steps into the back seat. She mouths, "Good luck," but Johnny isn't sure which of them needs luck more.

The 1988 Mustang LX has a manual transmission. Revving the lawnmower engine like it's the good kind of Ford Mustang, Derek Darius lets out the clutch and backs out of the parking slot skidding to a stop on the delicate spare tires. He has one elbow resting through the open window.

"If you die while we're out," he says, "you're going to be dead a long time."

Johnny watches the old sky blue car skid away as Julie Black, Nathan Montgomery, and Derek Darius drive into the distance. He has that thought about last words people say to each other. There's something profound about a last word, the last thing someone hears you say before you never cross paths again. He wants to be remembered as the person he's always tried his best to be. The last words he said to Julie Black and Nathan Montgomery were about the reasons he should sacrifice himself for the good of the group. They may not have been completely true, but they were good last words.

CHAPTER 16

The garden outside has thawed from stiff frost to limp dead brown. Most of these domestic plants are not adapted for the cold climate of an Idaho autumn. The tropical tomatoes have exposed tissue that is dead and rotting. The fruits that were full of liquid have frozen and burst so all that remains is scalded and broken. Wrinkled biomass still clings to wooden twigs, but it looks like with one loud footstep everything would splat to the ground.

Well-tended and pampered, until now. Cared for, until now.

Surrounded by death and rot, there is a single plant in the tilled soil that is alive and green. The living vegetable is hardy, not a delicate flower. Not only is it surviving… it's thriving. With decreased tomato competition this plant has come out of the shadows and is spreading its pedals in the sunnier daytime because it was better able to bear the frozen night. There may be less sun, but it has the sun all to itself now. A bigger piece of a smaller pie. A winter garden.

"Tragedy brings out the best in people," Tim says. "And also the worst."

The mailbox says *Montgomery*. Johnny Sparks is burdened with anxiety. He hates what's showing through the cracks. He thinks about mean people from his past, bullies and criminals. He worries how the grandpa will react when the two strangers show up on his doorstep. "I would feel better if Nathan were with us."

"It's fine."

"Should I just knock?"

"Just call him *sir*. Old people love that shit. Besides, we're like two hundred feet from the front door. Why are we talking about this?"

Tim is shaking, impatient and irritable. Sick. Under his army jacket are purple veins snaking outward in all inflamed directions. On his exposed neck are squiggling blood vessels that are fish hooking at unnatural varicose angles. He has a fever.

It has only been one hour, but to Johnny, Tim's wounds look badly infected. It should be impossible for infection to set in so quickly, but the discoloration is unmistakable. Tim needs penicillin or a shot of tequila, and he needs it soon.

The old person who exits from the front door is a kind looking shy looking guy. His deeply sunken colorless eyes hide between thick trifocal glasses, and they're set too far apart in his head. The timing is as precise as the whites of Johnny's eyes. He points a well-cared-for shotgun at Johnny's face. Patriarchal and gray, he looks like a returned check.

The old man opens his mouth and soft sounds come out. Every word is enunciated like a good education. Every syllable is tired as solitary confinement. When the old man talks, his sagging windpipe made of skin and wrinkles gobbles rhythmically.

"Are we... zombies?" Johnny echoes the old man's question.

The old man is not fat, but his hanging second chin gives him the look of an exotic rainforest frog that can inflate its neck sac to make it appear larger than it really is. In the wild, this tactic is successful at deterring predators. Evolution.

"Answer the d-d-d-damn question!" the old man shouts, quietly. He doesn't seem to be used to saying the word *damn* and by the time the exclamation mark escapes his mouth it is almost a whisper.

Johnny says, no, he's not a zombie and could he please put down the shotgun.

"I'm certainly not a zombie, sir."

"If you're not a zombie, what in the h-h-h-hell are you doing here!?"

Johnny explains that Nathan, apparently the old man's grandkid, sent them this way, and Nathan obviously looks up to his grandpa. He told everyone how great a person old Grandpa Montgomery is, his favorite trait being how he never shoots at strangers.

"He obviously doesn't know me at all, then."

"There are no zombies here, sir," Tim repeats.

The old man pauses. His rocket scientist mind appears tired. Broken with age and fear and exhaustion and grief.

"Take off your clothes. I want to make sure you're not bitten."

"Bitten, sir?"

A lifetime ago, way back in chapter two, Johnny told Autumn this is what he would do in exactly this sort of situation: strip naked. Now that he's here though, it seems ridiculous.

Johnny says, "Why would a bite even make us one of the infected, a 'zombie'?" At the word "zombie" he holds up his fingers to gesture that "zombie" is in quotes.

"That's exactly what a zombie would say."

"Actually, that's pretty fucking far from what a zombie would say. Sir." Tim says this, and everyone's looking at him so he continues, "I would think a zombie, if it said anything, would mostly be groaning… 'braaaaaaaaaaaaains'."

Grandpa is quick to point out that maybe if this were an actual George Romero movie that assumption would be correct, but in these new-fangled zombie movies the things can generally run and jump. Also, despite this being a conversation three grown men are having about zombie movie vocabulary, Grandpa Montgomery never smiles. The shotgun stays raised, and it's pointed at Tim now. The grandpa seems old like only a self-inflicted stereotype can. Only fake old people ever say something is new-fangled.

Behind his trifocals, the old man squints his gray eyes to focus on Tim. "You don't look so good."

"Look," Johnny is focused on the pointed shotgun, "there has obviously been a disaster. I don't know much about what's going on, but there is no reason to think it's even something that infects humans."

"No. *They* aren't human," the old man says like his tired brain is at its limits, "but they might have been human once. The thing I ask myself is, this might not be an infection. But then where are all the bodies? If people are *dying* instead of *turning*, where did the bodies go? And there's a reason movie zombie infections spread by biting – biting is one of the best ways to spread disease. Now take off your clothes."

"I'll save you the trouble," Tim says in an embarrassed voice. "I've been fish hooked, sir, and stabbed in the stomach. The cuts look infected."

The old man's red-rimmed eyes are shifting. He's the type of person where 87% of everything used to cost a nickel and 52% of everyone is a hoodlum. The gun starts trembling a little, but it's not trembling much so it would be easy to miss. Johnny notices. Grandpa's mind is clearly chugging.

"That's why we came here, sir. Nathan said you might have penicillin and guns. Nathan said you might be able to help. Sir."

Grandpa Montgomery seems like a good man, but Johnny thinks he's been pushed to his new-fangled limits. Old people have survival instincts too, and he must be looking for a way to get these two dangerous strangers to go away. If that means pulling the shaky trigger finger, then fine.

Grandpa says, "I want you two to turn around and leave right now."

"We need antibiotics or he's going to die. He was cut about an hour ago and it's already infected."

"He might be infected alright. But if it happened an hour ago it isn't bacteria."

Grandpa's eyes and his shotgun are locked on Tim like he's expecting the Southerner to strike out. Johnny is working his way imperceptibly closer to knocking the old man into uselessness with the sledgehammer. He sizes the old man up. *I could take him*, Johnny thinks, *I could knock the gun out of his hands before he could pull the trigger. If I needed to.*

He doesn't want to. Not if he doesn't have to.

But he *could*.

"Sir." Sickly sweat is beading on Tim's pale forehead. "I don't believe I'm turning into a zombie, but if it turns out I am then let me assure you, I have no problem at all with you shooting me in the face."

"Let's try the antibiotics first," Johnny says. He smells his own wet animal breath against his nose. Humid. "Let's see if he actually is turning into a zombie first."

The old man's finger is twitching on the trigger. It looks like all Grandpa Montgomery needs is an excuse to pull the trigger, and he is looking for that excuse.

"Where is Nathan? You said he told you all about me, so where is he?"

"He left town with a few others," Johnny says. "They thought their chances of survival would be better in Inkdon."

Behind the trifocals there is figurative blood dripping out of old man Montgomery's eyes as they water. Johnny thinks he might be working up the courage to kill. Every muscle in Johnny's body is full of adrenaline and blood. He's ready to pounce. The giant is so close to being in sledgehammer range now, but there are still a lot of unknowns and any move would be a Napoleonic rolling of the dice.

"Don't do anything stupid," Johnny says. "Please, just give us the antibiotics and we'll leave you alone."

"You'll turn into one of them, and now you know we're here. Then they'll all know we're here."

"Let's not have a brain breakdown, sir," Tim says. "Let's be reasonable, sir."

"I know I'm not being reasonable! I can't afford to be reasonable!"

"Okay Tim," Johnny says in his calm voice, "we really need to work on your negotiation skills. The *let's not have a brain breakdown* angle turns out, surprisingly, to not have a very high success rate at helping people prevent a breakdown."

The giant tells Grandpa to ignore Tim the idiot and that it's okay to be reasonable or even a little unreasonable. There's something unique about citing reason while the undead walk the earth and a shotgun is pointed at your face. Grandpa Montgomery's trigger finger tenses, and Johnny can clearly see that the old man is ready to fire.

But Johnny's arms are long, and he's close. He repeats, again and again, "Let's be reasonable" as he inches his way into striking distance.

CHAPTER 17

"I'm just saying," Nathan continues, "Julie sleeps in her locked bedroom in the basement. So does Tim. Johnny was walled up in a hotel room, and I have my windowless dorm room. I think that's the reason we're alive."

It's difficult for Julie Black to see outside. The back seat of the car is sunken in and low. The window is a small triangle that doesn't roll down, and she can only look on sideways as close objects whiz by. She keeps looking at herself in the rear view mirror to examine her injuries. The bruise on her forehead is already turning purple and well defined. Her crimpy dark brown hair is falling out of formation, green streaks messy. She wrinkles her forehead. "Why do you have your own room? I thought everyone shared a room in the dorms?"

"How else am I supposed to masturbate?"

There's an awkward silence. This must be awkward silence number seventeen.

Nathan shrugs. "What? Everyone does it." He says this as a truism, as if the entire Internet is backing him up on this one.

"Not me," Derek Darius says. "Why in the world would I masturbate when I could just use any girl I wanted?"

Julie is not attracted to powerful people. Unattainable, she just can't imagine sleeping with them. She's dealt with people like this her whole life. Obviously not as powerful as Derek Darius, but popular. Strong. They always make her feel useless and unimportant. She hates the cocky attitudes and the smug superiority. There's no doubt about it, Derek Darius is physically perfect. He's brilliant and funny. But she wants to be the most important person in the world to someone, not just something they use to masturbate with.

"Sorry." She smirks from the backseat. "You're not my type."

Derek Darius is driving, but he turns around anyway and takes off his sunglasses. He is too lean. Too angular. He doesn't look like he spends hours in front of a mirror, but he'd have to so that his shirt has no wrinkles and hair stays expertly styled, right?

"Are you sure about that?"

He looks right into her eyes in this way, and she can't help it, and she hates that she does it, but her stomach drops and she becomes warm between the thighs.

The narrow road is dynamite blast in the mountain, winding with the stream so there's never a dotted yellow line that says it's safe to pass. Blurry pine trees and shale pass through her window, nauseating to focus too hard on.

Nathan is popping the Marathon protein power bars like crack. The ingredient list mentions it has enough caffeine for a thousand truck drivers, and it also contains an assortment of mystical sounding Chinese herbs that have not been fully evaluated by the FDA. It's great for weight loss, the wrapper says. Julie has a bite. It tastes like grainy soy and chewy artificial sweetener, and also something that's supposed to taste like chocolate. The wrapper calls the chocolate taste *brown flavoring No. 5.*

"I'll admit it. I did sort of enjoy watching Tim fight the vampire," Nathan says, slumped in his seat. "And I enjoyed it for all the wrong reasons. It's exactly like that time my mom made me go to this Special Olympics wheelchair basketball game."

Whenever Nathan talks, Derek Darius groans out loud. He turns on the radio but there is only crackling static. The 1988 Ford Mustang doesn't have a digital tuner, it has a turn dial. The celebrity moves the tuner all the way left and slowly moves it all the way right. The only sounds the whole way are screeching white noise and sharp popping. Still, it's that or Nathan, so the celebrity turns up the white noise.

"Maybe it's my personality, but making mentally handicapped people compete in athletic sport seems like it should be the opposite of inspiring," Nathan says. "On the other hand, making myself feel good by comparison left me with a strange type of inspiration. Let me put it this way, I had way more fun at those games than I thought I would."

Derek Darius groans. Out loud. Again.

There is no oncoming traffic on the empty canyon road. The asphalt winds around deep under the sliver of sky above, snaking with the water through steep granite and sandstone. Nathan keeps staring at his phone, but even on a sunny day with no chance of vampires, there would be no signal here. Not in this canyon.

"No matter what happens, at least I have the Pac Man app on my phone that I can play from anywhere, signal or no signal. Cellphone Pac Man, a Pac Man app for today's modern man. Pac Man on the go."

Anyone with any type of social awareness can see Derek Darius is deeply annoyed with Nathan's blabbering. Julie Black is living through, first hand, an awkward scene from *Borat* or anything starring Johnny Knoxville. Being in the middle, it's not as funny, and it wasn't even that funny to begin with. Derek Darius scoffs. He shakes his head. He rolls his eyes. His body language is obvious enough that it almost even reaches the threshold of Nathan Montgomery's awareness. Almost.

"Driving, performing surgery, etc. It doesn't matter. Pac Man anywhere."

"Nathan. Shut up," Julie says.

"Don't tell me to shut up. I'm sitting in shotgun. I've got the second most power in this car."

Derek Darius has a scowl on his face that has *I'm going to turn this damn car around* written all over it.

"So, Mr. Derek Darius, when you shot that vampire… that was pretty cool."

The road is narrow and the slope is steep downhill, around

ten percent grade, but this doesn't stop Derek Darius from slamming on rusty breaks. In his natural environment he would be skid spinning to an angry stop in a red five hundred thousand dollar Ferrari, and it might have a more dramatic surprise effect. Instead, because of the steepness of the hill and oldness of the car, the forward momentum doesn't stop immediately when the breaks are slammed, and he has to pump the pedal and down shift. Coming to a stop on this slope takes some time.

The pulsating of the brakes is worse somehow for Julie. More suspenseful. Derek Darius's face is horrible and twisted, the worst kind of face a person can make. He is not the kind of person who pumps breaks. He might as well be shoveling manure as a farmhand or waiting tables.

Derek Darius is slamming on the brakes because he's annoyed with a Pac-Man-loving meaningless-word-blabbering Nathan. Obviously. For Julie, it's the feeling after you're caught but before you're sentenced. Nathan, of course, is oblivious. He asks, "Why are we stopping?"

The air smells like black asphalt and burning rubber, and Derek Darius's face has that terrible focus and cold anger it always has. He glares at Nathan with constant eyes that predict the unpredictable. The mask of an unchanging face with the deceptiveness of a random action.

Derek Darius could do anything he wanted, and not in a Thanksgiving special kind of way but rather in an unpredictable Charlie Manson kind of way. Julie could see him shooting Nathan in the forehead, opening the door to dump the body, and then continuing the drive with her still in the back seat.

Instead, with a Halloween smile stretched in a rictus of

politeness, he says, "Nathan, get in the back seat next to that Black girl. We need to… redistribute the weight. For the tires."

Since he learned her last name, Derek Darius has joined in referring to Julie as *that Black girl.*

…

Driving again, Nathan is in the back seat now. He still never shuts up.

There's a comfortableness people sometimes have with each other where silence can be nice and you don't have to say anything. You can think your own thoughts uninterrupted and you can be together but still alone. This is the opposite of that comfortable silence.

It's weird, but Nathan seems more nervous of her than of Derek Darius. He talks too fast and he's trying too hard to act natural. It's like he doesn't know what to do with his hands. They make fists, and then they rest on his lap but instead of resting they clutch his skinny legs for support. Then, just for a place to put them, he folds his arms to tuck his hands out of sight.

"Wild creatures like wolves are sometimes injured by their own food," Nathan says out loud, maybe to himself, maybe to everyone. "In the early nineties when they reintroduced wolves into Yellowstone they attached radio collars to track how they lived and how they died, and they publish this sort of data on the Internet. Causes of death like *gored by bull elk and then finished off by cougar* or *mauled on dead tree during hunt* are actually pretty common. It's not as rare as you'd think."

If Derek Darius is the one who randomly does the expected, then Nathan Montgomery is the one who is expected to be random.

"Of course, a more common cause of death for a wolf is *death by grizzly bear*. And vice versa. Some of the most interesting and bloody things in nature happen when two separate species of predator compete for a limited resource. Those are the lions and the hyenas. The Burmese pythons versus the American crocodiles. These are the pairs of elite carnivores battling ferociously at the top of the food chain to make *National Geographic* wildlife special headlines. *Eternal struggle for food in the wildlife preserve* and whatnot."

Nathan tries to put his awkward hands in his pockets, but he's struggling in his seat with the seatbelt. He's looking at the roof of the car, blind with his thoughts. He never seems to make eye contact with anyone.

"So I guess the question is, if the vampires are wolves, then what does that make us? Are we the cougars locked in a *National Geographic* eternal struggle with vampires, or are we just the elk that luckily got away while accidentally injuring the wolf chasing us?"

"I think it's clear what we are," Julie Black says. "An entire town of thousands is dead in an evening. We're less than the elk. We're an earthworm the wolf choked on."

"*We* are earthworms?" Derek Darius corrects Julie, emphasizing the word *we* in italics. And it's true. Julie has a point about the rest of her species, but it's impossible to think of Derek Darius as anything other than a top-of-the-food-chain cougar. Or another wolf.

135

…

"Well, this isn't a good sign."

The chrome of the F-150 pickup truck has a bumper sticker, and written in bubbly pimp color purple it says, *Jesus wuz here*. The steel of the truck is cringingly crumpled like tin foil chewed up with human teeth. A puddle of reddish dark fluid is smeared on the asphalt. It must have come from the truck, because there's too much of it to have come out of a human. It is unclear what happened. This huge vehicle that must weigh six thousand pounds is crunched and upside down and twisted, alone in the middle of the road as if the hand of some Greek god reached out of the sky to smash it against the pavement.

The easily readable and brightly lettered bumper sticker looks new and out of place, like the slogan had just arrived straight from the Internet. Nathan turns his head sideways to read the yellow text, as if a clue. His mouth opens and shuts as he mouths the words.

"*Ominous* is the word you're looking for, Mr. Montgomery," Derek Darius says. "But don't worry. With enough patience and determination, you'll figure out this whole English language thing yet."

There is no body.

Julie runs her slim fingers through her hair, and they come away sticky with hair product. "Thanks to denial, I'm actually not worried about this situation at all."

Derek Darius steers the car cautiously around the twisted metal wreckage. Following normal driving regulations here is impossible.

The weather feels like it's becoming darker, like there's a black storm cloud blocking the sun. It's unnatural. There should be more sunlight than this.

It isn't long after the F-150 that there's another piece of crumpled metal, a Suburban. Then there's what's left of an old Bronco leaning against a tree.

It keeps getting darker and there continue to be junkyard automobile pieces strewn about. A leather interior seat here, a sport chrome rim there. Smashed glass and broken fiberglass is everywhere. The cars lay upside down. American made. Abandoned and crumpled like dried out cockroaches, there are dozens of them.

"Still, on the plus side," Nathan says, "at least we're not in Utah..."

Everyone agrees and they continue to drive down the steep canyon, slowly circling the junkyard cars as they tread toward the ever increasing darkness of a Tuesday morning.

There is no suspense in a car crash. Even in the middle of the apocalypse, inside a car a person can feel safe. Surrounded by metal. There are airbags and seatbelts and five star safety ratings. But it's a false feeling of security. Cars can be bigger killers than cancer.

Before she has time to brace herself, Derek Darius turns the steering wheel violently to the left. Julie is thrown against the triangle window in the backseat. She reflexively puts her arm out, but her head bangs against glass.

In the back seat she can't see what's happening. It's like a Michael Bay movie where the camera is shaky and the plot unintelligible. All she gets are glimpses. The car is skidding sideways, inches from the side of the mountain. They almost hit another overturned car. Did she see yellow eyes? She feels nauseous.

Deafening gunshots are coming from the front seat.

Before she can look, she's hurled the other direction, toward Nathan. Her seatbelt digs into her collarbone, deep enough to cut skin. Nathan is struggling not to touch her.

There's an explosion noise that sounds like another gunshot but isn't. The drifting turn was more than the spare tires could take, and something had to give. Sideways axels vault against the asphalt, spearing it, and the car trips over itself.

Julie has a floating sensation, which isn't surprising considering her body is hurtling through the open air. Upside down in the 1988 LX, she notices that the driver side door is open and Derek Darius is not in his seat.

CHAPTER 18

When a beautiful lady walks out the front door holding a baby, the first thing Johnny Sparks notices is an American flag hanging limply behind her in the stale air. The well-cared for flag fabric has always been hanging red white and blue in the front of the Montgomery household, but Johnny had missed it earlier. Distracted by the shotgun pointing, maybe.

"I am so sorry about my hair," the mother says. "It's a rat's nest."

She hides behind an absence of the makeup she usually wears. Her hair is not a rat's nest, not compared to Johnny's own hair. She's wearing an extra-extra-large Walt Disney t-shirt featuring the Hundred Acre Woods gang. Pajamas. Johnny realizes he's still wearing the same clothes as when his marriage ended. A blue plaid button-up collar shirt. One of the buttons is missing, now.

The woman could be called Italian the same way Little

Caesar's can be called Italian. She has olive skin, and her hair is dyed blonde all the way to the roots. It's impossible to tell what color her hair used to be.

Currently, Johnny has the sledgehammer wound up for Grandpa. Tim has his hands up as if he's surrendering. Grandpa Montgomery has a shotgun pointed at Tim's face. The Three Stooges.

There's this feeling of being walked in on. If Tim and Johnny are two parents having sex, then this Italian lady is a child opening the door to see what cannot be unseen. And old Grandpa Montgomery is the crazy old Grandpa waving around a shotgun and looking creepily through the window, and how did he get here anyway when he's supposed to be in the nursing home. This analogy works on multiple levels.

"Um. Hi," Tim says.

"Hi," she replies. "Mr. Montgomery, what's going on? Why do you have the gun?"

"Go back inside." The old man's words bite back. Johnny suspects that with his generation, there are certain things women should stay completely out of, and one of those things is the messy process of putting a rabid dog down. Also, voting.

"Who are these people?"

"We're *friends* of Nathan," Tim answers, and with his raised hands he makes Richard Nixon quotations marks with his fingers around the word *friends*. "We're just on our way out."

"They're trespassers. And no, you aren't going anywhere."

Grandpa's knuckles are too big, and they stretch the loose skin on his hands tight. They're the hands people show when they talk about the greatest generation, and the caption says words like *resolve*. The gun has stopped shaking. Johnny suspects this means he won't be shot, not in front of the mother and baby. But the old man's grip on the shotgun is still tight and his aim direct. If Tim and Johnny pose an immediate threat, that trigger would hammer down in a hummingbird heartbeat.

"Why did you come here in the first place?" the mother asks Johnny. The baby seems to be sleeping, or anyway, the eyes are closed and it isn't moving or making baby sounds.

"We need antibiotics for Tim," Johnny explains. "Nathan told us you might be able to help."

"Did you try to sneak in and steal the antibiotics? Mr. Montgomery, why are you pointing the gun at them?"

"They... zombies...bite..."

It doesn't take long for the mother to completely defuse the situation. Johnny believes the mother saved Grandpa Montgomery's life. He would be surprised to learn that Grandpa Montgomery believes the opposite.

...

Old Man Montgomery's living room reeks of the *Reader's Digest*. There's no sense of taste to the furnishings. On the bookshelf it looks as if there are scrapbooks full of unorganized pictures. There's this smell of hidden dust under the carpets, a stench that can't be covered up with scented candles and air fresheners, although it seems they've tried.

"We've been calling them vampires, not zombies," Tim says. "When they move they're agile and not mindless zombie-like at all."

The yellow haired mother doesn't live here, Johnny thinks. The house is too clean to be a baby house. There is a grandfather clock and a sleek black grand piano in the front room, and a framed painting of Jesus flying through space in some sort of karate stance. There are no pets and the white carpet looks like it has just been vacuumed, every day for the last fifteen years. No child proof locks protect the electrical outlets. No diapers, and not a colored plastic thing in sight.

"My point is, if the armpit cut and the hole in my stomach are just vampire claw wounds and not a zombie bites, I think I should be fine."

The old chairs are dark polished wood and purplish felt. Everyone is sitting like it's a book club meeting. The lady holds the baby boy/girl tightly to her chest. It is a wrinkly pink thing with joints that are locked in fetal positions. Its eyes are still black and squinty. Johnny isn't sure how old that makes it. Young.

"A standard vampire characteristic is not being able to go out during daytime." Grandpa Montgomery's neck gobbles when he talks, and he speaks quietly. "Obviously, that's not a problem for these creatures."

"Daywalkers," Tim retorts.

"And it is true they don't come out during the day as much," the old man speaks barely over a whisper. "Not nearly as much."

"I hate this theory," Johnny says.

"Then you must hate the movie *Blade III,* because the entire plot pretty much revolves around this."

The infant is wrapped in a burrito blanket so tightly that it can't move its arms or legs. Joints are pointing out at contortionist angles. The blanket has butterflies and other cute foresty creatures, so Johnny supposes that makes it a girl.

Johnny turns up both his hands. "Why do the creatures need to be based on movies at all?"

Tim looks back at him sideways, wet-looking hair in his eyes. "What else is there to base them on?"

The old man still has his shotgun out, suggestively pointed in Tim's general direction. He cradles the weapon with every bit as much care as the mother cradling her pink baby fetus. When grandpa had suggested the living room shotgun pointing strategy, Tim seemed surprisingly fine with it. "Seriously, if I start to turn into a zombie feel free to blow the shit out of me with that thing, sir," he had said. "Although it *would* be nice if you made sure I was actually turning into a zombie first."

Tim has high doses of penicillin in him. They tried to give him food, but he can't hold it down, and everyone huddled over him nervously as he was vomiting. Grandpa Montgomery says the dose of penicillin is what they'd give to someone who just had their leg amputated with a bacteria bladed chain saw. Tim swears he feels better already, and can feel the drugs working.

He still looks pale.

Plastic flowers sit on the black piano in a glass vase full of polished rocks. They're too bright to be real. Blue, yellow, green. They sit colorful as the autumn world outside dies for the winter.

"Nathan told us you have a town emergency response plan with the ham radio folks," Johnny Sparks says. "A plan where you search for survivors in a disaster scenario.

"Everybody has a plan," Tim says, "until they're hit in the face by Mike Tyson."

"We had a plan all right," Grandpa Montgomery bobs his head. "And it was a pretty good plan too, I think, for most realistic scenarios. Imagine a disaster for us in Rockwell. It isn't a nuclear bomb, and it isn't a horde of d-d-d-damn vampire zombies. Our type of scenario is a snowstorm that blocks access to and from the only canyon road and we don't have electricity for a few days."

"So your disaster plan consists of what happens roughly six times per year."

"But there's a plan for a scenario like this too. Someone from the core group should radio the six other operatives. From there we would coordinate and fan out by foot to make sure everyone is okay at their houses, verifying they have food, water, heat. There is a ratio of overlap so that if any four out of six fail to respond we can still check all the people in the most danger."

"That does sound like an incredibly reasonable disaster plan."

A tiny pink wooden rocking chair obviously not meant for

sitting in is sitting next to an old radio. It's almost a dollhouse chair, and there's a stuffed bear sitting in it. The chair looks very old, and the stuffed bear is showing some serious signs of wear.

"Yes, it's really very well thought out. I have an alarm set to go off whenever the power fails, for example. All the operatives do. So when the power went out last night... well, the power does go out fairly regularly so I really wasn't worried at first."

The hallway is full of family pictures framed with kids and grandkids. One has a captioned matte. It says, *The LOVE of a family is life's Greatest BLESSING.*

"My job is to touch base with all the operatives, operatives one through five, to make sure they're able to do their jobs. I'm kind of a coordinator, Operative Zero." The old man pauses. He's not making eye contact with anybody, except maybe his own thoughts. "I never asked for Operative Four directly. I don't know why. I asked for everyone but him."

The mother starts crying, but she's trying not to. She holds what she can in. Tries not to wake the baby.

Johnny Sparks knows the rest of the story before tired Grandpa Montgomery can even mouth the words. The Jesus in space painting, the vacuumed carpet, the purple velvet chairs, and the plastic flowers. Some potpourri full of dead flower leaves that sits next to a heater. These are remnants of a woman's touch.

An old woman.

An old woman who isn't here.

Johnny doesn't have to ask where Grandma Montgomery

is, or where the baby father is.

Only a few feet from Johnny, a battleship siren goes off in the *Reader's Digest* living room, blasting at decibels meant for the outdoors. Red lights, discretely hidden behind bronze flush mounts in the ceiling and powered with backup generators, flood the room.

"Something tripped the motion detectors." The old man is bustling. He reaches into a hidden place in the wall and pulls a mechanical handle. A twenty seven inch monitor pops out, showing the world outside.

The screen is darkening, almost as if the world outside had a dimmer switch dialing down to zero. As the fix-it person in the College of Engineering, Johnny has a good deal of experience with audio/video solutions, and Grandpa Montgomery has some bitchingly nice monitoring equipment. The screen wouldn't be darkening like this unless it was exactly how the world was looking outside.

Except it's impossible. This darkness isn't like a cloud in front of the sun. This is like a sped up time-lapse of dusk... and there was hardly a cloud in the sky.

"They're here," the old man says.

CHAPTER 19

"Derek Darius is my hero."

The phrase is looping in his head like a song set to repeat. Every thought is disjointed and groggily separate. He thinks, "Am I asleep?" and then he thinks "It's so awesome how he wears a trench coat all the time. Am I upside down? Derek Darius is my hero. Is something burning? It's so cool how he always wears a trench coat."

Is someone screaming?

When Nathan realizes his heavy eyes are closed he opens them, which is harder than it should be. He's not wearing his glasses, and the world is indeed backwards and blurry. *Wait. No. I'm hanging upside down from somewhere.*

A girl is screaming as a part of the background noise. "Nathan! Get out of the car!" Her scream is hysterical.

At this point Nathan realizes he's inside the back seat of an upside down 1988 Ford Mustang LX. Also, it appears

147

the engine is on fire. There's black smoke billowing up and in, and sometimes an orange flame flickers. The air is thick with the smell of burning oil.

As he's dangling there, seatbelt strap digging into his lap, his mind stumbles trying to backtrack how he landed in this situation. He fumbles with the aluminum release button, which is imprinted with a cursive FORD. He presses so hard his thumb hurts, but the latch won't release under the weight of his dangling body.

He hangs his extra-extra-large t-shirt over his face and breathes through his nose to try and block out the engine smoke. It doesn't work. The thick smell burns through, cooking his throat and chest.

He tries pushing the seatbelt release again. This time he kind of jiggles himself and times the seat belt release for when the belt goes slack. It works almost immediately, and he falls hard on his head against the Mustang ceiling with a clunk.

The backseat is cramped and turning over is tight. He keeps hitting parts of his body against cheap plastic American car pieces and rear hatchback windows. Maintaining a hunched over posture with his feet on the roof of the hatchback, he shuffles around with tiny steps. Standing right side up makes it even harder to breathe.

"What are you doing!? The car is on fire Nathan, get out of there!"

What he's doing is trying to gather his marathon power protein bars. They're spilled all over the place so he's stuffing them into various coat pockets one handful at a time.

He coughs, and it isn't easy to stop coughing. He manages to chokes out, "We might need food. One sec!"

Two protein bars drop from his open coat pockets. There's overpowering heat inside his winter coat. He's fumbling even worse than usual. With shaky hands, he picks up his glasses and tries to put them on, but they're dark with smoke. Julie Black doesn't stop screaming at Nathan to get out of the car. Inhaling more smoke than oxygen, he still feels like he's in the middle of waking up. He has about thirty of the power protein bars stuffed in his pockets now, about half.

Julie is jumping up and down and her arms are waving. "The car is going to explode!"

Protein bars and glasses are stuffed into his overflowing pockets and bunched up in his coat. He tries to cradle them all, but one drops, then two. The world is a teary blur. He's one-handed and upside down. *Where is the latch that moves the seat forward?*

Nathan is coughing hard, the shallow kind of cough that doesn't do any good. He tries to shake his head clear. He tries to find the latch. But the world is gray. The air poison. Hunched over in the car, he falls to his knees. He fights to keep his eyes open.

A form shimmers in front of him. Black against the fiery mirage, she extends a terrible celestial arm toward him. Maybe angels are real. With one arm he still clings to the protein bars, but with his other hand, he reaches toward her.

Julie's slim arms wrap his elbow and then under his armpit like the Jaws of Life. She doesn't bother trying to get the

149

seat down. With him a sack of potatoes, she manages to drag him over the seat and out of the car.

"Why in the shit did you take so long? Do you not have any common sense of urgency? The car is on F-I-R-E. Do you understand that? Do you not understand that cars are full of *gasoline*?"

"Actually, that's a common misconception. Cars don't really explode in real life. We're so conditioned because of Hollywood action movies-"

Nathan is interrupted mid-sentence by the heat wave of an exploding car. The explosion is so big he thinks it might've mushroom clouded.

...

Somehow, neither of them is seriously hurt.

"I am so pissed at *Myth Busters*. They totally busted the car explosion myth," Nathan starts to drift off. "Or in retrospect, was that the exploding *helicopter* myth?"

"We need to decide if we're going to walk the rest of the way to Inkdon or go back to Rockwell. It's something like 8 miles versus something like 17 miles."

They've moved off the main road and into some Idaho shrubbery, which seemed like a good idea at the time. It's the old fashioned western kind of hill, steep with thorny plants that cling to sedimentary dirt. More dry roots are exposed than leaves, digging in and eroding. With every step, rocks are tumbling down to the narrow road below. The whole idea of climbing up the hill was to hide, but looking up from the road there's pretty much a clear trail of the path they took, and worse, they're both still clearly visible. They haven't gone very far.

Nathan says, "I was having this dream where I was in a car and I kept pumping on the breaks but the car wouldn't stop."

"The only thing I love more than hearing all about a person's dreams is hearing all about a person's dreams when I'm in the middle of a life threatening situation."

"Yeah. So instead of slowing down, when I'd press on the breaks it would speed up. But I kept pressing them anyway." Nathan feels cloudy, like he's high on laughing gas. "What happened? Like before the car exploded, I mean. I don't remember anything."

"You look loopy. If I had a flashlight I would shine it into your pupils."

His nose feels like it's running so he sniffs loudly and it sounds like a giant glob of snot. He puts a knuckle lightly against his nostril and it comes back gloopy red. A drop of blood lands on his coat and he says, "Whose coat is this?"

"Your nose is bleeding. I think you might have a concussion."

"I'm getting blood all over this coat. No, I don't have a concussion, my nose bleeds like this all the time."

He closes a nostril and farmer blows dark red gluck onto the ground. This does not slow the nose bleed.

With sticky red teeth he says, "Gross. Whose coat is this?"

"Geez Louise," she says. "Pinch the bridge of your nose and tilt your head forward." She reaches toward his nose to help, but stops halfway. Her fingernails are painted an earthy green.

"This is no big deal. Aren't I supposed to tilt my head back?"

"I honestly can never remember."

He tries tilting his head forward and blood pretty much streams out. He tilts his head way back and it's better. The clouds haven't changed but the sky visible from the canyon has taken on a color like Swiss cheese. Blood is trickling down his throat.

He gurgles, then swallows, then spits a glob of red. "Where's Derek Darius?"

"You really don't remember?"

"I can't even remember what I just asked."

"Yeah, so what happened was actually really weird... It's like piecing together a dream where I have to fill in the gaps." It must be hard for her, trying to put the story into words so soon after it happened. Everything was fast and she was in the back seat. "Derek Darius like... perked up and got super intense. Well, he's always intense, but this seemed different."

Nathan remembers how the celebrity's forearms were flexing to grip the fuzzy steering wheel cover tighter, his whole body taking a posture of readiness, and it's kind of how he acted right before the vampire attacked earlier in the morning.

"Everything got dark. There's a sort of continuous shadow in the canyon, but everything.... *blackened*." She looks at the Idaho hill, like it might trigger a clue. "I don't know another word to describe it. Ordinary objects were hard to focus on. It was like we entered a tunnel."

When she's thinking hard, her eyes squint and her mouth turns up a tiny bit, almost like a smile. She has a tiny overbite that Nathan thinks is perfect. The dark freckles on her nose are hardly noticeable unless you're standing close to her.

"I opened my mouth to say something to him," she says, "but I don't remember actually saying anything. The car slid sideways. The cold rear window pressed hard against my cheek. Eventually the car flipped over, and here we are."

For some reason the face of a vampire flickers in Nathan's memory like a rogue frame from a movie clip. Eyes as obsidian black as Julie's mood ring. Julie seems to be holding back something also. Her mouth is pursed, and her green eyes are a mask.

"Anyway," she says, "He's gone now. And we need to figure out what the devil we're going to do."

She doesn't say how many times the car tumbled along the asphalt. Nathan thinks a lot, but it was so hard to see. His neck feels whiplash rubbery, and he has a feeling that in a few hours he's going to have a hard time turning his head from side to side.

The blood from his nose has slowed to a seep. He moves his head slowly forward, and sniffs in loudly.

"Well," he says, "If I'm stuck with anyone in an apocalypse-like situation I'm glad it's you. You're pretty... and you're smart... I mean... if we had to repopulate the planet..."

"Nathan," she says with a flirty smile, "are you trying to hit on me?"

"Haha... no. I mean if it were just me and you then our kids wouldn't even have a big enough gene pool to survive most likely... haha."

Pause.

"I mean our kid's kids would be all inbred..."

Pause.

"Actually, I think I might have a concussion."

She looks down at the clearly visible road and their terrible hiding place. "We should get to some higher ground."

Nathan ponders that for a second with a furrowed forehead. Concerned, he says, "Is that supposed to be some kind of metaphor for Derek Darius being dead?"

"He must have been thrown from the car." She bites her upper lip, sounding unsure of herself. "It happened so fast."

"Could he have jumped out?" That seems unlikely. They had been traveling too fast, and there was no body on the pavement.

Julie shakes her head. "I honestly don't know where he is. By the time the car came to a stop he was gone." Her voice is flat and terrified. Nathan understands the fear. For some reason not knowing exactly where Derek Darius is gives him the shivers.

CHAPTER 20

They've been sitting in darkness for hours.

At first nobody said a word. Even after the blackness had passed and they triple checked the monitors, they all held perfectly still. Grandpa moved slowly, and when he did move, he tried not to disturb the air. It's the sound of everybody with teeth clamped shut, holding their breath. The infant is sleeping, peacefully unaware of the danger he's in. The silence is thin and tenuous. Noise and potential energy is just below the surface.

When Grandpa Montomery was a child, in another age, the county fair would come to town and they would have freak shows. The point of a freak show was to invite the public to view the grotesquely unusual. Johnny Sparks is a size that people would pay money to see. At his size, it's hard to notice anything else about him.

Unlike the performers, Johnny has a rabid look, like a caged animal newly trapped from the wilds. Old angry scars jig jag on his face. His blue shirt, the size of a picnic quilt, is coming apart at the seams. He's practically scratching through walls with his short fingernails. Even with the giant's polite words and respectful manner, it is impossible to relax in the same room with someone capable of such powerful violence.

But it's normal sized Tim who the old man is more wary of. His tan has turned yellowish, and the whites of his eyes are too dull. Grandpa Montgomery never takes his eyes off of Tim.

"I want to tell you all a story." The old man speaks in almost a whisper, but his voice shatters the quiet. What he says is a lie. He doesn't *want* to tell them a story. What he needs is to say these words out loud. "I'll start with when I woke up."

His stomach aches. The wounds are too fresh to bury, but he'll only ever say these words once. He speaks in paragraph form. Like a high school valedictorian, he articulates his thoughts with structure and complete sentences.

"When you get old, you sometimes forget things like beginnings. It's only later that you try to pick up the pieces and make sense of what you can. The first thing I remember this morning, I was pleading with the ham radio microphone. Asking, again and again, 'Is anybody here?' Every few words I would wait for some hidden response in the static of radio transmission retrieval. 'Operative one?' Static. 'Operative two?' Static. 'Operative three?' Static. Operative five?' Static. 'Anybody?'"

Nobody asks for context, or even says a word. Tim is leaning in, and Johnny has stopped fidgeting. All eyes are glued to the old man as he speaks. The dark clouds have passed by, and there's no reason to whisper anymore. Yet still he whispers.

"I keep a notepad in the second drawer of my desk that I call *the Rockwell Emergency Response Checklist.* The pages are preformatted with text, and there are of course redundant copies stored in separate geo locations. After no responses on the radio, I neatly tore out page 57 and made a note."

For many emergency response groups, having *Contact Other Operatives* as Box One may not be the right choice. For this specific emergency response group, through extended practice they've discovered the Step One that works best for them is to begin with a radio call.

"I once dreamt about a fire drill where there is real fire blazing and everyone's busy not panicking. Crowds of people filing out in an orderly fashion, repeating DON'T PANIC while skin burns from their bodies. I thought of that dream this morning, as I called into the empty radio."

It's called the Emergency Response Checklist, but it's really more of a flow chart. Step Six is, *If possible, identify and summarize the nature of the emergency.* He checked the *Power Failure* box and the *Other* box along with the time and readings. His handwriting is small and square, developed through years of graph paper. The meticulous print takes longer to write than most common scribble, but it's as legible as a typewriter. He could come back years later and still be able to read the emergency response checklist, if he wanted.

"Part of the reason we have the plan begin with *Contact Other Operatives* is that there are always people online, whether or not there's an emergency. Like me, every operative has a generator and an alarm rigged to go off when there's a power failure. I can't stress this enough: there is *always* someone there." Without any sort of response at all from the radio, despair had risen in his old throat like vomit. The part of not knowing is the worst. "Under the *Post Apocalyptic* box, I put a neat and square question mark."

The zombie boy Tim has half a smile. He rubs at his sideburns, which have grown thin and stringy. "What's an Emergency Response Plan if not for the Post Apocalyptic contingency?"

"Of course I was prepared for this situation. If nobody answers the radio call then there's a flow chart arrow pointing back to Step One, *Contact Other Operatives* and by it there is further clarification, *if this loop repeats more than three times, reevaluate situation. For guidance, skip to step twenty.* At the bottom of the page there's a comment that says, *Prevents infinite loops.*"

The old man lets his head drop, cradling his head in his hands. "Eventually I looped again for a third and final time, asking for anyone on the airwaves. I didn't want to, but after nearly a minute I had to move on to avoid being caught in an infinite loop. Still, I lingered for a response. If I moved on, I did so slowly."

It was five seconds or maybe fifteen minutes later, and he had still been muttering, "Is anybody there?" into the radio transponder when he finally heard a human voice over the crackling radio waves.

His daughter-in-law sits in front of him with her eyes closed. Her forehead, usually care-free, looks permanently lined with worry.

"When I heard the voice on the other end, it was more familiar than I could have hoped. It was clear through the static. 'Dad, is that you?'" The voice was adult and male. Operator Four. A six feet three inches tall voice. It should have been strong but it wasn't, instead sounding like a child through an analog home video. "The voice on the other end told me, 'Dad, everyone's dead.'"

There are more wrinkles on his face than there have ever been. His gray eyes look through thick glasses into the past, and he can see with a clarity that escapes the young.

"In the radio room, I keep a gun safe. The combination to unlock the safe went through my brain, but I stayed with Operative Four.

"'Who's dead? What's going on? Over.'

"'Everyone. I can't talk now, they're coming back. Save my wife. Save my kid. Over.'

"Static.

"I asked questions. 'Where are they?' 'What are they?' 'Operative Four?' But there was only static."

To receive incoming messages, he had to take his finger off the transmit button. By default, a radio just listens, even if there's nothing to hear but amplified noise. He did not push the transmit button when he had said out loud, "I'll get her, Operative Four. Over."

Grandpa Montgomery realizes that both fists are clenched tightly as he speaks to these strangers sitting in his wife's spot on her purple couch. Although everyone has their heads tilted toward him, struggling to hear his quiet voice, it's as if they have all disappeared.

"I carried the pump action shotgun with me as I opened the door to the dark bedroom. My wife's name is Mildred but she likes to be called Grandma, even by me. It's how she defines herself, and she hates her name because it's an old person name, even though it was popular when she was young. As if *Grandma* isn't an old person's name."

She had turned from the hallway when the light poured in. It was a tired and loud roll. She muttered something, probably meant to be *go away*, but it came out unintelligible.

"I love her so much, and she was so beautiful."

She is fifty-five years of marriage and a million memories; all the laughing and the stupid flirting and sometimes the fighting but more often the only one he talks to when he talks about that funny thing that happened.

She was lying on her stomach like how she always does in the morning. He had touched her bare shoulder, still elegant. His engineer finger traced her straight spine, still softly curved and distinguished. He rolled his old knuckle between vertebrae. She was half asleep but he knew it felt good to her, and even her sleepy body language let him know it felt good.

The old man swallows air so he can keep spitting out his story. The words are insufficient. Can't keep up. "She's always been someone out of my league by any American standard." She was the only girl he had ever dated and she could have had any guy she wanted. She did have a few when she was younger. "But she asked *me* out.

Otherwise we never would have gone on so much as a first date. I never would have asked her. I never would have thought she'd say yes."

She had asked him to marry her too, in her way; not in a way a girl does when she's trying to settle a guy down, but in a reassuring way to a sensitive friend she knew didn't like to take chances.

"And I think about the kind of husband I've been," Grandpa says, words blurring with thoughts. "Distant. Focused on work or projects or hobbies that seem more and more trivial as the years pass."

"I like how you have hobbies," she had told him once. "The worst thing in the world a person can be is boring, and you have always been interesting. I wanted that, and I wanted someone who would let me raise children the way I wanted, which has always been *my* dream. That's why I chose you." Then she had kissed him.

His friends would always be jealous of her, and she'd always flirt with them innocently because that was her personality. He's never been concerned with that sort of thing. They have always had that type of relationship. It's trust, he thinks.

"She was the one who raised our children. I know that. I wasn't around much. I didn't ever change a diaper. But when my children needed me, I would be the one to save them."

Telling the story now to his daughter-in-law and these strangers he says, "That was the last time I ever saw her. Beautiful. Lying on that bed." Less than a day, and he's already using the modifier *ever*.

"On the Rockwell emergency response checklist there isn't exactly a contingency flow for saving a daughter-in-law and grandchild from an undefined *they* entity that has apparently killed *everyone*, but it does contain specific instructions for rescuing people who might be hurt or in immediate danger."

Before he had left on Operation Rescue-Daughter-in-Law, he transcribed everything onto the checklist on the radio desk. Using a rolling ball pen with black ink he wrote, *5:25: I am going to attempt rescue of family at Operative Four's house at the following address. I am armed, and will have my portable radio set to channel 13. Judging by previous communications with Operative Four, I expect there to be high risk involved.*

Mildred, if you read this I have battened down the hatches. Nobody should be able to get in except through the front door.

Don't open the front door for anybody.

"Operation Rescue-Daughter-in-Law was uneventful to the point where I was starting to wonder if fire fighters have it easy. With all the things that could go wrong, everything fell into place. She was right where I guessed she would be, at Operative Four's house, at the front door. The walk was short, a few hugely spaced houses away. If the world was so quiet that it felt unnatural, well, I haven't been able to hear well for twenty years anyway."

The daughter-in-law's brown eyes contrast sharply with her professionally bleached hair. She listens to her own story, hiding behind the sleeping baby. Her face clings to her beautiful youth that's just starting to slip, and she wears its symmetric features like a mask. The old man talks past her. This story is not for her.

"She was awake and wide-eyed terrified when I got there." His grandson had been crying hysterically while he stood in the doorway. She had tried to force feed him, shoving his head into her boob. He tried to look at everything but her partially exposed chest. The house was a mess. Papers were scattered on the floor and a greasy pizza box was left empty on the carpet. It was probably a mess because of the kid and not because of zombie things that killed everyone, but it's hard to say for sure.

"She didn't know where my son was, or what *they* were." Grandpa looks at her now. She opens her eyes partway to meet his stare, and they share something with the eye contact. "With all the questions I asked, the only thing she told me was, *they're coming.*"

"The air turns black when they're coming." She sits like a statue, unblinking. "It's a feeling. You can sense the blackness inside as much as around you. By the time you came to my door it was already too late. Your son said his goodbyes."

Was there accusation in her voice?

"On the way back everything looked familiar but eerie," Grandpa Montgomery says. "Approaching my own house everything was perfectly in place. The little gnomes that Grandma had placed used to be facing north, and they were still facing north. The flag of the United States of America was still hanging on the front porch. The grass was still mowed. It was hard to imagine a disaster had happened here, but at the same time it was impossible not to imagine things were silently wrong."

He had called to her. The steel-framed door had been locked with heavy deadbolts. Black, wrought iron bars covered the windows. His whole house is like this. There are no sliding glass doors here. It's a Rockwell Idaho house, but it's prepared for life in the ghetto.

"Not a thing was out of place. Glancing through the open radio room door, my Emergency Response Checklist was still lying untouched on the desk." His note to her, unread.

His grandson had been crying, making it hard to think.

"I opened the bedroom door and light poured in." With all the senses he's lost in old age, his sense of smell is as good as ever. Maybe better. It might be that his brain has compensated for a lack of hearing and seeing and he now has the freakish super sense of smell of a blind person. The bedroom smelled like nothing was out of place. "Mildred was gone."

But even now it smells like she should still be there.

The room was exactly how he left it. The blankets were how they should be; as if Grandma was hidden in the folds of sheets. So he looked, but no, she wasn't there. There was no sign of a struggle.

He had called her name louder, trying to force his quiet voice over the screaming baby.

"I checked every room and I checked again as if I were looking for misplaced car keys, but she was nowhere."

When he ran out of obvious rooms, he started to look for her in impossible places like under the kitchen sink and in the dryer. A new tiredness came over him then. He's afraid it will never leave for the rest of his life.

He had checked the Emergency Response Checklist for anything about losing everything he's ever cared about. It had not been listed. He makes a mental note to cover this in the next iteration.

"Hours later I was checking under the sofa cushions for Grandma when my perimeter cameras detected two strangers approaching the house. One of them was an ugly giant with no sense and the other looked sick, like he might turn into a zombie any second."

This situation has made the old man open up, and he reveals details about himself that he usually would keep private. But one thing the old man doesn't tell Johnny Sparks and Tim is his instinct telling him to do anything at all to defend his remaining relatives. The rest of his old life should be dedicated to this cause above anything else. He must protect his baby grandson, his daughter-in-law, and Nathan (wherever he is). For a dead wife whose children meant everything, he needs to protect what's left of his family at all costs. For her.

CHAPTER 21

The theme is abandonment, sort of the way high school proms have a theme.

The city of Rockwell has a feeling of preternatural nighttime emptiness. Despite the afternoon sun sitting at a noonish angle overhead, it feels like a 3:00 a.m. winter night where white ice reflects back the heatless photons of a full moon. There are times when it's normal for the busiest Rockwell streets to be empty and the cold air to be quiet. Noon on the same day as the Derek Darius talk is not one of those times.

All the tires on all the cars are flat. They haven't seen any cars with inflated tires in over twenty-four hours, but Johnny Sparks is still obeying the jaywalking regulations with all the clean cut compliance of a Mormon missionary. He walks on the concrete sidewalks and crosses the street at crosswalks.

In his right hand he carries the gigantic sledgehammer. On

166

his left ring finger, a tarnished wedding ring.

A lifetime of thick hand calluses and brain calluses and mechanized labor makes this whole thing easy. There's a clear objective for Johnny, and that's rescuing Autumn.

"She would be in the attic section of the old town dormitory," Johnny had said. "There's roof access, a fire sprinkler system, food storage, and a high ceiling with a retractable ladder entrance. It was her zombie escape plan number one."

Tim and Johnny are alone in the open middle of some extremely dangerous unknown thing, and even though it terrifies them, they're doing it anyway in an attempt to save the people they love. Neither of them even has to think about it (this doesn't stop them from thinking about it).

Tim is walking in the gutter and sort of swaying like a pale drunkard. Johnny forces himself to use similes like *drunkard* and keep away from comparisons like *zombie* or *infected*. Grandpa Montgomery had a lot of guns, and Johnny did take one along with a holster, but Tim is strapped second-amendment style. Every time he stumbles, Johnny likes to think that maybe it's because the kid is overloaded with guns.

"I have a confession to make," Johnny had said. "The real reason I stayed is because of Autumn. I love her, and I need her to be okay." He had blinked away a picture of her sliced hand, dripping blood.

"The truth is," Tim had said, "I stayed because I love someone too."

The street they're walking on is an old type of

neighborhood and every house is different. One house is 1950s stucco, and its neighbor is 70s brick. There are no homeowner's associations here. Mailboxes stand next to the sidewalk, personalized but regular, just like they always have. The sidewalks have very few cracks, and the black paved roads have few potholes. The town takes pride in things like that.

It's both eerie and terrifying for the two men to walk in the open streets when there are thousands of people probably recently dead. Competing survival instincts located in their spinal cord brains are screaming in protest to this strategy, releasing bio-chemicals that tell them to find a safer place and get to higher ground.

Mostly they walk in silence. Once, Johnny asks, "Who's this someone you're coming back for?"

"Their names are Hooker and D-O-G." He pronounces D-O-G as *dee oh gee*. "They're my two dogs."

Tim hits his toe in-between sidewalk squares and barely catches himself. He clips a black mailbox with his arm and takes three stumbly steps before regaining his balance. The sidewalks are too skinny to hold him.

Every time he trips, Tim talks to himself. He says things like, "Man up" and "You can do this." The phrases started with encouragement, but have gradually become more depressing. "Just do this one last thing before you die."

Johnny has been careful not to comment. He badly wants to give encouragement, but he has never been able to lie.

"I can't stop thinking about the dark times in my life and how D-O-G was always there," Tim says to Johnny. "The memories come in flashes. Flash: there's D-O-G putting her squarely dog head on my lap. Flash: Hooker is sleeping in a curled ball and spasming in pursuit of some dream squirrel. Flash to puppies so excited they'd pee on the carpet when I walk through the door."

Johnny's is a face of concern. His rock square jaw doesn't seem so hard, and his angular head seems softer. He listens.

"There's a responsibility I have toward these animals that makes it a stronger bond than many types of love," Tim says. "It's a love where if something unthinkable ever happened it would be my fault. Both Hooker and D-O-G are just mutts I picked up from the pound, but they're like my kids. Most dogless humans would laugh... it's something someone who doesn't own a dog could never understand, like those cat people mother fuckers."

This is where most people would ask Tim what kind of dogs they are, or mention the dogs they have, or talk about how they're allergic to dog hair.

Instead, Johnny says with almost inhuman empathy, "There's love and then there's love."

...

Autumn Sparks isn't hiding in zombie escape place number one, the attic section of the old town dormitory. She isn't in zombie escape place two either, which she likely would have deviated to if she were starting from the university. Escape place number three is also empty.

Wobbling pale or not, Tim has proven invaluable to the survival effort. There's a lot of back watching and covering the other around the corner and eyes in the back of the head going on. Some of this is simply not possible with only two binocular eyes. While Johnny forges ahead, Tim scans behind. What they lack evolutionarily when compared with a cow's sideways predator scanning eyes, they make up with good American teamwork.

But realistically, what could the two of us really do if we did run into a vampire. Stampede?

Escape place four is this abandoned building that's being transformed into a vacuum cleaner museum. Construction here is rampant. Autumn liked this place because it was three stories of concrete construction where most zombies of the uncoordinated variety would have an impossible time escalating floors. There's a lot of surface area on the roof, and it's locationally close to a pawn shop and 7-11.

It's getting hard to ignore that Tim is in a state where he's a lot like a slow moving zombie. He drags his feet sideways when he walks, and he groans. Johnny is the one to climb to the roof and search for Autumn while Tim waits below, decomposing but still alert. "BRaaaaaaaaiiins," he said one time. "Just kidding." He had smiled weakly, and there was something insanely sad about it, like a terminally sick baby trying to smile.

Autumn isn't here, either.

One thing about escape place number four is that it's also close to Tim's house. "It's time we found those dogs of yours, Tim," Johnny says. "Let's take a detour to Hooker and D-O-G."

Tim smiles again, as happy as a make-a-wish kid.

"Dogs can sense what you and I can't," Tim says. "There are bad things just below the surface, and we might be able to feel them, just barely. But it's always smart to watch the dog. They'll tell us what to do."

Tim says that he is a home owner, in the sense that the bank owns the house he lives in and he has a mortgage. He lives in the house with just his two dogs, but he's trying to find a roommate to halve the cost because he's still a student.

Johnny Sparks understands completely. Despite emigrating from some other state, Tim is an Idaho man, completely different from the Silicon Valley types and people like Derek Darius. Johnny says, "Maybe this is the vampire crisis bringing two people together, but you and I are more alike than I ever would have guessed."

Tim shambles across his overgrown lawn toward an old gate, and Johnny follows with deliberate steps. Dying dandelions have taken over, dozens of them, and it looks like they've been poisoned with some chemical from Home Depot. The dying weed flowers are twisted and shriveled and growing sideways while gray seeds cling to what's left of deformed seed heads. The gate and fence are made out of wood that's maybe a faded cedar that's never been stained. There are a few places where the dogs have evidently dug holes under the fence which are blocked with concrete cinder blocks to prevent the animals from escaping.

There is a noticeable absence of barking. No wagging tails in sight.

"Hooker! D-O-G!" Tim yells at the top of his lungs, and it sounds louder than it should, perhaps because of the

171

contrast with the silent world around them. "Hooooooooker! D-O-G!"

Two steps in and there's a furry pile of intestines and guts. Unidentifiable pieces of blood and skin and shit are spread all over the yard. Pieces are splattered yards apart, some high against the side of Tim's house. The corpse could just as easily be a raccoon as a dog.

"D-O-G?" Tim says with recognition. Pieces of brown and tan hair are torn apart and matted with blood. "D-O-G-girl, is that you?"

Tim squeezes his eyes shut. He is obviously crushed, every bit as much as Johnny would be if this corpse were Autumn's. Johnny doesn't know what to say, but it feels like he has to say something, so he starts talking. "Did you check her pulse?"

Tim's eyes are hard with Idaho resolution. He takes a deep breath. "I only see one body." Scanning the small yard with his eyes he yells, "Hooker!" When he gave her this name, he had told Johnny earlier, it was pretty much as a joke. In a predominately conservative Christian neighborhood, there's something innately funny about a story where Hooker crapped on the carpet and he had to shove her face in it and yell at her so she wouldn't do it again. Or shouting for Hooker to get her ass inside.

"Hooker! Hooker! Hooker!"

There's nothing funny about the name now.

Below the old wooden fence a wild animal face pokes through a small dirt divot. A feral dog with wild yellowish brown eyes and a silver muzzle. The tiny fence hole looks too small for this animal to fit through, but the tufts of matching hair suggest that despite the impossible size, this was the animal's escape route.

Tim's voice softens. "Hooker, come here girl." He is on his knees and he snaps his fingers in a loving bidding motion. He coos, "Hooker, come here."

The dog is part black lab and part border collie and part Rottweiler, although Rottweiler is never included in things like apartment applications. She has a patchy undercoat. Tim had to vacuum every day. Slim. Brave. Independent. Survivor. She was a rescue, abandoned when Tim found her. Day by day, Tim had gained Hooker's trust. Over the years, she seemed happy.

She looks at Tim without any hint of recognition, and then her mangy face disappears behind the fence. By the time Tim is able to pull himself over, Hooker is a quarter mile away with her long legs gracefully bolting like an Ethiopian marathoner. She's running away from both Tim and Rockwell with unadulterated animal instinct.

CHAPTER 22

"It's a goddamned slightly biased coin flip." Julie's head falls back and she talks to the sky. "The moss on this tree is on the exact opposite side."

Nathan draws a tally on the scratchpad app. "So that's seven tallies for that way being north and five for the other way… and three tallies for undefined."

The moss-growing-on-the-north-side-of-trees compass strategy is working about as well as the early-afternoon-sun-compass strategy, which is to say not well. The sun is surprisingly useless as a navigation device from the vantage point of two o'clock in the northern afternoon hemisphere. The idea with the moss-growing-on-the-north-side-of-trees strategy is that with enough tallies they should arrive at a probabilistically likely direction for north.

"Aren't you supposed to be smart?" She presses her finger to one of the spots her head hurts and pushes gently until she has to wince away. Already she can't remember if this one was from the vampire or the car crash. "Isn't there an electrically charged safety pin you could put on a leaf to figure out magnetic north or something?"

"I've never been good at physics. If we could just get a signal, my phone does have a compass app I could use."

"Hey, great idea Nathan! That's what we should use your phone for if you get a signal!"

"Hey! Sarcasm! I love sarcasm!"

They've decided to continue to Inkdon rather than back to Rockwell, but after a few hours of walking they could be anywhere. In the name of not being vampire food, they've traveled further away from the only road and into rocky mountain terrain. There's an overwhelming massiveness about everything. The rocks are all boulders. The hills, mountains. With no path and no sign of living things, the world is dwarfed by granite and sandstone and the overall earthiness for gigantic stretches of space.

The terrain is not built for a casual stroll. More often than not, they hug the side of a steep hill so that their tired right legs are always downhill bearing their body weight. They take short awkward steps on the steep rock and dirt. The only plants managing to cling to the sides of the hill are rank weeds.

Whenever Julie looks in his direction, Nathan seems to forget how to walk. He says, "Whenever you look at me, I try and walk all naturally and cool, but it's harder than it looks. I'm aware of every piece of my body, and there are too many pieces to control." He stumbles again, whether from her presence or the uneven terrain she could not say. The hill is so steep that every stumble is inches away from a fatal mistake.

This makes Julie smile. What kind of person says that out loud? She looks at him every chance she gets.

"Have you ever heard of an Idaho right-legger? It's like a cow."

Julie glances at him, and he trips. "A what?"

"You know, a cow. Anyway, you know how when you drive out of the canyon there are hundreds of these cows on the side of the road that stand on hills that look like these? Well, I remember looking at them as a little kid, and my dad told me how the world was perfect. He said everything was adapted to fit so perfectly, and then he pointed to the Idaho right-legger cows standing on the hills.

"He said, 'Nathan, there are these two types of cow: right legged cows and left legged cows. It's kind of like how people are right or left handed. The right legged cows always face one direction on the hill, and left legged cows always face the other. That way they're able to run at full speed, even when they're walking on the side of a steep hill.' In other words, what happened is my dad basically inceptioned me.

"I remember thinking how awesome cows were, and when I got older eventually thinking that evolution was awesome. I grew up with left legged cows as a staple of knowledge, this sort of axiom I built on top of to help shape my view of the universe.

"So earlier this year in Biology 201 we were talking about evolution and I commented on how awesome right legged cows were, and I was in the middle of explaining how they can escape most standard equal legged predators when the Professor stopped me.

"Cows don't have one leg shorter than the other.

"I told him, 'no, but these aren't regular cows. These are Idaho right-leggers.'

"'No', he said, 'That wouldn't even make any sense.'"

Despite herself, Julie laughs genuinely, and it's the type of laugh that blurts out. Maybe it's the multiple head impacts, but she's feeling something she hasn't felt in a while. She's looking at Nathan differently, and starting to care about his opinion. Instead of survival, she finds herself smiling a lot, and wanting to look pretty.

Nathan's cheeks are rosy in a way that's not uncomfortable. He pushes his glasses up his nose. "Yes. Laugh. But I spent days on the Internet attempting to verify the existence of right legged cows so I could show Professor Wolfworth for a fool. I eventually asked my dad about it, and he was amazed I even remembered that. He asked if I still thought the road signs for 'Falling Rock' referenced an ancient Native American warlord."

"An ancient Native American warlord?"

"It's a long story but don't worry. I stopped believing in *The Legend of Falling Rock and his merciless band of Native Americans* when I was sixteen."

Nathan Montgomery would rather go to Rockwell than Inkdon. Julie disagreed. "What if the whole world is like this?" she had said. "Then it doesn't really matter where we go."

He had shrugged like she didn't understand logic. 1) Rockwell is closer to where Derek Darius wrecked the car. It could take over a day to make it to Inkdon, especially if they stay off the main road. 2) The only way to Inkdon is through an ambushably narrow canyon. 3) Rock paper scissors lizard Spock.

"I'm not going back there," Julie said definitively. Just the thought of returning to Rockwell makes her feel like she'll never sleep again. It's a coldness that buries itself past her gut and into her bones. There's an oppressive gloom from just being in the same area code as Rockwell. Only death and misery are there. She had told Nathan that she would never go back to Rockwell, not even if he wins rock paper scissors lizard Spock eight out of fifteen.

"Are you hungry?" Nathan offers her a marathon power protein bar. He has plenty.

Julie's guitar t-shirt is tied in a knot to show off her slim middle. There's no practical reason for this, it isn't hot outside. She's always been proud of her stomach, the slim way it tucks into her jeans. Maybe it's the weird sense of humor or possibly it's the apocalyptic scenario, but for the first time Julie realizes she likes Nathan Montgomery the way girls sometimes like boys.

And another thing; it doesn't matter. Everyone in her family is dead, and who knows how far Apocalypse Idaho reaches. The entire world could be dying. Nathan and Julie could be the last two people on earth by now, and more importantly their chance of actually surviving seems low.

"You know what my biggest fear in all this is?" Julie says. "I just don't want my life to end like HBO's Deadwood, right in the middle of plot escalations with no real resolution."

"We can at least take peace in that if it really is the end of the world, then the people who cancelled the show are probably dead."

"Well, however I die I want to be cremated."

"Me too."

"And my ashes spread throughout Rockwell College's ventilation system."

"That is a good thought. Whenever somebody coughs they might think, oh, it's just that Black girl again."

Amidst the vampire terror there's a feeling that if this were a first date it would be going pretty well.

"There was a story on NPR about this old electrician guy," Nathan says. "He wanted to be cremated and then shot out of a cannon he made himself."

"Ah, the age old debate of fulfilling a dead guy's last request versus basic sanitation/safety."

"Yeah, Disneyland has strict instructions to not allow people to spread remains on Pirates of the Caribbean anymore."

She takes a bite of a protein bar Nathan gave her and her stomach doesn't feel empty. Julie is not tall, and Nathan is only an inch or two taller. He is stick thin. Bad in a fight. Yet she's happy he's the one she's with. She tells herself the reason is simply that if you can't outrun a vampire, make sure you can outrun the person you're with.

But if Nathan had been the one to disappear at the car crash... If it were Derek Darius with her now.... She shudders.

"What do you think we should eat when the protein bars run out?" Nathan asks. "Do you think we could trap a squirrel? Maybe I could throw a rock and hit one."

Julie hasn't seen any squirrels. Not one.

"You want to know something funny? You know how the joke is to call me *that black girl* because Black is my last name? People refer to me as *that black girl*, like how you just referred to me as *that black girl*. They do it at work and school too."

"Well, it is kind of funny."

"The thing that's funnier is that I am actually part black."

"No." Nathan stops and turns to her. "NO."

"Yep. Kenyan Grandpa."

Awkward pause.

"You... um... you don't look black."

"One fourth."

Just like two certified purebred Idaho right-leggers, Nathan and Julie continue the sideways trek along the steep hill that's almost a mountain. Everyone is dead and they're lost in the woods and they're both wearing billboard smiles. When they laugh it's in a way that communicates they're having a good time. One foot in front of the other, she avoids the thought that at any moment they could end up another moderately priced meal for something inconceivably higher up on the food chain.

"So here's an ethical question. Now that you know I'm part black, are you more racist if you continue to call me that *black girl* or if you stop?"

"I'm pretty sure it's more racist if I keep calling you that black girl?"

"Could be. But wouldn't that be a decision that's based solely on the color of my skin and not the content of my character? Isn't that what being racist is all about?"

"Wait. Are you the one being racist now? I can't tell."

"I'm black, so I pretty much have racism immunity. I can say the N word and everything."

Ahead of them there's an area that looks like many others. On this infinite hill they can never seem to see the other side, but every so often there's a local peak that *looks* like it will give a good view. At one of these, Nathan stops jerkily ahead of her. She can't see what's on the other side, but he can. He turns around slowly to face Julie. "Do you want the good news or the bad news?"

She waits for the worst. Her breathing is shallow. "Both?"

"The good news is we are going toward Inkdon. We were going the right way all along, so yay!"

She rushes past him. Below, she can clearly see the narrow canyon. The walls are steep, and junkyard cars are piled high. The air itself is sinister. Shadows spill across open areas where there isn't anything to cause them. Her stomach drops into her intestines. She can smell the vampires down there. Hiding. Waiting.

And it's the only way across.

"We can't go that way." She tries to make her voice strong, but it shakes. There isn't any alternative. It's the feeling of being buried alive. You know you're already dead, but you might as well claw on your casket until your fingernails fall off. "We have to turn around. We have to go back to Rockwell."

CHAPTER 23

After Tim's house is when they start seeing the melting people.

"D-O-G died protecting my life - it was just in her nature…"

Tim's condition has deteriorated since the dog incident. Arteries in his neck are turning from red to brown to a squiggly blackish. The surrounding skin is bruise yellow. A combination of odors like you could only get in an old taxicab, he smells like some acrid combination of burning human hair and French person.

"What hurts the most is how I yelled at her for barking. I was always trying to change the way she was because in modern America there just aren't many things more annoying than a dog's protection instinct. This morning when she was busy saving my life I heard her barking like mad, and my reaction was to dog-whisper at her to shut the fuck up."

Mostly silent, Tim sits and stares at the insides of his wallet. Johnny imagines a picture of dogs behind the leather where the animals are wearing those expressions associated with dog happiness. Maybe their ears are relaxed, and their tails are in the middle of a wag.

"That's an interesting looking wallet." Johnny smiles solemnly, trying to divert the college kid's pain. "What's it made out of?"

"Eel skin. I'm not sure what kind of eel."

Escape place number five was empty, along with six, seven, and eight. Depending on the definition of empty. For Johnny, it means that Autumn was not there.

"Hooker was always wild. It doesn't surprise me at all that she ran away. I've thought a lot about how she grew up, like before I met her, and the way I see it is she's always been a survivor."

If the antibiotics were a placebo for Tim, the hope crushing encounter with his dogs was a reality pill. The realization he's going to die young is medicine that's tough to swallow.

"Hooker loved me. I know that. But she's a survivor first."

...

Johnny tries to place the accent of the old man. Russian maybe. He's propped up and dirty like a train-hopping hobo, and it's an accent that could be from any of the former Soviet states. Johnny has never left America, and everything he knows about Eastern European accents he's learned from movies. If he had to guess, he'd guess this accent is from Yugoslovia.

Guts are falling out of the wounds, and the first thing he said to Johnny Sparks and Tim is, "Kill me."

"Yugoslovia?" This was the second thing the dying Soviet had said, shaking his head with disbelief at the ignorant Americans. He coughed blood and spoke with great effort. "That is not even a real country."

This dirty Eastern European is the only living thing they've seen in what seems like a very long time. If you could call this living.

It's hard to focus on the something-a-stan accent when there is skin-toned pus oozing out of broken stumps where there should be legs. The bones sticking through are extraordinarily white, twisted like tree roots. The skin hanging on looks like reheated salmon that was melted in the microwave for way too long. The horribleness is hard to look at and simultaneously hard not to look at. It smells like Tim in here but more pungent.

The Russian struggles to speak. His breathing is shallow, and he appears to barely be holding back coughing fits. "They are the color of evil."

"Apparently *evil-color* is now an off-black," says Tim as he looks around the basement with a feigned type of indifference. "Thank you for this incredibly useful piece of information. You can now rest knowing that you did not die in vain."

"What did this to you, Russian?" Johnny asks.

As if for an answer, the hollow man coughs blood. Bits of lung and phlegm spray into the air. He continues coughing long past the point of sadness. "You must kill me before dusk," he finally manages to say.

"Why dusk? We've seen them out at day."

"The sun is not their weakness. It is just... they hunt at twilight."

This man looks tough, down to his guts and bones. Yet there is a longing in his accented voice when he asks Johnny to kill him. What pain must he be in to make this man not just want death - but *long* for it?

"Very strong fear, do you understand what this means?"

The burning air contrasts somehow with the rot-like melting decay that's visible. It doesn't hit Johnny until later that there were never any flies. With so much rot, there should be maggots and pus, but there is nothing except the sharp smell of melting bones.

"Try to imagine this scenario, and for you, it should not be difficult to imagine. This is something every real soldier encounters. You are at war, and you have friends. Imagine a friend you have thought was dead, but you find him lying on the side of the road where he is left by the enemy; meant to be found. Most pieces of him have been carved out. He no longer has ears. He has no eyes, no tongue. His arms and legs are cut. Obviously, he cannot speak. He should be dead, but somehow he is still alive. He is left in this state by the enemy as a symbol... maybe not a symbol of anything in particular, but most definitely symbolic."

The guts spilling out are the worst. They keep falling out, and the old man puts them back into his own belly. The image is horribly graphic. Most people would pass out after seeing this, but after a million zombie movies Johnny has a ridiculously strong stomach for gore. Even so, it's a gut wrenching image that can never be unseen. Johnny can't believe this man is still conscious. At the very least he must be in some kind of deep shock.

His old eyes are hard and intelligent, but there's this tortured madness to them. He's wearing a dusty military uniform with medals that must be from the Soviet Union or Czech or wherever (apparently not Yugosolvia). When people talk about seasoned veterans in the context of war, they could almost always be talking about this guy. Johnny has no idea why he's wearing the uniform, but he is unable to picture him without it.

"According to army protocol this kind of broken person should be taken to the hospital. But after seeing one, every soldier tells his friends, if you ever find me in this sort of condition, in this sort of shell… kill me. Just kill me."

When this eastern European told Johnny to kill him the first time, his voice had been horse at first. The unexpected "kill me" words escaped his mouth like someone who forgot to put up the Do Not Disturb sign on a hotel door. Tim and Johnny had intruded into the middle of this intimate dying moment. Johnny told him he was the first person they'd seen alive, to which the old man had responded, "I am not alive."

"Watching a person in this state, the kind of state I am in, it can make someone go crazy. We all of us think about death for our entire lives, and we imagine we fear death more than anything."

His lungs breathe shallowly.

"It is not until you see a person like me that you realize," he says, "there truly are things worse than death."

The old man's heart beats weakly.

"There is more than one method to win at war. You can kill your enemy, that is one method. Or you can strike fear into the heart of your enemy, and kill not only that person but terrorize his family, his friends, everyone that person speaks to. The terror spreads like disease. When these people close their eyes they have nightmares with melting legs and guts falling out."

His heart could continue beating broken blood for days.

Johnny tightens his grip on the hammer.

"And what rules this world? Fear." The old man makes eye contact with Johnny. With the slight strength he has left, he nods.

As Johnny Sparks swings the sledgehammer, the collapsing skull breaks the eye contact. Bits of skull and brain splatter onto his jeans and blue shirt. Johnny takes a moment to think about the old man's last words. Last words have always been important to Johnny.

...

More bodies were strung out on display; these melting dead left in places where they were meant to be found. Every one sticks to Johnny's brain, but the old Russian sticks the most.

Tim is a good person, but there's only so much even a good person should be expected to give. Tim found his dogs, so his part is over. Also, he's dying, and dying people should basically get what they want. Tim croaks,

"Should we go back to Grandpa Montomery's?" and it isn't really a question.

Even people on death row usually get a decent last meal.

"A couple more places on the way," Johnny Sparks says. "Then we should head back for the evening." He would search for her all night if he were alone, but leaving Tim is just not who he is. Johnny lies. "I'm getting tired and I need to go back anyway."

It seems like the only birds should be vultures, but there are not even those. It's getting dark. It seems like it should be too early, but the sky is darkening anyway like daylight savings Fall Forward.

He somehow knows Autumn is alive. It's the way people know their church is true, the same type of knowing when people say they *knew* something. When he thinks about her alive it is true that there is cold fear in his stomach, but there is also a burning warmth that fills his chest. Some would call that warmth faith, or even hope.

He knows she's alive, but he doesn't know where she is.

"Your house?" Tim manages to say as they walk up to Johnny's property.

"Yesterday it was. I'm not sure the specifics on how divorces work."

"Huh. Well, on the bright side if she's dead you can probably keep the house."

Johnny glares.

"I mean, it's not like it's a win-win," Tim says, "but at least all your bets are covered."

Johnny keeps glaring, but there's no malice in it. *I know she's alive.*

At the front door, Johnny reaches into his left pocket where he keeps his house keys. They aren't there. Autumn kept them when she threw him out of his house and out of her life. The door is bright red and welcoming, Johnny had repainted it only one year ago. Before kicking his own door in, he knocks first to see if anyone's home.

At escape places one through eight they went through the houses acting like trained Israeli military, kicking open doors and waving their pointed guns around corners while they yelled things like "The kitchen is clear!" and "Is there anyone alive?". This contrasts with the way they walk into Johnny's house. They tiptoe inside almost reverently, as if they're trying to be respectful of people praying inside. When Johnny shuts the broken door he turns the handle beforehand so the latch doesn't make a noise.

On the linoleum floor is a clear drop of blood that looks wet. It had dripped off Autumn's fingertips when Johnny was leaving. *Shouldn't it be dry by now?* He swallows the thought before it can surface. On his way inside he squashes the red blob with his black rubber boots, obscuring it to unrecognizable dirt. Tim doesn't seems to have noticed.

Johnny unloads the dishwasher every day after dinner, and there the dishwasher is, unloaded. A chess set is next to the couch where Johnny reads books and he doesn't use bookmarks, he folds the corner of the pages. It seems odd that his book is still sitting there and he hasn't lost his place.

The omnipresent sense of dread is almost absent from Johnny/Autumn's home. Instead it's replaced with a feeling of familiarity and also of creepiness. In a way, the creepiness is there because of the familiarity.

Hanging on the hallway wall there's a reflective black framed picture of when Autumn and Johnny were getting married, and she's wearing a white dress and Johnny is wearing a camera smile. They're both standing in front of a beach with fine-grained sand and green ocean. Her eyes are cold, even on the day they should be warmest. Despite gravity constantly pulling it toward the center of the earth, the picture still clings to the wall, hanging from the nail Johnny had pounded in years before. Since he left last night, there must not have been any time for her take the pictures down.

Was it only last night I left?

Autumn used to say she never understood the point of standing in front of pretty things and smiling. She's always preferred covert photographs snapped when nobody's looking.

"Autumn?" He calls to see if she's home. It comes out a whisper.

The house is only one story and in about ten seconds they've covered every room but one.

"This is her office," Johnny says, "If she left any sort of clue it would be in here."

Solemnly, he opens the door. *This is it. If there's nothing here...*

Her room is sterile and completely uncluttered. As usual.

191

There's a slight smell of Lysol. On the computer desk there's a paper notebook. It stands out as an item out of place in the carefully categorized area.

Johnny steps slowly toward it. He can see the paper is covered with black ink long before he can read the words. He inches closer as if the notepad is dangerous.

Written on her notepad, again and again, are two words scrawled in a spiderlike script, so different from her usual compact handwriting: Derek Darius.

Johnny reads it. He mouths the words but doesn't make a sound above a whisper. Derek Darius Derek Darius Derek Darius.

"Autumn never writes things down," he says. "Literally never. She always uses her laptop or phone or *something* electronic. She says anything written on paper might as well be forgotten."

The words are scrawled in black ink, between the lines and in the margins. The way it's almost enshrined on the desk it must be important. Sometimes the letters are angular and sometimes they're written in circles. Everywhere they are terrible. Derek Darius Derek Darius Derek Darius.

"What does it mean?" Tim asks.

Johnny has made a connection, and everything about it immediately feels right.

"Derek Darius is a vampire."

CHAPTER 24

The October sunlight is broken. Clouds are swimming black against the distant sky. Something is definitely up atmospherically; sounds sound different, breathing tastes funny, and everything is darker than it should be. If this were the Midwest and Rockwellian old people were still alive to sit on their front porches, various anatomical pieces would be swelling up to sense a serious storm coming.

Is this what the end of the world is like? Julie thinks. *A world where I'm pretty much oblivious to everything and I spend my time hiding in the mountain trees?*

"Am I allowed to talk yet?" Nathan says kind of loudly.

"No."

To Julie, maybe the most interesting part is how she's already moving on. Except for her possessions, her career, her loved ones…. as long as she stays away from the billboard specifics, she moves on. It's not as bad as it sounds. Yes, the surface is filled with sadness, but past the sadness there's something more primal that's being fulfilled, and it turns out it's bigger than the things she's lost.

She's cooling off and her skin is the salty smell of drying sweat. Her heart rate has slowed and her instinct tells her that it's safe enough to climb out of the tree. Not safe, but *safe enough.* Her hands are covered with dead pine needles and sap. She nods at Nathan, and they climb downward. Pine trees are fairly difficult to climb, and the ground isn't very far away. Nathan is talking before they hit the ground.

"So back to what I was saying, I think the reason why Sisko is so under-rated as a Starfleet captain is due to older generations looking back nostalgically at Spock and Picard and even the Borg. I admit, the assimilation idea is very cool and very eighties cold war, but you'd think this super advanced species would have adapted to consider humans wandering around their ship a threat by now, after like every episode where a *harmless* human manages to thwart the mighty Borg."

"Okay."

"Then look at the Dominion. Not only are they an intelligent adversary to the alpha quadrant, but the founders can shape-shift to look exactly like anybody in the entire galaxy. It's like *The Thing* combined with *Star Trek*. I think that in and of itself makes Deep Space Nine the best television series of this or (with recent events) maybe any generation. Have you watched it?"

"A little."

"What did you think?"

"To be honest, I had a hard time making it through the first season. I hope we can still be friends."

The roots of twisting trees are gnarled in rock and swollen at the joints. Her sandals dig into the webs between her toes as she walks over the black soil beneath her. Such a poor choice of shoes.

Her instinct feels inhibited by a hundred years of human couch potatoing, but she can still feel sharp survival processes hidden away somewhere in the back of her hypothalamus. It just needs some fine tuning is all. There's no way to move safely through these woods, and no amount of tree climbing can change that.

Her spidey sense is tingling. Right now.

We jumped down too soon.

She's overcome with a desire to jump or dodge or something. The last time she felt like this was like sixty seconds ago. She and Nathan climbed into a pine tree, even though logically vampires can probably climb trees. She doesn't understand why she feels this way, and doesn't have time to put effort into trying to understand.

"My instinct is now telling us to run up the hill. As fast as we can. Also, it's saying no more talk about Star Trek. Firefly only from here on out."

"Your instinct said all that?"

"I know it's specific, but so is the human genome."

He follows behind her shouting, "Wait, you like Firefly?" but it's already hard to hear over the sound of her own breathing.

She hears something else behind her too. It's something too quiet to hear with her ears, but with a deep sense in her core, she can just make it out over the lack of birds chirping. Maybe there's something chasing them, and maybe this thing lost sight of exactly where they were when they climbed up the tree. But it waited. And it knows where they are now.

Nathan strides up next to Julie, and the thought crosses her mind that he's running like a retarded person. This is not meant in a derogatory way. His arms are just flailing sideways randomly and there's white drool coming out of his mouth. His legs are bowlegged at his knobby knees. She tries not to think about how she's running top speed, and he still managed to catch up with her.

"The bad news is there's something out there," she pants out over several breaths while running.

"What's the good news?" he manages to say through the slobber.

"False dichotomy," she manages to say. "Just. Because. There's…. Bad news. Doesn't. Mean. There's. Good news."

Computer science school does not build muscles very often (other than the hard core universities, like CMU). Despite both Julie Black and Nathan Montgomery both being skinny enough to be varsity cross country runners, neither has really ever *ran* per se. They both go anaerobic almost instantly and it doesn't take long for their muscles to start burning. Julie's legs feel heavy and slow. She can barely lift them.

Darkness surrounds them now - an unseen presence that's silent but overpowering. It's nightmare-like, being chased by some unseen thing they can't escape.

Julie can feel it. But she can't see anything. She can't hear anything.

Especially not over Nathan's retarded running.

Skin Slap. Drool. Skin Slap. Thump. Arm Slap. Click. Thump. Skin Slap. Thump.

Nathan cocks his head. "What's that clicking noise?"

"I don't know, maybe it's you trying to run?"

Skin Slap. Skin Slap. Click. Click. Click. Thump. Arm Slap. Click. Thump. Skin Slap. Thump.

"No it isn't. Stop."

Julie stops, but she doesn't want to. Her instinct screams at her to run. The quiet clicking sounds are getting closer. They are quiet like a silenced gunshot is quiet.

Click. Click. Click.

The clicking sounds are getting louder. Closer.

"If we don't move maybe it can't see us."

"This isn't fucking Jurassic Park, Nathan!"

Click. Click. Click. Click.

"Nathan, we have to go." But she knows they can't outrun something like a vampire. Not both of them.

She tugs on his sleeve. Nathan doesn't respond. How did it get dark so quickly? They really need to leave. Why is it so quiet? She reaches out for Nathan, barely able to see him, grabs a handful of coat in her hands and tugs twice.

"If we believe in ourselves we can do anything." He says like a holiday special. "Don't be scared and they have no power over you."

"Nathan, we have to go. Now."

He still doesn't seem to respond. She looks in his direction, looks away. She takes a step and thinks about waiting longer, but instead she takes another step. Before she knows it she's running reactively away and leaving Nathan behind. There's no thought at all behind the action until it's already too late, and by then it's only sadness. *I'm sorry, Nathan.*

She is legally blind now, the world has gone almost black. She has lost most sense of direction and stumbles aimlessly into various types of plant life. The ground feels like a staircase where you're continuously taking one non-existing step too many.

A concussion echoes behind her. She tries not to make the simile too specific, but maybe it sounded like a vampire ripping Nathan's skull from his spine and then tossing the severed head at the nearest tree.

Sounds are sharp in the darkness. She stops breathing and runs softly. She points her ears in the direction of the collision and she listens harder, which turns out to not be necessary because what she hears next is a decibel order of magnitude louder.

An inhuman scream.

Haunting is the best word Julie can think of to describe it, but the word is inadequate. It feels like there's a foreign word for the scream that just doesn't translate to English. The *haunting* is the difference between watching a pre-recorded wolf howl on television and that same howl when you know the creature responsible is hunting you.

She closes her eyes bracing for death, not sure why she bothers. It's so dark she won't see it coming anyway. She wonders if it will hurt.

In wall-clock time it only lasts four seconds, but in Julie Black time the screaming lasts for several days.

"Hey, wait up!"

Nathan's voice.

He shouts, "Where are you? I can't see anything!"

Nathan is alive?

She hears him running retardedly in her general direction and she says she's over here, and he eventually manages to find her.

The jacket she's wearing is thin, style over utility. She finds herself shivering, but whether from the inhuman scream or from the cold, she cannot tell. Without a word, Nathan takes off his own jacket and drapes it over her shoulders. It is warmer than it was.

"What was that?" she asks, but the words themselves seem to be shivering as she speaks.

"Yeah, crazy right? What *was* that?" He talks as if nothing has happened. His tone of voice is not all that different from how he was talking about *Star Trek Deep Space Nine*.

Dread floods through her blood vessels. "You don't know what was just chasing us?"

"Well, I assume it was probably a vampire, but who knows for sure?"

"Why aren't we running?"

"Yeah, we should probably at least be walking away."

Julie looks around in the dark, trying to will her eyes into being able to see what direction to go.

"In my pocket I had this dog discipline thing that's basically a whistle. The idea is you can attach it to your dog's neck, and then over wireless you can signal the discipliner to emit an ultra-high-pitched noise that's above the hearing range for humans. Dogs apparently find it really annoying. I thought that since it was so dark and there was obviously something chasing after us, maybe the frequency would act as a deterrent or at least confuse the thing if it could hear it."

"You thought about that on the fly?"

"We can't outrun a vampire." He chuckles when he talks. He actually chuckles. "*You* might be safe since technically I'm the slow one, and maybe you would only need to outrun *me*, but the fact is I couldn't even outrun most down's syndrome five year olds."

Her eyes glisten. Her mouth is a little apart, with an expression impossible to read. One second she feels relieved. Even happy. The next, a deep sadness comes over her. "Nathan, why on earth were you carrying around a discipline dog whistle?"

"Oh. Well, later today I was planning on hooking it up to my ATmega board along with..."

She interrupts him, lips kissing first his face in the dark and then finding his lips. She's still running on instinct only now it's sharper. She kisses him with an open mouth, and she presses every inch of her body against his. Nathan is frozen at first, but he kisses back as if he's had a lifetime of practice. The only surprising thing about the kiss is how awkward it isn't. Any observer would expect a punch line here, some kind of joke or fluke by Nathan the nerd. Nathan the geek. But instead of awkwardness there's only chemistry and sensitive nerve endings recording every point of contact from soft lips to tightly pressed belly buttons. In wall-clock time, the kiss only lasts four seconds, but in Nathan Montgomery time it lasts for several days.

And it still isn't long enough.

CHAPTER 25

"I don't think we should go in there," Tim says.

They're faced northeast, away from the descending sun. Long shadows make deformed shadow people in front of them. Black and tall and sinewy, they exaggeratedly mimic their every movement on cracked gray asphalt. These shadow people make Johnny uncomfortable.

"There's no choice." Johnny grabs a clump of his thick hair when he talks. "Escape plan number eight. This is the last one."

Western sunlight glistens off a polished metallic red roof in a way that makes it blinding to look at. The supermarket parking lot has fresh asphalt that contrasts with the gray road, and the parking spots are marked with bright yellow lines. The newly painted asphalt felt soft to walk on. Thirteen cars are parked neatly between the lines, leaving plenty of open spaces. The store is relatively large, but not Wal-Mart large. If there were a neon sign it would be readable and decent quality, but one letter would be flickering. Every tire of every car in the parking lot is slashed.

Tim struggles with a deep breath, using watery sounding lungs. "I'll follow you. I've got at least this one more escape place in me." The whites of his eyes have turned a splotchy yellow, and there are red clouds where blood vessels have burst. He smells bad, like cheese that's been in the refrigerator too long. Grandpa Montgomery's house is only a few blocks away, which is a good thing. Tim could probably do that, if just barely. It would take every ounce of strength he has, but he could make it that far.

The supermarket must run on a gigantic generator, because bright electric lights are visible through the unbroken windows and a metal billboard sign that says "THE PIT STOP" is rotating slowly out front. Rust is spidering up the once white metal of the sign, partially splotching out the E and I. There is a grinding metallic screech every time it completes a rotation.

The unbroken automatic doors open menacingly for them as they walk to the entrance. They stand there long enough so that the doors start to close again, detect them, and then open again. And again.

Johnny readies the sledgehammer, resting the handle in a way that's ready to swing. He cautiously steps through the door...

And is surrounded by nineties elevator music.

It seems so out of place in this broken town, like a pornography featuring Monterey Jack from Disney's Rescue Rangers (which exists by the way, thanks a lot,

Internet). They are playing a song Johnny knows. It is dispassionate music, and he can understand every one of the inoffensive words and can guess the formulaic tune. The song feels Canadian or maybe Hollywood. Probably some twisted and evil hybrid like Celine Deion.

"Autumn!" Johnny bellows his deep voice against the music. "Are you inside?"

"Check this out." Tim lets his shotgun drop and grabs a magazine from a family-safe checkout aisle. The magazine is the National Enquirer and on the cover is a picture of a costumed vampire. Underneath an implausible celebrity sex-change story, the title says, *WORLD EXCLUSIVE: ALIENS INVADE SMALL TOWN! APOCALYPSE IDAHO!* "We're finally on the map."

"I applaud the investigative integrity of this fine publication." Johnny's eyes roll back into his skull.

Bright fluorescent lights buzz from the warehouse tall ceiling, barely audible over the nondenominational nineties music. The linoleum floor is clean, and the shelves look fully stocked.

"That's why I try to get my news from out of country, like from the BBC," Tim says. "It doesn't have as much American bias as most newspapers in the States."

"You should try Al Jazeera. I hear it doesn't have much American bias either."

They begin their search left to right. There are no signs of struggle on aisle one: dairy. Some of the milk and yogurt have passed their *sell by* dates, but all have their *use by* dates set firmly into the future. On the right side of the aisle are frozen food freezers. Cool water vapor floats in the air as precious energy is wasted by the refrigerator uselessly trying to slow the rot.

They inch to aisle two. Chips/bread.

Tim is hunching a little as he shuffles weakly, and he makes a face like he's chewing grass. He bumps lightly into Johnny's shoulder. For some reason, it's Johnny who says, "Sorry. Excuse me." He would apologize for bumping into an inanimate object.

Johnny has never been in this store before, so he searches every corner like Autumn might be waiting for him with her pale blue eyes and cold smile. He is beyond caution into borderline reckless desperation. They make their way through beverages and cereal to baking items and condiments. They travel from pasta/rice to crackers/cookies with nothing out of the ordinary.

It isn't until aisle seven, canned goods, that they see blood.

There is no sign of a struggle. Not a single can is knocked off the shelving, and there are no tracks in or out. The blood is congealed in a perfect Leonardo da Vinci circle.

"Clean up on aisle seven," says Tim. There is no one left to laugh over the terrible grocery store music playing above. "Hold on one second."

"Where are you...?"

Tim holds up his index finger to illustrate what one second looks like. Wearing a tragic mask of pain, and also perhaps a mask of comedy, he drags his feet around the corner and picks up a yellow sign he's found.

Johnny hunches down in a catcher's stance to get a closer look at the blood. It could almost be spilled Coca-Cola for its sticky brown consistency and how it's spilled on the floor. But there are differences with blood. Unlike soda, if scratched the dry parts of the stain would turn to dust and flake off. There are wet parts too, glumping together the way only congealing blood can. The puddle looks as if it were dumped from an aluminum can instead of pumped from a beating heart. There are no streaks where someone tried to crawl away. There is no blood spatter evidence of what happened. He sticks a finger out to feel how wet the blood is, then thinks better of it and pulls his hand back.

The triangle sign Tim is dragging over says, CAUTION WET FLOOR, and has a picture of a stick figure slipping on something black. Johnny guesses in this case, the sign is illustrating a person slipping on the sticky blood. Tim takes his time positioning the sign. The process must be difficult for him because his right shoulder is melting off and he's still fumbling with his shotgun.

A shit eating grin is plastered on Tim's face as he turns around to face Johnny. Three teeth short of a California supermodel smile, Tim laughs. When did he start losing teeth?

The lights go out. There are windows, but this is not the darkness of a light switch. The store is turning black. Johnny can barely see to the end of the aisle.

Johnny reaches out to Tim with urgency, silently begging him to be quiet.

There is a sound. A screeching noise like a metal blade being sharpened. Johnny can feel the movement, and it's close. No more than a few feet away. "Stop moving," he commands Tim quietly.

"I'm not moving."

Another noise, from the other corner of the store. Footsteps can be heard over the non-confrontational music. Sideways to the music maybe. The sound is stealthy, but not too stealthy. Like it wants to be heard.

A bead of cold sweat rolls down Johnny's forehead. Splashes onto his knee. He tightens his grip on the sledgehammer, holding it more like a shield than a weapon.

A creature slips fluidly to the center of aisle seven. In the unnatural darkness, it looks more like a shadow than a living thing. Maybe it is more like a shadow than a living thing. Johnny turns for the other side, and there's another with a single yellow eye and comic book muscles blocking the way. Its mouth hangs open in a silent scream of fury.

"I've never been a numbers person," Tim says, "but I think our odds have just dropped from bad, to winning-the-state-lottery worse."

One-Eye creeps forward, past Campbell's tomato soup and well into Progresso territory. It's smaller than the vampire they fought earlier. On its pale face it wears an inscrutable expression, alien and unrecognizable. Johnny can't take his eyes away from it, can't watch out for the other one behind him. It flashes long bleached sharp teeth in what might be construed as a smile. Only monsters have teeth so white. Johnny smiles back.

Tim begins firing his semi-automatic shotgun wildly. He pulls the trigger as fast as he can. Too fast. Bang-bang, frantic pellets destroy the ceiling and the floor.

Johnny raises his Bigfoot sized rubber boot and kicks the shelving down. Tomato Paste and soft meat explode as canned goods impact the hard floor.

Tim's legs are a tangled mess he can't seem to keep straight, sliding clumsily on the slippery blood in front of the CAUTION sign. He looks barely conscious and wobbly. Without thought, Johnny picks him up underhanded and sprints over the toppled shelving toward the back of the store. There's an arrow that points to restrooms, and Johnny follows the one that says "Gents". At some point Tim must have dropped all of his guns.

Beside the dairy aisle there are two industrial looking stainless steel doors. *That has to lead to an exit.*

Johnny can't hear anything following him. It would be better if he could.

He kicks at the double doors with all his adrenaline weight. They aren't as heavy as they look, and they bang open and swing back shut, hitting an already dazed Tim in the head. Johnny shoves into the doors again with his shoulder. The way is narrow, barely wide enough for him to drag Tim through.

He practically throws Tim to the ground in a rush to shut the metal doors. The stupid thing won't latch because of how he kicked it. He sees what the problem is, but he needs both hands, so he drops his sledgehammer. *Pull the spring, push the latch. Ignore the vampires. Don't worry if they can see in the dark and you can't.*

Like a head-on car crash, the doors bang at Johnny and hit

him squarely in the nose. Things go white, but he shakes his head back to reality and pushes back. The ground sticks as well as it can to the soles of his shoes, but he is losing ground to the creatures pushing on the other side of the doors. Millimeter by millimeter, he slips back. The latch won't click with this pressure.

"Tim, help me." *Help me what?* There's nothing to brace the doors with, and Tim is barely conscious. There will be no help from Tim.

The giant grinds his teeth.

The doors have an inhuman force behind them, but Johnny is an inhuman force too. He grabs the doors by the frame, and screams at it with the strength of a thousand men.

All pressure from the other end releases.

The doors bang shut, and the latch clacks neatly into place. Severe pain blinds Johnny as his left ring finger is smashed inside the latch he had been gripping for leverage. Stuck.

The room is a loading facility full of wooden crates and Styrofoam. There is no good barrier between the refrigerated milk and aisle one: dairy - nothing tangible separating them from the vampires outside. But the metal door and perceived wall should hold the creatures back for at least a few seconds. It has to.

Johnny needs the Jaws of Life. His finger is twisted inside the gears and springs of the door locking mechanism. Even if there wasn't death on the other side and he wanted to open the doors again, his finger is acting like a wedge, making the doors immovable.

Black strands of air are whisping under the doorway.

On three. Ready? One. Two. Wait wait wait… should I pull slow or fast?

He breathes out through his nose.

Jerking his hand once, pieces of the finger tear but the hand is not released. His teeth are clamped shut in a snarl, but he does not wince. He jerks again, and twists back and forth like a stubborn wine cork. The wedding ring must be caught. He braces his right leg against the door and pulls through his back. He can feel the pulp of his finger budging and slipping between metal gears. *Yes, only a bit more.* His arm comes away free. His finger free also.

The finger is mangled, hanging on to the rest of his hand only through sinewy tendons and red strands. Somehow, his tarnished wedding ring still clings to the fleshy lump. It would have been better if he could cut the finger cleanly. Blood drips from Johnny's broken nose and down his face. His eyes are already puffing up, and he hopes they don't swell so much that he can't see. He feels broken irreparably, but nothing hurts. Pain will come later.

Tim is slumped on the floor in a crumpled heap, exactly the way he landed after Johnny dropped him. *He smells like the Russian.* Tim manages a half smile and says to Johnny, "You look like shit."

Staying with Tim would almost certainly mean death for both of them. They might as well have put the courtesy lock on the bathroom for all the protection the latched door gives them. Even with the one in a million chance that they could both get out of here, Tim is already dead – rotting away like the Russian with his wasting illness. And his death could mean life for Johnny. For Autumn. Johnny turns his head toward the exit and takes a step away. He tries not to look at Tim. *Out of sight out of mind* would be easier to dismiss as cruel if it didn't work so well.

"Go," Tim says. "I'll hold them off."

Johnny's breathing is hard and shallow. He nods and takes a step away, keeping his eyes on the exit. He can't look back.

"Gosh darn it." Johnny turns to Tim.

"No! What are you doing?"

Johnny slings the sick man over his shoulder effortlessly. His finger has stopped hurting for now. The adrenaline has masked all pain.

"We'll both die if you take me. Do you *want* to be a martyr?"

No.

Johnny could never be a symbol for anything important. He is too big and too honest. People are too threatened by him to ever relate.

"I don't want people to feel sorry for me."

Just because someone isn't a martyr doesn't mean that person can't sacrifice everything for something he believes in. Just because what's right is a lost cause, doesn't mean Johnny isn't going to try with everything he has.

"I have to be more than just a sad story."

Johnny clings to the sledgehammer, slippery in his mangled hand. He never notices how he never contemplated leaving the sledgehammer behind.

"Grandpa Montgomery's house is close," the giant says. "Hang on."

Johnny barrels outside with Tim bouncing over his shoulder. Clammy wind bites into his face, but at least the air is clear. He can see out here, like how he can see the wooden fence surrounding the alleyway, the locked metal gate, the no escape death trap scenario...

"They're coming through the door!" Tim's head is bobbing behind Johnny as the giant sprints at the fence. With a rubber neck, Tim's hollow cheeks are smacking into Johnny's broad back and shoulders. "Go faster!"

Johnny runs directly at the fence with true lumberjack grit. His lungs are burning. There is no time for a plan. The fence is only around six feet tall, maybe he can just jump over it.

He pushes off the ground with his left leg, his right extended to clear the fence like a track and field hurdle. He doesn't come close to clearing the six feet. His leg jousts into the fence and brings fifty feet of supported structure twisting to the ground.

Somehow, toppling over what's left of the fence, he stays mostly on his feet.

"We'll never make it," Tim yells. His sideburns scratch against Johnny's greasy shirt. "They're right behind us!"

Black streaks are curling through the air now, filling it like cold death. Grandpa Montgomery's house is just across the street. Johnny has his head down and he focuses on the ground. His arms are locked in an embrace of the heavy Tim. He's lightheaded. Like a machine, he mechanically forces one foot in front of the other. His nose is spouting blood, and the sledgehammer is slipping out of his deformed hand. A car burning gas without engine oil. At any time his body's function could become malfunction.

"Don't tell me I'll never make it," Johnny tries to say, but he is breathing too hard to say anything.

The red door to the Montgomery house is already open as they reach the stoop, Grandpa Montgomery standing to one side and waving them in. Johnny and Tim tumble inside, clumpy blood smearing over the carpet like red wine. The heavy door locks behind them.

Grandpa Montomery's eyes are wide behind his horn rimmed glasses. "Did you find your wife?" He's clutching his shotgun tightly to his chest, and his fat neck bobbles when he speaks. "Did you find my grandson?"

Behind them, Aunt Montgomery is staring into a monitor. She talks in a flat voice devoid of emotion. "Something is behind you."

CHAPTER 26

In certain cold North American climates there is a terrifying type of person. In Idaho they are called *mall walkers.* Overwhelmingly AARP card carriers, these corpses wake up long before the rising sun to wander the echoing hallways of suburban city malls. With drooling mouths and eyes focused only on some unseen destination, these ancient creatures from another time stroll past the closed gateways of Zumiez and American Eagle with the deliberate strides of their stainless steel walkers.

Sometimes a mall walker will continue walking through the mall even after the stores open. This special and rare type of mall walker creature is called a *day walker.*

"I should go." Grandpa Montgomery grabs the shotgun, which is never far away. The intelligence in his eyes shine gray through thick glasses. "I know what you've said about Derek Darius, but there's a chance he's on our side. There's a chance he's human."

Day walkers are especially terrifying because unlike a normal mall walker, their undead paths regularly cross with those of the unsuspecting early morning shopper, who is just trying to snag a good deal at Old Navy. A day walker will not change paths, not for anybody, and especially not for somebody trying to conveniently pick up a pair of shoes before work. The day walker strides conversationless and with purpose. When these early morning shoppers cross paths with a day walkers, the shopper always gets more than they bargained for.

In the surveillance monitors, this is how Derek Darius walks at the house. A cigarette is lit in his mouth and his trench coat flaps behind him like a stereotype. He walks like a day walker.

Johnny, Tim, and Grandpa Montgomery are glued to the monitors while Aunt Montgomery is trying to keep the distracting infant quiet. They've all noticed strange things about Derek Darius. His unnatural intelligence, his unnatural quickness, he's too pale, he wears a lot of black, etc.

"This is important so listen carefully." The hair on Johnny's arms is growing longer now. Darker. His clothes feel itchy like they're too small, and there's an angry rip up the arm of his flannel sleeve. The legs of his jeans are hard with blood. The shirt is still tucked in tightly. "She never writes anything on paper. Not ever. And his name was written hundreds of times like a warning."

They all concede, okay, so Derek Darius is important and different, but does that necessarily mean he's a vampire? He did kill a vampire, after all. He hasn't tried to kill any people yet, he's generally been a famous person long enough to visibly age, etc.

Tim says, "What if there's a power struggle going on between separate vampire groups?"

They all concede, ok, so Derek Darius is dangerous.

Grandpa Montgomery's words command the authority of old age. "But is being dangerous enough to shoot in the face?"

"Let's use some logic here," Johnny says. "If he is a vampire, shooting him in the face probably won't hurt him. If he's not a vampire, then congratulations, we collectively just murdered somebody."

God," Tim says. "This is just like the Monty Python *it's a witch* sketch all over again."

"I'd still feel better knowing one way or the other."

"Maybe if we shot him in the... leg? Would that tell us whether or not he's a vampire?"

Apparently there's a lot that reminds both Aunt Montgomery and Grandpa of when Johnny Sparks and Tim were approaching the house. The uncertainty about who is human, the threat to survival, talks of one versus the many. The baby and protecting it. The baby is always the most important thing.

"Everything about this is exactly the same as when you guys came here," Aunt Montgomery says. "Is there a word for déjà vu, but for things that repeat in real life?"

Johnny says that the word is experience.

Grandpa says that word is a rut.

Tim asks if there is a difference. It's getting so that his voice creaks and cracks with effort. Small bits of skin are peeling away from cracked lips.

"I should go with you," Johnny says.

"If anything happens to me, you need to stay here and protect my grandson."

"I will."

"Promise me. At any cost."

Johnny promises.

Like before, Grandpa slips outside. Like before, Grandpa holds his shotgun hip high.

Derek Darius is close now, striding like there is no loaded shotgun pointed in his direction. His features are all sharp and perfectly proportioned. Slender and trim, he isn't as big as he looks on T.V., but his presence is somehow bigger. Prominent cheekbones cut through his face into a strong jawline, and there is almost no color to him, except his red rimmed glasses, and a burning cigarette.

"Are you a zombie?"

Derek Darius does not alter his pace. A normal person, even a movie star, has blemishes on their skin or hair in their nose. Not Derek Darius. There isn't even a single freckle on his face or wrinkle in his milk bath skin. Like a day walker, he takes long strides. Black eyes straight ahead, there's nothing he would stop for.

"Are you a d-d-d-amn zombie?" Grandpa raises the shotgun to his shoulder.

Derek Darius keeps speed walking.

Grandpa takes stumbling steps backward. He never gets the time he needs to convince himself whether he should shoot.

"May I borrow your gun?" Derek Darius says. "I'm afraid mine doesn't exist."

He is unnaturally fast when he swipes Grandpa's shotgun from slowly reflexing hands. In one smooth motion of Derek Darius's arm, he shoves the butt of the gun into the middle of Grandpa's chest, sending him tripping backwards and ultimately onto his old back.

"Good, a shotgun. One of the things I needed."

Through the monitors, everyone sees Derek Darius stride with long confident steps to the door and turn the door handle. It's locked. He mall-walks back to the helpless old man stuck on his back who is trying to roll himself over like a marooned turtle. He points the tip of the shotgun at the old man's face. Grandpa Montgomery freezes.

"How were you planning on getting back into your house, old man?"

Derek Darius inches the shotgun barrel closer to the old man's face until the cold barrel metal is pressed against his cheek.

"I don't have a lot of patience," Derek Darius whispers. "Tell me."

"I know which side you're on, zombie."

"I am not even going to pretend to understand what you're

talking about. And I'm likely the smartest person on the planet."

The old man could have had a key hidden somewhere like his pocket. But he doesn't, and Derek Darius seems to know it. The celebrity looks directly at the camera that's supposed to be hidden and says, "If anyone's in there you better let me in or I'm going to shoot Grandpa. And if after that I still can't manage to get in I'm going to light the house on fire. I've noticed it's built with fire resistant material, but I assure you, with enough effort I can figure out how to burn this motherfucker down."

Grandpa Montgomery has never had a gun pointed at him before. He is so terrified that he is unable to move. But in his mind he's made a decision. Better for his grandson to burn than to turn into a monster. Derek Darius can't be let into the house.

"Alrighty," the celebrity speaks to the people inside, "On the count of three I'll shoot for the foot, but you should realize my only gun right now is a shotgun. It's notoriously difficult to be precise at this range, even for me."

"One."

Grandpa Montgomery closes his eyes and prepares for death. Instead of his life flashing before his eyes, he pictures his wife, Mildred. Not old, like this morning, but young, like twenty something. He pictures photographs of her on their wedding day.

"Two."

He has had a good run. He's seventy-three now. He has regrets, but few enough. The biggest regret is how he can't see his grandson through this.

"Thr… any last words old man, in case I miss?"

"Fuck you."

He says it clearly and strong. He does not stutter.

"Would you rather be right legged or left legged? Wait wait wait. Don't tell me. I'll be on the safe side and blow off both."

Johnny Sparks bursts through the front door. The giant, twice the size of most people, has a sledgehammer strapped to his back and a scoped hunting rifle with an image of Derek Darius in the crosshairs.

CHAPTER 27

Johnny Sparks and Derek Darius are both killers. The difference is that Johnny has never used that statistic as a conversation starter at a cocktail party.

The giant isn't a timid person because he's afraid of losing. He isn't polite and respectful because he has any doubt at all in his own strength. If anything, he's respectful because he is too strong. He spends his life being gentle because it would be so easy for him to break the things around him. He could kill any person he wanted to in a fight, and he's done it before. It's a difficult strength to imagine, this surety that he could stop almost any person from breathing in an instant. He just never has, except that one time.

A gladiator from another age, the giant is inhumanly tough. He focuses. With this kind of mentality he has never lost a fight, not once. With this kind of focus he can beat Derek Darius. He has the element of surprise on his side, and a rifle pointed at the billionaire's head. There is no doubt he can win. There cannot be doubt.

221

So it comes as a surprise when Derek Darius smoothly draws a revolver and shoots the hunting rifle from under Johnny's square fingers. The giant reflexively tries to pull the trigger as the gun jumps out of his hand, but the bullet flies wildly off course.

Johnny grabs the sledgehammer strapped to his back and swings at the celebrity. Without breaking stride, the comparatively tiny Derek Darius slips his head an inch to one side and the sledgehammer whistles harmlessly past. One punch, two punch, Derek Darius casually T.K.O.s Johnny in about three seconds.

CHAPTER 28

"My my my," Derek Darius says, "I see the gang's all here."

Johnny Sparks, Tim, and the Montgomerys are sitting hostage-style on the hardwood floor inside the secret panic room. There are no windows, but the LED lighting is constant bright. The small room is too crowded, and with the monitors and bodies the atmosphere is already hot and muggy. They aren't tied up, but they don't have to be. To the side of them in the kitchen, Doctor Derek Darius is rummaging through Grandpa's drawers and cabinets.

"There are five creatures hunting me, and they will be here any minute." Derek Darius's hands are busy, and he talks with a cigarette crunched between his teeth. "I will kill them, but not here. My equipment is at the mansion. Right now we need to make sure they don't find us."

Nobody could be as quick as he is, Johnny Sparks is thinking, *Not anyone human...*

"The panic room isn't meant to stop an intruder," Grandpa says. The ground in the panic room is unfinished cement, and the old man is shifting around like he hasn't had to sit on the ground since one of the great wars. "It's meant more as a hiding place; it's almost invisible with the door shut and there is some sound proofing. But the good locks are on the front door and windows, not here."

Derek Darius says he knows.

"Five is a lot of vampires. You need our help," Johnny Sparks says. He can't stop what's left of his finger from bleeding. He has it wrapped in blood soaked cloth, dripping steadily on the concrete.

"Ha," Derek Darius snorts with derision. "No, tall guy, I really don't. What I do need is for you to be absolutely quiet when I tell you to. The creatures seem to have an uncanny sense of hearing."

Derek Darius is going through various over the counter medicine, which the Montgomerys appear to store in a plastic bin over the stove. "Do you have a hidden stash somewhere for the Ambien?" He reaches for a dark bottle of Nyquil and looks at the label. "How much acetaminophen is an infant able to take before the dosage is lethal?"

Johnny's broad face is tight, and his square chin clinched. "I hope that's a hypothetical question."

"It's really more of an ethical and survival concern."

The baby is quiet for now, sleeping peacefully in his mother's arms. He opens and closes his mouth in the air.

The celebrity tosses the bottle of Nyquil to Johnny. "I know more than one way to keep people quiet." He doesn't say anything about the baby, but his glance darts to the infant with coldness in his eyes.

"I'm only going to say this once so listen carefully: Not so much as a whisper."

Derek Darius rummages through the kitchen cupboard and tosses out coffee, pepper, and vinegar with the casual professionalism of a lifelong drug smuggler.

"You're trying to mask our smell," Grandpa Montgomery makes the statement. The top of his bald head wrinkles as the slow gears in his brain turn. It seems most of his fear has been replaced with a sense of purpose. "I have bleach and nail polish remover in the other room… if you'd like the help."

Derek Darius smiles. "Finally someone with half a brain. Why yes, old man, by all means. You don't happen to have any used tampons do you?"

Tim is lying on the ground in a bad state. He had to be dragged into the panic room. His skin is seeping sweat everywhere it makes contact with anything. He's delirious and murmuring odd phrases that are weirdly interesting like, "Ugh… I hate being sick… I usually avoid getting sick like the plague," and, "I keep falling asleep. I think this is my body's way of telling me I need more caffeine."

Derek Darius took one look at him and said, "I have a feeling that lad is going to go on and live a long, full life."

Grandpa Montgomery makes it clear that he doesn't want to be in the same room as Tim. "No offense, but not without a gun." He keeps eyeing the dying computer scientist with the obvious distrust that only the very old can effectively pull off.

"Come to think of it, I can think of one thing you guys could do to help," Derek Darius says to Johnny. "If one of you went outside and started walking directly east, that would throw the vampires off my trail, and it would give the rest of us enough time to better prepare."

"Wouldn't that person die?"

"Well, yes, but I think Tim ought to be the perfect candidate. Point one is it looks like he's already well into the process of dying anyway."

"We are not sending Tim."

"Point two, and this may be kind of controversial," Derek Darius continues, "but he was kind of a loser."

Derek Darius inhales deeply and exhales cigarette smoke into the front door. He is sprinkling a chemical cacophony full of interesting smelling things. The mixtures and placements look precise and well thought out. When a few minutes of not-talking pass, Johnny still isn't sure whether the celebrity was serious about sending Tim to his death.

"They've been slipping in and out through here." Derek Darius points his cigarette at the backdoor. "A six year old could bump that lock open."

"How did you know they got in at all?" Grandpa Montgomery runs a hand over his bald scalp. "How would a zombie pick a lock?"

Ignoring the question, Derek Darius begins kicking apart wooden furniture. Barricading the back door with table legs, he says to Johnny, "I assume you don't want to die either? Why don't you at least make yourself half useful and watch the monitors. Let me know when you see anything out of the ordinary."

Grandpa Montgomery bends over the door, peering into the key hole with a flashlight and a magnifying glass. "You must be right. This is a new lock and there are scratch marks that are smaller than the key. How did you know that?"

Johnny can't shake this feeling of dread he has about Derek Darius. It isn't just his dangerousness or his arrogance. There is something deeply terrifying about a tentative ally who's untrustworthy.

He walks slowly over to the monitors located in the panic room. Blood is streaming off his finger stump, but his brain is elsewhere. Derek Darius's gunshot was impossible from that distance. Shooting the revolver so accurately it made the rifle jump out of a good grip from what must have been thirty meters away. Impossible. He finally asks, "How were you able to shoot the gun out of my hand? How were you able to hit your target from so far away?"

The pieces of chair the billionaire is nailing across the door appear to have an antique kind of craftsmanship. The wood must be a hundred years old, polished regularly all that time. "What are you talking about? I *didn't* hit my target. I was going for your chest cavity," his eyes narrow, "and I missed."

A second passes, and a smile creeps over the celebrity's face. His teeth are toothpaste-commercial white. "Nah, I'm just kidding. But this just proves once again how many of life's problems can be solved with a well-placed bullet."

The celebrity walks to Johnny with a threatening gait, and without a word he unceremoniously tears away the makeshift finger stump bandage. "I see you're on the rag. May I have that please?"

Johnny bites down to keep himself from screaming. Where his ring finger should be, there are instead only ligaments clinging to the rest of his hand. It's like a hangnail, the way it can get caught on anything. Something needs to be done, medically speaking.

Cradling his arm, he walks cautiously toward the medicine cabinet. He finds a role of gauze. Iodine. A foot long kitchen knife. His wounded hand is lacking in basic mobility, and he is unable to lay his finger flat on the table. He looks around for help, but there is no one. Some things you have to do yourself. The Montgomerys have no alcohol. Just as well.

"Goodbye, finger."

He cuts hard just above the knuckle where his wedding ring used to sit. The cut is clean and easy. The knife slices through the meat and drops to the counter with a thud. He had expected resistance, but the knife is sharp, and there wasn't much left to cut through.

Johnny staggers, vision blurry. The pain is sharp, coming from where his finger should be, but also spread throughout his entire body. His legs feel weak. They could go out on him at any time.

He is still holding the knife with a shaky right hand. The handle is slippery with blood. He sets it messily down on the counter to grab the bottle of iodine, which he pours on the stump sloppily. He does not scream. He fumbles one-handed with the bandages, trying to apply pressure. By the time he can wrap the gauze around his finger, it is already soaked through with dripping blood.

His vision is cloudy. The knife still sits on the counter, waiting to be used once again. *I am better than stabbing someone in the back, under any circumstance. On the other hand, stabbing a vampire in the back…*

He tries to blink back the fog. No. In his current state there is no way he would be able to kill Derek Darius with a knife. He can barely stand. His voice is thick when he speaks. "I could help more if you give me a gun. I know how to shoot."

"Well I would, but I don't like people pointing them at me or shooting me with them. I'm sure you understand."

"If you're not a vampire you really shouldn't have anything to worry about."

"The fact that witchcraft isn't real has never stopped people from burning witches."

The conversation is interrupted by the world outside darkening. In an instant the air has dropped temperature. Johnny feels a feverish cold. His good hand feels weak. Tim and Aunt Montgomery and the baby are in the panic room while Grandpa Montgomery is sprinkling Derek Darius's smelly concoctions across the floor. With a crisp clarity, monitor 1A shows the dying garden outside, dead brown plant strands looking burrowed out and empty. On monitor 1B, the limp American flag has folded in on itself. All the red, white, and blue colors fading to vampire blackness.

Johnny doesn't have a chance to give any sort of warning to the group about the things he sees on the monitors. Before he can breathe, the celebrity stretches his neck out like an alert meerkat. "It's time."

The sun itself has turned against the human race. There are times to fight and there are times to run and there are times to hide. This is no time for fighting, the vampires are too strong. There is no chance to run, the vampires are too fast. They know what to do.

They efficiently shuttle themselves to the panic room. Johnny has a Lysol rag and wipes up the blood he's dripping, while Grandpa Montgomery shuts the concealed door behind them. To a viewer outside, the room looks like an extension of the wooden kitchen cabinets. The bat cave entrance from Wayne manor isn't better concealed.

"Be absolutely quiet," Derek Darius warns. "Not a peep."

He's still the only one with a gun, and he stands close to the dark monitors. The others crouch down and try to force themselves quiet – for whatever reason crouching just seems like it should be quieter than standing. There are parallels to a hostage negotiation scenario, but the distinct difference is that instead of police trying to rescue hostages there are vampires trying to eat them.

Nobody breathes.

It's completely quiet. Aunt Montgomery holds the sleeping baby tight against her involuntarily trembling body.

It seems like it should be dark in their secret hiding place, but it's not. It doesn't need to be, Grandpa had assured them, since no light would be seen from the kitchen. There are no real shadows below the blue industrial lighting. The useless monitors blaze black against the light. They sit in between a bright red panic phone with no dial tone and an army camouflage radio terminal with no reception, and maybe no one alive on the other end anyway.

Johnny's square jaw is clenched and on his good hand, dirty fingernails dig into sweaty palms. If it were just him, that would be difficult, but there are good people here. He won't let anything happen to them. He can't.

The longest minute in Johnny's life passes.

There's nothing to look at in the panic room. Widely terrified eyes sit generally facing each other, but nobody makes eye contact. It's like riding in an overcrowded and terrifying subway. Whenever two peoples' eyes accidentally meet they both break almost immediately. With nothing to see they're reaching out with their ears, trying to hear as hard as they can.

A muffled thump. Curious and probing.

Johnny's lungs burn, but he still can't bring himself to breathe. There's a second thump. Slightly louder.

They are all acutely focused on the quiet noise. Pumped full of pituitary survival hormones and unable to see clearly through the monitors, they've all temporarily obtained the superhero hearing ability of the blind. The sounds are not loud, but they might as well be the sound of thunder.

More thumps. The sound Johnny hears in his dreams sometimes. Or nightmares.

It's Grandpa who tries to mouth a word. The loose skin of his triple chin is shakily pulsating with fear. *Front door*, he mouths. He barely breathes the syllables, a hardly audible whisper escaping from his thin lips. After all, he and Derek Darius are buddies now, ever since he built up that rapport with the chemicals.

Derek Darius fires back a glare full of malice. It's a look hot enough to turn sand to glass; some temperature that to imagine you have to start multiplying by the temperature on the surface of the sun. It's clear what sort of thing the look is communicating: Shut. The fuck. Up.

The thumps are louder now. Angrier.

Tim's red rimmed eyes are open in a bit of survival clarity. He'd been muttering deliriousness earlier, but he is silent now. Johnny puts a finger to his lips as a gesture toward Tim, and Tim nods in acknowledgement. When Tim nods he does so slowly and deliberately, with every effort to make the nodding motion completely quiet.

The infant is still asleep as Aunt Montgomery cradles his head tightly with a hand gently over his mouth in case he starts to wake up. Her eyes are wide in a constant expression of terror. For the most part Derek Darius's venomous gaze is locked on her and the baby.

A sharp bang silhouettes against the muffled quiet like a billiard ball breaking. With blind superhero hearing, Johnny can almost see the entire front door bending out of the protective frame, succumbing to the inhuman force of a vampire.

The metal sound jolts the sleeping baby. At first he just moves his head from side to side, waking up from his nap. The skinny neck is so weak he can't even support the weight of his own cartoon-proportioned skull, much less struggle with his mother's snug muzzle.

The silence outside is palpable. Much like how this darkness seems more than the absence of light, this silence seems more than the absence of sound. There's almost a physical property to it.

Time passes, either a second or an hour. Grandpa had said the doors had some sound proofing. Johnny doesn't know much about the science of sound, but he trusts the old man's judgment. There are certain things Johnny does know a lot about, like monitoring equipment, and since Grandpa has clearly done his research there it's a good bet that the old man puts that kind of thought into everything.

But is it enough?

There's a tap tap tap tap outside, and even with superhero hearing abilities it's hard to deduce what the ominous sound is. Other than it's close.

A giant crash with broken glass. Johnny wonders if it was a stack of dishes from the adjacent kitchen or a vase from further away. *Do they even have vases?*

Derek Darius is a lot of things, but he's right about being quiet, and there's one obvious way things could go terribly wrong: the baby. Johnny can't take his eyes off the kid. The infant is struggling with the mother. Obviously wide awake now, he's kicking his pudgy legs into the air and turning his head with more and more effort as she cups her hand over his mouth and nose. There's a fine line between suffocating a baby and keeping him quiet. If anyone can convince the baby to be quiet, Johnny has faith that Aunt Montgomery can. She has to.

A moment ago Johnny had almost lost consciousness from losing his finger, but he is now more awake than he has ever been. He clutches the stump tightly. The pain keeps him sharp.

All eyes are on the epic struggle quietly happening. The baby seems set on letting his annoyance be heard, that he's uncomfortable or something. She's trying to take out her breast to feed the baby, but he turns his head away. The positioning is awkward and she takes her hand off the kid's mouth as she shoves her boob at his face. For decency's sake, Johnny looks away.

A small squeal escapes from the baby.

It isn't much of a sound, but the tapping outside is immediately replaced with an alert silence – the kind of sound that happens between aiming a gun and pulling the trigger. It's hard to breathe. Johnny takes short breaths, like he's had a lung removed. It's so quiet he can hear himself blink. His heart is racing past the anaerobic zone into this continuous tachycardia state, and he's briefly worried the heart beats will be loud enough for the vampires to hear.

They've heard us, and now they're just figuring out where we are.

Silently fast, Derek Darius snatches the baby from the struggling grip of the petrified mother. He clamps his hand firmly over the infant's mouth and nose. Where Aunt Montgomery was persuading silence over the baby, Derek Darius imposes it.

Johnny tries without much success to conjure up the proper emotion for this. Relief. Guilt. Hatred. Hatred is what sticks.

Aunt Montgomery looks like a brand new rape victim. Vulnerable and exposed with her t-shirt torn, she has a perfect breast still half exposed through the stretched neck hole. She is unable see her son. Derek Darius has positioned the infant behind Johnny. Her eyes are wide, looking at Johnny. Trying to look *through* Johnny. It looks like she's smiling, but she isn't smiling. Her facial muscles are flexed because every part of her body is flexed.

Derek Darius's hand is tight over the baby's face. The child is obviously becoming increasingly agitated as he struggles with powerless muscles. Like a constricting snake, every time the kid squirms Derek Darius's hand only squeezes tighter.

The infant's legs are kicking at air. His bald head is red, and blue veins are sticking prominently out the top where there isn't even a full head of hair. His skull skin is almost transparent, and it's possible to see the soft spot in his skull pulse with his rapid heartbeat.

At least he isn't blue yet.

And then the child starts to turn blue.

Johnny's beer barrel chest is expanding and contracting along with the gasping infant. The giant can't seem to get enough air in his lungs and he can't breathe through his nose. He's gasping through his mouth, but although his breaths are as deep as he can inhale, the vacuum air seems hollow. This is what asthma must feel like.

Only a bit longer, we can revive the baby if necessary.

Aunt Montgomery begins to stand up, beyond frantic. Even

without being able to see her boy, it seems she is able to sense what is wrong. She looks like she could pick up a car to rescue her baby. She looks ready to scream.

Derek Darius's venom glance shifts from the baby to the dangerous mother. Johnny pleads with his eyes for her to notice him, to understand, and it's a miracle that she does. Their eyes meet. The large man shakes his head silently no, and the mother listens. She steps down. The life and death situation is defused, for another moment.

Johnny isn't sure why she's decided to trust in him, but she has a look on her face that says she does. She's put her life and her baby's in Johnny's giant hands.

If the baby lets the vampires know where we are, the baby dies with the rest of us anyway.

Time has slowed to an agonizing pace. The infant's head has gone from blue to purplish. It's obvious that if the celebrity lets up at all now, there will be noise.

But it's quiet outside. How would we even know when they're gone?

The soft spot in the skull is pulsating slower. Johnny can't see the baby's mouth, but he imagines a brook trout out of water, opening and closing its dying mouth seconds from death.

It's then that Johnny makes a decision. He lifts his four fingered arm to save the baby. Derek Darius be damned. Vampires be damned. This isn't right. The cost is too high.

A noise outside comes crashing through the quiet. *Is that laughter?* More voices join in. No, not voices. A terrible sound that comes from a place where light itself is shrouded in darkness. The mirthless laughter floats through the air and pierces Johnny's soul. He squeezes his bandage wrapped stump. This is no time for superstition. It's nothing more than noise. But one thing is for sure. Vampires are still inside the house, a lot of them. Right outside the door.

His arm is still reaching out toward the baby. He lets it fall.

Aunt Montgomery is staring at Johnny, the color in her cheeks drained. She clearly wants to move around the giant so she can see her son, but she appears to be frozen in place, as if the laughter had paralyzed every part of her but her earthy brown eyes. "Is my baby okay?" her eyes seem to say.

Johnny has both honor and strength, or at least he used to have these things. He held the hand of his father while he was wasting away with leukemia and spoke at his mother's funeral after she killed herself. But he can't watch this. He tries, but he physically can't do it. He can't help but look away.

Until the breathing stops.

And there is no miracle CPR. The child is dead and isn't coming back.

CHAPTER 29

The ground feels electrified, barely insulated by the rubber soles in their shoes. The emotions in the air are all too hot, and the breathing is empty. Laughing and crying and hope and despair are running so close together now that they might as well be the same color. An ugly brown.

Julie and Nathan skid to a stop over a large drop. The edge isn't the kind a person would fall off as much as it's something someone might stumble down and find it difficult to stop stumbling. The familiar town of Rockwell comes into view, sort of. A dark cloud is hovering above it, and in that, black smoke clings together like a thick cumulus cloud. There aren't words to describe how it feels when the weather itself is turning against mankind, but it's an ancient feeling of when gods were thunder and lightning, spectral and apocalyptic.

Nathan says, "W.T.F."

The world looks photoshopped, like the colors have gone

through some sort of evil filter. It's a water color painting with too much dirty water. "Did you ever wonder why they started naming hurricanes?" Julie asks, "I mean, ultimately a hurricane is just a weather pattern, and what kind of weather pattern deserves to be elevated to proper noun status."

Unnatural black wisps swirl in dark patterns above the city. It is not windy outside, but the menacing black vapor is pulsing and swirling in living clumps. The possessed air is breathing itself.

"Well, mystery solved, because now I know exactly how it feels to want to name the sky. But I will admit, now that I know what it feels like, I can't seem think of a name for it."

When Julie was young she thought she would be struck down by lightning for thinking bad thoughts. She feels like that now. As if the atmosphere were responding directly to her, lightning strikes jaggedly in the sky, sideways, the bolts obscured by black sand. Thunder roars savagely with white fire, shaking the earth below. "Cloud Marv," Nathan says, and it seems as good a name as any.

They go quickly, because Nathan told Julie he's not sure why the high pitched noise threw the vampire off, and they both agree the fix is temporary at best. Something about the surrounding blackness gives a perpetual and dream-like feeling of being chased.

There's no other way to go but down. Julie puts her feet sideways and side-shuffles while Nathan takes baby steps and walks in tight S shapes. Close up Cloud Marv looks like something you should be able to reach out and touch. As they go down and drift into blackness, Julie expects to feel something sharp. She hears Nathan ask, do you think this stuff is poisonous?

"Only one way to find out," she says.

Together, they dip into darkness.

Julie tries to taste Cloud Marv, but the air only tastes like air. She can't feel anything, either, and it's not a surprise she can't see much of anything. She keeps looking over her shoulder, despite or maybe because it's so hard to see.

"You know," Nathan says as they're descending, "I can actually think of several ways to test if it's poisonous besides strolling into it and trying to taste it."

Cloud Marv seems almost alive. It's constantly shifting and swirling around them. One minute the world is blackened into obscurity, and the next the air is clear. Every time the shadow passes over them, there's the feeling of passing from sunlight to underground darkness, cool and wet.

At the bottom of the hill is a barbed wire fence, and Julie finds her bearings. This is Mr. Manwaring's house. She remembers him keeping horses in the pasture, but he eventually sold them and let the grass grow so it's now a field of waist-high grass and weeds. Julie has memories of taking care of the horses when Mr. Manwaring would go out of town. She was younger and he was still ancient. She can't imagine a time where he wasn't ancient. He always reminded her of Master Yoda.

"Sometimes when a cat lady dies," Nathan says, "it can take weeks or even months for anyone to notice her bloated corpse rotting. When somebody does finally notice it's usually not because people miss her or because the mailman smells something, or even because the insane cats are howling. The world notices she's dead because she slowly runs behind on her bills. First they turn off the power, and next the water, and eventually they turn off the gas. This all has little effect on the rotting resident except the lack of climate control changes the decomposition rate on a cold winter, or a hot summer."

There are open spaces, a yard, a house, a street, a fence, another yard, and it goes on and on. The lawns are mowed short and the paint unpeeling. These are the same modest houses seen across those states that seem to start and end in vowels. They speak of reliable roofs over sturdy families. Perfect one-acre squares pass by as they make their way to Grandpa Montgomery's house.

Chad Harrison's house. He and his brothers like poker. The biggest parties have always been when his dad makes a trip to Vegas. Julie never enjoyed them, although she showed up, talked, left. Chad Harrison's dad went to Vegas every year.

"It can take months before someone from the utility company is sent to investigate; some poor sap who walks into a nightmare of cat piss and corpse remains." Nathan is stumbling further behind her. "This sort of thing happens all the time, and who would've thought it can happen to an entire town."

Thunder cracks in the sky. Closer now. She's making an effort to control her emotions. She had imagined these houses gone. Obliterated somehow, maybe with hellfire. Yet here they stand. Nothing below the turbulent sky feels that different. Here it is. The potholes are still patched in the street. The wood fences are newly stained with sensible colors.

In a place like Rockwell, everyone knows everybody else, but this neighborhood is especially familiar to Julie. This is where she grew up. "That is how it feels," she whispers to herself. "The starving cats are the only ones who know the cat lady is dead. They're howling but not even the mailman notices."

Adam Eddington's house. She's never been inside, but she knows the exterior brick chimney and white re-painted aluminum siding by memory. In ninth grade Adam Harrington was in her biology class, and they watched a lot of National Geographic movies in the dark. Julie doesn't remember why she put her hand in his pocket, but she does remember it was her first time feeling the alien hardness that's a part of the opposite gender. The suppressed memory comes back only in flashes of teenage immaturity. Awkwardly adjusting pants caught on the pulsing organ. Underwater starfish on screen, and a hole cut in his jean pocket. A narrator with a British accent. The teacher, Mrs. Something, who had no idea what was happening. Julie realizes she can't recall the teacher's name or picture Adam Eddington's face.

She had a hard time making eye contact with Adam after that semester; she usually kept her eyes on sidewalk cracks when she walked by this house just in case he was looking out a window so that they didn't accidentally see each other.

It's strange how the legacy of an entire complicated and real person is reduced to one embarrassing memory that swirls in and out of darkness. It's entirely possible Julie and a game of pocket pool is all that's left of Adam Eddington.

That all other memories of the entire Eddingon family have disappeared from the entire planet for the rest of history. This is what losing a bloodline means.

She hears Nathan lagging behind her, or rather, she *can't* hear him following. Her heart stops beating. She doesn't have time to synthesize what she thinks is wrong, but not hearing him feels terrible. She whips her head backward like it's a matter of life and death, and she sees Nathan about fifty meters away playing with what looks like a piece of rebar sticking out of the ground. He's okay. There's no emergency. The panic she felt says something about her current state of mind.

"What are you doing?"

"I don't like to be weaponless."

"Yes," she says, "because we all fought so valiantly the last time we had weapons."

"Look at the scoreboard. We're doing okay."

"I'd rather not look at the scoreboard."

Nathan is wiggling the rebar back and forth until it comes out of its hole in the grass. Metal stick in hand, Nathan poses without smiling as he looks Julie squarely in the eye. He beams proudly. "I was voted most likely to get a Darwin Award in high school."

"So… you're the most likely to die by doing something stupid?"

"What? No. A Darwin Award means I'm the most likely to evolve and improve myself." He pauses as a look of humiliation crawls across his face. "Doesn't it?"

Julie says, look, the vampires move like *the chosen one*. It would be next to impossible to kill those things with a metal stick.

"I prefer to think of this as a metal *stake*. Besides, *Killing-vampires-with-sticks* is my middle name"

"Your parents, were they the type that used to eat a lot of special brownies?"

There's something morbidly sad about the use of past tense from what was supposed to be a joke. *Were your parents the type*, she had said. Not, *are they the type*. The short-term memories of new love are replaced with memories of death.

They pass by where Kirk used to live. He was a civil engineer who used to work for the forest service. Now he's dead.

That used to be Robert's house, until he moved to the other side of town in sixth grade. He and Julie *went out* in fifth grade, which basically consisted of passing notes. He used to smile awkwardly at her whenever they ran into each other. He won't be smiling awkwardly or otherwise anymore, of course. Dead.

Cody. Dead.

Melissa. Dead.

Dead. Dead. Dead.

She closes her eyes until she's walking with her own cloud surrounding her, nearly as dark as Cloud Marv.

Then they're standing in front of Grandpa Montgomery's

house. She didn't know what she should have expected, but the door is barely clinging to its strong-looking hinges. The house is dead, like everything else. Evidently a vampire has forced its way inside to kill the morning's survivors.

Julie sees Nathan stuttering and trying to say something, the way he can in tense situations. In her deathly dark mood, the last thing she wants to listen to is his babbling. Nathan says, "I've always thought it's interesting how concrete is used with rebar like this."

She rolls her eyes and glares at him with an obviousness even he can recognize.

"Raw concrete is super strong when it comes to compression, but it turns out it actually crumbles relatively easily if you apply tension. This is where steel reinforcement comes in – it has the tension strength concrete needs so that the combined product doesn't crumble. They work well together in other ways too, like both steel and concrete expand at similar rates with the temperature so neither one destroys the other."

He's draws his eyes up from the ground, and through his dorky glasses and long eyelashes he looks at her. The skin on his face is silk smooth. "It's cool how two materials so different can be combined to do something neither one could really do on their own." He has straitened his back and is standing up straight. "Does that make sense?"

His eyes say what he can't. They tell Julie, "Maybe in some ways we're like those different materials. Maybe individually we couldn't survive, and sure, we're completely different. Things are terrible, but I think we complement each other in some pretty amazing ways. Maybe together we can do this. Maybe together we can do anything."

She melts.

Julie grabs Nathan's hand and they look at each other. She can't bring herself to smile, but the corner of her mouth turns up. What's left of the front door hanging from the metal hinges, they push it open together.

The scene inside is not what she expected. Derek Darius is holding Johnny, some lady, and evidently Grandpa Montgomery at gunpoint. The lady is sobbing and holding what looks like a baby, no more than three months old. *No, not a baby. The skin is too clammy. That poor child is dead.*

Nathan says, "Hey, guys. What's up?"

CHAPTER 30

Their hair all has a story to tell.

"It's easier to ask forgiveness than permission."

"You killed a baby." Heat boils deep inside Johnny's chest. There is no longer room for fear. "You murdered an innocent child by deliberately putting your hand over his mouth until he suffocated."

"Yes, yes, yes, and I'm very sorry."

Julie's kinky dark hair is sticky with the goop she used to spike it up with this morning, looking worse because of her effort to look better. Nathan's albino blonde hair hangs limply over his forehead like how it always hangs over his forehead.

The childless mother is the reality television version of somebody falling to pieces. Her eyes are focused in the distance, i.e. the wall. She rocks while she clutches the tiny lifeless body close to her chest. Her entire body sobs violently and sometimes she starts making unrecognizably sad sounds. Whenever she's coherent, which isn't often, she just murmurs, over and over again, *why didn't I make him take the Nyquil*?

Derek Darius gestures a revolver in Aunt Montgomery's direction and says to no one in particular, "Shut her the hell up."

"Classy," Johnny Sparks mumbles.

"I'm the richest person on the planet out of everyone who isn't oil, and I own a goddamn 24 karat gold monocle. I am the very fucking definition of class."

Johnny's hair is a rat's nest. On a usual day, combing it hides most of its true length, and it's surprising how long it actually is. Thick strands now loop in random directions, and he spends a lot of time pushing his fingers through, trying to tame it. There is blood in his hair from both himself and others.

The whole gang is under Derek Darius hostage control now. Grandpa Montgomery is just staring nearsightedly at the spot where his grandson died. He hasn't had hair on his head for years. Julie and Nathan are cuddling together on the Montgomery kitchen floor sitting next to Tim, who seems to be in the last stages of dying. Even the bone from his arm is melting into liquidy goo. Julie is stroking his hair, which looks like it might start falling out in clumps.

It's only after the baby is dead that Johnny learned the child's name.

"Why don't you just leave," Johnny says to the celebrity captor. "Go off by yourself."

"I intend to, but the timing needs to be right." He glares at the constant sobbing from the ex-mother. "In the meantime, seriously, shut her the fuck up. Don't make me repeat myself again."

Aunt Montgomery counted on me to protect the baby and I failed her, Johnny thinks, *I've failed everyone. And most of all, Autumn is still out there. Alone maybe. Dead maybe.* Johnny pictures her, with her wet wound on her hand. Her arm melting into goo. He swallows as he stands. "I need to leave so I can find my wife."

Derek Darius snorts. "Good luck with that."

"Are you saying I can leave?"

"Of course not. I'm saying she's dead. Sit back down."

"We're still alive," Johnny gestures grandly to the group. "And if we can make it, she can too."

"No, it doesn't."

"Yes, it does."

"Let's use reason to see which one of us is right." Derek Darius's hair is jet black and perfectly spiked. Not one strand is out of place - it's like his celebrity makeup artists have just finished with it and he's ready to go on stage. "You people have no chance at all of fighting a vampire. They're better than you. Really. In every way. The only reason you all are alive is because I happened to be with you when shit hit the rotating shit flinger."

It worries Johnny out of his mind to think about Autumn, but he's never going to find her sitting here. It's hardest to do nothing in moments like these, when people you care about could be in serious trouble. Still, he sits.

Tim has slumped over himself, as in prayer, but Johnny knows from earlier conversations that the Californian is not religious. "I wish I had a marriage like that. I never even fell in love." He looks the way processed meat looks after it's been put through a very fine grinder. His green jacket is zipped up and seems to be holding him together. His jaw is slack. Eyes glazed over.

"Yeah, well, maybe love is overrated," Johnny says. "Autumn is still my wife, but the truth is that she's been cheating on me with some asshole named Derek."

Tim coughs his words out at Stephen Hawking speeds. He takes his air in sips, as if through a coffee straw. It's clearly difficult for him to speak, and the sheer effort involved in producing an audible sentence makes every communication poignant. The ideas carry much more weight than they otherwise would have - last words seem to have that effect. "It doesn't matter. You're going after her. That's what's important. That's love."

Johnny isn't sure why he has to find her, like if it really is love, but he does know that he has to. Beyond love or dedication or desire, this is simply who he is. He has to try to find her, even if she'd rather sleep with some asshole.

And she's alive. I know she is.

He doesn't know what to say back to Tim, to someone dying. He grabs Tim's hand in a gesture meant for comfort, but as soon as there's skin contact he jerks back because of how clammy Tim's hands are.

Derek Darius says, "Johnny, you don't live on Third Street

do you?"

"Yeah, why?"

"No reason. Just wondering…. Hey, is your wife's name Autumn?"

"How did you know that? I never mentioned her name…"

Johnny's eyes narrow with suspicious realization. The cheating. The cigarette smoking. Derek.

The celebrity is smiling slightly, trying to suppress a bigger smile. "Hey, so out of curiosity… does your wife happen to have a small black tribal tattoo on the top of her right foot?"

"You mother fucker."

His first reaction: *Out of all the people in the world to sleep with, and she chose Derek fucking Darius!*

But then with almost Zen-like composure, Johnny inhales deeply. Calmly. This detail doesn't matter. This tiny thing doesn't change anything. Autumn still needs to be saved.

The celebrity does not move on. He has a smirking look on his face. "I take it back. I'm not wrong often, but if there is still one person alive in this town, that girl is. I've never had a girl like her!"

Aunt Montgomery has quieted with her head down for a moment, but her silence doesn't last long. Her hair is wet and hangs in yellow seaweed strands. She looks too pale. When she raises her head she looks hatefully at Derek Darius out of the top parts of her eyes. She looks hardened and scary when she points a shaky finger at the celebrity and gives a hexing curse, "YOU. You killed my son. He didn't have to die. You are a bad person."

Derek Darius shrugs. "You know, you try to do what you can to protect your children. You have childproof locks and baby monitors. But this whole situation just goes to show that no matter what you do, sooner or later, you will eventually have to smother the baby to death one day for crying while trying to evade a man-eating predator."

"Yep," Nathan agrees. "That's exactly why I don't have kids."

Johnny can feel the world bending to a point where it's about to break. He grits through clenched teeth, "Now is not the time or the place." He's not sure exactly who he's talking to. Maybe all of them.

With the only gun in the room, Derek Darius is almost smiling at Johnny. "Oh, I'm sorry. Are you under the impression that you're in a position to make any sort of demand?"

The situation has become untenable. Aunt Montgomery is right about one thing, Derek Darius is not a good person. Not to mention he is probably a vampire. That doesn't mean now is the right time to try anything. If this continues, Johnny is confident more people will die.

But she keeps getting louder.

"YOU KILLED HIM!"

"YOU'RE A MURDERER!"

"YOU KILLED MY SON!!!"

The best way to picture the way Aunt Montgomery is acting

is to imagine an overdramatic actress playing at what it feels like to lose everything. The screaming is awkwardly loud, the type of yelling usually reserved for New Jersey reality shows. Most everyone is looking at the ground and the walls without knowing what to say. Even dying Tim is managing to look awkward. But her Judge-Joe-Brown-level yelling is no match for Derek Darius's poison intellectualism.

"If you think about it, it's really a victimless crime." Derek Darius's ugly words dance off his tongue. "Or it would be as long as we can find an acid bath to throw the corpse in."

She screams with caps lock on, and far too many exclamation marks for her sentences to be grammatically correct.

"Get it? It's victimless if we had an acid bath because there'd be no body."

"Calm down," Johnny Sparks tells Aunt Montgomery, and he pronounces the L in calm. "Think about what you're doing and where it will lead. Things can get better."

"I am worn down with your reassurances." The ex-mother laughs crazily. "The last time I listened to you, you let that monster kill my baby. I don't believe I will ever again listen to anything you have to say."

"What else would you have done?" Johnny asks. "What else could you do now?"

Spit bubbles at the corners of her mouth, she focuses her mad attention back to the billionaire. She points a crooked witch finger at him. "You killed him!"

"Blah blah blah," Derek Darius says. "You're boring me.

This would all probably be much more interesting if I were on drugs. But I'm not. So please shut your mouth."

To Johnny's eyes, it's a blur how fast the ex-mother moves. It's as if she's summoned up all her motherly-super-powers and focused them directly at Derek Darius's throat. There is no thought in her savage eyes. There was no plan. She's going for a kill.

There's not much distance between the two. Derek Darius steps back. However, even as he does so, he raises his revolver like a finely tuned machine. He squeezes the trigger with the casual accuracy of a lifetime of practice.

The inside explosion is deafening as the walls echo the gunshot. It's so loud Johnny's vision is blurring, his body not sure how to handle the sensory overload. The noise. The loss of blood. His broken nose. Nathan sticks his hands up. He looks completely shocked, like he had no idea this was coming, which is probably the case.

Bullet in her brain, Aunt Montgomery's momentum doesn't slow as her legs keep moving underneath her, but something is wrong with the way she's moving. When she reaches Derek Darius, the celebrity doesn't put his arms up or make a movement to defend himself. Rather, he steps calmly out of the way as she runs past him and clumsily into various household appliances.

It isn't until she rolls over, arms still stiffly extended out in a grab at Derek Darius's throat, that Johnny sees the bullet hole entering her skull between her eyes like a Hindu dot. There's no intelligence in her face, but she's clearly still alive and twitching, despite the bullet hole.

"AAARRRGHHH!" Grandpa Montgomery seems to have

snapped awake from his daze and struggles to stand up with the calcified slowness of the old. It's clear he's trying to tackle Derek Darius, although he's going about it at wheelchair speed.

The old man never makes it to his feet. A bullet in his chest stops him. A few seconds later, another bullet in the face makes him stop gurgling blood.

Ears ringing and full of adrenaline energy screaming at him to do something, Johnny Sparks begins to stand up into a tackling pose. Derek Darius points the gun at him. He talks flatly. Bored. "Stop. No. Don't."

Aunt Montgomery's face is twisted with her dying thought, stuck in a contorted snarl while her legs kick at the air. Her pearl white teeth are showing because her upper lip is curled in rage. Her well-manicured fingernails are broken and clawing at a throat they will never reach. The back of her head is not visible, but the blood beneath her is beginning to pool.

Julie turns to the wall and vomits. When she turns back, stomach acid stringing from her lips, it is not sickness in her expression, but shame.

"Shoot her again," Johnny says. "Put her out of her misery."

"Why would I waste the bullet? She probably can't feel much now anyhow."

"Why would you… waste the bullet?" Johnny asks. "Jesus, give me the gun."

"No way Jose, even if you do call me Jesus. If you feel strongly about it, just smash her head in with something."

Johnny risks a glance at Nathan. The boy's face is pallid and his eyes unfocussed. He looks like he's in shock. Good. Johnny prays he will stay silent and unmoving.

As Johnny Sparks stands up, he moves slowly and deliberately. He can't help but think about the way the celebrity shot Grandpa Montgomery while he was trying to stand. Johnny can feel the gun pointing at him, even if technically it's not. He imagines being shot as he struggles to his feet. He would die without last words, like how the old man did. Grandpa "Bullet Hole" Montgomery is the kind of thing people have recurring nightmares about. It was a terrible thing, witnessing him murdered. Definitely in the top five worst things Johnny has seen today.

Despite reservations, Johnny stands up anyway because he has to. He can't just leave her there like that.

Aunt Montgomery's eyes are vacant with hate or vacant from dying. Her mouth is opening and closing, like a goldfish.

Johnny says to Derek Darius, "Will you please give me the gun?" but the celebrity does not respond. He's apparently made up his mind.

Johnny instinctively wants his sledgehammer, he even reaches for it, but he dropped it when Derek Darius knocked him unconscious. Outside isn't far, but he doesn't have much time. He can't bear to watch what's left of Aunt Montgomery suffer like this even a moment more. He looks around the room a little frantically, looking for something to put Aunt Montgomery out of her misery.

A rock. No, a stone. It's a decorative piece of earth that the Montgomery's have placed on a clean shelf between two vases, a little bigger than a coffee mug and the edges are too smooth to be natural. When Johnny picks it up it feels heavy. Blood from his hand smears across the polished surface.

This will have to do.

Aunt Montgomery's eyes are rolled back in her head and jerkily moving. Johnny wants to fast forward her out of existence. In a way, that's what he's doing. Her mouth is twisted further into a rictus of biting nastiness. Johnny touches the stone to her head. One hard hit should do it. It seems like the kind of thing where you should count to three, so he pulls the stone back and forth. One. Two. Three.

When the stone crashes into her eye socket with all the formidable strength of Johnny's right arm, it sounds like an axe hitting a wet log. The orbital part of her skull shatters against the force. With no bone to hold it in, gooey parts of her left eye goop out, clinging to dark pink nerve-like wiring. The rest of the skull has a sagging look to it as well, like the overall structure has lost its integrity. As terrible as it is to look at, at least this is done. She can finally rest in peace with her baby.

But her legs keep kicking air. Her face keeps snarling.

Oh God, she's still alive.

Without thinking he brings the stone down again, hitting her deformed forehead, but she doesn't stop. She's kicking, snarling. Her one non-goop eye remains open, and it looks alert, and didn't it look lifeless before? He hits her again and again. He brings the stone down on her good eye so it will quit looking at him. He slams it into her head long after she stops moving. Blood from his finger is flying out of his hand, spraying the walls and mixing with her blood. He hits her until all that's left to hit are the bits of skull and brain that are spattered into the carpet, just to be sure.

"I think we can finally say this house is now a home," Derek Darius says. No remorse.

This is all his fault.

Johnny isn't sure why he understands the hate so well. He quietly makes a promise to himself. At the first opportunity, he will kill Derek Darius.

CHAPTER 31

The pain in Johnny's body, his phantom finger for instance, lacks any symmetry. It comes and goes in waves. One moment it's barely there, and the next it's sharp and demanding attention, wanting him to bend over and howl. He no longer wears his wedding ring. It is bloody and in his pocket. His vision is clouded and every heartbeat pumps blood from his body. His head pounds with concussion ferocity. He feels broken. Leaky and full of holes. Still, he bites his lip and forces any sign of weakness deep inside. The words "Turn to God." squirm out of his mouth. He can't think of anything else to say.

"Turn to God."

"Yeah… every time I turn to religion I pull some muscles or tendons or something."

Derek Darius is pacing in the graveyard house. It is too early for decay to set in, but there is a dead smell in the room and it's stronger than Tim. An undead reaper come

259

to collect souls of the living. The carnage is a liquid thicker than water. Where there are bodies, Derek Darius steps over them or around them.

"Well shit," the celebrity ignores Johnny's blathering as he berates himself. "I knew she was going to attack me but I didn't think she would attack so quickly."

Blood is everywhere. It seeps into the off-white carpet like spilled barrels of red wine. It drips from Johnny's soaked bandage, his blood mixing with everyone else's on the dirty floor. The gore pools into the linoleum of the adjacent kitchen and dries into sticky pools as platelets try to coagulate. Some of the blood cells might not know they're dead yet.

Nathan hasn't moved. His skin looks hollow, a shell that would shatter on impact. "This is starting to feel an awful lot like a George R.R. Martin book."

"I shouldn't have shot her." Derek Darius lights a cigarette. "I should have snapped her neck."

Not for the first time, Johnny notices the reflective sunglasses Derek Darius always wears. They're what people call aviators, now that people who fly planes are called pilots. When Johnny tries to look Derek Darius in the eye, he ends up seeing a warped version of himself reflected back in the aviators.

"The vampires will hear the gunshots." Johnny sees his warped reflected self say. "And they'll come back. Soon."

Aviator Mirror Johnny's features are similar but exaggerated and inverted, like seeing yourself caught off guard in pictures. The deep scar on his forehead looks like it was carved out by some kind of razorblade. It criss-crosses across the reflection the wrong way. His left is Johnny's right. His right, Johnny's left.

Behind the red rimmed aviators, Derek Darius appears to be thinking furiously. Since he killed Aunt Montgomery and Grandpa Montgomery, all traces of humor have vanished and he's pacing and angry. Looking at him, Johnny thinks of a gigantic machine, bigger than life, churning toward some conclusion. It might be powered by huge amounts of steam and have gears the size of Australia.

The celebrity stops, reaching the end of his brain chugging. "I'm going to go kill the vampires. You four, come with me. Excuse me, you three."

"Why would we ever go with you?"

"First, I'd like to point out that I am giving you a choice. I've had the observation that people generally respond better when they're given the illusion of choice. Choice one: come with me and maybe live. Choice two: ultimately die an untimely death where you're turned into human melt. "

"Choice three." Johnny turns away from the celebrity toward the Computer Science kids. "The four of us stick together and figure out what to do next on our own."

"Which would ultimately be... vampire meat. We don't have time for this. Are you coming or not?"

Derek Darius is leaning toward the group. His feet are pointed slightly outward, and one hand is rested on a trench coat pocket. On most people the stance would be natural, but it's so unlike Derek Darius that Johnny has the sense it's calculated somehow, like he's posing for something. Insight flashes. Johnny says, "You need us..."

Over reactive anger radiates as Derek Darius takes a step away. "Every good king needs his pawns." He mutters at himself through tight lips. The whispers are quiet enough that most people would not have been able to make out the words, but Johnny's hearing has always been acute.

Turning back to Johnny, the celebrity's anger has seemingly vanished. He smiles disarmingly with a plastic calmness. "I know where your wife is, and can take you there."

Johnny freezes and unconsciously moves a hand to his pocket, feeling the wedding ring inside. He has had a look of deadly acceptance on his face for a while now. The ring in his pocket is tarnished, he knows that. It probably doesn't fit his broken ring finger anymore, and never will again. "How would you know where she is?"

"Are you coming or not?" The celebrity shrugs, like he doesn't care what they decide. But his eyes are piercing and almost desperate.

Of course Derek Darius knows where she is. Why wouldn't a vampire know what other vampires do with victims? Johnny doesn't trust him, but with all Autumn's escape places empty, he doesn't have much choice. He looks at his hands as if they have answers. Inexplicably, his wedding ring has found its way from his pocket to his finger stump. He doesn't remember putting it there. It seems impossible it would still fit, with the bandages and the swelling. The pain of putting it on seems like something he would have remembered.

The giant sighs deeply and speaks slowly. "I'm not

speaking for everyone else. But I'll go with you."

Even if it's one in a million chance at saving Autumn, he has to try.

Nathan and Julie say they're going too. They look like they're still in shock, like the micromillimeter roots of their hair are already growing in bone white.

"Good." Derek Darius claps his hands and turns on a heel so his back faces everyone. He walks briskly out of the room.

Nathan says, "Were we… supposed to follow him?"

Before Johnny can answer, the celebrity is back, and he starts handing out guns like presents. He gives a bolt action .30-06 rifle to Nathan, and a smaller rifle without a scope to Julie. He hands Johnny his sledgehammer. "If any of you even point them in my direction, or don't do what I say, I will shoot you. You don't get another warning; this *is* your warning." He adds that they may have noticed he turned his back on them to grab the weapons, and he mentions that will be the last time he turns his back on them.

It feels good to have the heavy sledgehammer in his giant hands again. Nine fingers and a wedding ring, his grip is still strong. On the head of the hammer, blackish goo has dried. That must be vampire blood or whatever, and Johnny doesn't remember that being there. He does, however, remember how it got there.

"I don't need to add," the celebrity adds, "that if you were to try anything, and I wanted to stop you, there is absolutely nothing you could do."

It feels good to stand up and be armed. Powerful. He might die, but if he does he'll die on his own terms now. A warrior.

Just don't forget that Derek Darius is the one watching your back.

The celebrity's mood has improved also. "We need to move, now. Adios, bitches."

Presumably he says *adios bitches* to the dead bodies they're leaving behind, since there is no one else.

"Wait," Julie says, "What about Tim?"

"Oh, he died like five minutes ago."

Johnny's heart stops. Everyone turns to look, but not because they don't believe the celebrity. They look because they can't believe something like this could happen with them in the room. How could they miss this? How could it just slip by? It's difficult to accept that death could be so silent.

It is no surprise that Tim doesn't look good, and he's sitting too still to look alive. He has a chemotherapy kind of thinness. His chest isn't moving, and though his eyes are open, he isn't blinking. His skull looks soft and caved in on itself. Every piece of him is melting skin and blood colored wax. Even through his cotton shirt the thick goo is seeping through like a bandage that needed to be changed days ago.

"Tim... he's dead?" Julie says, with panic and concern in her voice. She's visibly shaking and pale, obviously deeply saddened and shocked at the loss of a true friend who she was hoping, at some level, would pull through somehow.

Derek Darius says, "Well, don't thank me. The vampires did most of the work."

Nathan Montgomery's voice is also strangely sad. "I always wanted to beat him at vampire killing, but I never wanted to beat him like this."

Johnny looks around the room for a first aid kit. He's sure Grandpa Montgomery has one, meticulously labeled and stored away somewhere. But even if he manages to find one, he's not sure what to do with it. A bandaid? More antibiotics might be a start, if he is still alive. Johnny thinks about Aunt Montgomery's kicking body, how she stayed alive for minutes. Snarling. They need to check Tim's pulse. "We should make sure he's dead."

Everyone is startled by Nathan Montgomery's rifle blast. His smooth skin seems to have stretched this past hour, too thin now, making his face gaunt. "Yeah. I'm pretty sure he's dead now. I don't think even a turned vampire could come back from the dead when its head has been blown off with a thirty aught six."

CHAPTER 32

Nathan Montgomery takes another bite of his chocolate flavored energy bar. The vampire/zombie apocalypse was fun, for a while, but there's too much death for this to be enjoyable anymore. There always was, but for some reason it's more real now. The deaths seem so needless and casual. His cousin, his Aunt, his Grandpa, and Tim, all dying within a chapter and a half. He feels wrung out and tired. When he realized Tim was dead he was already so emotionally drained from the other three that another one didn't seem to matter as a piece in the bigger picture. That fact bothers him a lot.

His only job is to keep the rifle pointed to the right, called "protecting the right flank". It's tough to walk and chew and carry a rifle, but Nathan is hungry and fidgety. He scans the right side of the group, and jumps at any movement.

It's dusk, and the wind is screaming at a hundred miles per hour. The blackness, Cloud Marv, seems to have mostly disappeared from outside with strands of eerie remnants whisking along with the strong wind. The invisible sun is probably in the last stages of setting somewhere beyond the dark gray world. A storm is coming, and hearing is already nearly impossible with the wind blowing at these dry class two hurricane speeds. Clouds in the distance are dark and raging wildly. It's not raining, but cold sideways rain looks imminent.

So basically the Idaho weather seems to be getting back to normal.

"There are at least two dozen vampires," Derek Darius had told them. "They seem to vary in size and speed. The not-bad news is almost all of them following me seem to be babies; considerably weaker and slower than the one we fought this morning. The bad news is there's at least one that definitely is not weaker. It looks <u>Really Really Fucking Big</u>." The underlined capital letters in Derek Darius's voice were audible. It's an inflection point that says, this needs emphasis. *One of the vampires is really really fucking big.*"

"This is worse than I thought." Nathan had shaken his head in disbelief. "It's just like when Shredder turned into Super Shredder."

Johnny had said, "So, the vampires are all different?"

"Yes. But don't get me wrong with the not-bad news. Fun fact: a baby vampire is still a vampire. Even a single baby vampire could still kill all of you."

"They all look alike to me."

"Vampires are like fingerprints. They all look similar from a distance, but no two are exactly alike, and they all want to destroy you."

In formation, they're crossing an open city field leading to Derek Darius's mansion. Sagebrush and yellow grass sprout in clumps about waste high. The plants here are dry and tough, with shallow roots squirming their way into the frozen October dirt.

They're walking because Derek Darius had said to. Nathan wondered why not try to fix Grandpa's car, but he can't help but rationalize for the celebrity, who offers so little in the way of explanation. Perhaps the best way to the mansion *is* taking a stroll through this exposed looking field with hard soil and vampire fox holes.

The young billionaire had brought everyone tidbits of knowledge like room service for when vampires attack. Stab this way. Shoot that way. Swing the sledgehammer like this. The knowledge was always peppered with caveats, like none of you could ever do this properly. It would take years of training and you would still fail, so realistically you might as well not even try.

"So are we supposed to blow off their heads so their brains are scrambled or stake them through the heart?" Julie had asked.

"Both, I guess." Nathan nodded gravely. "It's the only way to be sure."

"Neither," Derek Darius said. "They don't have hearts and their brains aren't in their heads."

"What if I did both? Chop off the head and stab through the middle."

"Hey, don't spend the rest of your probably short life wondering *what if*? Go ahead, see if that works. Science!"

Here is what "in formation" means: Julie Black and her rifle are taking the left rear flank, from ten o' clock to six o' clock. Nathan has better shooting skills thanks to video games and being a boy (misogyny aside, Derek Darius added) so he's responsible for two to six o' clock. The right behind flank is the more likely direction in terms of vampire attack. Johnny is in front of the formation. If the vampires get close, Derek Darius's explicit instructions for him were "Johnny SMASH". The celebrity is in the middle, a giant revolver dangling from each arm. He's taking twelve o' clock around to twelve o' clock.

"The point of this formation is to turn us into a vampire-defending cow herd," Derek Darius had said. "With eyes on the sides of our head and the ability to stampede to protect from predators. It will be especially nice to have you along, Johnny. In a pinch I can always shoot you in the leg and I suspect the vampires will go after you rather than chase me down."

Nathan is not the most observant person, but even he could see the unmasked hatred on Johnny's face.

"Don't worry, I'm just kidding big guy," the celebrity had added. "I could just outrun all of you without firing a shot."

Nathan is sweating like Steve Ballmer at a boxing club. A trickle of perspiration runs all the way down his back. He squints at the sun and makes a face like he's waiting for the bus. It's terrifying to walk like this, and not only for the obvious reason. They're completely out in the naked open. At least in the woods they had the trees to… climb. So maybe the trees wouldn't help that much, but at least they were there, and it was something. Even in the streets they were generally surrounded by houses. Here, there's nothing except the sagebrush, exclusively there to allow vampire sneak attacks.

"Most of the remaining vampires are little babies, and these ones are easy to chop up," Derek Darius had said. "But the only way to kill an adult creature involves several steps. First, they have an armor plate over this area." He pointed at a precise point exactly one inch below his sternum. "You can smash that several ways, for example, by shooting point blank with armor rounds or maybe even a large impact with your sledgehammer."

Johnny wrinkled his forehead, making the deep scar split into two. "Is that all?"

"Now it gets interesting, because after the sternum armor is smashed, you have to pry back a scale thing that looks like part of a vampire trench coat." Derek Darius gestured to a second precise area on the right side. "It's probably the most straightforward to peel it back by hand. Then you just shove a gun through that, aim for the nervy area behind the shattered sternum piece, and... bang."

"I assume throughout the entire process the vampire would be deadly functional?"

"I mean, there are other ways to kill the adults obviously, but it's not as if I can just carry those sorts of military grade weapons with me to a University talk... thanks a lot, liberals..."

Despite the ridiculousness of the scenarios, Johnny Sparks said, "If chance and God wills it, we'll be able to do this." Eternal optimists like that make Nathan a little sick.

The wind is tearing at Nathan's big hood on his big coat,

further complicating his continued effort to eat and chew and walk and scan for vampires in the two to six o' clock range. Regardless, he meets the wind as it surges against him, and he continues eating. *You never know when you'll get your next meal.*

He wants to know how Derek Darius knows so much. Can he sense the vampires coming? Where did he go after the car crash?

Garbage can! Nathan clumsily jerks the rifle in the direction of the metal and trash being blown on the road adjacent to the field. He was startled by the noise, which is one of the only noises he's been able to hear over the squealing wind. With his reaction times ridiculously slow, he has the feeling of being helplessly blind. *Why am I guarding a flank? I couldn't even spot a vampire in the open, much less one trying to sneak up on us.*

But there is nobody else.

The garbage can continues to bang down the street, and it has the effect of a tumbleweed in a John Wayne western. Then, at the exact moment he's thinking about how the garbage is taking the place of a tumbleweed, an actual tumbleweed blows around in the same field. COINCIDENCE??? Yes, it is totally a coincidence. Why would those two things be related? When it's windy outside things will blow around. Also, the actual tumbleweed doesn't have the same ominous tumbleweed effect.

Nathan's body is exhausted. He's trying to walk in his ready-for-anything pose, but his skinny nerd muscles can't handle it for the length of time required.

"It could be worse," he says out loud, and he immediately

regrets it. It's windy, so he hopes that nobody heard the words. Saying that "It could be worse" is pretty much the worst thing you can say in any apocalypse vampire movie. He might as well be a jock and go have sex in the goddamn woods.

His grip tightens on his rifle, and his eyes narrow at the windy rear-left flank. He takes another slow bite of the protein bar.

"There," Johnny shouts over the weather. "Three o' clock."

Derek Darius says he sees it. He says there's another at five and another at six, and he suggests everyone walk faster. *Three vampires, and they're all on my flank.*

Even Nathan, world's worst lookout, manages to spot the one at three o' clock. The thing makes no effort to hide as it trots along on two legs beside the group. This is the closest Nathan has really looked at a vampire, and there are details present he hadn't been able to make out before. They aren't tall or short. Skinny or fat. It looks human, resembling the kind of invisible kid who disappears in the back of a high school classroom, wearing dark clothes and never a smile. The most remarkable thing about this creature is how unremarkable it is.

But there are differences too. Its nostrils are kind of slit and snake-like. Its mouth is so angular it reminds him of a jack o' lantern. Its evil eyes are black pits that actually sparkle with malevolence and hatred.

Oh my God. Stephanie Meyers was right all along. Vampires do sparkle.

There is nowhere to go. The vampires are too close and

the field is too open. In the middle, they couldn't be farther away from everything. It seems significant that the creatures waited until now to start trotting along. Nathan can feel it in the air. Stampede time.

"Nobody fire yet," Derek Darius says. "Head toward the vacuum museum sculpture. We're almost there."

Nathan looks up. It does not look like they are almost there.

The vacuum museum sculpture is a twenty-five foot tall upside down triangle shaped a bit like the cloud city buildings from Star Wars. It's not immediately clear how it can offer any sort of protection from the surrounding vampires.

At Derek Darius's order the group shifts in the direction of the vacuum sculpture with military precision. The group isn't running, it is speed walking.

Nathan keeps his eye on the vampire, which is staring back at him with solid black eyes. It doesn't need to trot to keep up, but it keeps slithering smoothly back and forth within Nathan's rear left flank. The black vampire eyes are hatefully playful. It's not the hate, but the playfulness that is scariest.

"Another one at eleven," Johnny says.

"I spot six altogether, but no sign of King Vampire." Derek Darius is dancing forward, gliding through the dry Idaho plants. "Keep mall walking."

They're mall walking so fast now that it might as well be a job. But the field is open and it feels like they're walking in place, burning calories on an inclined treadmill.

273

Nathan's heart is beating into his skull. Sweat drips down his brain. It seems like the vampires are playing with the group. Nathan saw a documentary once where dolphins did something like this with fish they were eating. They would jump and play and even though they're in the ocean you could almost hear them laughing as they ruthlessly rounded up and massacred the entire school. Fucking evil dolphins.

He glances up to see how far they've gone. So much time has passed, they've got to be close to the vacuum museum sculpture by now. Only when he looks up he sees they're not close. He can't tell for sure, but they seem to be in the exact same spot they were several hours ago (or whenever he last looked). Adding infinity with infinity just equals infinity.

And meanwhile, the vampires are casually trotting closer. Playing with their food.

Derek Darius doesn't tell anyone to fire, he just starts firing. Nathan pivots on his right foot, aims the rifle through a scope (which is difficult with a jumping target) and he fires like its Grand Theft Auto III.

The rifle kicks like a bully's punch. Between the rifle's jerk and the moving target, he doesn't bother to investigate the impact of the shot through the scope, but he's sure his aim was good. He still imagines the creature smiling with jagged edged teeth at the thought of feisty food. Let it smile. Nathan bolt actions out the old shell so the next bullet can mechanically come into place. He aims, which gives him a chance to see the vampire coming unnaturally quickly toward the group. He fires again and it turns out it's not actually smiling. It just looks pissed.

Bullets fire at an incredible constant rate, and 95% seem to have the sound of Derek Darius's twin revolvers. Another vampire is coming at the formation head-on. Johnny swings his sledgehammer as soon as it's in range. Nathan is somewhat aware of this peripheral movement, but his focus is on the left rear flank. The shots have slowed the vampire's advance, but not enough. He has maybe time for one more round before the flank vampire reaches him.

He aims for the middle place where Derek Darius shot the first vampire, somewhere above the belly button. He exhales to aim. He pulls the trigger.

The shot seems accurate. The impact is visible. But also the vampire seems fine. Johnny is too busy trying to fight a vampire in front to be any sort of help when the vampire reaches the group.

"Secret weapon, bitches!" Nathan shouts as he fumbles out his dog whistle and blows with all the air in his lungs. All five of the visible vampires turn toward him, snarling and startled. Ahead of him, Johnny's hammer connects with a distracted creature, connecting solidly and bringing it down. Derek Darius's bullets cause one of them to fall backward. One of the creatures seem to have fallen down on itself. "Mess with the best, die like the rest!"

Nathan laughs manically as the creatures struggle to regain their balance and retreat to a safer distance. They round back, seemingly regrouping for an offensive "Haven't had enough yet?" He blows the whistle again. The vampires focus on him. One takes a stuttering step, but none seem frozen. The dolphin playfulness Nathan was projecting onto the creatures has disappeared, replaced by unmasked malevolence. As full of hatred as a snake.

He whistles again. There is no reaction.

The creatures have altered their course from a direct kill to something more tangential. Nathan raises his rifle and fires another round, but he pulls the trigger too quickly and he isn't sure if the bullet connected. The word helplessness comes to mind.

"Everyone forward," Derek Darius orders. There is no trace of fear in his voice.

Nathan realizes he, along with everyone else in formation, is going to die here. For the first time in his entire life death is more than an abstract thought, and he's already come to accept it. If he dies here, then fine, but he's taking this left rear flank vampire with him. Nathan knows there's not much time until the vampires are on top of them. He bolt actions another bullet.

The formation progresses slowly. The people who want you to choose between fight or flight have set up a false dichotomy. You can actually have both at once. The rifle magazine holds five bullets, and Nathan's rifle is out of ammo other than the bullet in the chamber. He yells to the group "reloading," but he can't even hear himself over ringing ears and hurricane wind. He shoves a bullet into the chamber, but it must have been misaligned because it falls to the ground. His hood is blowing in his face and he still somehow carries both the protein power bar and the dog whistle. The ammunition feels slippery in his hands, like he's gripping it through ice water. He wishes he could just shoot off the screen.

The vampires are following along on the periphery; far enough out where they have a bit of cover and even Derek Darius would have trouble scoring a direct gunshot at this range while mall walking. The creatures dart in and out with Japanese anime agility, never committing to attack but always looking for weaknesses to exploit. They look so unremarkably human that the movement seems even more unnatural. It's scary to watch the vampires dart in at Interstate speeds, eyes black as midnight. But as fast as they are at darting, Derek Darius is equally fast with the revolvers. Continuous shooting where every shot counts. The open space, which seemed so ominous before, gives Derek Darius a sort of bullet buffer the vampires have to make it through before they reach the chewy center.

Blink.

In the time it takes to blink, three vampires are on top of the formation. Derek Darius is a blur of bullets and empty brass. Nathan fires his rifle. Julie fires her rifle. They both fire like mad, but they fire at human speed. The bullet barrage slows the creatures, and two turn back, but one gets to Nathan as he's reloading. And it's not just a vampire. It's *the* vampire, the one that's been watching him. White skin that looks almost rubbery is stretched across the creature's hollow cheeks. Its teeth are human, but carnivorous too. The canines are steel like a saw blade, too long to fit in a person's mouth, and have they extended? Nathan has been projecting emotions onto the vampire. Playful. Hate. Now the vampire is only death, if that counts as an emotion.

The creature is so close that this is where he should be pressing the left "knife/punch/hit with the back of the rifle" button, but he hasn't got a knife and the thought of punching this demon in the face seems more ridiculous than anything. He winds up for a geek punch anyway, because what else is he supposed to do?

277

Between the constant gunshots and warzone wind and ringing ears, a sledgehammer crashes into the vampire above the nose. It's a head on car wreck, a relatively smallish creature running full speed into an oncoming brick wall. Johnny's forearms are as wide as Nathan's middle, and Johnny has put all of his massive weight into the fully extended swing. The direction of the vampire reverses instantly, from like 60 mph to like negative 60 mph. Johnny hit it out of the park, as they say. Derek Darius fires at least eight continuous rounds into the creature's backside as it limps and scrambles its way back to the periphery. It may be dazed, but it's not seriously injured. Nathan projects a feeling like getting the wind knocked out of you. Nathan projects record breaking seventh level of hell anger once it catches its breath.

Amazingly, everyone is still moving in the direction of the vacuum museum sculpture. With everything happening, in theory this should be difficult, but the formation is holding remarkably. They're working fluidly as a team, and despite Derek Darius very recently killing his Aunt, nephew, and Grandpa, Nathan has to admit he still likes following the celebrity's lead. Hope floods through his veins when he risks a glance at their destination. He never thought they would make it this far. The vacuum museum sculpture is close enough to reach out and touch. Almost.

Bullets are firing from all directions and the pace is picking up. This is the final sprint at the end of the race.

"Run!" Derek Darius yells as he breaks out of formation and runs full speed ahead. He's faster than everyone, of course, and easily outpaces the group before anyone else can even begin sprinting.

Nathan obeys orders, and runs as fast as he can. He isn't slow compared to the average North American human being, especially considering all the fat people, paraplegics, and babies weighing that statistic down, but in this situation an average speed is pitifully slow. When Nathan sprints on his toes and picks up his knees it feels slow-motion and dream-like.

The vacuum museum sculpture is still maybe fifty meters away. Nathan keeps his eyes on the prize. With tunnel vision he doesn't see the vampires closing in, but he knows they're there. It's going to be close.

His heart is so full of blood it feels like it's ready to burst. Ventricles press into ribcage bones and pump oxygen into his sluggish legs. When it comes down to it, Julie can apparently run faster than Nathan; she's pulled out a few steps in front. Johnny is in the back, which makes no sense at all. Johnny would be significantly faster than both Nathan and Julie in any life or death sprint, which of course this is. Nathan glances back mid-run, expecting to see Johnny being eaten or something, but there he is pacing himself behind Nathan and protecting their rear flank. It's clear that with his long legs and easy pace he is not going full speed.

When Johnny sees Nathan's backward glance, he says, "Keep going." He says it encouragingly, as if they might actually have a chance. Nathan puts his head down and sprints at dangerous speeds.

One Mississippi. Two Mississippi. Three Mississippi.

The base of the museum vacuum sculpture is cylindrical cement, maybe two meters in diameter. It has an arch cut out of one side to act as a way in. Julie slips through the entrance just ahead of Nathan. Inside, metal rebar rungs are bent into the cement to act as a ladder. Derek Darius is already standing at the top, two stories above, looking down at them over a hatch as wide as a sewer manhole opening. Nathan is a little surprised to see that the celebrity hasn't already shut the hatch.

There is no transition time as Julie goes from sprinting to climbing; she kind of runs up the side of the wall at first. Nathan is a split second behind her, with Johnny pushing him forward. Nathan climbs the rungs in much the same way he was running, he simply moves his legs and arms as fast as they will go. The rifle is awkward and slows him down, and he wonders how Julie (also holding a rifle) is managing to climb so much faster.

He scrambles through the top of the hatch onto the roof of the vacuum museum sculpture. A theme-appropriate raging wind blows into his face. He's past the finish line and he can't help but blurt out a bit of a laugh past his anaerobic breathing. At Nathan's side, Johnny is having a bit of trouble making it through the hatch, but it looks like he's made it too. Nathan crawls to see what the problem is. Derek Darius and Julie are gathered around the hatch as well. It looks like Johnny is caught on something. *Ah, there's the problem.*

A vampire has latched itself onto the shoe of Johnny Sparks. It's hanging on with a finger. Or claw. Whatever.

Nathan doesn't hesitate or even think. A bullet is already in the rifle chamber. He points without looking through the scope and fires. It's only after he pulls the trigger that he feels uncertainty, like what would happen if he missed and shot Johnny in the leg or face.

The vampire falls to the ground with all the regularness of gravity. No amount of super agility will speed it up. It might as well be an apple or any other ordinary 9.81 meters per second squared object.

Johnny wriggles his massive body through the hatch opening, and Derek Darius swings shut the rusty hatch at the top of the ladder, but in the last moment a very human hand punches through. The fingers are sharp and white. A vile thing, made worse because it looks so close to what a normal hand should look like. It slashes blindly in search of flesh. The celebrity kicks the top of the hatch like a karate black belt would punch through cement blocks. The sound is similar too. It sounds like how a human forearm breaking would sound.

The creature's broken arm darts back below. The hatch clanks shut. Nathan breathes.

In the wind, standing outside on top of the small vacuum museum sculpture, Nathan takes a bite of his chocolate power protein bar. He's managed to hang onto it somehow, and you never know when you'll be able to eat next. The hood of his coat flaps behind him in the wind like a tattered American flag.

CHAPTER 33

The city of Rockwell doesn't have a visitor's center, but if it did, it would have postcards picturing the vacuum cleaner museum sculpture. The two story building is the closest thing Rockwell has to a monument. In the 1920s, a vacuum entrepreneur founded a company that manufactured and sold industrial and household vacuum cleaners. This guy held seventeen patents in the science of sucking, and he was made very rich. Even in the Great Depression, the vacuum cleaner as a durable good was commonly said to be "recession proof". During World War II the factory was converted to fight Nazis somehow, where it undoubtedly helped pave the way for an allied victory. The entrepreneur eventually died, and his vacuum company acquired. The museum has been abandoned now for over twenty years. It had been full of signs with bible quotes and religious overtones, and there was a Noah's ark at the front for some reason. No one ever bothered to take out the exhibits, which aren't even worth sentimental feelings anymore. Today, the abandoned building's primary function is for middle school kids to dare each other to go in. But despite the decay of the original museum itself, the museum sculpture outside still shines as a shiny beacon of cleanliness and… dust free carpet.

Also, the sculpture has a rare quality - the vampires can't seem to easily reach the top of it.

Johnny guesses this makes sense, considering the space needle shape and the slick stainless steel construction. The sculpture is about as tall as a two story house, and the top is a circle about twelve feet in diameter. Initially, the vampires got scarily close to the top by running up the slick metal sides. After a bullet from Derek Darius, the creatures seem content to wait at the base. Their prey has to come down to eat sometime.

It seems invisible dust is blowing with the wind, and it's in everything. Johnny shields his eyes from the worst of it, but he can feel the grit building up in his nostrils and ear holes. One way to look at this current situation on top of the structure is temporary safety. Another is overcrowded prison. It's opinions like these that separate the optimists from the pessimists "There's a 99% chance we're going to die horrible deaths here," the pessimist might say. "No," the optimist would disagree. "There's a 1% chance some of us might live." It's the classic glass half empty half full question, but with probabilities of dying.

Fact: Derek Darius has two bullets left, and Nathan Montgomery has only one. If the group wanted to shoot themselves, which they don't, but even if they did, they wouldn't have enough bullets for everyone. Two of them might have to double up behind the rifle.

The sun has finished its sunset. Even if there were city

power, there aren't any street lights here at the top of the vacuum cleaner museum sculpture. The only sound louder than the howling wind is the freezing rain as it stabs the world sideways. Johnny keeps pulling his coat over his square face to cover as much of his skin as possible from the stinging of needle water. He's wearing jeans, and if he wrung them out he could fill a bucket.

Fact: there is not a lot of talking, but silences are never uncomfortable when the wind is howling. In fact, in howling wind scenarios it's trying to yell over the noise that's uncomfortable.

"Do you think they're gone?" Julie asks over the wind. "One of them left pretty quickly when Nathan and I climbed a tree."

"What?"

Johnny and Derek Darius have been toting around backpacks of miscellaneous supplies that they grabbed from Grandpa Montgomery's end-of-the-world bunker. As an answer to Julie's question, the celebrity casually grabs a Montgomery flare and tosses the hissing light to the ground. When it hits, a dome of light is created, and it doesn't even take a single second before two vampires trot through the light dome. They look like NFL wide receivers running for a ball thrown out of bounds. They had acted on casual instinct with reaction times that are really really fast.

"Maybe they'll leave eventually," Julie says optimistically, like there's a one in a hundred chance they'll just leave. Sometimes problems really do just disappear.

"They have to eat too." Lines, wrinkles, and dirt cover Johnny's flawed face now. It makes his brown eyes stand out in a haunting way. "They'll lose interest and leave well before we run out of food. Nathan has enough snacks we can make it up here for days".

He can't stop the bleeding. His whole arm is weak with dull pain from his ring finger stub. It's not frigid outside, but between the rain and cotton jeans, the wind chill factor, and the complete lack of shelter it's easy to imagine falling scalp deep through thin ice. He's been shivering for a while, and he's already starting to shake uncontrollably. His muscles feel exhausted as they spontaneously jerk. His face feels lumpy and deformed to the touch. His nose is crooked.

He doesn't remember for sure, medically speaking, if he's supposed to try to stop the shaking or to just let his body do its thing to generate heat. Should he be flexing his muscles? Should he elevate his hand? Other questions start to go through his mind, like how long is the time between when a human body starts shivering and critical hypothermia. Forty-five minutes? Is this shock from blood loss? He doesn't feel pain from his broken nose, comparatively, and that seems worrying.

Derek Darius still wears the red rimmed sunglasses into the night. He grins widely against the dark ice rain. His teeth are so white they could use him in a dentist commercial, and they sort of glow in the dark. They're too white in fact, as if something terrible had to be bleached away. "Thinking about cuddling with me for warmth?"

Blood rushes into Johnny's ears and his face feels hot. The thought had barely touched his mind. *How did he know?*

There's a vampire darkness to the howling night. Johnny's

eyesight is usually good in the dark -he's always eaten a lot of carrots – but now he is blinded. The air sounds like sand beating and blowing against them all. Occasionally, the ground below will swarm with the creatures, dozens, visible only by their yellow eyes. But it's never for more than a moment, and the oily darkness always returns. A blackness that gets in his mouth.

It's hypnotic and surreal, peering into the void with universal sensory deprivation. There's something similar to, but deeper than, looking into a burning campfire. Almost hypothermic in the windy darkness, this must be what a vision quest feels like. He keeps trying to picture her face, and finds that he can't remember it.

Instead, his mind keeps drifting to how Derek Darius overpowered him so casually. Him, Johnny Sparks, who is bigger and faster and stronger than anyone he's ever met. A little over six feet tall and a slender build, Derek Darius is a tiny person compared to Johnny's hulking frame. But the grace and smoothness of the celebrity is phenomenal, and Johnny can't help but feel helpless around him. This emotion is so alien to the giant that he almost hopes Derek Darius *is* a vampire.

Yellow eyes streak across the night below, blurry with movement, and then are gone. Will they wait below until the end?

The sideways rain eventually dies down, but the wind doesn't and the cold doesn't. This is about as uncomfortable as it gets, but as time passes and he can make out a star in the sky, Johnny knows his body will recover. He can withstand more cold than this. The ominous shivering dies down to persistent chattering teeth and non-functioning fingers. His muscles are achy and tired, but his vision has lost the tunnel effect. The pain has gone from blinding to aching. He's not going to die from exposure tonight. Anyway, he was more worried about the computer science kids getting hypothermia, but although he can't see them in the darkness, they also seem like they're doing basically alright. "How are you holding up?"

Dressed in real winter clothes they say, "A little cold. A lot tired."

"If you can, you should try to get some rest," Johnny says, and he adds for Nathan's benefit, "It does actually help if you cuddle."

The kids seem to agree, and soon they're cuddling together on the small metal rooftop, either sleeping or at least collapsed. Things have slowed down. Even the wind and chattering teeth eventually die down.

Derek Darius, as a vampire, likely doesn't need sleep. Johnny isn't going to sleep as long as Derek Darius is awake.

No one speaks.

Johnny asks the question that shatters the silence in the darkest hours of the night. It's the question that matters above all else. He can't see much, but he can see the celebrity's silhouette darker against the darkness. "How do you know where Autumn is?"

The silhouette shrugs. "She told me where she would go."

"She... told you where she would go when exactly?"

"Right after we were done having sex."

"No, I mean…" Johnny isn't sure what he means.

The celebrity talks fast but his words are always articulate. He enunciates like he's had years of manners trainings from a good British school of etiquette. "Sometimes I just have to spell it the fuck out for you, don't I? She's in the safe room at my house. I have a place setup similar to but better than old Grandpa Montgomery's. A few days ago we had a conversation about end of the world scenarios, and she told me that my safe room was her new *zombie escape plan number one.*"

"Oh," Johnny says, and his mouth feels sluggish and stupid. There isn't really anything else for him to say. It sounds like her words coming out of the celebrity's mouth. She's always looking for zombie safe places, and this is a reasonable story.

So what's wrong? Something invisible stabs at Johnny's throat and he tries to swallow. The fact that she had talked with Derek Darius about apocalyptic scenarios hurts so much more than the sex for some reason. Sex is just sex, but Johnny had always thought zombie escape plans were their special thing, an intimate window the two of them shared only with each other. It's stupid. This isn't even the part that's supposed to hurt. He can feel emotional damage running into his heart like poison, but he tries to push it aside.

None of this matters. I love her. I have to save her.

"Anything worth having is worth fighting for," Johnny says, but the saliva is thickening up and the conviction in his voice sounds shaky.

"Ah, truisms. It's like my couch. It's a pretty awesome

couch, but I wouldn't necessarily call it something worth fighting for. Worth having though."

"Can't you ever look past the surface?"

"Reductio ad absurdum." The celebrity shrugs and pops an unlit cigarette into his mouth as he talks. "It's one of my favorite things."

"I don't know what that means."

"Haha, big guy. You crack me up. That's why I keep saving your life. Your vocabulary is as bad as, like… whatever."

The big mystery for Johnny has been Derek Darius's motivations. If he's a vampire, and Johnny is convinced that he is, then why hasn't he killed everyone else yet? And why is he fighting with the other vampires? Is this a trick? Are the other vampires in different packs or tribes or something?

Less of a mystery is the question of whether or not Derek Darius is a vampire. He is. It would be impossible for a human to move that quickly or with so much strength.

"Why are you going back to your house?" Johnny tries to ask casually. He wants the truth, but more than that, he hopes the answer isn't Autumn.

"I'm going to kill the creatures." His cigarette is lit now, although Johnny doesn't recall him lighting it. "Although the timing couldn't be worse. Not only did they choose Rockwell as ground zero, they picked the same morning as my computer science lecture."

"Maybe that saved your life. Maybe the fact you left your house is why you're alive."

289

"Unlikely." The celebrity says this scornfully, but with no explanation.

"There's no other reason you're trying so hard to make it to your house?"

"I also plan on saving Rockwell."

"Is that like how you saved the Montgomery mother and child?"

"So when I say 'saving' what I mean is like *saving* a document or *saving* a stamp collection. This is part of a larger event that will change human history, maybe end human history, and I have little doubt there's extremely important information here that needs to be 'saved'."

Pieces are missing. Why would a vampire celebrity care about human history? It wouldn't make sense for a vampire to wait to kill the Montgomerys until they attacked him, rather than just killing them earlier. Is it because he enjoys killing, and he likes to draw that pleasure out?

Why is Derek Darius letting me live?

A thought forms at his center. *Is Autumn a vampire?* She was acting so different, and the cut on her hand so unnatural. *Was it turning her?*

Sometimes it's best to be direct.

"I know you're a vampire."

The celebrity raises a perfectly arched eyebrows. "A vampire."

Johnny has his arms folded against his chest like a parent who's found drugs hidden in the sock drawer. His back is straight, and his superhero shoulders wide.

In the dark wind there's the orange flame of Derek Darius's millionth cigarette. A single point of light. He breathes deeply and exhales smoke with the kind of coffee and cigarette pick-me-up that only an addict can understand. When he talks, he whispers. "How... how did you find out?"

"That's not important."

"I need to know."

"It's not really a single thing as much as a series of events." There are hundreds of examples, some so small they're barely worth mentioning. Derek Darius is staring through the darkness into Johnny, willing him to continue. "The strength, the quickness. There was nothing human about the way you took my shotgun."

"So does it have anything to do with how smart I am?"

"I guess."

"Or how handsome?"

"This is serious."

Derek Darius says seriously, "It's not like I'm just asking you if my handsomeness tipped you off out of curiosity. This is important. I need to know how I... how I gave it away."

Johnny nods. He *knew* Derek Darius was a vampire. He felt it in his gut. "No, it wasn't your handsomeness."

"Good, because there isn't much I could do to fix how good looking I am." The celebrity exhales smoke. "Truthfully, and when I raise my right hand it means I'm telling the truth, I am a vampire. But I am NOTHING like them." Reluctant, he pauses. "I have more to tell you, but look - if we survive, you can't tell this to anyone. Do you understand?"

It's too dark to clearly see whether or not the celebrity's hand is actually raised. Regardless, Johnny agrees. He doesn't know what's changed, but he's eager to take advantage of Derek Darius's surprisingly open state of mind.

"Do you know how you only use ten percent of your brain? How do I put this? *We vampires* use a lot more of our brain than ten percent. It helps us be faster and stronger than a normal human."

"I suspected something like this all along." Johnny's words are coming out too quickly, and he isn't breathing at commas or periods. "That's why you were able to take me down so easily and how you're able to shoot with such precision. You use the extra brain power to predict how the world around you will behave. When we were fighting it felt almost like you were seeing into the future."

There's a quiet pause.

And Derek Darius snorts. He laughs almost uncontrollably, so loud that Nathan Montgomery and Julie Black stir in their sleep, and the monsters on ground level begin to rustle. "Seriously, a vampire? So I suppose the creatures down there that *actually aren't* human are capable of unhinging their jaws by using this *extra 90%* brain functionality?"

Johnny looks at his boots. It's too dark to see them, but he's spent enough time looking this direction to know what they look like. "Well, you did say you're not exactly like them…"

"This isn't some eighties sitcom plot device that… Oh, I'm sorry, I was going to complete my sentence but suddenly I can't even remember who I am because I've contracted a remarkable case of 80s plot device amnesia!"

"Ha ha."

"No, no, no. I'm completely serious here, I'm raising my right hand and everything. We need some time apart to think about this, so I'm going to draw an 80s plot device line in the middle of the roof. You stay on your side and I'll stay on mine, and neither of us can cross the line. Do you have any duct tape or a sharpie?"

"What were you saying about the ten percent of your brain?"

"Mr. Janitor, I know this whole science thing is tough for you to grasp, but that ten percent of your brain thing ain't science. That was just me leading up to a punch line where you were the butt of the joke." Derek Darius laughs. "You really think I'm a vampire?" Then he laughs more.

"This doesn't explain anything," Johnny says. "Like how when you're shooting you never, ever miss. Not once. It's not humanly possible from the ranges you're firing. Not to mention how someone your size was somehow able to take me down with so little effort."

"And me being a vampire is somehow the best explanation for me being better than you at everything. That's fucking brilliant. I guess that explains why I've been going around with you *killing* vampires during the day and eating

Nathan's protein bars. I guess that would make me a vampire like Blade? A daywalker?"

"All you're doing is evading. If you're not a vampire then what are you?"

"You know Johnny, if I wanted to, I could've killed you already." He points the gun at Johnny. His tone has become bitter cold. "If I wanted to, I could kill you right now."

Johnny agrees that it is actually a good explanation and leaves it at that. He's noticed a new quality about himself these past couple days where he tends to agree with people when they're pointing a gun at him.

Derek Darius's mood spins on a dime as he holsters his gun. He yawns and stretches as he lies down gracefully on the metal roof. He says, "I'll sleep soundly tonight."

"Derek, you smothered a baby to death today."

"Yes Johnny Boy. I did. But I'm also tired." He doesn't seem to have any fear whatsoever that either Johnny or the vampires below will hurt him while he's sleeping. "Did you know nearly every single animal species on earth sleeps? Even mosquitos need sleep."

CHAPTER 34

A million invisible needles are acupuncturing into Nathan Montgomery's sleeping left arm. There's a girl stuck to his side, so he doesn't dare move or this foreign creature might realize his presence and bolt. The top of the metal roof isn't a comfortable place to lie down. Nathan's back hurts, but she's on his arm. The swollen lump on her forehead blossoming purple does nothing to make her less beautiful. He can smell her morning breath as she breathes out her mouth, and it smells sensual somehow.

The sun will rise soon, strange in its clockwork normalcy. It's as if it doesn't even realize it's moving through the sky in the middle of an apocalypse. Quiet, as if it were any other morning.

Julie Black jerks awake from whatever nightmare she was having. Terrified, the adrenaline girl looks around with dinner-plate eyes. When she exhales her eyes narrow. She settles her crinkled gaze on Nathan. "You killed Tim. You are a terrible person."

The look she gives really captures the awkwardness of when you're just getting to know a girl, and it seems like you're really hitting it off, but then she wakes up cuddling next to you the morning after she watched you shoot the corpse of her old dead friend.

Johnny is standing on the platform, apparently having been awake all night. Dark eyes set deep in his massive square head, he glances at Nathan with a look of heavy-handed disapproval. The skin on Johnny's face is so damn leathery.

Why are they mad at him for shooting Tim? It had been Derek Darius who killed his aunt and cousin. At worst, Nathan is only the second most terrible person here. He stammers. "Tim… asked me to."

"Yeah," Julie says, "and dad really took Wolfie to the farm."

Johnny Sparks says lecturingly to Nathan, "This is not a videogame. You need to be careful when you're handling a weapon like that. Not only could you shoot someone accidentally, but you could give our position away. Basic gun safety exists, even now."

Derek Darius groans as he wakes up. "It's really very simple. At all times keep the gun pointed directly at your own face, so you're able to shoot yourself at a moment's notice if a vampire sneaks by." He stretches his arms behind his head. He yawns widely. "That's like rule number one of gun safety."

Julie has a frown, set deeply in sadness for all her easy smile. The green streaks are fading from her hair, driven away by the night's rain. "You shouldn't have shot him. He deserved a proper burial or something."

"Yeah, or something." Then Derek Darius says to Nathan. "Hey, give me a protein power bar."

At the center of attention in the middle of the vacuum museum sculpture roof, Nathan has nowhere to look but down. He absentmindedly hands a peanut butter protein bar to Derek Darius and takes another one out for himself. Vanilla flavor.

"He was already dead," Nathan gasps quietly as he tries to tread water. "I was being cautious."

"It's just common sense." Julie Black shakes her head, and her freckles seem more pronounced when she's angry. "Even if you thought it was necessary, you should have warned us first and told us you were going to shoot. It was just so inappropriate and random. *Like every single thing you do.* Even if you do manage to survive this, if you keep acting this way you're going to end up as a thirty-five year old neck-beard non-practicing heterosexual living in your parent's basement."

Derek Darius laughs. Everyone glares at him so he adds, "It's funny because he has no social skills."

The funny thing is, Tim really had asked Nathan to shoot him. According to Tim, Grandpa Montgomery had apparently discovered (or at least mentioned) that a bite would turn a person into a creature. Grandpa Montgomery knew (or at least suspected) the vampires around town were actually the former residents of Rockwell, Idaho.

Tim had said, "Make sure it doesn't come to that for me. Promise me."

At the time, minutes before the Midwesterner died, most

people weren't exactly paying attention. Aunt Montgomery had been flipping out. But Nathan had heard. Those were Tim's last words. "Promise me." Nathan has his doubts about the Grandpa Montgomery zombie vampire reincarnation theory, but regardless, Tim had asked for a bullet through his brain. And Nathan delivered.

The protein bar is chewy, grainy, and manufactured, which would have tasted good except for all three of those things. The texture is plastic like, but it gets in your teeth and absorbs all moisture from your mouth.

"I'm not saying you shouldn't get a gun," Johnny Sparks' lecture continues, "but if you misuse a weapon like that it puts all of us in danger."

Nathan nods. Less in agreement and more as a way to communicate that he's following along. He doesn't know how he would begin to explain that Tim had asked to be shot. *Worst Doctor Kevorkian ever.* He stares down at the metal roof, and despite having food already in his mouth, he takes another bite of the protein bar. With how full his mouth is, he can barely keep his lips closed while he chews.

...

She turns the hopelessness over and over in her mind. She is a logical person, and no logical person would be able to see a happy ending from here. Life seems so fragile since everyone died.

"So, the long term strategy is to starve to death?" Julie drags a green-painted fingernail over her cheek. Yesterday's makeup feels grimy, caked into her pores. It seems strange that this is the probable outcome, given how unlikely starving to death while perching on top of the vacuum museum sculpture while surrounded by vampires seemed only yesterday.

Derek Darius points his cigarette as he speaks. "The long term strategy is that I'm going to kill the vampires. Let me emphasize once again for the sake of Johnny the Janitor; as I am not a vampire, that no, killing the vampires does *not* include killing myself."

Below the sculpture, the dark creatures aren't bothering to hide. At least half a dozen are coming and going as they wait for the humans to eventually come down. Julie suspects that they could climb to the top of the sculpture with a bit of effort, but it's simply easier to wait for their meal to come to them.

"Why don't they go after easier targets?" Julie stares at the creatures below. "There has to be more people to eat somewhere."

"Maybe there are no easier targets left."

"Maybe it's the same reason I would go after them if they killed Autumn," Johnny says. "The same reason Derek Darius is going after them now. Some things go beyond food."

Derek Darius is stretched out across the rooftop. There's nowhere to put his feet up, but it looks like he has his feet up on a desk. "What makes you say I'm going after them?"

"Well, aren't you?"

There is no response.

...

299

"...so once the vampires are distracted," Johnny talks to the computer science kids as slowly and dramatically as an overacted soap opera, "That's when you two follow Derek to jump off the side – you'll have to hang first and the fall shouldn't be too bad. I'll hold them off for as long as I can with the sledgehammer. Derek still has a few bullets left, so with those you can make a sprint for the mansion and hopefully make it to this safe room."

Johnny creaks and cracks as he lays out his years of Apocalypse Wednesday movie watching experience. He can feel himself wearing out. They need a plan, and Johnny knows that at this point in the plot there's nothing they can do to survive without sacrifice. Derek Darius seems to have gone quiet for now, meditating off to the side while Johnny spells out a plan for Nathan and Julie to escape.

"So I overheard you saying something about an escape plan while I was eavesdropping," Derek Darius butts in. "Seriously. Don't worry about it big boy, you can leave the escaping to those of us who have half a brain. So me."

"I just offered to sacrifice my life to save yours, and this is really your response? I'm sorry this plan doesn't meet with your *genius* expectation. Spending all your time insulting everyone isn't constructive – if you have a better plan, then please, let us know."

"I have a better plan." Johnny waits for the celebrity to go on. He doesn't.

"*Derek*, if you haven't noticed, there aren't any babies to sacrifice this time, so you might want to take advantage of what's probably the only option you have for saving not only your life, but the lives of these kids."

Derek Darius radiates anger. "Holy fucking expletive deleted, how many times are you going to bring up this baby thing?"

"How many times am I going to bring up *this baby thing*? You mean that time *yesterday* when you *murdered* an innocent child? I'm sorry if I think that's an event that warrants a little discussion."

Derek Darius takes off his sunglasses and stares uncomfortably direct into Johnny's eyes. His unblinking gaze hits Johnny like a metric ton of dynamite. Eggs would fry on that gaze. "Killing the baby was an unethical dilemma," he says calmly, "and whenever I find myself having to choose between two evils, I generally pick the more interesting one. Let's leave it at that."

Nathan asks, "Is it even possible to have an unethical dilemma?"

"I am not going to just *leave it at that.* Murdering a child – a family - is already evil. But where is your remorse? That is the truly inhuman part. Terrible things are sometimes necessary, but then you laugh and you joke about the very people you've slaughtered. You should burn in hell for what you did."

"An *ethical* dilemma, sure. But an unethical dilemma?"

"Tell me Johnny," Derek Darius hisses, "How much time did you have between when I left in the Mustang and when I came back? Do you think a hard core survivalist like Gramps might have some sort of opiate somewhere in his medical stash? Ether maybe? Or maybe even goddamn Benadryl?"

"I don't see your point."

"You had an entire seven hour window to prepare for this and you didn't. Did you ever stop to think that *gee, we have an infant and it might cry?* Shit Johnny, crying is just about all they do. If you would've been even somewhat prepared with an opium rag to put over the baby's mouth when the vampires came, the kid would have gone right to sleep and woken up in a half hour feeling fine. You say you don't see my point? The point, Johnny, is you're the one who killed that baby. Not me."

Johnny opens his mouth. Closes it.

"By the time I got there that baby was already dead," Derek Darius continues. "All I did was save the rest of you."

Derek Darius puts his sunglasses back on. "Look. If it makes you feel any better, if you gave the kid gasoline in a bottle, he would probably drink it, because babies are just not that smart."

Nathan is standing on the side mostly watching, but just involved enough to blurt things out inappropriately. "Babies are ridiculous."

"How on earth is the fact that babies would drink gasoline supposed to make me feel better?"

"Nathan's right. Babies *are* ridiculous. Even a mentally retarded cow wouldn't drink gasoline, and we kill cows all the time."

"Are you suggesting we… start eating babies?"

"What? No, psychopath, of course not. I'm trying to make you feel better about killing the baby."

"I didn't..." Johnny's voice trails off, and he bites his lower lip. There's something about this he can't quite get by. "You're trying to be nice?"

...

Waiting around to die, there isn't much to say. You'd think it would be the opposite. With only a very limited time left to live you'd think a person would try to convey something about himself; a life flashing before his eyes but out loud. It isn't like that. For the most part, people sit very quietly. If they talk even a little, they mostly spend the time talking to themselves.

"You see, in the end, all we really need is each other," Derek Darius explains once again why Johnny doesn't get a gun.

Nathan asks himself the really hard questions like *would I rather starve to death or freeze to death*? He says things out loud like, "As a kid, I always knew people should be taking vampire movies more seriously."

When Johnny had tried to ration out the remaining protein bars Derek Darius had said, *Fuck that, I'm not going hungry – I'm a billionaire*. Since then, they've been eating relatively well, considering. Practically the only time people talk at all is to ask Nathan for a "Peanut Butter" or a "Chocolate". The threat of running down to only "Vanilla" seems somehow more dire than the impending death and starvation that follows. Nathan probably has enough protein bars for everyone to eat like dog food kings for at least a few days. After that, it will be only "Vanilla".

Nathan spends most of the time feeling sorry for himself, his parents, Tim, Grandpa Montgomery, all those people recently eaten, but mostly himself. Despite being trapped on the metal rooftop by surrounding vampires, he's young, and the end of the world seems very far away compared to Julie's disappointment. It's a feeling nobody over thirty years old could really understand, except through distant memory.

If only I could talk to her and explain...

But he knows he can't. He's only ever been able to communicate effectively through IRC, and he doesn't even know her alias.

Below them, a vampire shrieks inhumanly, a reminder of their mortality.

"Do you think that's vampire-speak for 'Vanilla'"?

Sitting Indian style, Nathan rests his elbows on skinny inner thighs and hunches over to rest his forehead in open hands. He doesn't close his eyes, but keeps them open to stare at the cold metal below.

He feels a light touch on his back and he never wants it to leave. All his focus and all his nerves strain to feel the human warmth emanating through the outlines of the fingertips. They trace lines across his spine, communicating millions of words per second.

"You were right to shoot him," Julie whispers. The sound is soft, but Nathan doesn't have to strain to hear. "It scared everyone, but it's what he would've wanted."

She leans closer and kisses his cheek softly. Electricity comes out of her lips. "I'm falling into something. Maybe it's you?"

"Why?" is the only thing Nathan can say.

Julie smiles a sad smile full of the future. Her soft eyes communicate only hope and love. Despite evidence to the contrary, Nathan feels like maybe everything will be alright.

CHAPTER 35

When Johnny wakes up, his sledgehammer is gone.

He doesn't remember falling asleep, but he must have nodded off. It couldn't have been for more than a second, could it? His stomach boils.

Nathan is talking. "I had a dream where I was naked in school. I don't know if it was a dream actually... I didn't do well in school."

The weapon had never left Johnny's hand since he made it up here. It couldn't have dropped. Even with his bloody finger stump he would have felt it slipping. It wasn't dropped. It was taken.

"Wait. You're twenty-five percent black?" Derek Darius is saying this to Julie Black after he had called her *that black girl.* "Let me just say that I'm not someone who is easily surprised. When I was a kid I used to be surprised every day, but as a grown-up the entire world has become predictable and boring. But wow, with the vampire thing and now this – that's two surprises in two days."

The area on the sculpture isn't large, and a sledgehammer that size would be difficult to conceal. It would be too bulky and long to fit in Derek Darius's trench coat. There aren't many places to search. The hammer isn't here.

Julie has a vanilla protein bar in her hand. She winds up and throws like a major league pitcher. Her aim is true, and the hard synthesized "food" hurdles toward the back of a creature below. At the last moment, however, the vampire moves minimally out of the way to avoid being hit upside the head with all the nutrition a human body needs. So close.

Nathan is scowling like a coach, arms folded. "You almost hit it that time."

"I can use my blackness as an excuse here. Throwing things is generally for white people. Rugby, baseballs, ultimate Frisbees, vanilla protein bars, etc."

"As a white male, I'm not allowed to comment on anything you say about race," Nathan says.

"We all have problems," she shrugs. "Mine is that I am actually extremely racist."

"I'm an equal opportunity bigot," Derek Darius chimes in. "It doesn't matter if you're black, white, Asian, or even Canadian. All races are equally inferior to my incredible *übermensch* genetics."

Johnny's square teeth are grinding and his eyes narrow. He doesn't know where his hammer is, but he does know who's responsible.

"I am nearly positive the part of that sentence where you just said *black people's genetics are inferior to mine* is pretty racist," Julie says. "Also, I want to point out again that I don't think the vanilla protein bars taste all that bad. What if tomorrow we collectively get sick of the chocolate flavors and we want to mix it up? Shouldn't we mix up vanilla and chocolate for variety? There's no correlation with that and the racist thing, by the way. I'm just saying."

"Uh, yes, there is a correlation between what you just said and racism," Nathan nods. Everyone looks at him.

He says in a hushed voice, "The Jews."

They're all smiling and joking, but the enjoyment seems calculated. The smiles too broad.

Johnny spreads his mass out and beefs himself up until he covers two thirds of the rooftop surface. He doesn't speak loudly, but there's a weight to his words that silences everyone. "Where is it?"

"Where's what?" Derek Darius responds immediately cool. Nonchalant.

Johnny sucks in the surrounding air like a whirlpool. He booms as deep and powerful as the industrial revolution. "The hammer. Where is my sledgehammer?"

"Oh, that." And it seems like that's all he does to acknowledge Johnny's accusation. He winds up and throws a vanilla protein power bar at the vampires with the same fluid grace he uses for everything. The motion is like skipping a stone. A flick of his wrist sends the processed vanilla goo hurtling at the vampires below faster and more accurate than a no-hitter, but it doesn't matter. The vampire dodges this as well, and it turns to glare at the celebrity with unadulterated malevolence. "As you can see, the creatures and I are engaged in an epic battle where they hide below and I rain terror from above. I simply needed more ammunition."

Johnny is horrified at the waste in a time like this. Not only the food, but his only weapon as well? "You threw my sledgehammer at the vampires as part of some game?"

"Congratulations on solving the entire vampire problem," Derek Darius says. "You must have, or you wouldn't be spending all your time thinking about a useless toy."

Johnny sucks in gallons of air. Barrels of it. "A toy?"

"A useless toy for a useless game."

Nathan tosses a vanilla bar awkwardly at the vampires. It looks like a right handed person throwing with their left hand. The bar lands on the ground several yards away from the nearest vampire.

There are maybe a dozen protein bars left. At most. Their best chance of survival is rationing these out. Waiting. The creatures below will leave. The group has already made it one night. They're as safe here as they can get.

Derek Darius hands over a chocolate bar, the vanilla bars are gone now. He gestures Johnny toward the vampires, clearly motioning that Johnny should throw the bar. He says, "Untuck that flannel shirt and live a little."

Johnny turns the protein bar over in his massive hands. The label on the back is loaded with vitamins and minerals and polydextrose, rice starch. BHT for freshness. In the fine print it says *not kosher certified.* "Why would I waste our only food when not even the great Derek can hit one?"

The world freezes. Derek Darius's mood has shifted to heat of some kind, but Johnny is left to guess as to why. Was it because of his refusal to throw the bar? The sarcasm? Was it because he had called him Derek and not Derek Darius?

"You *really* think I can't hit one?" Derek Darius's voice is ice. "Do you even realize who you're talking to?"

Electric current is rushing from the celebrity and through Johnny. As the giant looks away, he can still feel the pressure of the stare behind the shades, sapping strength out of him. The vampires are fifty meters away now, not nearly as close as they had been. *They're too far.* And the creatures are moving too, facing the building so they would be able to see projectiles coming head on. *He'll have to wait until they come closer again.*

Derek Darius moves without reserve, snatching up protein bars by the handful. He splays them like playing cards in his left hand as he dishes them out two at a time. Three at a time. He swings his right arm from above his left shoulder and down through his hips at ninja star speeds until every last ration is in the air.

The protein bars give a whirring ninja-star sound as they hurl above the high Idaho desert. Less than a second after the foodstuff leaves his hand, the vampire in the distance is ducking and dodging, and it evades one protein bar and it manages to duck under the second. But the third drills it in the leg. While it evades the fourth, fifth, and sixth, the seventh makes contact between the creature's black eyes.

They all bounce off harmlessly of course.

The expression on the vampire's face goes beyond hatred. The demonic emotion the creature projects is so alien that it doesn't have a name. More like unnamable. Its canines are completely extended in its snarl from the deepest reaches of Hell, and the angular nostrils are flared wide. The expression is evil incarnate.

"Haha, that one looks pissed," Nathan says.

Perhaps unable to restrain itself, the struck vampire charges at the vacuum museum sculpture. It's there faster than should be possible, in times reserved for particle accelerators and computer processors. Planting feet into the side of the building, it uses the side of the base to jump parkour style and grasp the top of the structure. Pulling itself up with a single hand, it uses the grip as leverage to swing the rest of its mass to the top.

Derek Darius already has the gun drawn.

He fires into the chest area before the vampire can establish a base for balance. He sidekicks high and hard, and the vampire tumbles off.

"Come on guy," Derek Darius leans over the edge and laughs at the creature below. "You were so close!"

Johnny feels empty at the loss of his sledgehammer, like how an amputee must feel. He's pumping his fingerless hand looking for it when it isn't there. *How did the creature jump up so easily?* With everything, it's that illusion of safety that scares him most. How he had thought he was safe here. How he had thought vampires couldn't reach this height.

With one less bullet, only two remaining now, Derek Darius

shouts trash talk at the creatures blow. Pigmentless skin stretches over their skull-like heads. They snarl back, seemingly understanding the celebrity's words. The vampires back up to try scaling the ledge again.

CHAPTER 36

"I'm so scared for her." He talks out loud because he knows nobody is listening. His wide fingers press against the inner wall of the yellow wedding ring like a tree choked at the root. At the pain of his missing finger, he winces like he deserves it.

"I always wonder why birds choose to stay in the same place when they can fly anywhere on earth," Autumn had told him once. "Then I ask myself the same question."

Johnny had said he didn't like flying because he was too big to fit in the seat. Autumn replied that what makes him think the quote has anything to do with travel.

People can forget the darkness of being alone. One against many. But it's something Johnny won't forget. No matter what she might do later, Autumn had saved his life. As smart as she was, she could never understand what she had done for him. More than his wife, she was someone when he needed somebody so badly. She was always there for him. They have years of that history together, the best years of his life. Johnny isn't the same person he was then. He's better. Stronger. And it's because of her. As cold as she is, she has this uncompromising goodness inside her. Even at her worst, she has always been a bright light in a terrible world.

Johnny has spent enough of his lifetime outside to be able to sense that this coming sunset will be a beautiful one. The sky will have oranges and purples that are impossible to describe or even remember. The dream-like white clouds above are just the right consistency to reflect light waves at beautiful rainbow angles. It will stretch before them like a gothic watercolor painting, unfinished sketches with miles of oil stretched onto canvas where abstract oranges bleed into the earth. It already feels more vivid than any sunset he's ever seen. Possibly because it might be his last.

Night is coming.

He breathes deeply through his nose. Exhales through his mouth.

Even if he does survive today, this might be the last night ever where he's not starving. Full on scientifically engineered protein power bars, he savors the feeling of an unempty stomach. Already broken, this might be the strongest he'll ever be again.

In this state of mind, wounded and at the edge of exhaustion, he's aware of every piece of himself. His brain is transparent and empty. He senses his fingertips and toes, even the fingertip of his missing finger. His entire horse-sized heart beats rhythmically. He feels his blue shirt lying against the curly hair on his shoulders.

The last thing he said to her was, "You can be a horrible person."

Breathe in. Breathe out.

I don't know why this evil has come here, and I won't pretend to understand. But if it is Your will for us to help ourselves, please, choose her. She is capable of so much, please, choose her. But before that, help me help her.

Almost as an afterthought, his thoughts draw to the deep slice on her hand. *Please let it just be a cut.* His breathing is stuttered. He's hesitant to voice his worst fear, even in his mind. He doesn't want to give it credibility.

Johnny buries thoughts about what kind of God would allow an entire planet of people to be so easily wiped out of existence. An Old Testament supreme being full of wrath and vengeance. A jealous creature that turns cities to dust and floods worlds. Johnny has never believed in a God like that. Johnny's God has always been merciful and caring – a wise and powerful Father who is trying to help His children. More than him or Autumn or even humanity, there's a very real piece of him that's simply praying for his God to exist.

I want to live. The words form in his head before he thinks about them. *But her life means so much more than mine. If it is my time to die, then let me die a good death with honor and courage. I'm not going to stay up here and rot... I guess you know that. What I'm trying to ask... when I die, please help it mean something.*

I will always come for you, he had promised her. *And I will.*

He breathes in and out again while he looks at the broken horizon. One last sunset.

Johnny is only peripherally aware of Derek Darius standing behind him, smiling his twisted smile, as if death hilarious. By the time Derek Darius enters Johnny's field of view the cigarette-smoking genius is already running at speeds quicker than life. Johnny doesn't know where the machetes came from, but Derek Darius has a slightly curved knife in each hand, each with a slick-looking blade about the length of a forearm. He cartwheels off the top of the vacuum cleaning museum sculpture in a one handed summersault, and in the open air he spins like an Olympic gold medalist high diver. His duster flaps behind him.

He lands on the ground between two vampires camping below. Derek Darius's movement was so quiet that the vampires are still moving slowly. As the celebrity lands sliding, he simultaneously stabs outward with the knives, impaling the two creatures in what seems like a specific spot. Two-point-three inches above where their belly buttons would be or whatever.

The vampires soon slump to the ground. Kill strike.

Faster than a muscle car there are almost half a dozen creatures rushing at Derek Darius. Each one bares a mouth of white razor teeth. Sharp objects move too quickly for the human eye to meaningfully comprehend. Derek Darius runs through formalized sequences of practiced movements as enemy claws instinctually go for the throat. He moves in a circular pattern while the vampires are continuously gravitating toward the center.

The scene is as fluid as water ripples and just as impossible to comprehend. Zooming in to just one vampire, Johnny watches as it moves in for an attack, is deflected, moves in again, only to be deflected again. Again and again. Except one time when it moves in it must have opened an imperceptibly small opportunity weakness, because the million dollar machete darts into and out of that special belly button sweet spot. The vampire falls.

The vampire assault on the center continues. All four of the creatures fall to the stabbing motion of Derek Darius's pointy ninja blades, one by one.

But there are many more out there, just out of view...

Ten or twenty hungrily rush one over another toward the celebrity. They come in different human shapes and sizes, some are thin and feminine while others are stocky masculine. All are dark and without color, like they're on their way to Goth-Con. As fast as Derek Darius is, these creatures are faster. But they lack grace and form. They're clawing their way at the victim, in some sort of frenzy. They've smelt blood.

Johnny blinks. It's like he's moving through thick syrup compared with the fast forwarding world below. *The sledgehammer!* Johnny knows where it is, lying head down in the dirt below, but the time it takes to retrieve that information from his brain takes another agonizing .1 seconds, and then yet more time as he sends electrical impulses through his neurons to move his feet.

Feeling a little religious, Johnny leaps blindly off the tall vacuum museum sculpture. It's tall enough it should jar his human body – overextend his knee or twist his ankle – but he feels no pain coming down like a meteor next to the

317

sledgehammer. His blood is boiling. The earth shakes when he lands.

He grabs the blunt weapon one handed. It feels good in his four fingered hand.

It's impossible for Johnny's human eyes to count how many vampires have already surrounded the celebrity. The action is moving too fast, and the monsters are hard to focus on. The giant's optical nerve tries to send these total motion-blur speeds of ten thousand frames per second to an uncomprehending brain. But from this new lower vantage the battle is just a mosh pit of hyperactive hungry hungry hell spawn.

Johnny barrels into the mess at full speed. No fear. The first creature in his path appears to have its entire attention focused into avoiding Derek Darius's pointy things. Good. Johnny is left with a t-ball target. He swings his sledgehammer with every ounce of his massive strength. As the blunt weapon smashes sideways against the vampire, Johnny yells animalistically, but it's quiet compared to the sweet sound of sledgehammer impact. The smash echoes over everything, even over the sound of battle.

The creature tumbles backward in somersaults but manages to maintain some control. The crash landing becomes graceful, and eventually the vampire lands on its feet and sprawls backward. By the time the motion has stopped, the evil looking bastard might or might not be fazed from the impact.

The vampire ahead of Johnny is much smaller than the one fought earlier. Skinny and long. Johnny realizes the thing is naked, and that they're all naked. They don't wear clothes over their hairless bodies. They look like they're wearing teenage getups from Hot Topic, but where the clothes should turn into skin there is only seamless dark armor. There is no penis, although the lanky demon seems masculine. It could easily pass for human as long as you don't look too hard. Maybe it was human, once. Obsidian black eyes focus on Johnny.

Ok. Take a breath. On his right ring finger, the one that wasn't cut off, Johnny wears a ring that says, WWJD. *What would Jesus do?*

The creature moves first. It slithers toward him, quick and graceful. Johnny stamps back toward it, thundering and powerful.

When they meet in the middle the force is like a hash collision attack. The vampire impacts Johnny in a head-on car crash kind of way, with all the confidence of a thousand dead bodies behind it. But with all its alien power, it isn't ready for the Samson strength of Johnny Sparks. The huge man runs through the vampire, and on his way he grabs a monstrous arm with enough torque that if it were a natural mammal the arm would have torn from its socket. With all the strength of adrenaline this creature is light as a feather. It seems impossible something so small could have inflicted so much damage. He slams it into the hard ground Macho Man Randy Savage style.

Johnny Sparks is a hulking mass of rage and veins and muscles on top of muscles. He stomps the heel of his size sixteen shoe into the middle of the vampire's back, and it's the sound a battering ram makes.

He doesn't let up. He smashes the huge boot into the vampire's guts again and again like a two-year-old temper

319

tantrum. He picks the ragdoll creature up single handed and throws it against the side of the metal vacuum museum sculpture. It droops down the side. There are words painted in pretty black cursive where the vampire is sliding that say, "Clean speaks with a clear voice that all is well and in control."

Is Derek Darius dead? Johnny doesn't dare turn his head to look. *He must still be alive and fighting, or else they would have all already turned on me by now.* Johnny feels like he's winning this side battle, but even this runt-of-the-evil-litter-from-hell still poses a critical threat. Johnny hasn't forgotten the poisonous strength of the earlier vampire even after a hundred bullets, and he isn't about to underestimate this alien creature. One deep cut is enough to kill. Tim taught him that. He's going to keep pummeling until the thing is dirt.

The vampire is sagging against the sculpture wall, between a hard place and a metal place, but it can still stand. Its body is deformed and broken – not like a human body would break but more like crumpled steel. Shapeless gray matter oozes from pieces torn off or bashed in. Johnny takes three steps and swings the sledgehammer at full force into its middle. The vacuum museum sculpture reverberates at the foundation.

Don't let up for a second. Finish this.

Johnny winds up for a final superpowered sledgehammer strike, one that will reduce the creature to dirt. The kill strike.

A recurring action scene that happens in climactic battles of good vs. evil plays out like this: The protagonist is beaten and battered. He falls to his knees or slouches

320

against a wall. The antagonist goes in for a final critical blow. Somehow, the protagonist finds strength from within, and is able to dodge at just the right moment so the antagonist impales his evil self. The opposite never happens. The antagonist never finds newfound strength from within.

So it's a surprise when the vampire does this.

The creature rolls sideways to avoid a crushing blow from Johnny's giant sledgehammer of pain, which instead of killing the creature connects directly with the vacuum museum sculpture. The building doesn't lose structural integrity, but the steel reverberates dangerously hard. Johnny's fingerless hand betrays him and he fumbles the sledgehammer.

Survival: it's a motivator regardless of moral persuasion.

The vampire is obviously hurt. As quick as it is, its smoothness has become lockstep and jerky. One more solid connection with the hammer should do it. It's still faster than Johnny; it could run away. But it stands its ground with alien resolve. Emotionless black eyes peer through Johnny, and he has the feeling that it's reading his mind. Claws sharp as knives extend over an inch from otherwise primate hands, and Johnny wonders if its fingernails have extended because he didn't notice that before. Shadow radiates around the creature, making it blurry and hard to focus on. Johnny shakes off the terror starting to build, and charges in once more to finish the job.

One step, two step, wind step, swing step. The swing is hard and accurate.

Once again, the injured vampire dodges the blow.

Johnny doesn't waste even a microsecond. He uses the momentum from swing two for swing three and four. The vampire dodges again. And again. Johnny swings, the vampire jumps and ducks and dodges and slashes. But it isn't as if the vampire is having an easy time of it. Its movements are too slow and jagged. The head of the hammer misses by centimeters.

Johnny barely pays attention to openings he might be creating. As long as he can keep the creature continuously reacting, eventually it will make a mistake and the swing will connect.

Just one solid hit and I could finish this.

With every swing the hammer whips through sound barriers. As quick as the little monster is, Johnny's reach spans football fields. The creature barely stays out of range, but none of the swings really connect. Even in the cases where the hammer is too close to avoid completely, the creature turns in a way that deflects 99 percent of the blow, which puts Johnny somewhat off balance while the hammer bounces off harmlessly. Every time this happens, the vampire will quickly jab an appendage with a sharp claw and slash at Johnny flesh.

Just one bite and my flesh would rot off like Tim.

The claw cuts aren't deep, but Johnny is already bleeding from half a dozen places where rusty vampire nails have torn through clothing. The bloody wounds are like broken glass, and although a sort of battle fever is blocking all pain receptors, the slices are bleeding strength out of him. His arms feel heavy, and the sledgehammer swings aren't as quick as they were twenty seconds ago. There's no time to think about if the claws are as poisonous as the teeth.

The tide is turning in all the wrong ways. The gaping wound on his finger has come wide open, covering the sledgehammer handle with slippery blood, so that it's difficult to grip. Johnny's sledgehammer swings are wilder and vampire claw cuts more frequent. The creature is wearing Johnny down. Too fast to touch, it's biding its time. Johnny tries to focus but his latest swing misses wildly, and the vampire flips in the air over his head. On the way down, it drags a heavy claw along Johnny's spine. It cuts deep.

These outside creatures come into my own home and massacre everyone. They kill my friends and my family. Brutally. The creature inflicts another quick cut on the forearm and darts out of range. Dodge. Dodge. Dodge. Scratch across the cheek. There are so many of these cuts. It's the eighth wonder of the world Johnny is even standing.

In all likelihood, Autumn is already dead.

A dangerous rage is growing within; a quiet thing that started as a seed, but with the blood seeping from his body the conditions are right for it to grow and flourish. It replaces hurt and terror and civility and eventually maybe even love. Putting the RAGE back in courage. He has tunnel-vision, and there's a terrible enlightened focus just behind his eyes. One might even call it a *Derek Darius-like* focus.

I can see the future.

The trick is to use its own speed and strength against it.

Johnny sees where the vampire is, and where it will be. In his mind, he can predict how it will react to his attacks. The vampire, ten times faster than Bruce Wayne, seems slow and predictable. He swings for a home run swing and it connects perfectly. The small vampire sails into the metal base of the vacuum museum sculpture, where it looks dazed and surprised.

Before the creature comes to a stop, Johnny is running at the sculpture – it isn't far away. He isn't going to miss this time, because he knows not only where the vampire is, but where it's going. The giant man gathers all his remaining strength and swings the sledgehammer with all his momentum. It connects.

A sledgehammer sandwich, the vampire squishes between the weapon and metal. With nowhere for matter to go cleanly, black vampire goop spews outward in nearly every direction like Nickelodeon slime. Whatever skeleton used to hold the creature together seems shattered, and bits of flesh cling to it only out of habit. What little movement remains is twitchy and unintentional – signals sent while there were still functioning nerves to send them. There are no blood or organs, the insides are only gray and black. It smells like pumping gasoline or peeling an orange in that it's a distinctly sharp smell that will follow you no matter how well you wash your hands.

Every ounce of Johnny's giant strength used up, and shallow breaths gasp out. He feels like he might vomit. His arms are so full of acid he can't hold onto the sledgehammer as the handle slides from his bloody hands and falls to the ground. He can't hold on. He can't even stand.

Movement from the corner of his eye is his only warning. It all comes flooding back. *Oh yeah. There are dozens. Right now. All around me.*

Johnny manages to raise his eight hundred pound arms to avoid a fatal neck bite. The force pushes him diagonally and he lands heavily on his back. This vampire is half again as large as the runt Johnny just smashed, and ten times as strong. Its movements are fresh and smooth, there is no jerkiness to them. It stares into Johnny with eyes like bottomless pits. No gray matter is showing. No injuries.

This is death, then. Beyond fear, even the deeply rooted survival instincts within Johnny's lizard brain have given up. There is only exhaustion. He puts on his brace-for-impact face and closes his eyes. If he were still capable of moving, maybe he would curl into a fetal position. Moments pass and Johnny is shaking, but the creature hasn't left. Johnny can feel it standing there. It's breath. Slowly and deliberately, it moves its face inches from his. Although his eyes are closed, he sees a smile of enjoyment creep across its almost human face.

The noble giant trembles.

Thap. Pwap. Wrap. Wait. What?

Johnny squints his eyes straight into bizarro world.

Derek Darius, Silicon Valley celebrity billionaire, has tackled the large vampire like a linebacker, laying them both flatly on the ground. They roll to their feet with Japanimation agility, but the creature is just slightly off balance. Derek Darius throws one of his curved blades with precision into the sensitive belly button spot. The vampire knocks it away with its right hand. Derek Darius exploits the opening to stab the vampire in its vulnerable spot with the second knife. He kicks the vampire to the ground and turns his back to the dead creature.

"You make… that look… so easy," Johnny gasps out the words from exhausted lungs.

Black blood paints the landscape. The ground is littered with dead. Some of the fallen look like mannequins, lifeless sculptures in a crude representation of a person. Others now look more like Korean barbeque cow stomach. While Johnny Sparks had been battling a single insignificant runt, Derek Darius had slaughtered this alien army.

The aviator sunglasses are still clinging to Derek Darius's ears, but they're badly broken. What's left is a spider webbed mess of gorilla glass clinging to the bent red titanium frame. One lens has completely popped out of its socket and lies in pieces on the dirt. He takes them off gently, studies them for an empty second, and tosses them aside.

Above them, Nathan Montgomery and Julie Black are cheering. Julie yells, "That was amazing! You just saved all of our lives."

"You did okay too, Johnny!" Nathan shouts.

The celebrity stands tall and arrogant below, the People Magazine '13 pose. With the duster artistically splattered with black blood, he's still wearing a practiced look of cool control. Johnny can't help but look at this idol in wonderment and almost hero worship. Johnny is one of the most physically powerful people on the planet, but his strength is so frail compared to this five-time sexiest man alive winner.

But something is wrong. There's a chink somewhere in his celebrity armor, and the broken sunglasses have to be symbolic for something. The air is tragically poignant somehow. Johnny isn't sure what the difference is, maybe it's the way his hands are resting, but something bad is tangible.

He's been bitten.

Vampire teeth marks are visible on his carotid. Derek Darius notices Johnny looking at his bloody neck and he pops up his collar.

"You must've been trying to murder me," the celebrity says, but venom is noticeably absent from his voice. "If you were trying to help me, then you did a really terrible job. If you wouldn't have jumped down like a fool I wouldn't have had to tackle the one that was about to kill you."

He was bitten while tackling the one to save my life.

Johnny Sparks doesn't know for sure if the vampire bites are always fatal, especially for someone like Derek Darius, but it's clear the celebrity believes the bite will kill him. He stands perfectly still, but it's the hands that give it away.

"Derek..." Johnny says. He can't bring himself to say the celebrity's full name, and for once Derek Darius doesn't correct him.

Dusk is over. The sun is below the horizon now. Johnny was right, it was the most beautiful sunset he would have ever seen.

CHAPTER 37

American darkness. Cloud Marv has vaporized, and what's left is the kind of sky where it's possible to squint into the fuzziness and see galaxies. The stars shimmer naturally through what remains of a depleted o-zone. Hovering in an invisible dome over the world, these savage gods of the northern hemisphere twinkle suspended over the planet without so much as a thought regarding humanity's struggle for existence below.

"Why did you save my life?" Johnny Sparks asks. "I'm not yourself."

Human-looking blood trickles down the billionaire's famous neckline. Derek Darius refuses to acknowledge the wound exists, much less apply basic first aid to the torn flesh. Drip, drip, drip. He's tried to hide the bite behind his duster, but the freely dripping red blood is clearly visible. Red, not black.

What if Derek Darius isn't a vampire at all? He tries to

picture Derek Darius shopping at the mall to buy gothic clothes and finds it impossible.

"How could you kill three people so carelessly," Johnny whispers, "but then save all of our lives when it would have been so much easier to save yourself?"

The machetes are black with sticky vampire guts, so Derek Darius is making an effort to clean the weapons before the next battle. It's not as easy as wiping the blade clean in green grass. The tarry goo has caustic properties and has eaten into the expensive machete steel. It's a lengthy process just to wipe the acidic roof-tar off the blade. With most of the stuff scraped off, he's now sharpening the weapon with a smooth stone.

"Your question is *how?*" Careless and arrogant tone. Nothing is wrong. "Suffocation, a couple gun shots, and lots and lots of stabbing."

When Derek Darius dies, will that be my fault or will it be my accomplishment?

Johnny replays the sentence over and over in his head. "You must've been trying to murder me," the celebrity had said. "Because if you were trying to help me, then you did a really terrible job. If you wouldn't have jumped down like a fool I wouldn't have had to tackle the one that was about to kill you."

The sharpening stone has two sides, the tar side and the clean side. After the tar is scraped off, Derek Darius flips the whetstone over and begins to sharpen the weapon back into its deadly shape.

I am responsible for destroying one of the most brilliant

minds on the planet at the precipice of human survival. Johnny can't help but think about the celebrity's death as inevitable, not only because of the vampire bite, but because it is apparent that Derek Darius himself believes it is inevitable. Johnny pictures the billionaire's proud strength wasting away to skeletons. A melting cancerous mess. How long did it take Tim to die after he was bitten? Twenty-four hours? It sends retching pangs of sadness even in his phantom fingertip.

And Johnny caused this.

Yet all of this badness had been built upon the best of intentions. Johnny was just trying to help. He had even been ready to sacrifice his own life to help. Why is it that this feels so much less noble than if he had saved everyone? Why is it that heroes are the ones who succeed, whereas the ones who give everything and fail are nothing? Johnny can suddenly relate to that guy who tried to kill Hitler, and almost did, but failed and died. Whatever his name was.

Grinding against the makeshift whetstone, the knives are getting sharper. There's a professional harmony to the moving parts. The knife whisks flush against earth, moving circularly away from the celebrity. He does this with the practiced look of a samurai warrior. Although the deadly knife looked like it would never be sharp again, Johnny has little doubt that by the time Derek Darius is through the weapon will once again cut through bone like it's easy spread margarine.

"They say a dull knife is more dangerous than a sharp knife," Derek Darius says, "but it really depends on your point of view."

He slips.

The knife comes off the whetstone in a way that slices open the billionaire's left trigger finger. The cut is deep, maybe to the bone. Blood pools quickly out the open veins. Derek Darius doesn't wince in pain. His eyes shoot fire with intensity, and he attends to the cut hurriedly before sharpening again.

Autumn could save us. I know she's alive. That cut on her hand was nothing.

He sharpens until the knives are sharp. All the original polish is gone and what's left is this savage gray color. It's hard to tell at a glance, but Johnny is pretty sure that the edges are just a single atom wide. Derek Darius stands up, holstering the knives with a sort of Wyoming gunslinger knife spin.

"Ready?" Johnny says. He's not sure what he's ready for.

Derek Darius holds a finger out and sits back down. From his duster breast pocket, he fishes out a piece of paper and lays it on his lap. He spreads a measured amount of tobacco evenly with practiced skill as if he's been doing this type of thing his whole life.

"Do you believe in God, Johnny?"

"Of course I do."

"Yes," the celebrity snorts, "of course you would."

The man with the broken glasses smokes like he's been to prison. He's smoking like he taught Autumn how to smoke.

"Did they ever teach you what an axiom is in janitor

community college?"

An axiom? It rings a bell.

"The easiest way to think about a mathematical axiom is as a starting point - something we mathematicians agree is true. Axioms are truths as simple and as fundamental as possible. Like if A equals B then B equals A – that is actually an axiom, by the way. There isn't a proof for that, and there never will be. We all simply accept these assumptions, and then on top of these assumptions we build proofs and theorems. Eventually from these axioms we build semiconductors.

"The most complex ideas in the world are built one step at a time, and it always starts with this axiomatic kernel of faith. There are (or were) people who don't understand rational thinking or logic, but I'm not talking about those Glenn Beck crazies. Rational people have axioms: fundamental beliefs we build our lives on. These seeds of truth grow within us and form what shred of consistency we have."

The cigarette smoke has hellish properties, and it surrounds them all. The smoke breathes itself into evil looking shapes from childhood nightmares. Derek Darius is damned; one of the Fallen.

"You're a logical person, Johnny, as far as most idiots go. One axiom for you is probably something like: *I believe God exists, and that He loves me.* Everything you believe in is based on that, even if you don't realize it. That little bit of science you know? That's because God is rational and loving. For you, science exists because God wants us to think for ourselves."

Falling is such an ingrained part of Johnny's western civilization culture that nobody thinks about what it is to really fall anymore. There's even the capitalized version that's called *The Fall*, which refers to the story of when Lucifer, one of God's greatest angels was cast from heaven by God Himself.

"So in other words Johnny, if you weren't so stuck in survival mode and were capable of thinking rationally for seven seconds, right now your brain would be going crazy trying to justify this whole vampire apocalypse thing with a god who cares about you."

Here's the thing people forget about falling: the only way it's even possible to fall so far is to have risen so high.

Johnny tries to sound casual, but he wants to hear a truthful answer more than he wants to hear almost anything. "What's your axiom?"

In response, the celebrity smiles devilishly and offers a single professionally rolled cigarette. Johnny hadn't even realized he had rolled a second.

"No, thanks," Johnny says with the forceful habit of Nancy Regan tradition. "I don't smoke."

"What, are you afraid of coming down with a case of lung cancer?"

"There isn't time for this." Derek Darius has maybe twenty-four hours of breathing left, and Johnny doesn't intend to waste what's left of his short life feeding a pointless nicotine addiction. He needs to somehow convince the celebrity to use what's left of his strength to help find Autumn and save the planet.

Derek Darius shrugs. "I could stop smoking much easier than you could start."

"That has absolutely no merit."

"Here. Take a breather." He holds out the cigarette.

"No, why would I want to be addicted?"

"You call this not addicted? You can't even inhale one time. It's incredibly easy for me *not* to smoke for one inhalation, see?" He deeply breathes in regular air.

"You seriously need some kind of rehab."

"Rehab is for quitters."

Smoke from two cigarettes drifts stagnantly in the gunslinger's hands. He looks crooked in a way that can never be straightened out. It somehow makes him more... lifelike.

"You did well," Derek Darius says. "I don't know anyone else who could've taken a vampire with a sledgehammer."

"You killed twenty. To be honest my self-esteem has taken quite a hit."

"Yeah, well..."

It's odd and abusive-father-like how after everything a single encouraging phrase can carry so much weight. All previous meanness fades into the smoke and is replaced with rotting sadness.

Johnny's head feels too big and too heavy. He allows his chin to slump down to his chest.

What can Johnny say? You can't give up? The game isn't over? I mean, literally, yes, most of humanity appears to be dead and you do have a vampire bite that's going to slowly eat away at you until you're dead, but... you... um...

Blood is trickling in a constant stream from Derek Darius's neck, and the fatal wound is already turning an angry yellowish red. "Don't worry, cowboy. I'll save Autumn, even if it kills... well, someone. Probably you, Johnny."

Derek Darius's metal cut features seem dented. His smooth skin, blemished.

"We're all marked men. The creatures pick us out and hunt us until the end. No matter where we go, they will follow." The wound in the celebrity's finger has bled through the cloth wrapped around it. The makeshift bandage itself looks wrapped tight enough to make pulling a trigger impossible. When he talks, his voice sounds nothing like his television self. "There was one that marked me, I know that. I'll kill it, of course. But its laugh... it was... You'd like this one, big guy. It might have even been as big as you."

"I really hate analogies." Johnny forces a smile that looks more like a scowl. "Like how..." He trails off, struggling to think of an analogy.

One corner of Derek Darius's mouth turns up slightly. "Perhaps you should leave the jokes to those of us who are funny."

Derek Darius has eyes so dark they're almost black, swirling with storms of blacker black. Without sunglasses on, Johnny Sparks is able to look into Derek Darius's eyes, and he notices that they are the same color as his own. Derek Darius meets the giant's gaze.

"You want to hear my axiom Johnny? Everyone dies. You're going to die, Autumn's going to die... I'm going to die," Derek Darius talks with gravity. It's not unlikely what he says next won't be his last meaningful words, so full of meaning. Johnny hangs on every syllable. Whatever the celebrity says next are words that Johnny won't forget as long as he lives. "What I'm trying to say is, all things being equal, showmanship matters."

CHAPTER 38

They have the rations they need so they can go anywhere.

For as much life as she can remember, Rockwell has been Julie's home. As a girl she always planned on leaving Idaho someday, but never for forever, and never like this. Obviously. Inappropriate memories flash, like the boy she gave a half handjob in seventh grade Biology, Adam Eddington. Did he ever end up knocking up some clueless girl from Inkdon? He's dead now, of course. She mouths the word goodbye as she overlooks the nighttime version of what's left of Rockwell. From this angle it looks pretty much the same as it always has, all fixed up for one last viewing. Like a cadaver in a casket.

"Nobody asked you to," Derek Darius had said when Julie told them they weren't coming to help rescue Autumn. "You wouldn't be any help at all, and it's more likely you'd just get in the way."

Broken off from the warriors, Nathan and Julie are headed

north by foot. The celebrity had cautioned to stay off the roads, as if they hadn't been doing this all along. He had told them about a cabin he owned. Secluded, seventy miles from a drivable road, and stocked with a lifetime supply of survival stuff. A zombie fortress. Derek Darius escape plan number one. He made sure to add that they could alternatively stay put on top of the vacuum museum sculpture until they froze to death, for all he cared.

"We need to swallow our pride," Johnny had said, diplomatically using plural possessive. "Who cares about winning or losing? I say we rescue Autumn and then slip by the creatures if we can. There's no need for more death if we can avoid it."

"This is not about winning or losing," Derek Darius replied. "This is about winning." The celebrity had looked at Julie with those black eyes. "But if the creature does manage to escape us, it will come for you at the cabin. Even there."

Julie smiles at Nathan, the last man on earth. They hold hands briefly, but they have to let go as soon as they start moving. The broken forest is too uneven, and they need all their appendages to make their way.

"I want to help your wife, Johnny. I really do. But it's too dangerous and we just wouldn't be any help." She had said this after Johnny told them to go because rescuing Autumn would be too dangerous and they wouldn't be any help.

Why the celebrity is going along with Johnny is anyone's guess.

It's a stupid thing for Johnny to do in any rational sense, still trying to rescue his dead wife. According to Derek

Darius, there's the king of all vampires remaining, and the creature is probably hanging out exactly where they're going. "For all intents and purposes," Derek Darius told them, "I'm *trying* to find King Vampire."

Nobody even thinks Autumn is still alive except Johnny Sparks. There's really no reason to think she's still alive.

"Given the choice between going to try and rescue a dead girl by trying to fight my way through a creature that's trying to eat me alive, or not doing that," Nathan Montgomery had said, "I'm going to choose the latter every time."

The thought that Autumn is hunkered up in Derek Darius's panic room is a guess at best. But to this Johnny had simply said he loved her. That was that.

"Love. It's the most important ingredient, as we all know from the Fifth Element," Nathan says, but Julie has a hard time accepting it. She loved her mom, but her mom's dead. She accepts that.

"Autumn is probably dead," Derek Darius had said, "but if she *is* alive it wouldn't surprise me if she's where we're going. We had sex there several times, and that was when she told me the room would be a great place to hide from vampires."

There aren't words to describe the deepness of feeling the college kids have over the dying Derek Darius. Despite the Montgomery Massacre, the dying hero represents the last hope from being destroyed. Him melting away shows how even the strongest things can be corrupted.

Julie isn't used to carrying a real backpack, and the weight of it digs into her shoulders and hips. "With all he's done and all he's accomplished in his life, the thing that makes me saddest is how it seems like he never found happiness."

Nathan looks at her through his long eyelashes and smiles. His forehead is wide. His jaw, narrow. "Being happy isn't about the things we own or what we've done - it's about the journey. The only part of the destination that matters is how we get there. I promise you, Luke Skywalker wasn't happiest after he finally defeated the Empire after an epic struggle. In his whole life, if Luke Skywalker was ever really truly happy, he was happiest when things were at their worst and he saw an opportunity to set them right."

"Do you really think someone like that can be happy when things are so bad?"

"I think most everyone. Show me a person who's finished achieving their dreams and I'll show you someone miserable. With Luke, his happiest point was probably in Return of the Jedi right after he had surrendered to Imperial troops and was being brought to Emperor Palpatine. There's a reason they don't tell you the *happily ever after* part of the story."

"What about in Star Wars 7? I heard they got Mark Hamill back..."

Nathan's eyes narrow behind his glasses, and he speaks in a low voice. "There is no Star Wars 7."

Their movement is slow.

Julie tries to step around trees in the dark without much success. Mountains jet out from the ground like nobody's business, and her footing is always tentative. The forest is heavy with plant life. Branches reach out to scratch her arms. Her jeans feel heavy and sweaty. Thorny grass brushes against her legs, clinging to them. These are old woods. Thick woods.

Julie is tired and full of grief, certainly not happy. Yet as counter-intuitive as it seems, she's found purpose inside herself that was never there before. In her head she's always had this picture of what being happy is, and it involved a chimney and a fire and family and charity work. Afternoon soccer games even though she's never liked soccer, and hot chocolate even though she doesn't especially like hot chocolate. Disneyland was also involved somehow. Yet when she pictures moments that include these things, they aren't what happiness is. She loved her family, but they could never make her happy. Not by themselves.

This purpose in her gut, it's gritty and rugged. There's something darkly powerful about it, the difference between confidence won and self-esteem given. Despite being different from what she has been told happiness should be, she wonders if this is what true happiness feels like. She asks Nathan, "Are you happy now?"

He stops in his tracks and thinks for a minute, and makes a face like he's trying to get corn-and-the-cob unstuck from his teeth. "Yeah. I think I am happy."

And something inside Julie says that Nathan's right. Dying or not, Derek Darius might be happy too.

Branches snap with every step. Making their way off the path, they sound loud as elephants. It's amazing how much noise there should be. An engine. A bird. A plane.

341

An insect. But there is only them, broadcasting their progress into the silent air.

Even without a path, there is sometimes only one or two ways to go. Rocks and cliffs will block a side. Fallen trees can be in the way. They feel through each step as much as see. A lot of the obstacles are too big, and they have to go around them.

Ahead, there are two ways to go. Right or left.

And the right way is blocked.

Trees are uprooted or cut and piled in heaps. In the otherwise untouched forest, a tornado of viciousness has come through here. Boulders are piled into an unpassable barrier. There are deep tracks where objects were dragged. This happened recently. Julie thinks of the cars piled in the road. Objects placed in order to herd them. Or trap.

"On the other hand," Nathan says, "maybe I'm not so happy."

They aren't alone in this forest. There are predators here.

CHAPTER 39

It feels like this is the beginning of a brand new disaster. Apocalypse Idaho, part two. Johnny and the world famous Derek Darius walking into the mansion to try and rescue a dead girl and kill the King Vampire, it feels like this moment is something they would show in a documentary about how the last remaining survivors of Rockwell died. Johnny thinks of the Donner party and how they tried to make it over the pass based on false information, forever remembered for eating each other. When Derek Darius says, "I know the creature is in there. I can smell it," it seems like a sound bite they'd play. The people watching the show would shake their heads with the perspicaciousness of retrospect.

DANGER: 10,000 VOLTS.

A ten foot high electric fence surrounds the gigantic Derek Darius estate, standing intimidatingly tall behind the moat, but in front of the surveillance cameras and booby traps. Basically, the place is a giant shit storm of security devices.

"The good news is this fence was designed to keep out the Mormons, not velociraptors. You should be able to get in."

"What are you talking about?"

"The Jurassic Park style electric fence in my yard, obviously. Velociraptors are smart, but I'd bet you're even smarter." Derek Darius has this tone where he's making a special effort to be insulting. "You are to velociraptors as I am to you. That's a compliment by the way. You're welcome."

First is the moat. The banks are utilitarian concrete. Wide, maybe 25 feet across, it's too far to jump. Unchlorinated water is running through the channel, fast enough that it's producing the sound of a river more than a stream.

Johnny's muscles are dangerously over-exhausted. He holds his sledgehammer above his head and jumps into the trench without hesitation – just another obstacle in the course. His open vampire scratches sting when they submerge in the freezing water. The moat comes up to his armpits, sapping strength and strangling every knotted muscle in his legs and hips. Never trying to show weakness to Derek Darius, Johnny keeps his backbone straight and his chin up. Despite deliberate steps, his tired legs are slow to respond to his brain's commands, and he slips on the cool mud on his way to the other side and face plants.

"Don't worry," Derek Darius says when Johnny is already pretty much done clawing his way out. "I took all the really dangerous chemicals out of the water after the Jehovah Witness Incident of 2009."

The superhuman easily hop scotches across the moat surrounding the fence, securing himself a Guinness world record in the long jump.

"I hope I don't sound arrogant when I say this," Derek Darius says, "But I'm the most awesome person in the world."

"I don't know how I got so lucky," Johnny says, "to end up with you at the end."

"I was thinking the exact same thing. I don't know how you got so lucky either."

There isn't much space between the moat and the metal fence. Unclimbable and deadly, it stretches into the air with chain link and razor wire. Maybe it's the ten-thousand-volt warning signs that are displayed at regular intervals, but touching the metal seems like it would feel like touching lightning.

"Should we... throw something at the fence to make sure it's not still electrified?" Johnny says, dripping, but Derek Darius grabs the fence without any sort of test. Maybe there's a light somewhere or something that turns on when it's electrified, or maybe there's some sort of buzzing sound that indicates whether or not the fence is turned on. Maybe.

Derek Darius climbs the fence like an animal, like Spider Man. He grabs a center post and scales over protruding arm-band-tattoo-quality barbed wire with smooth quick motions.

Johnny starts climbing at the same spot, and the first thing is his feet are too wide to fit into the chain link holes. He wedges a corner of his sopping wet boot and grabs high. *You don't realize how much you need your finger until it's a bloody stump.* He doesn't know what to do with the sledgehammer so he tries to awkwardly hold it. The fence is solid, but Johnny's tremendous mass makes the metal post flimsy, and images flash of the structure crashing down into a tangled mess of barbed wire and cut flesh. When he finally fumbles his way to the top, he's already cut his arm several times, barbed wire cuts on top of vampire claw cuts, and there's still no easy way to get over the remaining sharp pieces. He's stuck, clinging on with nowhere to go. *I wish I would have paid closer attention to see how Derek Darius made it over this part.*

The giant leaps. In mid-air, there's a cartoon moment where time freezes. He hits the ground hard as gravity forces him down. His knees have no chance at absorbing the megaton impact, and his feet hurt. It's loud. The last seismologist on earth, holed up somewhere, watches a needle twitch.

"Well," Derek Darius says, "if they didn't know we were coming, they do now." It isn't an exaggeration. The impact of Johnny hitting the ground is still echoing across the greater part of the Western United States.

Inside the estate grounds, there's no obvious direction to go, and no clear sense of distance. The mansion is nowhere in sight and could be miles away. There is no lawn. It's interesting as to why there's even a fence around the property. If anything, the land inside is more wild and untamed than outside. Thick vegetation juts out in every direction, and even around the perimeter the plant life is varied and Johnny doesn't recognize half the species. They aren't native to Idaho.

"We go this way," the celebrity says. "It isn't the most direct route, but we should avoid most of the land mines."

Imagine your best talent, whatever it is. This talent might be something you instantly had a knack for, and you might've spent hours and months and years perfecting it. You're probably not the best person in the world at whatever it is, but you certainly have the ability to recognize the ineffable greatness here where other people don't. You've put sweat into your talent, and people who haven't might nod their heads and listen, but they can never recognize the kind of awesomeness the giants of your talent possess. Whatever your talent is, Derek Darius is better. He's better than you ever were and better than you could ever be. Unless your talent is something dumb like kindness.

Johnny Sparks can't help but look up to the celebrity as a kind of role model. It's sickening, yet everyone needs heroes.

"I honestly don't get it. You have this incredible intellect, but then you put yourself in a situation where you had to kill the Montgomerys. It seems so senseless, like something that could have easily been avoided."

"It does seem like that, doesn't it?"

Derek Darius is leading Johnny through his property in a zig zagged and random seeming pattern. The dark northern jungle is thick and ancient. This is old growth forest, untouched by lumberjacks. Trees grow blanketed in moss and fungus and point at random angles. Some of them are giant, growing a hundred feet high and looking a thousand years old. There's the smell of rotten wood. Ferns and other things are everywhere, ferns on top of ferns. It's too wet for Idaho, like they've entered another more humid world. Humans haven't walked enough here to make anything resembling a path. Even Johnny Sparks, human compass, has lost all sense of north.

"Do you believe in Karma, Johnny?"

"I believe that things come around. But you're evading the question. I don't see what Karma has to do with this."

"I'm not evading. I'm saying you can relax. Because if you believe in Karma then bad things happen to bad people, so you can rest easy," Derek Darius turns to face Johnny, eyes narrow. "The Montgomerys got what was coming."

Western hemlock conifers are bending to the side. Sad. These types of trees grow better in the shade. It can take hundreds of years to have a western hemlock forest, but given enough time they become dominant. Eventually, they shade themselves. These types of conifers are dominant now. The trees are all too close together. There are hardly any openings.

"Look. I would've had to kill them both sooner or later. Ever since I killed the kid, his mom was bending her mind trying to push herself to kill me. There was no talking her out of it. I just nudged her into doing something she was already going to do, and made her do it sooner."

"What about the Grandpa?"

"Take a minute to think about what you just asked."

Fall is a time when people are confronted with their own mortality, and it seems appropriate that this is the time of year when the world ends. The ground has give. Spongy almost. It's covered with dead pieces of trees that used to be green and soak up sunlight. Now they're rotting on the dark ground, turning into the ugly brown colors of compost.

Derek Darius is right. The childless mother and grandfather would have tried to kill him at some point. Johnny remembers the way the mother was sitting there - having to stare at this person who murdered her only child - she could never have understood that killing the baby probably saved her own life. If the child crying might have meant everyone's death, well, she would have taken the risk if it meant the baby would have a chance at surviving, no matter how small that chance was.

Johnny isn't sure he could risk it. Not if it meant giving up on Autumn.

"Why provoke them into attacking you? I would have killed them right away."

I would have killed them. Johnny said, *I would have killed them.*

"Why didn't I shoot them?" Derek Darius says. "I have a little something called ethics."

"Ethics? What kind of ethics does someone like you have?"

"Don't murder people."

"What do you call what you did?"

"Self-defense."

"Provoking someone to attack you and then killing them for it is not self-defense."

"Look. There's the Johnny Sparks way to do things, and then there's the fun way."

One explanation Johnny has heard for why leaves fall is that trees are able to use the nutrients in the soil when spring comes. In this new world, he can't help but think of other organisms providing nutrients for spring. He imagines the ground littered with dead. The Russian. Tim's dog. Tim. The Montgomery baby and his mother and grandfather. Even Derek Darius. All of them decomposing to feed giant trees. Johnny can feel what's left of some organic goo crunching and squishing underneath his sopping boot. He hopes there will still be another spring.

Derek Darius had said he can save Autumn if she's alive, but the fact is he doesn't care about her, and he doesn't care about Johnny. He has some sort of agenda. Johnny trusts that the celebrity would probably save Autumn if it were convenient. He would probably save her life if it were on the way to the grocery store.

"So it's kind of like two birds with one stone for you," Johnny had said.

"One stone. Eighteen birds."

The giant scans every dark place looking for movement, and with a breeze above, he finds it everywhere. The forest is dark in the cool night, but seventy-two hour stubble on Johnny's face can feel trees thinning. Overhead, a big yellow moon outlines shadows with its pale light. Ordinary objects are stretched disproportionately against the world. Tree branches are haunted hands, reaching out to snatch the human stick figures traversing through them.

The Derek Darius mansion is illuminated yellow. This is where the king of earth lives. It cuts into the land against the dirt, an enormous man-made fortress stretching formidably against the surrounding Idaho frontier. The structure seems to be built out of pyramid rock, surrounded by a lawn chopped like a Marine's haircut. Unreal moon shadows stretch horribly across the short grass, a twisted outline of the house consuming all the shadows around it. The few windows that exist are buried deep into the thick walls, almost like arrow slits. In a nationally broadcast interview a few years ago, Derek Darius described windows as a distraction.

Autumn is in there. He had told her he would come for her, and he's coming. The end of the world might have happened at the beginning, but the end of the story is somewhere inside.

CHAPTER 40

Late twilight and the world might've died with the sun. The forest is too silent and dark. Cloud Marv might or might not be gone. In the shadow under the trees, it's so dark that it's impossible to tell.

Nathan and Julie are not alone.

The idea is to run away from the sound of bullets. The most dangerous way is not this path, but stuck in the middle of a world set on fire, every direction is dangerous. It seems like the vampires would focus on populated areas, right? It seems like they would stay out of the scary forest where there's nothing left alive for them to eat, right?

Julie wishes she would've asked Derek Darius whether or not they should turn on flashlights. There seem to be pros and cons, but mostly cons.

The fear is in Julie, but it doesn't paralyze her. She's thinking clearly and her senses are adrenaline sharp.

Every bit of her awareness focuses on the sounds of the forest crunching and squishing beneath her feet and Nathan stumbling over uneven terrain. More than sounds themselves, she can hear the absence of sounds. These are noises she's not even aware of until they're gone; birds chirping, wind blowing, her breathing. But the darkness doesn't stop her. Julie can see in the blackness. Her last name is Black.

When she walks, she doesn't just let her feet flop to the ground like some McMerican. Instead, her quadriceps are flexed and she moves her legs with control. She walks on her toes, and thinks of ninjas and night games.

The menacing knife feels small and worthless in her hand, but her slender fingers wrap tightly around the handle anyway. She feels naked without guns. Nathan only has one bullet left in his rifle, and he has his rebar that he pulled out of the ground. He's holding one weapon in each hand.

Overhead, a hole in the shadows opens. It could be trees or clouds parting to allow pale moonlight through, but it feels timed. Whatever is in charge of stage lighting has allowed the ghostly light through.

It's setting the mood for the vampire.

The creature stands terrifyingly in front of them as it sucks in the light around it like a black hole. *Wanting to be seen.* Bigger than the others they fought at the sculpture, this one heaves tall. What might be flesh clings to what might be bone. Slabs of soft pieces have been torn off by bullets; what's left is spotty with partially dried patches of black goo and gray gunk. Out of a deformed human face, one non-human eyes glows evil with hatred. The other is shot out.

The only way to describe this creature is to call it Death.

"Nathan," there's cool urgency in her voice. "Blow on the whistle."

He does.

The vampire does not react.

Julie recognizes this particular creature. It stares at her, looking human but strange. The Derek Darius bullet holes are unmistakable, as is the black eye that never blinks. This is the vampire they fought on the quad, the creature that killed Tim and almost killed them all. She always knew this was coming, this creature from the place where shadows come from. She knew it would be back.

Her knife might as well be a twig. Nathan's rebar might as well be NERF. Storming the beaches of Normandy with cubicle warfare weapons.

The creature struts at them, full of powerful scariness. Its body is twisted, joints at angles, and hair is sticking in every direction. Clearly, it is not in a rush. It steps heavily.

With all the action happening, there is actually very little sound. So the click Nathan's rifle makes when he pushes the safety pin is deafening.

Then he fires.

The vampire doesn't bother to dodge as a bullet tears into its middle. It continues a casual march forward. Its black skin is rusty and torn, peeling back in places to expose its gray innards. It's missing a jawbone. The bullet is hardly even an annoyance, on top of all the other bullets.

Maybe it's not capable of dodging anymore.

The vampire has to be hurt, she hopes. Its head is massively deformed and dozens of openings are oozing black goop that looks like crusty pus. It looks mutated. The smell is overwhelming, like being stuck inside a closed barrel full of decomposing animals. The sort of smell that gets in your hair for weeks. On top of survival adrenaline, the fact that she can notice the smell at all is significant.

The point: it might be that the creature is acting more confident than it really is.

The strength might be deceptive, but one thing that isn't an act is its pure hate. Close enough to touch, the vampire bites the air around the college kids, an obvious attempt at scaring them. It's working. Without a bottom jaw to contract, masses of tongue and gums pulsate, and pieces of the gray goo splatter off like spit. It's like insects have eaten its face, picking at it. It basks in its grotesqueness. The scare tactics are sickly human. Usually this insane rage is associated with sick humanity, but here is a predator that would strip its prey's skin and wear it as clothing.

If I die it's going to be fighting.

She stabs her knife at the creature, and it laughs. With so much *alien* about the vampires, that laugh is unmistakably human. She keeps stabbing and it keeps laughing. She thinks of every one of the Montgomerys and she keeps stabbing. She thinks of her mom, and the vampire keeps laughing.

Until it stops laughing.

The creature knocks the blade away easily. The shift in its emotion jerks from sadistic amusement to hate, and the knife thuds against the wooden forest floor. There's a finality about the sound the knife makes as it hits the ground.

Julie takes a wobbly step backward. She isn't sure how to fight anymore.

There's something that comes after flight or fight, and that's giving up. They say it's the number one cause of death in the wild.

A shaky step back. It's reflexive. There's nowhere to run. There's no way to fight.

The vampire glares into Julie Black's face, all traces of laughter completely absent. Its empty eye socket is drooling. The vampire seems to savor the moment.

Nathan Montgomery steps in the way, between the vampire and Julie. With Johnny Sparks-like superhuman strength, Nathan drives the rebar into the soft spot where Derek Darius shot, that clavicle-like notch that's located about six point five inches above what might be a naval.

The slight college kids attack, standing enormous. She stabs. Nathan swings. Their hearts pound against their rib cages and they're incapable of any sort of higher level thought. Julie isn't sure what effect this will have. Battle fever surges through her arteries.

The vampire twitches mechanically to the ground, a victim of gravity as much as anything. Its muscles are tense, but its movement uncoordinated. Its one remaining eye doesn't stop bristling with hate until much later, when Julie finally uses her knife to dig it out of the vampire's skull. She will later say to Nathan that you can never be too careful.

When the creature hits the ground, a geyser of black goo erupts from the chest wound and covers the college kids with black blood and terrible animal smell.

Julie will later go on to tell Nathan how unnatural his incredibly strong swing looked. A miracle. This is how legends are born, she will say, a modern David and Goliath story for a new civilization. But for now, alive and with sticky goo on their faces, they kiss.

CHAPTER 41

The electricity inside the mansion works. A digital clock hanging on Derek Darius's kitchen wall is displaying the wrong time, 11:11. This is one of only two times in a twenty-four hour clock when all four numbers are the same. The minute usually passes so quickly that it's barely there at all. You look at the clock at just the right time, within sixty seconds, and there it is, 11:11. Like a four leaf clover. It's lucky because it's rare.

It isn't like that now. The clock is displaying this time because it's broken. The numbers flash 11:11, stuck forever.

"A broken clock is right twice a day," Derek Darius says. "Which, to be fair, is two more times than you usually are."

Whenever Johnny encountered this magical minute as a kid, he would make a wish. In his current state, whatever he wishes for seems pretty unlikely. Unless it's death by vampire. If he wished for that, he's relatively optimistic he

358

would get his wish.

There's a stab of pain in his bloody stump of a finger as he removes his wedding ring. He spits on his right hand and rubs the ring in tiny circles. He twists it on his shirt, brown blood flaking off with what might be rust, working to get it if not clean, cleaner.

Please, clock on the wall, let her be alive and here. I have nowhere else to try if she isn't.

Johnny picks up the telephone receiver on the wall, because he can't help but check. It's dead.

"I have a satellite phone by the safe-room on the west wing. Once we get there you can use that to call anyone who is still able to pick up. I have no doubt there are still plenty of cowards locked away and alive somewhere in this world."

The theme of the kitchen is utilitarian steel, and it looks barely used. There are no dirty dishes, and the appliances are all revolver gray, smooth and cold. Johnny suspects if he opened the fridge it would be spotless and mostly empty. The stools are made out of expensive wood that looks uncomfortable to sit on.

Johnny fumbles open a drawer and finds silverware made out of real silver. There are intricate hand carvings with each piece. Real seventeenth century style art, and there's a lot of old religion going on. Each piece is probably priceless. He kind of slams the drawer shut inadvertently. It's unfamiliar how smoothly the drawers slide.

"What are you doing?"

"I'm looking for a pen." Johnny glances at his thousand

cuts from the earlier vampire battle. The skin around the worst injuries has risen up like a yellowish three dimensional map of a sick mountain. His stomach and chest are a mess of flesh, volcanos covered in matted hair and they're all about to erupt. "I'm also looking for a band aid."

The next drawer is full of playboys, sorted by month and year. Then a drawer full of bottle openers. There are at least five - not nearly enough to fill the drawer. Johnny notices one of the bottle openers is shaped like a Bat-a-rang. The next drawer contains a single monocle.

There's nothing high class about the contents of the drawers, but it isn't low brow either.

The celebrity opens a cabinet to fish out a Band Aid box and tosses it to Johnny. The Band Aids are miniature sized and have Dora the Explorer on them. Johnny puts his hand under the kitchen faucet and the water runs red. He washes his wounds the best he is able, and tries to cover them with the children's first aid, but the gashes are much too big and the adhesive pieces don't stick properly to matted blood and hair. He tries to wrap his finger stump in Dora the Explorer Band-Aids, using the tarnished wedding ring as an anchor.

"A pen? If you're planning on writing your will to make sure Autumn can cover the cost of your funeral with your ridiculous Idaho state life insurance, I wouldn't. The bodies seem to dissolve so there's nothing left to bury."

Seeing Derek Darius like this is a front tooth short of a perfect smile. He's nicer, for one. It's like how he got Johnny the Band Aids, and even though they *were* Dora the Explorer and even though he doubtless has more functional first aid, he did help. The celebrity's tone is less caustic and spiteful. There's something missing from his voice, and maybe that thing is fire and arrogance, but it's like a piece of him is already dead.

"Also, by the way, I've left everything to her."

TV sportscasters will sometimes call a sports figure *at 90 percent,* as in *this sports guy twisted his ankle but he's on the mend so he's at 90 percent right now.* It's been two hours since the celebrity was bitten on the neck. Only two hours after he had been bitten, Tim was dragging his feet and almost getting shot by Grandpa Montgomery. When a vampire bites, the sickness spreads quickly. At this point Tim was barely able to focus on anything. With Derek Darius, the effects still aren't visible on the outside. He walks with the grace he always walks with, but he's a professional at hardening the fuck up. Derek Darius, looking good as new, must be at around 60 or 70 percent right now.

"I believe in hypocrisy just a little," the celebrity says, "but I still don't believe in fairy tale endings."

In an adjoining room to the kitchen, there is an office with a twenty thousand dollar desk. These offices look like they're littered across the house, a place where Derek Darius could go to work on ideas that occur to him. Johnny takes a step toward the office. It should have a pen.

The celebrity gun enthusiast is also looking for something.

He opens a locked drawer under the playboys and pulls out a Ruger. He puts the gun in his back belt.

He opens a hidden compartment beneath the kitchen sink

and fishes out a twelve gauge shotgun. In the same stash, there are two grenades that he fastens to his belt, and several more handguns he sets on the steel cabinet. There are other hidden places and other guns. He opens the fridge and there's expensive foreign chocolate from Sweden where they sell it by the milligram. Instead of that, he takes a Snickers bar. He closes his eyes and places the candy in his mouth. He doesn't chew. He lets the dark flavor melt on his tongue, eventually biting into the nuts and caramel.

Vampires are in this house, and so is Autumn.

This isn't a logical conclusion, but Johnny has never been so sure about anything in his life. He feels there's a vampire close, and he feels it in the core of his teeth. Despite the immaculate condition of everything in the mansion, the air tastes stale and ancient. Even though the interior lights are bright, it's too hard to see anything, and he has to squint his eyes to look around. The entire estate is giving an aura of foreboding.

Despite the absolute coldness of the Derek Darius mansion, there's warmth burning in his belly that says this is the right place to be, and it burns like the wrath of an archangel. Yes, there is a vampire here, but Autumn is somewhere inside this place too.

Returning from the office, Johnny enters a kitchen empty of food but full of stockpiled weapons. Derek Darius has more supplies stacked than Wile E Coyote. Weapons spread out over the counters and everywhere.

The celebrity smiles his sardonic smile. "He who sacrifices automatic weapons for food deserves neither." He lights a match and raises it to his lips to light a cigarette that isn't there. He must have forgotten. He looks coyly in Johnny's direction. Johnny pretends not to have seen. After a while, Derek Darius puts the burnt match in his pocket.

Johnny picks up one of the guns. It's loaded and the safety is off, which he can tell because there's a button switched to red. All the safeties are off.

"Good thing you're prepared to fire these at a moment's notice," Johnny can't help but remember Aunt Montgomery. Her face caving in as he hit her head with a rock to put her out of her misery. "You can never be too careful when a childless mother is coming right at you."

"Are you going to rub that in my face for the rest of my life?"

Yes, Mr. Derek Darius. All thirty minutes of it.

"Listen carefully." Derek Darius opens another counter and pulls out a bottle of priceless scotch. He drinks from the bottle. "When the time comes - I don't need help. Not from you. Not ever."

The gun feels too heavy. Johnny is holding the revolver in his uninjured right hand, and his sledgehammer in his four fingered left. In terms of pounds, the gun is a light thing, hardly weighing more than a stage prop. But in Johnny's giant hand, the gun feels so much heavier than his hammer. A hammer is for building things, but there's just no constructive use for a gun. At best it's construction through destruction. A predator culling the weak and elderly. The gun's entire purpose in life is to kill. Armed to the teeth has never felt so literal before.

"The revolution begins now. Over vampires and American

chocolate."

Derek Darius pumps the shotgun for effect.

"It will not be televised."

They're in the kitchen in the first place because this is where Derek Darius had led - the east end of the house on the close side of the estate. The room adjacent to the kitchen Derek Darius calls *the entrance hall.* This is what he came here for. This is a place where important things happen.

Johnny's breathing is unsteady and he's shaking. His stomach is sucked in tight.

Derek Darius looks at him with raised eyebrows. "You scared?"

The big man looks down and shakes his head. Smiles. Laughs. "Yeah."

Derek Darius smiles back. "Did you actually expect to feel anything *other* than fear right now?"

There is no battle talk. Nobody says, *are you ready*?

As they enter the entrance hall, it's easy to imagine the famous footsteps that have been received here. Very little is known about the famous Derek Darius to the outside world. There's something *Willy Wonka and the Chocolate Factory* about receiving an invitation to the elusive mansion in the middle of nowhere Idaho. The entrance room is as big as Las Vegas, but clean and polished and with the intricate detail of a thousand years of artisanship. Every inch seems to have detail carved into the wood or marble or other flaunted rich things. With how utilitarian the remainder of the house is, this room alone was designed to impress and maybe something else. Inspire fear.

It's a kind of power that most people can't even imagine. A 16th century power where every door handle is individually carved and intricate, and every piece is years of some skilled laborer's life. It's a Marie Antoinette kind of wealth where you literally have never needed to leave the palace and you can say things like "let them eat cake." Derek Darius has the sort of power that not even big oil can buy. The kind of wealth that could just go and buy Paris, or if they say it's not for sale then he could take Paris. It is a king's power, and is usually reserved for very old blood.

The second most eye catching thing in the room is a giant statue of Derek Darius. It's a nude statue, but in an artistic sort of way. Carved from the most expensive kind of marble, every detail from the angular jaw to the spiked hair is flawlessly reproduced. The statue must be fifteen feet tall, but if anything, it looks too short. If anything, the Michelangelo perfection of the stone is not perfect enough.

The entrance hall of the Derek Darius estate is a historic site full of expensive things designed to intimidate. It could just as well be the entrance to the house of Scrooge McDuck.

However, despite all the over-the-top grandeur and genuine historical significance, all Johnny notices as he enters is the vampire waiting inside. This is the first most eye catching thing in the room.

CHAPTER 42

The humans exit the kitchen like Roman gladiators entering an arena. Ready. Weapons in hand. Johnny has a gun alongside his sledgehammer, Derek Darius carries his twin revolvers. The safeties have never been on. Johnny could always sense the final battle would be fought here. His stomach is knotted with nerves, but he's ready, and anyway, what choice does he have?

In the middle of the room it stands terrifying. Hungry. Waiting. The vampire makes no attempt at all to hide or ambush its human prey. It waits with electricity eyes. It knew they would come. What choice did they have?

Solid black eyes are pools of malevolence. Its fingernails are razors. Its teeth are steel and its drool, cyanide. The most laughable thing is how Johnny thought they had a chance of winning against an immortal.

The creature stands tall, towering over the naked Derek Darius statue. While the celebrity is the perfect Vitruvian human form, this vampire is a comic book villain made from muscle. Every detail is terrifying. Most vampires they've encountered have worn a kind of mask to blend in as a Goth human, but the king of the vampires makes no attempt to hide its true self. It isn't surrounded by darkness – it *is* shadow. There is no hair on its demon head. Muscular arms hang powerfully from great, sloping shoulders. Its teeth are predator teeth, inches long. Claws extend fully from its fingertips, curved and sharp.

How can this creature be truly explained? It has a shape, a size. It has certain attributes and characteristics. But human words are incapable of describing the essence. The smell makes your throat swell into your mouth. It inspires a primal fear so deep that it creeps under your skin and makes your very core shrink.

Johnny Sparks realizes for sure that Derek Darius is not a vampire, and he realizes a lot of things. He sees with a life-flashing-before-his-eyes clarity that can elude most people even as they die.

Pure evil is real, and it can't be found in a lie or a cigarette or extramarital secretary sex or even Derek Darius. Evil is not Rupert Murdoch who disgusts you with corporate greed or the crazy child-microwaving mother you can't stomach because of her insanity. No, humans who are bad are not pure evil, because as messed up and psychopathic as humans can ever be, they are still only human.

This vampire standing before him is evil in the worst demonic sense of the word. It's the evil that has a voice almost too low pitched to hear. It's the evil that manifests itself within the darkest nights on the hair of the back of your neck, when there is no moon and nobody's around.

Sulfur smelling, eternally burning, hellfire evil. It makes Johnny taste copper just to look at. It makes his chest cave-in just to be in the same room.

Evil the way the seventh level of hell must be evil.

Infinite evil.

The Vampire King.

"The safe-room is right, left, straight, straight, left, then behind the bookcase." Derek Darius wears a suicide grin, but there is no fear in his world famous voice. He recites the directions as if it were a Super Mario Brothers cheat code.

They say if you are truly afraid, it is not possible to scream. Johnny freezes, unable to move. Trembling words pour from his mouth. "You're wounded... at sixty...seventy percent. That... *thing*" he can't vocalize the creature in front of them. He fears naming it will give it power. "...*thing* is bigger than any of the vampires we've fought so far" understatement of the apocalypse. "It isn't a fair fight."

Derek Darius exudes smoke, from his ever present cigarette no doubt, but still it's as if he's made of fire. "Yes I know, but I promise to give it a sporting chance."

The battle begins like the drop of a guillotine.

As full of hatred as a snake, Derek Darius shoots first and moves in like a cobra, slithering and shooting. From the other corner, King Vampire barrels toward the celebrity directly. It appears to be smiling.

When they are about to clash, Derek Darius drops down, sliding on his marble floor like a baseball player stealing second. As always, the his movement is sound barrier-breaking quick. Theoretically, the vampire would over commit so the celebrity could face the creature's weak side.

The vampire reacts at the speed of an electron. It sweeps the ground unnaturally, practically teleporting its arm to the ground. It hooks Derek Darius by his million-dollar trench coat, winds him up like a baseball, and flings him effortlessly against the solid entrance room wall at a hundred miles per hour.

King Vampire lets out something like a laugh. A terrible sound that passes through the ears and reverberates its way directly into the brain. Deep and sadistic and ancient. An ear grinding sound of inevitability.

The evil sound comes from everywhere at once, as if the primitive elements themselves obey the commands of this immortal creature. In this laugh, there is wind and earth and water and fire, and there is no room for sadness at the fallen vampires Derek Darius had killed. It's clear the creature is not in a state of grief. This fight is not about revenge. This is for entertainment.

Johnny Sparks is a super hardy dude. The climate in Idaho is cold, and although relatively clean-shaven now, he's spent almost his entire life with a beard. Mere hours ago, he literally crushed a vampire with a sledgehammer. But the giant man stands frozen. He wants to help - this is why he's here - but he can't force himself to move. It's the smell of the thing that's paralyzing. An evil stench. The kind of smell that the most haunted lunatics imagine before they're locked away forever. Johnny has a gun resting in his hand, but it's useless. His bloody hand won't stop trembling.

It's easy to forget Derek Darius is human, and how being thrown against a wall like this should have killed him. He droops to the ground at the slow speed of regular earth gravity, about 9.81 meters per second squared minus the coefficient of friction. Bones and internal pieces must be broken. He stifles a cough with blood, but then he stands strong.

Not even looking shaken, Derek Darius walks with his back against the wall while shooting execution style. Every bullet unrelentingly finds its mark. The eyes. The mouth. The soft spot one inch below the sternum, if it had a sternum.

The creature's black skin is thick. Solid as a tank. The bullets hardly leave a mark at this range. At any range.

The Vampire King laughs and laughs.

There is fire in Derek Darius's eyes. *It's been fun, vampire. A worthwhile endeavor. The humans on my plane of existence are weak compared to us – all boring and predictable. You're powerful and alien. Finally, a worthy adversary...*

But don't ever laugh at me.

Derek Darius settles into some sort of martial arts stance. He drops an empty gun and pulls out a Japanese looking sword, which probably has an ancient story involving Samurais and trips to mountaintops. There's a single second of stillness, him standing there, this grandmaster martial artist, katana in one hand, revolver in the other. For that second, the only part of him that moves is his eyes, moving the way a fire moves. Consuming.

HOW CAN I NOT LAUGH? The vampire stands amused.

IMAGINE AN ANT ATTEMPTING TO BATTLE YOU AS AN EQUAL. THAT IS WHAT YOU ARE TO ME. AN ANT.

Derek Darius explodes at the Vampire King with fury. His kick is meant to make the creature step back, and he follows with a roundhouse that would shatter the skull of any ordinary superhuman giant, like Johnny Sparks/Goliath/Robocop.

The creature hardly budges. It dodges haphazardly, moving in miniscule motions. When Derek Darius slashes hard with the katana, King Vampire only has to move three inches to avoid the cut. The celebrity roundhouse kicks, and the creature slides the length of a hand to avoid the force.

Derek Darius tries to shove the gun into the vulnerable clavicle cavity, but the creature brushes it aside. Derek uppercuts with the sword, but King Vampire nudges the blade harmlessly into emptiness.

He's pushing himself too fast.

The celebrity moves fast. A blur. Hardly visible. He was bound to make a mistake.

Derek Darius punches with his revolver hand and is deflected off balance. The vampire uses the opening to strike like a snake, slashing poisonous teeth deep across the celebrity's cheek, sending him stumbling backwards.

Johnny the spectator stares helplessly out his eye sockets. Even dying, the celebrity should be invincible. Derek Darius is not a person who stumbles backwards. Yet, here he stands, blood seeping out of multiple parallel slices on the side of his face. These are fatal wounds. More vampire

371

poison is undoubtedly seeping into the celebrity now. The claws might have poison, but the teeth are fatal.

Fire burns hotter in Derek Darius's eyes, hotter than hell. There is no fear or uncertainty, only rage. It might be that he's angry with himself for making a mistake. He might hate that he opened himself up to the strike.

But more than anything, he hates being laughed at.

Blood streaming everywhere, he inches forward in an ancient martial art pose, something passed down from generation to generation for ten thousand years. Inching forward in his stance, no part of him moves except feet. The vampire stands still, large hands dangling open at its side. The only piece of it moving are shoulders chuckling with barely contained laughter; taking delight at their suffering.

Derek Darius kicks high (blocked) and without bringing his leg down he kicks higher (blocked). He uses the momentum to spin a roundhouse kick (dodged) and slice with his katana (dodged). The celebrity has become a tornado of sharp objects.

Earlier battles involving Derek Darius were like deadly dances. This battle is desperation. And yet, the celebrity is on the offensive. The vampire blocks and dodges, but doesn't successfully counterstrike. Maybe it can't counterstrike. The vampire inches backward. To Johnny's untrained eye, something about the offensive nature of Derek Darius's attacks makes it seem like the dying billionaire might be holding his own. The vampire has stopped laughing.

Every kick carries the force of a freight train. He kicks hard, throwing his entire weight into it (blocked). He shoots the vampire's shoulder (a small irritation). He kicks hard again (blocked). He stabs (hit away). But with every collision, the vampire is moving backward.

And it looks like Derek Darius might almost be winning.

He swings the katana in a wide arc. The swing is hard enough to slice through the vampire, and because of the earlier tornado force it's awkward to dodge - but dodgeable. The vampire flips backward with that alien agility, rolling smoothly back to standing. But Derek Darius has never let up. He is glue.

When it tries to stand, Derek Darius kicks it in the head (impact). King Vampire braces for the katana, but is put off by a sledgehammer kick to its clavicle area (impact). It sprawls backward again, and Derek Darius sticks to it, katana ready for a kill.

The creature springs off its hands and launches toward the celebrity with a reversal in force, toe claws first. The eight inch nails tear through Kevlar and force him back several stumbling steps.

As soon as the celebrity regains control, he sprints back at the vampire. Rage. Desperation. Glue.

He swings the katana (easily dodged, counter punch). He fires his left revolver (the vampire swats it to the ground then knees him in the gut). He tries to throw the vampire again (and is punched in the ribs).

Joke's over.

Then it hits Johnny that the vampire isn't using deadly claws or teeth. The Vampire King is hitting Derek Darius with a closed fist, like how a human would punch.

Maybe the joke is just beginning.

The vampire's fists move so fast it's like bad special effects.

Punch punch.

With a constant barrage of punches, Derek Darius is on the ground now, on his back. He makes feeble attempts to cover himself. When he blocks his face, the vampire punches his ribs and groin. When he blocks his lower body, the vampire punches him in the face.

At some point in all this, the vampire has started laughing like a maniac. It sounds southern. From the *deep* south.

Derek Darius has dropped his katana now, but somehow he has managed to grasp a black revolver from his belt.

He fires it wildly without really aiming. Not one bullet hits the vampire. He kicks, more of a flail, and it weakly connects with the vampire's back. There's no weight behind the kick. He tries to get up and the vampire lets him, only to claw his face on the other side, bringing him back down hard.

It's been over a minute since Johnny last inhaled. He feels heavier than he has ever felt. Full of lead.

Once again Derek Darius struggles to his feet and snatches his katana on the way up, slashing for the vampire's head in a ridiculously slow and sadly avoidable motion. The vampire picks the celebrity up and pushes him against the wall. It pierces its claws through Derek Darius's biceps. It kicks his knees to shatter his knee caps. All weapons have fallen uselessly to the ground. Derek Darius doesn't seem to have the strength to block anything anymore. The vampire bludgeons the celebrity, sometimes using talons and teeth now. What's keeping the celebrity on his feet isn't his legs as much as the force of the vampire's punches and elbows and claws and teeth.

The sound is one of a mallet pounding on meat, of a cleaver cutting through it. But it's still the laughing that reverberates loudest - deep and terrible. Johnny's eyeballs vibrate against his orbital sockets so hard they might turn to mush.

After an eternity, the creature stops punching and allows what's left of Derek Darius to droop to the ground. Johnny isn't sure if he's dead or alive.

Poison seeps out Derek Darius's perfect face, now a grotesquely bloody balloon. The handsomest face in America could now belong in a circus freak show. Along his cheek, chunks of skin are already melting off in blobs to reveal sticky red tissue, and one of the cuts goes all the way through to reveal the remaining teeth. Dark spots of skin-colored slime are melting over what remains of the trench coat, in tatters now.

Immobile, his eyes are open and clear. They still burn a fire hot as hell.

Is a man judged by a single moment?

The thought passes through Johnny's immobile brain. He has no doubt at all that this demon will kill him if he doesn't run now. But it will find him anyway. Johnny is a dead man, sure as Derek Darius.

I won't die a coward.

His giant hand tightens on the toy sledgehammer. If he hits it on the rib maybe there will be some damage. Johnny could break the plate and give Derek Darius another shot. He will only have time for a single hit before he is killed. He gathers courage.

The creature paces in front of Derek Darius, looking at the celebrity. A cat fascinated with the mouse that thought it could win.

Johnny Sparks and Derek Darius's eyes meet. The celebrity shakes his head, such a slight movement that Johnny isn't sure he saw it. He remembers what the celebrity said. *Don't jump in, no matter what.*

"There's only one way to kill an adult vampire," the celebrity had said. "First, you need to smash the armor plate over the sternum…"

Is that what Derek Darius was doing with his offensive kicks and gunshots? Cracking the weaker sternum armor?

"After the sternum armor is smashed, you have to pry back a scale that looks like part of its trench coat over the right rib. Peeling it by hand is probably the most straightforward…"

Claws out, Vampire King leans in for a final blow. This is the end of the hunt. A gazelle barely twitching. There's no need to be careful with prey so weak.

"…Then just shove a gun through that, aim for the nerve area behind the shattered sternum piece, and… bang. It's a very difficult shot."

He meant for this to happen.

Johnny can see it now. The celebrity has played the entire battle out in his head. He had a plan, and screw Mike Tyson, it worked after the first punch, and it even worked after the hundredth punch. The plan was specific, and included things like allowing a fatal claw to the face here, a skull fracture there. It was all for this single moment.

Derek Darius moves faster than he's ever moved before, fast enough that even this immortal demon has no time to react. With his left hand he digs fingers under the scale that looks like part of the trench coat above the right rib. With his right he grabs a revolver from his back belt and shoves it into the gap. He aims for the bundle of nerves behind the cracked sternum armor plating.

Everything was for this single shot.

Johnny had once thought Derek Darius was a vampire. "It's like how when you're shooting you never, ever miss," Johnny had said, "Not once."

The bullet fires and travels through the sternum armor

377

plating as intended. It then harmlessly exits the other side of the vampire's body. Derek Darius was right. There is a vulnerable bundle of nerves inside the vampire.

The bullet had missed this mass by millimeters.

Even in this colorless world of black and white, Derek Darius's discarded cigarette burns red and somewhere her eyes are pale blue.

Vampire King screams with rage. It's a guttural sound spoken in a tongue that no human could ever pronounce, but Johnny understands the meaning. The reaction to the gunshot is swift. The creature slices Derek Darius's right arm from his body using its full muscle strength and every inch of deadly talons. When the arm separates from his body, blood falls like it's dropped from a bucket. There is no laughter anymore. The detached arm makes a thud as it hits the ground.

The human who stood up to the gods themselves. Thought he was better than the gods, even.

Derek Darius never once says *help me*.

The vampire king decapitates Derek Darius with a wide swing of its arm.

The creature has its back to Johnny, so Johnny can't see how it happened. Maybe the claws are retractable. Maybe the force is so great that the stuff holding humans together simply tears. Regardless, Derek Darius's head rolls off with a thud. The violence looks fake, like it was done with mediocre Hollywood makeup.

Johnny feels his knees trembling, knocking together involuntarily. His grip tightens around the sledgehammer.

This is as vulnerable as the vampire will get. He should take the opportunity to try something. Maybe that sensitive spot is weakened. He should jump in and smash it to bits.

Instead, he drops his hammer and runs as fast as he can.

CHAPTER 43

The Vampire King licks its lips.

The world is hot in the worst kind of way, but there is ecstasy in the kill. In life there has always been blood, but never has the blood been this sweet or plentiful.

The fast and powerful human killed many of the young, yes, but the vampire king knows his kind will evolve to become stronger and more resilient against the humans. They always have.

For now, it must go north. The heat is almost overwhelming.

We have killed many. The dead will be noticed, this time.

The humans are laughably vulnerable. Cows, disassociated from the reality of death. They do not kill their own food. They spend their time sitting. Distracted. They live long fat domesticated lives. This is going to change. The Vampire King will bring death to them, soon enough.

Now is not the time, but soon.

The fast and powerful one killed many. There must be time to repopulate the young. There are too many humans to continue, for now. A swarm of ants. But there will be a swarm of his own to face the ants.

Not now.

More than anything, it is much too hot.

But soon.

The Vampire King will return.

CHAPTER 44

It took nearly two days before someone made it past the road barriers and into Rockwell. One theory as to why there were giant boulders blocking the road was that a localized earthquake may have caused a large rock avalanche. This theory was quickly disproved by geologists, who hadn't detected any sort of unusual activity in the area. The earthquake theory spread anyway, because what else could it be?

The first person to notice the roadblocks had been an ice-truck driver. His job was to refill local freezers with bags of ice, and there was a convenience store in Rockwell that was due for a refill. Most ice is used in the summer, but people buy bags of ice all year round. Some people use it to make homemade ice cream. At four a.m., the ice-truck driver saw a wall of rock and turned his truck around. The truck was large enough that turning around on the skinny two lane highway was difficult, and it took around an eighteen point turn where he had to get out of the truck and spot where he was multiple times. He did not call 911. Why would he? If there were an emergency others would have already called the right people.

Eventually someone did call the right people.

Emergency construction crews were called in to help clear debris. It wasn't obvious at first that all contact from Rockwell had been severed. Once they put that together, a state of emergency was declared by the mayor of Inkdon almost immediately. His office put out a statement about the cold, and how people could be going hungry already.

When the rocks were first cleared, there was hardly any yellow tape. Family members who had been waiting were allowed to wander in. People congratulated themselves. Moving so much rock so quickly is not an easy job, and overtime was required. It's not like they would call themselves heroes, but it is true that without them the supplies would never be able to reach Rockwell's starving/freezing population.

The crowd inched past the wide path through the rock. Empty cars were the first things most people could see. They were everywhere. Cars pulled right up to the opening, piled up and wrecked. Every single tire was slashed. The general feeling was, *what on earth?*

Somewhere, somebody started vomiting.

Another screamed.

A young police captain named Jim Clemmons began urgently herding people out to the Inkdon side. He had a tightly pressed blue uniform, polished shoes, and he spoke with a clean-shaven aura of leadership that left no room for negotiation.

Miles of yellow tape went up across the narrow two lane highway then. It said, DO NOT CROSS. Some of it was written in unintelligible Asian lettering. They had run out of English tape. Not one person could read what the foreign letters said. Still, nobody tried to cross the line or to push that limit. Everyone was curious, but nobody wanted to get too close.

Rumors and speculation spread. People said the rock collapse was manmade. Terrorists. There was talk of the entire town going crazy. One insider news source claimed there was a cult and everyone in Rockwell was dead. Apparently the source asked not to be named.

One frantic person kept saying to anyone who would listen, "It couldn't have been a person. Could it? People have bones. This was pudding. It looked like leftover lasagna throw up. What could make a human melt into that!?" He was erratic and at first most people thought he must be asking for money, but he was wearing an expensive waterproof jacket and a nice hat.

The first police on the scene had never seen anything like it. Hundreds dead. More bodies were missing than not. They had to get an old census to try and identify everyone. Sometimes they would look for the next of kin and realize there were no relatives to call. Entire bloodlines cut short. Families had lived together in Rockwell. It looked like nobody had survived. It seemed like there should be protocols for this type of thing but nobody knew what they were. There wasn't enough police tape or body chalk to cover an entire town.

There were no black helicopters that swooped in

unannounced. It was Police Captain Jim Clemmons who eventually took the initiative to call the FBI. It seemed like the right thing to do.

When they got the call, Special Agent Jack Bauer was assigned as point. His partner gave him the message, "According to this guy on the phone, there is some Lovecraft shit going down in Idaho."

The journalists came before the Feds. Cameras were everywhere. They were pushy and loud, disconnected with the rural town. They came from national cable channels and big cities. They spent time panning wide angle shots. They would shove microphones into local faces and hope for sound bites. Everyone would be standing with hands in their pockets, and the press would shout with one hand on their ear like it was a war zone.

Nobody was allowed through the barrier. Captain Clemmons made it his duty to wait for the FBI.

The corpses inside the city were terrible. It was hard for anyone to imagine that these putrid remains were once people. Mangled and rotten. Old Swiss meat. You could locate them by a smell so strong it had warmth to it. The smell would grow stronger as you got close, and the body finders would say, *we're getting warmer*, or *we're getting cooler*. Many corpses were naked, stripped bare from the force. But from the force of what, the investigators could not say.

There were too few bodies. Far too few. Only a percentage point of the bodies there should have been, strewn out like trophies. Federal detectives would try to piece horrible scenes together. Infant corpses lying across the room from a topless mother's body. The detectives guessed that whoever (or whatever) did this would hold the crying infant away from its mother's nursing breast as the infant would cry and cry, naked in the freezing temperatures and starving.

There were never any flies. Not even insects were alive in this town.

In the west wing of the Derek Darius mansion was an office next to the kitchen. In the top drawer of the desk, government investigators found a letter written on the back of an advertisement from a 1995 April Playboy. It was signed, From: Johnny. Johnny was the name of one of the bodies they'd found and identified.

The media went crazy over Rockwell. The first headlines mostly contained the words *disaster* and *rural America* and more than one question mark.

To put it into context, markets have dropped percentage points on fake reports that said Derek Darius had cancer.

Derek Darius was publicly confirmed dead, although the cause of death was never released. His obituary covered all of his life accomplishments. It was a long obituary that spanned pages of newspaper. Millions of people would read it to the end hoping it would say something about how he died (it didn't).

Rockwell had a population of over 14,000 people yesterday. Down to zero today.

There was only one known survivor, and nobody really knew what happened to Rockwell. Not even her.

Survival supplies across the nation ran low. Companies that made flashlights and canned food and Bibles would report record profits in the next quarter. Even the anti-gun people would stock up on high-caliber ammunition.

The President of the United States addressed the nation trying to lessen the primal fear most people felt. He used words like *persevere, endurance*, and *bravery*.

If they were honest, most people would answer that they thought what happened in Idaho was the start of the end of the world. They weren't far off.

…

She looks hardened and tough, like she's a veteran of something. Her eyes are cold. Autumn Sparks steps into the white makeshift tent, built by the United States government. Her movements are precise, or rather, they jerk exactly into place as if calculated ahead of time. The pieces of her that used to make tears are calcified. Her tear ducts are harder than a fat Texan's arteries now, harder than bone. She has her grandfather's eyes. He never cried after his war either.

For days, people in suits have been asking her if she wants a cup of coffee or if she needs time to use the restroom. In the closets where they ask questions there are no windows and the lights are all the cheap kind of fluorescent. She usually can't figure out what the purpose of the questions are. Twenty people ask her about the healing cut on her left hand she sliced several days ago on a dropped glass, as if it had some significance. They make her talk with a psychologist, who asks things like, *have you ever tried drugs* and *how often do you masturbate*. They hide behind their procedures and checklists. Everyone is a little scared of her.

When she wakes up in the morning she's always shaking uncontrollably and covered with cold sweat. She dies in her sleep every night. The psychologist talking to her said that it's a myth that if you die in a dream then you die in real life, and look at her, she's still alive. He told her that the terror she still felt was *only in her head.* How she loved that 'only'.

The government official walking into the tent and toward her is carrying a letter. Even with the clouds outside, he's wearing dark sunglasses that look like they were made in Mexico. He has a familiar face, and although she doesn't know his name she knows they've seen each other before, maybe years ago. His suit is worn like he'd wear it to church on a Sunday, and it's nothing like the black suit uniform the normal Feds have been wearing. As he approaches her, he glances at the wedding ring she's wearing again, on a left hand that's bandaged but healing, and then he looks at what she's absentmindedly drawing. He points at something that looks like a tribal tattoo, black ink on a white sheet of paper. "What's the significance of this?"

She says, "I doodled it. I just draw things when I'm thinking."

"That's weird. I knew your husband, and he told me you never draw anything."

"How did that come up?"

"I don't remember the context, it just did."

"He was wrong then. I draw stuff all the time. Since I was a girl."

The government official bites his lips. "Read it and weep," he says as he hands her the envelope, but there is no maliciousness in his voice, only the overly apologetic tone of someone who has said something that came out wrong.

To: Autumn. From: Johnny Sparks. The letter is signed with a last name she shares, as if there were more than one Johnny who would write her a letter.

Even scrawled, written in just a few moments, she recognizes the blocky handwriting as well as she'd recognize her own. It says:

Stop this thing. If anyone can, it's you.

CHAPTER 45

She shivers lonely in the cold. Snow is falling deep outside, but she can't bring herself to turn up the thermostat. Cold is the temperature the world should be now. The question hanging on her mind is, *what's next*. There are weighty decisions to make.

Autumn Sparks is alone for the first time in weeks.

The cavernous Derek Darius mansion is the Autumn Sparks mansion now. He left it to her, along with everything else. She guesses this is how it feels to be one of the most powerful girls on the planet. She has fans. She's a celebrity.

In her pocket she toys with a plastic cylinder the size of a finger. Even with all that she now owns, the cylinder (or more accurately, what's inside) is one of her most prized possessions.

She hates this house. The smell of it. The taste of the air.

Every time she walks into a new room she's reminded of death. Maybe that's why she will never leave this house, or this town. She has to always remember.

She's carrying another prized possession in her left hand. It's a hard drive. On it, there's extremely valuable information that very few people know about. Perhaps nobody alive.

She presses a power button on one of Derek Darius's computers. It boots quickly in terms of seconds, but to Autumn it takes an eternity. A second clicks on the digital clock, a year passes. As a prisoner of time, there's nothing she can do about it. The operating system is still loading. Fucking OS X.

Just like the item in her pocket, the information on this hard drive has to be kept secret. The people in black suits that are asking all the questions can never know about this. They would bury it, like they've buried everything else.

She connects the hard drive. The digital clock clicks forward one second. She's grown old and lived a hundred lifetimes. She doesn't trust the clock's accuracy, but as a human she doesn't have much of a choice. Later, she will throw the drive in the fire, after consuming the information only one time. The fire will burn the computer parts toxically, creating poisonous acrid smelling smoke. Despite only viewing the footage once, the memories will be seared into her head forever.

Once it loads, it doesn't take long to find what she's looking for. The software for watching the video feeds is capable of skipping ahead when there's no motion or no audio. It's easily searchable by time.

Her husband snaps into view. She is still his wife. His large torso takes up the entire screen. Autumn can see everything.

Johnny Sparks barrels down the hallways running from the giant vampire that killed Derek Darius. Lost. The house is a maze.

"Right. Left. Does the closet count as straight?"

The vampire follows.

On the high definition computer monitors, he makes no attempt to be quiet. He runs right, left, straight, straight, left. He's panicky. He jerks through the mansion as quickly as he can. Something like a third of the doors are locked.

The software is smart enough to have Johnny on one screen and the vampire on the other. The creature takes measured steps, in no hurry. It doesn't make a wrong turn. Right, left, straight, straight, left.

Autumn stares unblinking. Her thumb strokes the cylinder in her pocket. Her teeth grind.

That's not even where I was, Johnny.

It doesn't take long for the creature to catch up. It's so fast, and he's so defenseless. He has no weapons. He's dropped everything.

The mansion is dark.

It's dreamlike, or nightmare-like anyway. This unseen thing following him in an unseen place. He's bumping into things. It's obviously too dark for him to see clearly. But it doesn't stop him from trying. He's squinting, looking in the darkness for her. But the video cameras can see everything clearly.

He shouts her name, and then screams it. "Autumn. Where are you?"

Inside the cylinder in her pocket is a grisly trophy of battle. Throughout history, the most ruthless cultures would carry away pieces of their enemies as proof of a warrior's prowess. A scalp. An ear. What's in the cylinder is like that. A trophy.

In the monitor, the vampire looks at Johnny in the dark. Smiling. Hateful.

Johnny stands cornered. He has nowhere to run. He puts his hands out ridiculously as if he's going to have a boxing match with the creature.

The vampire grabs him by his thick hair and begins dragging him head first. With giant neck muscles, Johnny rips his head free from the clumps of hair holding him. In a lightning strike instant the vampire has him by the neck and just drags him by that. The giant flexes his neck and shoulders. He appears to be using most of his strength to not choke.

He pushes with his feet. He flails his hands. He kicks. The creature relentlessly marches down the hall back the way they came. It smiles a twisted grin full of good intentioned reproof, as if to tell Johnny he shouldn't have tried to run away.

Autumn can't watch this any more than she can pull her eyes away.

Johnny is struggling the way a puppy might struggle

against a leash. This whole scenario should have an abrupt end, one way or another. A climax. But instead, it's perpetually and eternally ending. The creature drags the struggling giant down the hallway as indefinitely as a furniture warehouse going-out-of-business-sale.

Back to the entrance room, to where it started. The marble Derek Darius statue is toppled and broken like an overthrown dictator. The celebrity's headless body is limp on the polished floor, a bloody mess. Autumn can't tell where his head is. What's left of the body has defecated itself. The creature drags Johnny to it and shoves his nose in the celebrity's corpse like shoving a dog's nose in shit. *THIS IS YOUR IDOL. THIS IS THE BEST YOU CAN DO AND IT IS NOTHING.*

And the ending *is* abrupt. All this buildup and anticipation for a seven second death. An entire life comes down to this.

With a claw, the vampire slices Johnny Sparks from naval to sternum.

The cut is too clean for guts to spill out. At first. The creature steps back and watches. The process of dying starts before the actual death occurs.

Poison seeps in through severed blood vessels and three heartbeats later it's pumped into his superior vena cava. His breathing is shallow and irregular. He's making almost panting sounds. The world is darkening around him. Everything has become allegorical.

The world is darkening.

She strokes the cylinder case with the trophy inside. The

answer is in there somewhere.

It doesn't take long for the inside organs to begin to dissolve and collapse in on themselves. Johnny looks like he's trying to say something, but his dying tongue is too heavy to talk. Using an inspiring amount of willpower, his eyes find the camera and he looks directly at it, at her.

"Look me in the eyes," Johnny Sparks manages to say. Through the television camera, she does. "I want you to remember something."

"Anything," she says. Her thin fingers reach out and gently touch the monitors, brush the pixels of Johnny.

"I don't remember what I was going to say."

These are his last words. Last words have always been important to Johnny.

AFTERWARD AND CITATIONS

Thank you so much for reading. I love writing. It would be cool to one day write as a job rather than a hobby. If you liked this book, please leave a good review and share this with others who like weird stores.

I never thought this would be so dark. I wrote the sequel first – Apocalypse Idaho Volume 2. In that, Autumn Sparks is the main character. Nathan and Julie are there, along with Agent Jack Bauer and a few new characters. I knew before writing Volume 1 that Johnny Sparks and Derek Darius had to die. They have long shadows in the sequel.

The second book is a completely different genre. It's almost science fiction, exploring how the vampires work and where they come from. This book was meant to be more horror. One of the early themes I thought about was to have the first book be darker and scarier – the characters and audience knowing nothing about what's going on. For example, in this book they fear the darkness whereas in the second they spend time experimenting and analyzing how the vampires are able to make it hard to see. The second book is lighter all around, as if to say how knowledge can illuminate and make the unknown less scary.

It was really hard for me to kill both main characters in this book. Sorry, good-natured readers, but this is pretty much a tragedy. In the end though, I feel this is the better of the two books, and stands well on its own. I may never release Apocalypse Idaho Volume 2.

I've tried to cite whenever I borrow/butcher other people's words or ideas below:

Chapter 14: "Are you fucking retarded?" following a motivational speech was from Astonishing X-Men.

Chapter 16: "What if we used up all our best weapons and ammo to go beat the boss at the end of the game, but then it turns out it was just the mini boss at the end of the level" I heard Cory Doctorow say something along these lines at his 28C3 keynote.

Chapter 25: Several sentences from old Czech guy were taken from a former Soviet Union person interviewed in radiolab.

Chapter 30: The "victimless crime" joke is based on a Ken Jennings tweet: https://twitter.com/KenJennings/status/214847483371728896

Chapter 34: "Truthfully, and when I raise my right hand it means I'm telling the truth" is written by Kurt Vonnegut in the *Cat's Cradle* preface.

Chapter 38: Perhaps you should leave the jokes to people who are funny" is the title of this article: http://27bslash6.com/sarahsarms.html

Chapter 40: The karma joke is from Dilbert: http://dilbert.com/strips/comic/2005-08-06/

Chapter 41: "Front tooth short of a perfect smile" is from Lindsay Fuller's fantastic song, *Ball and Chain*.

Chapter 42: "Did you actually expect to feel anything else right now?" is taken out of context from Julie Andrews' commencement speech

Chapter 43: "Its fingernails are razors. Its teeth are steel. Its drool, cyanide." Is written by Kurt Vonnegut in *Breakfast of Champions*.

Chapter 45: "hardened and tough, like she's a veteran of something" is written by Kurt Vonnegut in *Slaughterhouse Five*.

Chapter 45: "Only in her head. How she loved that 'only'" is written by Jon Irving in *A Prayer for Owen Meany*.

Ending: The ending sequence of the book was taken from one of my favorite endings *Bible Camp Bloodbath*, by Joey Comeau. Although the words and phrases are different for the most part, how the death of the main protagonist is unfolded is the same (leaving a note, running from the killer, leaving the readers to find out later).

Thanks to my editor, James Thayer, for all his terrific feedback on the first draft. The cover was (roughly) designed by me, illustrated by the competent Kit Foster. Mostly, thanks to my wife and mom for all the support.

ABOUT THE AUTHOR

Rich Lundeen lives in Seattle with his family. He has a Masters degree in Computer Science and he currently works at Microsoft where he spends his days unethically hacking. Visit his website at http://www.richlundeen.com for any upcoming book stuff.

ALTERNATE COVERS

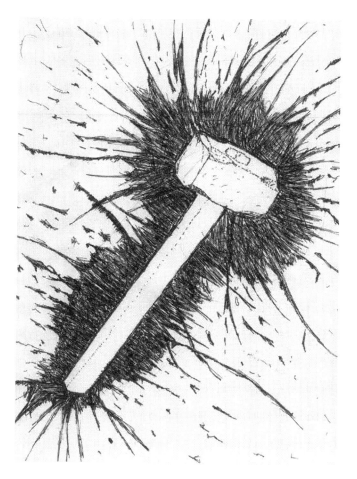

Original Concept Sketch

APOCALYPSE IDAHO

RICH LUNDEEN

APOCALYPSE IDAHO

RICH LUNDEEN

Proof

38071376R00233

Made in the USA
Charleston, SC
26 January 2015